Barbara Cartland

Three Complete Novels of
Earls and Their Ladies

Read These Other Compelling Collections of Dame Barbara Cartland's Novels:

Barbara Cartland: Five Complete Novels
Moon over Eden
No Time for Love
The Incredible Honeymoon
Kiss the Moonlight
A Kiss in Rome

Barbara Cartland: Three Complete Novels
A Night of Gaiety
A Duke in Danger
Secret Harbor

Barbara Cartland: Three Complete Novels
Lights, Laughter and a Lady
Love in the Moon
Bride to the King

Barbara Cartland: Five Complete Novels of Dukes and Their Ladies
A Fugitive from Love
Lucifer and the Angel
The River of Love
The Wings of Ecstasy
A Shaft of Sunlight

Barbara Cartland: Three Complete Novels of Marquises and Their Ladies
Ola and the Sea Wolf
Looking for Love
The Call of the Highlands

Three Complete Novels of Earls and Their Ladies

A Gentleman in Love

Gift of the Gods

Music from the Heart

WINGS BOOKS
New York • Avenel, New Jersey

This omnibus was originally published in separate volumes under the titles:

Published by Wings Books,
a division of Random House Value Publishing, Inc.,
40 Engelhard Avenue, Avenel, New Jersey 07001,
by arrangement with the author.

Random House
New York • Toronto • London • Sydney • Auckland

Printed and bound in the United States of America

Library of Congress Cataloging-in-Publication Data

Cartland, Barbara, 1902–
[Novels. Selections]
Three complete novels of earls and their ladies / Barbara Cartland.
p. cm.
Contents: A gentleman in love—Gift of the gods—Music from the heart.
ISBN 0-517-14772-6 (trade paper)
1. Man-woman relationships—Great Britain—Fiction. 2. Nobility—Great Britain—Fiction. 3. Historical fiction, English. 4. Love stories, English. I. Title.
PR6005.A765A6 1995b
823'.912—dc20 95-31433
CIP

8 7 6 5 4 3 2 1

Contents

A Gentleman in Love

Author's Note

Duels of honour were private encounters about real or imaginary insults. Duels with swords spread over Europe from Italy, at the end of the 15th century. In France political duels were frequent in the 19th century, and took place occasionally in the 20th.

In England famous duels were those between Lord Castlereagh and George Canning in 1809 and between the Duke of Wellington and the 10th Earl of Winchelsea in 1829. An act making duelling a military affair in 1881 resulted in duels being fought abroad at Calais or Boulogne.

Hatchard's bookshop still exists today at 190 Piccadilly.

Chapter One

1815

"*I* see nothing in this that is remarkable," the Honourable Richard Rowlands said, inspecting his newly tied cravat from every angle.

"There is a difference, Sir," his valet said respectfully.

"Well, to me it looks just a muddle," Richard Rowlands said disagreeably.

"I agree with you," a voice said from the doorway.

The Honourable Richard swung around with an exclamation.

"Vargus! I did not know you had returned to London!"

"I arrived late last night," the Earl of Hellington replied, "and I broke my own record, as I intended."

"With new horses?"

"With the chestnuts I bought at Tattersall's when you were with me."

"I thought they would prove outstanding," Richard Rowlands said. "Sit down, Vargus, and have a glass of champagne, or would you prefer brandy?"

"It is too early in the day for either," the Earl answered, "but I would like a cup of coffee."

His friend made a face.

"Beastly stuff except when one wants to keep awake."

"I thought you had more alluring attractions to do that for you," the Earl remarked mockingly.

He sat down in a comfortable armchair as he spoke and crossed his legs, his polished Hessians with their gold tassels shining in a manner which brought a look of admiration into the valet's eyes as he moved from the room to fetch the coffee the Earl preferred.

Richard Rowlands made no effort to continue dressing but turned around to sit in his shirt-sleeves looking his friend over critically.

"You look damned well!" he said. "I suppose it is the country air."

"I have been out in all weathers, training a new horse with which I intend to win every steeplechase in the County," the Earl replied.

"You always do," Richard said laconically, "and it is not surprising, considering you always have the best horses because you train them yourself."

"That is the secret, my dear Richard," the Earl said. "If you stopped chasing women and concentrated on horses, you would find yourself a better equestrian and very much better in health."

His friend gave a laugh.

"At the moment the only thing I could afford to train would be a mule for which no one else had any use."

"Under the hatches?" the Earl asked sympathetically.

"Completely," Richard replied, "and this time I cannot turn to my father for assistance. He swore to me when I went to him six months ago that he would never bail me out again, and as far as he was concerned I could stay in the Fleet until I rotted!"

"Strong words!" the Earl remarked, "but of course I will see that does not happen to you."

"No, Vargus. It is very decent of you to suggest it," Richard protested, "but you know I swore when we first became friends that I would not sponge on you as three-quarters of your acquaintances manage to do, and it is a vow I intend to keep."

"It is easy to be proud—if you can afford it," the Earl said cynically.

"Well, I cannot afford it, but I am still proud."

"In which case," the Earl replied, "I hope you will find it edible. I have no wish ever again to be as hungry as we were sometimes with Wellington's Army. I remember several occasions when I was so empty I would gladly have eaten my boots."

"I am not likely to forget that," Richard agreed. "But if we start talking about the war I shall forget everything else. Why are you back in London?"

The Earl hesitated and his friend looked at him in surprise.

Ever since they had served in the same Regiment they had been such close friends that Richard believed they had no secrets from each other.

When the war was over they both turned spontaneously to the gaieties of London as a relief from the privations and discomforts they had suffered in Portugal and Spain.

Even so, when reminiscing they had found it easier to remember the glory and triumph.

But Waterloo had not only brought the cessation of hostilities with the French, it had also brought young men back into civilian life with not enough to do except seek enjoyment.

This was not difficult in the case of the Earl who was an exceedingly wealthy man, but dozens of his contemporaries like Richard Rowlands found themselves with a champagne taste but unable to afford anything but home-brewed ale, unless they were prepared to run into debt.

The Regent had set the fashion for extravagance and the amassing of pile upon pile of unpaid bills which was being emulated in an alarming fashion by the friends he entertained at Carlton House.

When they were not there, they frequented the Clubs in St. James's Street.

Here they would gamble with what ready money they could find and discuss the merits of the latest social "Incomparable" and the fascination of the "Impures" who were to be found in the theatres and the dance-halls at which they were always welcome.

Despite the restrictions imposed upon him by the narrowness of his purse, Richard Rowlands had enjoyed not only the nightlife of London but the race-meetings, the Mills, the horse-sales, and every other event to which the *Beaux* and the Dandies flocked daily.

He had thought that the Earl was as fascinated as he was by every new excitement, so he was extremely surprised when three weeks ago he had suddenly for no apparent reason, left London for his country house in Kent.

He gave no explanation on his decision except that he had things to see to in the country.

Richard had missed the Earl more than he would admit and had waited expectantly for an invitation to Hellington Park, only to be disappointed.

Now the Earl was back and he said impatiently:

"Come on, Vargus! It is not like you to be mysterious. If it is a woman who is coming between us, I swear I shall feel like throttling her!"

"It is not any particular woman, yet in a way you are being clairvoyant, except that the woman you wish to throttle has, as yet, no name."

"What the devil do you mean by that?" Richard enquired.

As he spoke, his valet came back into the room with a tray on which there was a silver coffee-pot, a cream-jug and a large, man-sized cup.

He set it down on a small table by the Earl who thanked him.

When he left the room the Earl said:

"I went to the country, Richard, to think."

"To think?" his friend exclaimed.

He spoke incredulously, as if he had never heard of the exercise.

"I thought," he continued after a moment, "that you were finding Lady Adelaide rather a bore. At the same time that little dancer—what was her name?—Fay—was divinely alluring."

"I paid her off," the Earl said.

"You got rid of her?" Richard asked. "For whom?"

There was a pause before the Earl replied:

"I do not know yet, but I have decided I shall get married."

"Who is to be the fortunate bride?"

"As I say, I have not yet found her."

Richard gave a laugh.

"That is just like you, Vargus! You make up your mind about something and plan it out like a military campaign. Well, I think you are wise, in your position, to marry. It is obvious you need an heir, but for God's sake choose the right woman, or it will not be I who will throttle her, but you!"

"That is exactly what I thought myself," the Earl replied seriously.

He took a sip of coffee before he went on:

"I went to Hellington because I felt stifled in London and bored with the endless gambling and drinking, and having to toady to all those fat women at Carlton House."

Richard laughed.

"I agree with you. Lady Hertford ruins one's enjoyment of the time one spends there, but I am genuinely fond of Prinny."

"So am I," the Earl agreed. "But he has become too pompous lately and far too sensitive about himself. I suppose we can thank Beau Brummel for that."

Both men were silent for a moment knowing that because Beau Brummell had insulted the Heir to the Throne by calling him fat, it had made him long avidly for personal compliments in a manner which his friends often found disconcerting.

"Whatever else Prinny is," the Earl said, "he has excellent taste. In fact, it is outstanding except where it concerns his women!"

"I believe things were much better when he was with Mrs. Fitzherbert," Richard replied, "although I am too young to remember."

"So am I," the Earl agreed.

"Now, let me think . . ." Richard said, "you are just a year older than I, which means you will be twenty-eight this year. It is certainly time you married, Vargus. Most men of your consequence are married off almost as soon as they leave Oxford."

"When I was that age," the Earl said, "I suppose my choice would have been confined to either a Portuguese peasant or one of those aggressive camp followers who followed the Army. They would hardly grace my table at Hellington."

"That is true," Richard smiled. "And I have always believed that a wife is a very different 'kettle of fish' from the Ladies of Fashion who have a 'come hither' look in their eyes almost before you are introduced."

"That is exactly what I think myself," the Earl said, "and while I know exactly what you are hinting at, Richard, I have no intention of marrying Lady Adelaide or any woman in the least like her."

There was a smile of satisfaction on Richard's face as he thought of the dark-haired, tempestuous "Incomparable" who had been pursuing the Earl ever since he appeared in London.

She was beautiful and undoubtedly alluring in a serpentine manner that made her the centre of the social scene despite the fact that she was rivalled by Lady Caroline Lamb, notorious for her mad infatuation for Lord Byron, and a number of other beauties who dispensed their favours very generously on those they fancied.

Lady Adelaide was a widow and had made no secret of her determination to marry the Earl.

If Richard had been surprised at his friend's sudden disappearance to the country, Lady Adelaide had made no pretence of not being disconsolate.

"Go and fetch him back, Richard," she said at the last party at which they had met and there had been no need for her to explain to whom she was referring.

"Vargus will return when he is ready to do so," Richard had replied defiantly.

Lady Adelaide put her hand on his arm and looked up at him with an expression in her eyes which she knew could send a man crazy with desire.

"Do it for me, dearest Richard," she said. "You know I would not be—ungrateful."

For a moment she had almost hypnotised him into agreeing to do anything she asked. Then he had shaken himself free to say:

"I have no more influence over Vargus than you have. If he wishes to return he will do so. If not, he will stay away."

It was true that the Earl was a law unto himself.

He was used to commanding, used to being obeyed. Wellington had said that he found him an excellent leader of men owing to the simple reason that he made up his mind what he wanted and could never visualize for a moment that he would not attain it.

Looking at him now, Richard thought that, while it would be easy for him to get any woman he desired, she would be taking on a very hard task in trying to be the wife he wanted.

For one thing, he would expect perfection—nothing else was acceptable where the Earl was concerned.

Thinking over the women he knew, Richard could not think of one who qualified for that requirement.

As if he realised what his friend was thinking, the Earl said:

"It will not be easy. When I looked at Hellington which has been somewhat neglected since the war, I was aware it needed a woman's presence and something else which only she could give it."

"What is that?" Richard enquired.

"It should be a home," the Earl said. "That is what it meant to me when I was a young boy, and I know that it now lacks what—I suppose you could call 'atmosphere'."

"I think I understand what you are trying to say," Richard answered. "I felt the same when my mother died. The house seemed empty."

"Exactly!" the Earl said, "and also, if I do not get the heir you suggest, the next in line for the title is an uncle who is unmarried, and after him another uncle I have never cared for, with only four daughters."

"Good God!" Richard exclaimed. "You will certainly have to get busy to prevent a succession of that sort!"

The Earl drank some more coffee, then said:

"I came back to London to find a pile of invitations waiting for me. There are a number from women who, I believe, are introducing their daughters to Society. I thought you and I might go along to one or two of them."

Richard gave a groan.

"I cannot imagine anything more depressing," he said. "Have you ever been to one of those Balls where young girls predominate? It is about a thousand times more formal and more boring than Almack's."

"That is what I suspected," the Earl said, "but the only alternative is to ask someone like Lady Melbourne to introduce me to the right sort of young woman. And look what happened to George Byron."

He was thinking, as he spoke, of how disastrous Lord Byron's marriage had been and how Lady Byron, now he had gone abroad, was working up a case for divorce with details of cruelty and infidelity which were making the scandalmongers lick their lips.

"I am not going to have that sort of thing happening," the Earl went on firmly. "I will choose my own wife and I will have no meddlesome interference."

"She will have to be of the highest breeding," Richard said. "After all, your mother was the Duke of Dorset's daughter, and no one gives himself more airs than the present Duke."

He paused, then added quickly in case the Earl should think he was criticising:

"And quite right. The Dorsets were never part of the Carlton House Set. At least, that is what my father told me."

"It is true," the Earl replied, "and I certainly would not allow my mother's place to be filled by any doxy. At the same time, to be truthful I find a lot of my Dorset relations extremely dull. They have allied themselves with the King and Queen and spend most of their time decrying the morals, manners and extravagances of our friend Prinny."

"And of quite a lot of other people as well," Richard added, "but that is the sort of background your future wife must come from."

The Earl put down his cup with a little clatter.

"In books it is always so easy," he said. "The hero meets the heroine, they fall in love, he turns out to be a Prince in disguise and she is not the 'goose-girl', but the daughter of a King."

Richard drew back his head and laughed.

"Where on earth have you heard such stories?"

The Earl laughed too.

"My first Governess, who used to read to me fairy-stories every night before I went to sleep, was an incurable romantic. I suppose because children are impressionable, I remember them when I have forgotten a whole number of other much more important things."

"You will have to see that your children are brought up from a very early age on historical facts and Philosophy."

"It is no use telling me what I should do with my

children until I have them, and before I have children I have to find a wife! Come on, Richard, help me! You are not being very constructive."

"Ever since I have known you," Richard replied, "you have always set me impossible tasks. I remember at Eton you used to demand delicacies that were out of season and quite unobtainable within the School bounds. When we were in the Army I was sent foraging when there was not a pig or a chicken within a hundred miles of where we were camped. And now I have to find you a wife!"

He threw up his hands and exclaimed:

"Dammit all, Vargus, it is far simpler to provide you with a dozen doxies of the first water!"

"I can find those myself," the Earl replied.

"That reminds me," Richard exclaimed, "I promised to look in on Genevieve this morning. If you have not met her, it is something which should be a definite part of your education."

"Who is Genevieve?" the Earl asked without much interest in his voice.

"She is the latest addition to Madam Vestris's ballet at the Kings Theatre."

"I have met Madam, and although her legs are exceptional, she is too flamboyant for my taste," the Earl remarked.

He was speaking of the dazzling young actress, who, it had been said, "sang like an angel, danced like a sylph, and possessed the most shapely legs in the world."

"I agree with you," Richard said, "but Genevieve is different. She only arrived from France about a fortnight ago, in fact just after you left, and she has taken London by storm."

"I seem to have heard that story before."

"I know, Vargus, but she really is exceptional. She not only dances well, but she has a charm which does not come off with the grease-paint. Come and meet her, and you will see that I am not exaggerating."

"I will come," the Earl replied, "if you promise to accompany me to at least two of the Balls which are taking place tonight."

Richard groaned, and the Earl added:

"One of them will not be too bad, because it is at Ashburnham House."

"The Princess de Leivens!" Richard exclaimed. "At least she introduced us to the waltz, even though she has the sharpest tongue that ever graced an Embassy."

The Earl laughed.

"She is too clever to cause a diplomatic incident, but I often wonder how long it will be before the Russian Ambassador is recalled."

"He will not be, if his wife can prevent it. The Princess likes England—or should I say the English."

Richard rose to his feet as he spoke and shouted for his valet.

"Jarvis!"

The man came hurrying into the room to help him into the exceedingly smart cut-away coat with long tails which, because it fitted without a wrinkle, had obviously been made by Weston.

"You will find the Princess will be only too willing to assist you in your search, Vargus," Richard remarked.

There was as he spoke, a twinkle in his eye as if he knew he was being provocative.

"I have already told you, I will have no interference from women of any sort," the Earl replied, "and everything I have said to you, Richard, is of course in confidence. If you betray me, I swear I will call you out!"

Richard laughed.

"Since you are a far better shot than I am, it would be sheer murder, and you would have to flee the country. After all those years in the Peninsula I suspect you have had enough of foreign parts."

"I certainly have!" the Earl said fervently. "Quite

frankly, Richard, I am glad to be home. But there is a devil of a lot to do."

He gave a sigh.

"The people I employ have grown old, the estate has been neglected, and because everyone was concentrating on the war, there have been practically no repairs done on the houses, barns, fences or anything else."

"That should keep you busy," Richard remarked, "but enough, you are depressing me! Come on, Vargus! Let us go and call on Genevieve."

"I am not certain I feel very friendly towards French women at the moment," the Earl commented.

His friend laughed.

"Does it matter what her nationality is, as long as she is attractive? And let me assure you that French women, like French wines, are, I find, far more delectable than the English variety."

Carrying his hat and cane Richard started to walk down the stairs of his lodgings as he spoke and smiling, the Earl followed him.

Outside the house in Half Moon Street there was an exceedingly smart Phaeton drawn by two superfine horses.

Richard glanced at them with a touch of envy in his eyes before he climbed into the seat beside the Earl.

A groom wearing the Hellington livery released the horses' heads and as the Phaeton moved off ran to spring up into the small seat behind the Earl and his friend.

Driving with an expertise that had made him in the short time he had been back in England an acclaimed "Corinthian," the Earl turned into Piccadilly.

A number of people walking along the pavement stopped to stare at the arresting picture he made with the smartness of his Phaeton, his horses and of course, himself.

With his tall hat at exactly the right angle on his dark hair, the Earl drew the eyes of every woman within a small radius and appeared supremely unaware that their hearts beat quicker at the mere sight of him.

If there was one thing he disliked it was a reference to his looks, and he had already threatened to thrash any man who spoke of him as a "Beau."

"It is only a fashionable term," Richard protested.

"I do not care! It is insulting for any man to be called beautiful, or for that matter a 'Dandy', and it is certainly not the way I wish to be described."

Richard had teased him but had been too wise to use the term himself.

He was well aware that although the Earl kept his temper under control he had one, and he had no wish to have it expended upon him personally.

They drove along Piccadilly towards the Kings Theatre which was situated in the Haymarket.

"If your French woman is as attractive as you describe," the Earl said, "she does not live in a very salubrious neighbourhood."

They were passing, as he spoke, through the dusty streets around the theatre which, in the winter, were a quagmire of mud.

"She has wisely not been in a hurry to make her choice of a protector," Richard replied quickly, "well aware that she will have a large number of applications for the position."

"Which you are thinking might include me!" the Earl questioned.

"It has flashed through my mind," Richard admitted.

"Why has she refused you?"

Richard shook his head.

"Do you really think I qualify? If I cannot afford to buy a decent horse, I certainly cannot afford to keep an attractive woman."

"Then why are you so interested in her?"

"As it happens, she had an introduction to me from Raymond Chatteris. You remember Raymond?"

"Yes, of course I do."

"When he was in trouble over a married woman it was a question either of 'pistols at dawn' or skipping the country, so he went to Paris in April."

"And met your friend Genevieve."

"Exactly!"

"He has obviously been very generous in paying back an old debt."

The Earl's voice was somewhat mocking.

"I think, as it happens," Richard replied quite seriously, "he really wanted to do her a good turn and he trusted me to guide her for the first month she is in England. I do not think I shall be wanted after that."

"You are beginning to intrigue me," the Earl said, "and by the way, Richard, what is her full name?"

"Just 'Genevieve'."

The Earl looked puzzled and Richard explained:

"It is what she called herself in France where, I understand, she had a small part in the Théâtre de Variétés. When she arrived in London and found how the Vestris calls herself 'Madam' and names all the cast on the programme as Monsieur this and Mademoiselle that, she decided to do the exact opposite and be just Genevieve. It is original, you must admit."

"I wonder who told her that would be a good thing to do?" the Earl asked mockingly.

They drove on, and Richard directed the Earl to a small Hotel situated at the back of the Kings Theatre.

"She usually receives when she is having her hair done," Richard explained, as the horses were drawn to a standstill. "I hope we are not too late. You will find her very attractive *en déshabillé*."

There was a cynical twist to the Earl's lips, but he made no reply.

As he stepped into the small vestibule of the Hotel he thought that Richard was diverting him far from what had been his intention when he called on him this morning.

He was not for the moment interested in acquiring

another mistress. His last one had been selected, he admitted now, rather hastily when he first returned to London and had been a failure.

It was not the money he had expended on her that had irked him, but the fact that he considered he had wasted his time and shown, perhaps for the first time in his life, a lack of good taste.

Fay had, as it happened, been outstandingly lovely. It was only when he got to know her a little better that he had found her inane conversation, the way she giggled at everything or nothing, got on his nerves besides the fact that she was greedy almost to the point of absurdity.

It had been his own fault, he admitted, that he had ever become involved, and he told himself as Richard led him up the stairs to the first floor, that he would never again act in haste.

Richard knocked on a door which was opened by a maid somewhat theatrically attired in a mob-cap trimmed with lace and an apron which matched it.

"M'mselle expec' you, Monsieur," she said in broken English, then saw with a look of surprise, that Richard was not alone.

The Earl followed him into what was a quite decent-sized room.

There was a bed draped with chiffon curtains in one corner of the room and seated at a dressing-table in front of the bow-window which overlooked the street was a young woman trying on a fashionable bonnet.

Beside her stood the Milliner with one bonnet in her hand and several others arrayed in their round boxes on the floor.

"Monsieur Rowlands, M'mselle!" the maid announced from the door, *"et un autre gentilhomme."*

The woman at the mirror turned round.

"Richard! *Quelle chance!* I need your advice. 'Ow do I look?"

There was no doubt of the answer she expected, for

her small piquant face with flashing eyes fringed with dark eyelashes and a red mouth that curved provocatively at the corners was framed by a black bonnet trimmed with lace, red ribbons and scarlet roses.

Not only was the hat sensational, but Genevieve wore only a thin black nightgown which did little to conceal the perfection of her figure.

"Good morning, Genevieve!" Richard said, raising her hand to his lips. "You must forgive me for arriving late, but I have brought with me someone I particularly want you to meet—the Earl of Hellington!"

He stood to one side as he spoke and Genevieve held out her hand to the Earl.

"Enchantée Monsieur," she said. "Richard has told me much about you. I 'ope I not be disappointed."

The Earl, as was expected, kissed her hand.

"I hope so too, Mademoiselle."

"Asseyez-vous," Genevieve ordered, waving her hand in the direction of two chairs. "Richard, procure a drink *pour votre ami* an' both concentrate on me! I 'ave to buy *trois* or perhaps *quatre* bonnets and I need your advice. I need it *tout de suite!"*

She turned back to the mirror as she spoke and stared at her reflection for a moment or two before she said:

"I not certain if in this I look *très jolie.* What you think?"

She looked into the mirror as she spoke, not at the gentlemen reflected in it, who had seated themselves on two rather uncomfortable chairs, the only ones in the room that were not cluttered with clothes or theatrical trophies of some sort or another, but at herself.

"Personally, Mademoiselle, I prefer you in the green one. It is not so dramatic, but it does not detract from your features as this one does."

The words were spoken in a soft musical voice which was so different from Genevieve's and so unexpected from someone in her position that the Earl looked with curiosity at the speaker.

She was wearing a nondescript grey gown with a bonnet in the same colour and he thought he would not have noticed if it had not been for her voice.

The sides of her bonnet made it difficult for him to see her face, and yet he had the impression of a small, straight nose, a firm chin and a curved mouth whose soft pink owed nothing to artifice.

"Peutêtre vous avez raison," Genevieve said. "Put on again, an' I ask *les gentilhommes* what they think."

The Milliner produced the green bonnet and the moment it covered Genevieve's dark hair the Earl was aware how right the woman with the musical voice was.

As she said, it was far more becoming than the black and red one.

"You t'ink I am pretty, Milor? *Oui?*" Genevieve enquired.

"Very lovely!" the Earl agreed automatically.

As he spoke he was listening to hear the Milliner speak again.

"Then I take this one," Genevieve said, "and ze other two we 'ave already chosen. Put 'em on ze bed."

The Milliner took the three bonnets and moved across the room to place them on the bed which had a frilled cover decorated with large bows of velvet ribbon.

The Earl watched her and thought she moved with a grace that he might have expected from an actress rather than a saleswoman.

It was still impossible to see her face because of the way the sides of her bonnet obscured it, but he was sure that she had not looked directly at him.

She walked back again to the dressing-table to begin tying up the boxes in which the bonnets had been packed.

"You 'ave ze bill?" Genevieve asked.

"Yes, Mademoiselle."

"Vous savez what to do wi' it. *Les Anglais pas différents* from ze way they are *en Paris."*

It was obvious the Milliner did not understand, and in an amused voice the Earl said mockingly:

"What Mademoiselle means is that the spectators must always pay for the entertainment. Bring the bill to me."

For the first time the Milliner looked up at him and he saw the astonishment in her eyes. Then Genevieve gave a little laugh.

"Tiens Monsieur, vous êtes très gentil! It is not what I meant, *mais je suis très* . . . grateful. 'Ow shall I thank you?"

She sprang from the stool on which she was sitting and moving towards the Earl, bent and kissed his cheek.

He was conscious as she did so of the exotic perfume Genevieve used and for the moment the warmth of her barely covered body pressed against him.

Then she was moving towards Richard saying, as she did so:

" 'Ave you forgotten, *mon cher* Richard, that I also am thirsty?"

"No, of course not," Richard replied, "and I have a drink ready for you."

"Merci, mon cher."

He knew that she thanked him not only for the drink, but for the Earl.

He smiled at her in a slightly conspiratorial manner, studiously ignoring the fact that the Earl was counting out quite a number of guineas from his purse.

The Earl had not taken the bill, which was neatly written in a flowing hand, from the saleswoman, but had left her holding it.

She stood very straight and still beside him, and looking up he could see her face clearly. He thought she was not only very different from what he had thought a saleswoman would look like, but also unexpectedly lovely.

It was not only her large eyes in her small oval face that surprised him, it was her clear-cut features which had an almost classical look about them.

"Do you make these bonnets yourself?" he asked.

"Some of them, My Lord."

"You must be very skilful."

She did not reply, but merely acknowledged his compliment with a little inclination of her head.

"Do you enjoy your work?"

Again there was no answer, but she merely signified the affirmative.

The Earl had the feeling she was being deliberately aloof, and he was certain that she resented the fact that he was speaking to her as if it was an intrusion on her privacy.

Because he was determined to hear her voice again, he said:

"I asked you a question."

"I . . . work as a necessity . . . My Lord."

Her voice was still musical, but there was a note in it which told him she would have liked to tell him to mind his own business.

He now had the right amount of guineas in his hand, but he did not give them to her.

"It must be somewhat frustrating," he said, "to spend one's life adorning other women so that they should look beautiful."

Just for a moment the corners of her mouth twitched and he thought he saw the suspicion of a twinkle in her down-cast eyes as if she told him without words that for many women, whatever one did to make them look beautiful, and however much they hoped and paid, it was an impossible task.

It was strange, the Earl thought, but he knew that was what she was thinking, even though she had said not a word.

The Milliner stood waiting and now as if she felt he was being unnecessarily tardy in paying the bill, she held out her hand.

It was a small, exquisitely shaped hand with long thin fingers and she wore, the Earl noted, no rings.

"Thank you, My Lord."

She was prompting him, almost demanding the money, and as if she goaded him into a reply, he said:

"Here is the amount which is on the bill, and here is a guinea for yourself."

It was then she raised her eyes to look into his and he saw a flash of anger in them.

For one moment he thought she was about to refuse to accept his "tip." Then almost as if she recollected something, perhaps the position in which she found herself, she merely said in what he thought was a deliberately meek manner.

"Thank you . . . My Lord. I am . . . of course . . . grateful."

She curtsied, took the money from his hand and turned away with what was suspiciously like a little flounce of her gown.

Then she gathered up her boxes and had gone from the room without speaking another word, not even to her client.

CHAPTER TWO

Thalia came out of the back door of Mrs. Burton's Millinery shop and looked to where at the end of the street, a figure was waiting.

She hurried towards an elderly woman dressed like a respectable servant who smiled as she approached.

"I am sorry, Hannah, if I kept you waiting," Thalia said, "but there were a lot of boxes to pack up at the last moment. Thank goodness I did not have to deliver them."

"It's not right for you to do such menial jobs anyway!" Hannah answered crossly.

Thalia laughed.

"Beggars cannot be choosers, as you well know, and actually I have had a most entertaining day. I will not tell you about it now but will wait until we reach Mama. How is she?"

"As she always is," Hannah replied, "counting the days until your father's return and watching for a letter that never comes!"

Again Hannah's voice was sharp with anger and Thalia understood, because if there was one person whom Hannah adored it was her mother.

They walked briskly along the streets that were not so crowded as they had been earlier in the day until they reached Hay Hill.

At the bottom they crossed the road and entered Lansdowne Passage.

As often as Thalia walked along the passage which lay between the garden of Lansdown House and that of Devonshire House she invariably found herself thinking of Highwaymen.

The Prince of Wales and the Duke of York when they were very young men, were once driving in a hackney-carriage down Hay Hill when they were stopped and robbed by a group of Highwaymen.

Those thieves were never caught, and another time a Highwayman escaping from Piccadilly rode down Lansdowne Passage, put his horse to the steps at the Curzon Street end and galloped away.

It always seemed to Thalia a reckless and exciting escapade and she invariably found herself wondering if she, had she been in the same position, would have been so clever.

Hannah disliked talking when they were hurrying home and Thalia therefore continued with her own thoughts without interruption.

The gentleman who had given her the guinea in Mademoiselle Genevieve's room this morning had the look, she thought, of a Highwayman, or perhaps a buccaneer.

He was exactly the type of man she liked to watch either riding in the Row or walking down Bond Street.

She had not until now, had the chance of speaking with what she imagined was one of the Beaux, and his cynical, rather mocking voice was just the way she had anticipated he would speak.

Now they were in Curzon Street Hannah seemed to move even more quickly and a few minutes later they had turned left under an archway which led them into Shepherd's Market.

Here again Thalia's imagination made her people the place with the Fair which she had read about in books and had been described to her by many of the older inhabitants of the Market.

Shepherd's Market was still a little village with its own independent life, but in the past the Fair which had been held there for two weeks every year had been one of the sights of London.

It had started as an annual market, but in the surrounding fields and streets there had been booths for jugglers and prize-fighters, wild beasts and mountebanks.

A merry-go-round, swings, fire-eaters, and rope-dancers had drawn the gaping crowds who had found the pig-faced women, monstrosities and cannibal chiefs an irresistible entertainment.

But it had not always been fun, Thalia remembered. There had been tragedies too.

Over a hundred years ago there had been a

tightrope dancer known as "Lady Mary" who was said to be the daughter of a foreign nobleman.

She had eloped with a showman who taught her how to dance on a tightrope, and her performance was immensely popular as she had both grace and skill.

She had continued with her act after she became pregnant and one day she over-balanced and fell. She gave birth to a stillborn child and died almost at once.

Thalia would often think of Lady Mary because although it was a sad story, it was a very romantic one.

She must, she thought, have loved her lover very deeply to have left her luxurious home in Florence for such a strange way of life.

But now at one of the small houses at the far end of Shepherd's Market Hannah had stopped and drawn a large key from a pocket in her sensible black skirt.

She opened the door and Thalia ran past her to call as she hurried up a narrow staircase:

"Mama, I am back!"

She opened a door and entered what would have been a Drawing-Room, if such a tiny building could boast of anything so pretentious.

It was now converted into a bedroom, and lying on a chaise-longue in front of the window was a woman who still retained her beauty, although she looked frail and ill.

She held out both hands to her daughter and Thalia ran across the room to kiss her on both cheeks.

"I am back, Mama, and I have so much to tell you. Have you been very dull here all day?"

"I have been all right, my dearest," her mother replied softly. "But I admit to waiting impatiently for your return. You seem to bring the sunshine with you."

"That is what I would like to bring," Thalia said, "but instead I have brought you something which will make you laugh and will purchase food, which is more important at the moment, than the sunshine."

She drew the guinea from her purse as she spoke and held it up for her mother to see.

"My first 'tip'," she said, "and from a Gentleman of Fashion."

Her mother gave a little gasp.

"You cannot mean, Thalia, that you actually accepted money from a man?"

Thalia laughed.

She was taking off her concealing bonnet and now she flung it down on a chair and patted her golden hair which had tiny red lights in it, into place.

"I admit, Mama, I felt like throwing it at him, but then I remembered I was a humble milliner."

Her mother gave a little groan.

"Oh, Thalia, how can I bear to think of you working in such conditions and being treated as if you were nothing more than a servant?"

"That is exactly what I am," Thalia said. "But, Mama, it was such fun today! If you only saw the women who came in to buy bonnets."

She gave a little laugh at the remembrance of them and went on:

"One looked exactly like a cottage-loaf and her face was as big as a pumpkin. She kept saying to me: 'Do you really think I look pretty in this?' I longed to tell her she could not look pretty in anything."

"I hope you did nothing of the sort!" her mother said reprovingly. "That would be unkind."

"No, of course not, Mama. I told her she looked charming and persuaded her to buy three bonnets instead of two. Mrs. Burton was delighted with me."

She sat down on a chair beside her mother, taking her hand in hers.

"Do not be shocked about the guinea, dearest," she said. "It will buy you some delicious things to eat, a chicken, lots of eggs, cream and many more luxuries which the doctor ordered."

Her mother did not reply and Thalia knew that nothing the doctor could prescribe or they could buy could heal an anxious heart that was growing near to despair.

As she looked at the sadness in her mother's face Thalia asked herself why, wherever he was, her father had not written.

She had sent him dozens of letters to the address he had given them in America, but after the first six months he had been away, there had been no more news of him.

It was terrible to see her mother suffering so acutely, growing paler and thinner every day, and knowing there was nothing she could do about it.

The three years of her father's exile were nearly at an end, and she was sure if he was alive he would come home.

He could not be so cruel as to stay away when he knew how desperately they needed him.

As if she wished to divert her mother's mind from where it always lingered with her father, Thalia told her in detail about her visit to Mademoiselle Genevieve at the Hotel near the King's Theatre, and how, having chosen three bonnets, she had made the Earl of Hellington pay for them.

She told the story amusingly, omitting the fact that the ballet-dancer wore only her nightgown or that she had kissed the Earl in gratitude.

As it was her mother was shocked at the Frenchwoman's behaviour.

"How can I bear to think of you, my dearest, associating with such women?"

"I have heard Papa talking about 'bits o' muslin'!" Thalia said, "but I never expected to speak to any of them. She was extremely attractive, Mama, and I am sure she dances beautifully."

"Dearest, you must find something else to do."

The laughter died out of Thalia's eyes.

"Mama, you know as well as I do that I am very lucky to have employment of any sort, and it was actually you who thought I should be a milliner."

"I did?"

"Yes, Mama. When I was trimming that old bonnet of mine you said: 'You are so skilful with your fingers, dearest child, I do not believe that even Bond Street could produce anything more stylish than you have just contrived out of those old ribbons and the silk flowers I bought over five years ago.' "

"I did not mean you to sell your skill," her mother said, "even while I admit it is unusual."

"We had nothing else left to sell," Thalia replied simply, "and even Hannah disliked the idea of starving to death."

Her mother said no more.

She was thinking that when her husband had to flee the country he had thought that with what he had left them, they would at least be comfortably provided for until his return.

It had been one of those dramatic and unexpected events that had dropped like a meteor from the skies, to change the lives of people when they were least expecting it.

Sir Denzil Caversham had always been a charming but impetuous man who, ever since he was a small boy, had got into unexpected scrapes.

He had been in trouble at School, at his University and even at one time in his Regiment.

Then he had married and settled down and his relatives had thought their anxieties regarding him were over.

He would live the quiet life of the country squire, happy with his beautiful wife and content with the ancient Manor House and estate which had been in the Caversham family for five hundred years.

But Sir Denzil had been a man who needed friends and he had found it impossible to keep away from his Clubs, from the excitement and entertainments of London, where the companions of his more raffish days welcomed his return effusively.

Although he could not afford it, he and his wife had

rented a house in Mayfair for the Season and regardless of expense had entertained until they were back in the swim of what was known as the *Beau Monde.*

As Lady Caversham was extremely beautiful, she had enjoyed the Balls, the Receptions and the Assemblies almost as much as her husband had.

They returned to the country only for the hunting and shooting and gradually had begun to spend more time in London, arriving almost before the daffodils were in bud, and leaving often long after the Season had come to an end, with the Regent moving from Carlton House to Brighton.

It was only Thalia who missed the country even though she enjoyed the teachers and Tutors who came to the house in Brook Street.

But they could not make up for the fact that riding in Hyde Park was not the same as riding over the fields at home, and her dogs had to be left behind because she could not exercise them as much as they needed in London.

Then three years ago disaster had struck.

Sir Denzil, who was inclined to be unpredictable especially when he had been drinking, got into an argument at White's Club over some quite trivial subject that ended in his being insulted.

Thalia was never quite certain what was the real source of the quarrel in the first place, although she suspected it concerned a woman.

Whatever it was, it resulted in Sir Denzil being involved in a duel, his opponent being a Statesman of considerable importance.

They met at dawn in St. James's Park and Lady Caversham was not told what was happening until the duel was over.

Not that she could have done anything to prevent it because a challenge, once given and accepted, involved the honour of the participants and there was no going back.

The first thing Thalia knew about it was when she

went into her mother's room to bid her good morning and Lady Caversham said:

"I cannot imagine what has happened, Thalia. When I woke your father was not here. It is not like him to leave the house without telling me where he is going. It is too early for him to be riding."

Neither of them could imagine what had occurred until half an hour later they heard footsteps coming up the stairs.

"Here is Papa!" Thalia said. "Now he will be able to tell you, Mama, where he has been."

Sir Denzil had entered the bedroom and his wife had given a little cry.

"What has—happened? Why do you—look like that?"

"I have killed him!" Sir Denzil said.

"Killed—who?" Lady Caversham cried.

"Spencer Talbot," he answered, "and now I have to leave the country."

"Leave the—country?"

Lady Caversham could hardly whisper the words.

"I have already seen the Lord Chancellor," Sir Denzil explained. "It was the only thing I could do in the circumstances. After all, Talbot was in the Cabinet, and the first thing I realised was there must be no scandal which would affect the Government."

"How could you kill him? How is it possible?"

"I meant only to wing him in the arm," Sir Denzil said, "but he moved at the last moment, I think because he intended from the very first, to kill me. His temper is proverbial."

"Instead . . . you killed . . . him!"

Thalia heard her own voice say the words and was surprised she had spoken.

"Yes, I have killed him," Sir Denzil said, "and because Lord Eldon is insistent there should be no scandal, the whole thing will be hushed up and it will be announced that Talbot has died of a heart attack. But I am to go abroad for three years."

"Three—years!" Lady Caversham echoed faintly.

"It might have been five, or even life," Sir Denzil said, "but knowing Talbot's temper the Lord Chancellor has been lenient to me, as he pointed out in no uncertain terms."

"But three—years, dearest! Where will you go?"

"Anywhere in Europe is impossible, I realise that," Sir Denzil had replied, "and I have no wish to be a prisoner of Bonaparte. No, I shall go to America."

"To . . . America!"

Thalia's voice echoed round the room, because she was so astonished.

America seemed far away, a land of unpredictable people who had thrown out the British, a land full, she thought, of Red Indians and black people who had been brought there from Africa to work as slaves.

After that there had been a wild commotion of packing what her father needed and getting him off to Plymouth where he had already learnt there was a ship preparing to sail across the Atlantic.

His wife had wanted to go with him, but he would not hear of it.

"God knows what sort of discomforts I shall have to endure," Sir Denzil said. "It will be hard enough, my darling, without having to worry about you. Yet three years will pass quickly and I will soon be with you again."

It all sounded a sensible idea despite her mother's misery at being parted from the man she loved.

As soon as it was learned, and it was impossible to pretend otherwise, that Sir Denzil had left the country, the bills came pouring in.

Because her mother was so unhappy, Thalia, although she was only fifteen, had tried to help the family Solicitor whom she had known ever since she was a child, to sort things out.

Thalia was never certain how the rumour began, but the story got about that Sir Denzil had been exiled for life and could never return to England.

It was difficult to explain the true facts and as in all rumours, there had been no single person they could actually discover who had started the story in the first place.

The tradesmen grew more and more pressing and in the end the only thing they could do was to shut up the Manor House and move to London, renting a house in Shepherd's Market for a few pounds a month.

There they lived on the sale of Lady Caversham's jewels that were her own property.

Everything that belonged to Sir Denzil was either sold or mortgaged, the Manor House and its contents fortunately being entailed on to his heirs.

At first Thalia thought that if they lived frugally without any extravagances, they could just manage to exist until her father returned.

Then when the letters from him ceased and they had no news, her mother grew ill. There were doctor's bills and soon their little store of money disappeared.

Owing to the war, luxury foods became more expensive and when it was a case of their being actually hungry, Thalia knew she had to do something.

She had, in fact, for the last year been planning a way in which she thought she could augment their income, but that was a secret she kept even from her mother and it was unfortunately something that was not likely to show a return very quickly.

She therefore told herself she must get employment of some sort, and it was her mother who had given her the idea of trimming bonnets.

Since the war had ended the previous year, clothes had become more elaborate and bonnets were, at times, almost garishly decorated to match the gowns which were also trimmed with lace and ruchings, embroidery and bows.

Mrs. Burton to whom she went first had said she

had no vacancy in her shop and certainly not for somebody without previous experience.

Then she had been astute enough to realise that Thalia's beauty, the educated manner in which she spoke and her whole appearance might be an asset.

She looked her up and down very critically, and found it difficult to find fault.

"I will give you a trial in the workroom," she said at length. "But if you are not satisfactory, you can leave without notice and without making any fuss."

"I accept your conditions, Madam," Thalia had replied.

Mrs. Burton had offered a remuneration for her services which was so small as to be almost ludicrous, but Thalia did not complain.

She told herself that once she was in the position she would make herself indispensable and her finances would improve.

Mrs. Burton, although she was not prepared to say so, had been astounded not only by the artistry with which Thalia could trim bonnets but, when she was promoted to the front of the shop, the skill by which she would flatter a customer into buying more than she had first intended.

I could not do better myself, she often thought.

But she had no intention of saying so, knowing that if a shopwoman was praised she invariably expected her wages to escalate accordingly.

In April, when Mrs. Burton's shop was run off its feet in preparation for the Royal Wedding of Princess Charlotte and Prince Leopold of the Belgians, which was to take place on 4th May, Thalia became, as she had intended, indispensable.

Although her mother was still horrified that she must demean herself to work in a shop, she and Hannah were glad of the money that she brought home.

Now, as if she had been thinking over what Thalia had been saying to her, Lady Caversham asked:

"Is it really necessary, dearest, for you to come in

contact with the gentlemen like the Earl of Hellington? I do not remember your father speaking of him but if he does not treat you as a lady, it will be because of the invidious position in which you are placed."

"I told you, Mama, he treated me as if I was a Milliner," Thalia said with laughter in her voice, "and tipped me for my pains."

Lady Caversham shuddered.

"I cannot bear to think of it," she said.

Then with a little cry, she exclaimed:

"He did not know who you were?"

"No, of course not, Mama," Thalia answered, "and even if he asked my name, Mrs. Burton as you are well aware, only knows me as 'Miss Carver'."

Lady Caversham sighed.

"Such a common name!" she had protested when Thalia had told her it was the name she had chosen.

"That is what it is intended to be," Thalia had replied. "Carver is good old English and doubtless it derives from the butchers who carve the meat."

She had chosen it deliberately as being as near as possible to Caversham, knowing how hard it would be if she was asked quickly to remember not to give her real name.

Her mother had been as horrified by the subterfuge as she was by everything else which Thalia's working entailed.

But Lady Caversham had, in her ignorance, thought that being in a ladies shop was at least some protection from the gentlemen who wandered up and down Bond Street looking for attractive women who frequented that street.

Mrs. Burton did not only sell bonnets, although they had become since Thalia's arrival, her most important item of sale.

The Milliners furnished everything to Ladies that could contribute to or set off their beauty and as some writer had said: "Increase their vanity or render them ridiculous."

Lady Caversham had no idea, nor had Thalia until she worked in a shop, how many gentlemen escorted the lady of their fancy when she went shopping, or how many were expected to pay for what was purchased.

Mrs. Burton soon realised that Thalia was too attractive to serve the Social Ladies who were accompanied by their rich lovers and always waited on them herself.

Thalia was at her best with women who were so plain and unattractive that it was doubtful if any man would look at them with or without an alluring bonnet.

The gentlemen lounged in chairs on the other side of the room while some fashionable Beauty stared at her reflection in the mirror until the moment when she asked his approval pouting her red lips as she did so.

They make me sick, Thalia said to herself. *If I was a man, I would be put off by all those stupid affectations.*

She came to the conclusion however, that a great number of the Gentlemen she saw in Mrs. Burton's shop were as empty-headed as the women they escorted, and she noted critically the behaviour of both sexes.

Now, because she did not wish to go on talking about anything that might prove distressing or upsetting, she said to Lady Caversham:

"I am going to change, dearest, then when we have had supper, I am going to read to you from a book of Lord Byron's poetry which has just been published."

She saw Lady Caversham's eyes light up and she explained:

"On the way back from Mademoiselle Genevieve's this morning I stopped at Hatchard's in Piccadilly and bought the book. I know you will enjoy it, Mama."

"I am sure of it, dearest. But surely that was rather extravagant?"

"We can afford it," Thalia replied.

She was about to add that she had been feeling especially rich because she had the Earl's guinea in her purse, although the circumstances in which she received it, made it feel as if it burned a hole in her pocket.

But she had wanted to give her mother a treat and she had also had another reason for going to Hatchard's.

Now she bent down and kissed Lady Caversham saying:

"Stop worrying, Mama. It will not be long before Papa is home, and you know as well as I do that with the storms we have had this winter, half the ships carrying mail to England from the other side of the world, never reached their destination."

"Supposing—he never comes—home?" Lady Caversham said in a very low voice.

"He will, I know he will," Thalia said. "I 'feel it in my bones', as Hannah says, and you know you told me once, Mama, that because you and Papa were so close, if he had died you would have been aware of it."

"I suppose that is true," Lady Caversham agreed.

"Of course it is true," Thalia said. "You have to believe in Papa and trust him. He is alive, and if he comes home seeing you look as pale as you are now, he will be furious with me and will never believe I have done my best to look after you."

"Oh, my dearest, you have done everything anyone could do, and a great deal more besides," Lady Caversham said. "It is just that I pray that I shall hear from him, but somehow my prayers do not seem to be heard. If only I could have a letter."

"You do not want a letter," Thalia said firmly, "you want Papa! One day he will walk in when you least expect it."

"Suppose he cannot find us?"

"Now, Mama, we have talked about this over and over again," Thalia said. "Everyone in the country will be ready to tell him. Mr. Johnson who runs 'The Green Man' and old Hibbert who is looking after the house, are waiting for him to appear."

She paused then added:

"I also went to our house in Brook Street the other day. As it is empty again, I left a piece of paper stuck on the door saying that all enquiries regarding Lady Caversham should be made to this address."

"You think of everything, dearest."

"I try to," Thalia said, "but you have to help me, Mama, by getting well, and a great deal fatter than you are at the moment."

Lady Caversham smiled.

"If I do that," she said,"I shall have to ask you to let out my gowns, and you know you have no time at the moment."

"When you talk like that, Mama, I feel we are back in the old days with you and Papa, making a joke of everything and the whole house seeming to be filled with sunshine."

She saw the longing in her mother's eyes and added quickly:

"And that is what it will be, mark my words, by the end of the summer. Papa will be with us and we shall all be laughing at something absurd he has done."

Her mother was smiling as Thalia went to her own room.

It was hardly larger than a cupboard on the other side of the landing.

They had been lucky to find such a cheap house and she knew it was because the kind of artisan who lived with his family in Shepherd's Market usually had a number of children, and so small a house could not have accommodated them.

Downstairs was the kitchen where Hannah reigned supreme and a very small Sitting-Room facing on to the street.

It was here that Thalia kept her papers, and before she went into the kitchen where Hannah had prepared her mother's supper that she would carry upstairs, she made a few notes.

As she put her quill-pen back into its holder she looked longingly at what she had written as if she would have liked to go on writing.

Then resolutely she went from the small room, shutting the door behind her.

The Earl walked into White's Club to cause a sensation by his sudden re-appearance.

"Good God, Hellington!" someone exclaimed. "We thought you had gone rustic and we had lost you! Do you realise you have been away for three weeks?"

"I am aware of it," the Earl replied, seating himself amongst the Club's select "inner circle" as a matter of right.

They were all close friends including the Duke of Argyll, Lord Alvanley, Lord Worcester, "Poodle" Byng, and Sir Lumley Skeffington.

They sat in the bow-window which had been sacred to Beau Brummell. It was there he had reigned supreme and his pronouncements were listened to as if he had the wisdom of Solomon.

Not only the Earl but a great number of other members thought White's had never been the same since Brummell's debts had caught up with him and he had been forced to make a quick escape across the Channel where he was now living in a lodging-house in Calais.

"What was the country like?" someone asked, as if it was a foreign land.

"Hot!" the Earl replied.

Because he had no desire to talk about himself he asked:

"What were you laughing about when I arrived? I heard you from the pavement."

"Alvanley was reading from a new book that has just been published," Poodle Byng replied.

"A book?" the Earl enquired.

It seemed an unlikely subject for his friends at White's but Lord Alvanley who was noted as a wit, held up a small volume.

The Earl read what was written on the cover:

GENTLEMEN
by a
PERSON OF QUALITY

"You find it amusing?" he asked.

"Just listen," Lord Alvanley replied.

He turned several pages before he said: "Here is one the others have not heard:

"In the race for a Gentleman's affections, his horses come first, his Club second, his dogs third. Also ran are a number of pretty women, but they seldom last the course."

Those listening laughed and the Earl said:

"It certainly sounds amusing."

"Give us another!" Lord Worcester begged.

Lord Alvanley turned a page and read:

"A Gentleman does not listen at key-holes, but then he listens to no one but himself!"

"That is you, Poodle!" the Duke of Argyll said. "The 'Person of Quality' must have met you!"

"Here is another!" Lord Alvanley said.

"A Gentleman is too sporting to pull his horses or cheat at cards, but he has no qualms about seducing his best friend's wife!"

The Earl looked around his circle of friends.

"Which of you is responsible for this?" he asked. "I doubt if it is you, Skeffington, but I rather suspect Alvanley."

"I swear to you on my honour, that I have not written it, even though I would like to have done so," Lord Alvanley replied. "But now I think of it, it is too witty to be written by anyone who is not a member."

"Sheer conceit!" the Earl snapped. "A great number of the members of this Club are incapable of writing their own names, let alone a book!"

They laughed and teased each other, but while he was talking Lord Alvanley had put the book down on the table in front of him and the Earl picked it up.

There were not many pages but on each one there were six witty comments, and yet there was nothing vicious in what was said. The Earl read:

"A Gentleman has two sets of rules regarding infidelity, one for himself and another for his wife."

Below this was:

"A Dandy is like a peacock: all tail and little brain."

He thought that applied to all the Dandies he knew and whom he also despised. Aloud he said:

"I wonder if we shall ever discover who the author is? I think he will be far too discreet to admit that he is responsible for what a number of people would find uncomfortably true."

"You speak for yourself, Hellington!" the Duke of Argyll answered. "I refuse to admit that anything the book says is the truth, and what is more I resent the impertinence of somebody we might even call a friend putting us in print."

"I agree with you," Lord Worcester said, "it is unsporting."

"If you ask me," the Earl said, "you all have guilty

consciences, and are frightened of what you will read next. But at least as far as I can ascertain, the author mentions no names."

"That is one good thing, at any rate," Lord Worcester said. "At the same time, I shall try to discover who is the traitor in our midst, and when we know, we will make it extremely uncomfortable for him to remain in the Club."

"Personally I could not care what he writes," the Earl said, "and in the case of the innuendoes, if the cap fits, then one must be prepared to wear it."

"That is very high-handed, Vargus," Richard said, who had remained silent up until now. "You are only able to feel so 'cock-a-hoop' because you are quite certain there is no scandal written about you, but a lot of people are in a very different position."

There was silence after he had spoken. Then Lord Worcester said hastily:

"That is true enough. People have no right to go snooping around writing about their friends and acquaintances, then being too cowardly to give their name. I vote we find out who it is and have him 'black-balled'."

The Earl laughed.

"You are all making a mountain out of a mole-hill. As far as I can see there is nothing slanderous in anything that is written here, just generally amusing quips about gentlemen in general."

"If the newspapers get hold of it they will make us look pretty ridiculous!" the Duke of Argyll said harshly.

"Personally I do not care what they say," the Earl replied. "It is only women who read the gossip anyway."

The Earl spoke in the lofty tone which always made Richard smile.

He was well aware that he never gossiped and was never interested in even the juiciest scandals.

The majority of the members at White's were quite

prepared to talk about one another and a number of them were always ready to whisper in a corner about what had happened the night before and reveal whose husband was being cuckolded by his closest friends.

He was not surprised when a little later on the Earl rose restlessly and left the Club.

He did not invite Richard to join him and he watched him wistfully from the bow-window driving off in his Phaeton, up St. James's Street.

He wondered where he was going and wished he had asked.

Last night had been more amusing than he had anticipated. At the first Ball they had attended he and the Earl had found friends there who had been delighted to see them and they had sat drinking in the card-room and made no effort to join the dancers.

At Ashburnham House the Princess had held out her arms in greeting and scolded the Earl for being away for so long.

"London has been dull without you," she said, "but now you are back, My Lord, we must celebrate."

She had introduced him to a number of beautiful women, none of whom Richard thought would be of any use to the Earl in his search for a wife.

At least two of them had intimated before the evening was over that they would be willing to play a very different role in his life when their husbands were otherwise engaged.

Another tried determinedly to enlist his help in promoting a young man with whom she declared herself hopelessly and crazily in love.

All together it was an enjoyable evening, Richard told himself when he got back to his lodgings, *but extremely unfruitful from Vargus's point of view.*

He needed a vast amount of self-control to prevent himself from asking the Earl if he intended to further his acquaintance with Genevieve.

He knew if there was one thing his friend really

disliked it was being cross-questioned about the women in his life.

Richard himself admired Genevieve so much that he could not believe the Earl would be any less enthusiastic than he was and would not take the opportunity of capturing her before he found he had other rivals.

At the same time the Earl was always unpredictable and Richard would have thought him even more so if he had known where he was going at this moment.

The Earl drove his Phaeton to Bond Street, and when he was some doors away from where he knew Mrs. Burton had her shop he drew his horses to a standstill.

"Walk them, Henry," he said to his groom, then proceeded to walk leisurely down the street.

Thinking over his encounter yesterday with the French ballet-dancer, he had come to the conclusion that he was more interested in the little Milliner.

He found himself remembering not only the musical quality of her voice, but also the flash of anger that had appeared in her eyes when he had tipped her.

It was certainly unexpected, and that it had happened, intrigued him.

He also remembered the faint suspicion of dimples and the twinkle in her down-cast eyes when something amused her.

He might be mistaken, he might easily be disappointed, but he had the feeling that he would like to see her again. However, for the moment he was not quite certain how to go about it.

He knew where she worked because Mrs. Burton's name was inscribed on the bonnet-boxes which she had carried from the room when she left without bidding anyone good-bye.

The Earl was sure that the reason her departure

had been so precipitate was the fact that he had given her a guinea.

He had expended a great many more guineas on Genevieve and when he and Richard had left and she had thanked him even more profusely the second time, he had found her methods too obvious to be intriguing.

What was more, the blatant way she displayed her body robbed her of the mystery which the Earl liked to find in the women he fancied.

It continually irked him that when he was with Ladies of the *Beau Monde* or the "Fashionable Impures," they never allowed him to do his own hunting.

Almost before he made up his mind he was interested in them, they were making it unmistakably obvious that they were very interested in him.

Last night he had known that only a matter of time and opportunity would enable him, if he wished, to go to bed with both the women to whom the Princess had introduced him, and accordingly he found himself retreating rather than advancing.

He spent more time thinking of the troubles of the woman in love than of the considerable attractions of the other two.

He had known she was sincere and he liked the manner in which she spoke naturally and unpretentiously in order to plead the cause of the man she loved.

The Earl had long ago admitted to himself that one thing he hoped to find in a woman, was a certain unpredictableness.

It was like playing a game of chess with an experienced opponent whose move one never expected and was therefore exciting and stimulating.

Unfortunately the women he met up with were predictable to the point when he could anticipate every move they made and every word they said.

It was this which made him afraid of marriage.

How could he endure the boredom of knowing

what remark his wife would make before she made it? Of knowing there were no surprises in store for him tomorrow, the day after, or the day after that?

There was one thing about horses, he told himself often enough, that even the best trained and the most reliable could sometimes surprise, disconcert and even infuriate one.

When he thought of horses he remembered the phrase which Lord Alvanley had read aloud, and he told himself that it was unmistakably true that in a race for his affections, his horses came in first.

Nevertheless, he decided he would have a look at the little Milliner again.

He would doubtless be disillusioned, but at least it would be amusing, if nothing else, to make her eyes flash with anger, then watch her force herself to be humbly subservient.

Mrs. Burton's shop was the next in the street and he would reach it within a few footsteps.

He stopped almost as if he was reconnoitring his position as he had often done in France.

Even as he stared into a shop-window which although he was unaware of it, was a Pharmacist's, he heard a voice cry from a carriage:

"Vargus! Is it really you?"

There was no mistaking who spoke and as the Earl took his hat from his head he thought it was unfortunate that he had encountered Lady Adelaide so soon after returning to London.

He had, in fact, been relieved that she had not been at either of the Balls last night, knowing she would cling to him in that possessive manner that he found extremely irritating.

"You are back, Vargus!" she said.

She alighted from her carriage and was standing beside him and looking up at him with an unmistakable enticement in her slanting dark eyes.

"As you see, I am back," the Earl replied.

"Why did you not tell me?"

"I only returned yesterday."

"You knew I would be waiting breathlessly for your return! Surely Richard must have told you how perturbed I was at your long absence in the country?"

She paused and looked suspicious.

"If it was the country which kept you?"

"If there is one thing I find tiresome it is being expected to make explanations about what I have done or have not done," the Earl replied sharply.

Then an idea came to him. In a very different voice he said:

"To make reparation for my misdeeds, I will give you a new bonnet. Why do we not repair to Mrs. Burton's shop and see what she has that will suit you?"

"Vargus!"

For a moment Lady Adelaide's breath was taken away.

Never until now, had the Earl offered her presents of any sort with the exception of flowers which she knew were ordered for him by his secretary, as a matter of form.

"A bonnet!" she went on. "But of course, I would love one."

It struck her that a bonnet was a rather intimate present: something a man might give to a woman to whom he was attracted, but not if his intentions were serious.

Then she told herself quickly she was not a young girl to be compromised by a present, whatever it might be, and that the Earl should give her anything was certainly a step in the right direction.

"I can imagine," she said, "no better way to celebrate your homecoming, and as you say, Mrs. Burton's is next door."

"Let us go there," the Earl said. "I have a feeling, Adelaide, that no woman has enough bonnets in her life."

"Of course not, nor enough Beaux," Lady Adelaide

replied with what was meant to be a glance of admiration.

She did not realise that the Earl's lips tightened for a moment at the name or that he had a strong desire to tell her that he had changed his mind.

Then, Lady Adelaide chattering gaily, they walked into Mrs. Burton's shop and the Earl, as he had expected, saw a slight figure in a grey gown, waiting on a customer.

Chapter Three

The Earl driving his Phaeton down a somewhat scruffy street into which he knew the back door of the Bond Street shops opened, thought he had been very clever.

One glance at the little Milliner he had seen the day before told him she was even more alluring than he remembered and her hair particularly, was a colour that was unique.

He realised that it was a hue chorus-girls attempted to attain with the use of dye-pots, only to be disappointed.

There was no doubt that in the Milliner's case it was natural and a perfect frame for her large eyes.

She was very thin and it gave her a spiritual grace which made Lady Adelaide look heavy and somewhat clumsy.

The Earl was far too shrewd to stare too obviously

across the shop or appear to be interested in anything except the lady he was accompanying.

Lady Adelaide was in her element.

She was so elated at the thought of the Earl giving her a present and seeming to be more effusive than usual that she chattered away, flirting with him with side-long glances and an invitation on her red lips which she felt he must find irresistible.

Mrs. Burton produced a number of extremely attractive bonnets for Lady Adelaide to try on.

Each time she turned to ask the Earl's opinion she was sure there was a look of admiration in his eyes and as she was determined to spin out the time they were together for as long as possible she kept on asking to see yet another creation.

She must have tried on nearly a dozen when the Earl said to Mrs. Burton:

"I saw a bonnet I rather admired yesterday. One of your assistants was showing it to a client at Fletcher's Hotel near Drury Lane."

Lady Adelaide was still.

She was immediately curious as to who the Earl was visiting in that vicinity and suspected it was a performer at either the King's Theatre or Covent Garden.

In the circumstances the woman was not likely to trouble her particularly. But she had no wish for him to take another mistress, having learnt from Richard that his interest in one he had recently housed and provided with some quite outstanding jewellery was now at an end.

If he was going to be generous with jewels in the future Lady Adelaide was determined to have them herself, although what she really craved was nothing more expensive than a gold wedding-ring.

She was, however, wise enough not to interrupt but to listen to what was said as Mrs. Burton replied to the Earl:

"Can Your Lordship describe the bonnet in any way?" Mrs. Burton asked.

"I think it was black," the Earl said vaguely, "with some trimming that might have been red or pink—I really cannot remember. Perhaps your assistant can recall the one I mean."

"That would have been Thalia—I mean Miss Carver," Mrs. Burton said as if to herself. "I will ask her."

She crossed the room to speak to Thalia who disappeared into the back of the shop and returned with the black and red bonnet that the Earl remembered perfectly well. But he had discovered what he wished to know, the little Milliner's name was Thalia Carver!

It was only when she had been promoted to work in the front of the shop that Thalia had been called by her surname prefixed with "Miss."

The work-girls were all addressed by their Christian names, but because she was so popular and unlike the other assistants who gave themselves airs when there were no customers present, everyone from Mrs. Burton downwards still called her Thalia.

Lady Adelaide was delighted with the black and red bonnet, and after she had ordered it to be sent to her house and the Earl had told Mrs. Burton to send the bill to him they left the shop.

He deliberately did not even glance in Thalia's direction, but he was aware that she did not look at him —which for him, was an unusual experience.

He thought now as he drew up his horses outside the shabby door that she could not help being impressed by his Phaeton, if not by him.

As the groom ran to the horses' heads he climbed down to wait with a feeling that surprisingly, was nearly one of impatience.

It was a long time, he thought, since he had felt interested in a woman who was not already flirting with him over a supper-table, or contriving in the most obvious manner that they should be alone in the

Conservatory or the garden of a mansion in which a Ball was being given.

Last night the two Beauties to whom the Princess had introduced him made it quite clear what they wanted, and he had therefore found himself bored after a very short time in their company.

Some cynical part of his mind told him that the pursuit of the little Milliner would be no different.

At the same time he could not help remembering that when she had flounced away from him in Genevieve's bedroom she had certainly not shown any anxiety either to speak to him again, let alone meet him.

I shall undoubtedly find I have been over-optimistic in expecting her to be any different, he told himself, *although her hair is certainly an unexpected colour for someone of her class.*

The shop-door opened and the Earl waited expectantly, but it was not Thalia who came out but a number of other women.

Most of them were middle-aged or elderly with the exception of two very young girls who the Earl suspected, were what was known as "matchers," and occupied the lowest and least paid position in Mrs. Burton's.

Because he always made it his business to know the details about anything and anyone in whom he was interested, this afternoon he had, when he left White's gone to a bookshop to find out if there were any publications about shops and their assistants.

He had an account with several bookshops, but the nearest to White's was John Hatchard's at 190 Piccadilly.

He was the bookseller to Queen Charlotte, while Nicoll at Pall Mall, was patronised by the King.

As the Earl expected, the shop was filled with a number of men and women from the Social World and a number who were not, most of them talking to each other while they imbibed cups of coffee.

The Earl was immediately recognised by John

Hatchard who hurried to bow respectfully his pleasure at receiving His Lordship in person.

Although he regularly bought a number of books they were usually ordered by his secretary and delivered to Hellington House.

The Earl told John Hatchard what he required.

"That is not a difficult request, My Lord," Mr. Hatchard replied. "I have here William Abbott's *Reminiscences of an old Draper* and there is quite a lot about a shopkeeper who ranges from grocer to cheese-monger, to Men-Milliners in *Cranford* by Mrs. Gaskell."

The Earl glanced at the books and decided they would tell him a little of what he wished to know and ignored Mr. Hatchard's expostulations when he said, instead of having them delivered, he would take them with him.

He had driven back home to peruse what he had bought, and now seeing the women leaving the shop staring at him with surprise and curiosity, he thought it was unlikely they had ever had what the servants called a "follower" waiting for them at the back-door.

They continued to turn their heads even when they had reached the end of the street, but the Earl waited, feeling it was unlikely that Thalia would leave by the front.

In this he was correct, for ten minutes after Mrs. Burton's other employees had left, she stepped out into the street.

She was wearing the concealing grey bonnet which she had worn in Genevieve's bedroom and because her head was bent as she closed the door behind her, she did not see who was waiting.

It was the horses which caught her eye first, then as her head went up to stare at them the Earl was in front of her, blocking her view.

"Good evening, Miss Carver!"

For a moment it seemed as if because she was so astonished to see him, she could not find the words to reply. Then she announced in the low, musical voice he remembered:

"Good evening, My Lord."

She made an effort to proceed but with the Earl blocking her way, it was not easy.

"I hope," he said, "you will allow me to drive you home. I have brought my Phaeton, as you see, in order to do so."

"I thank Your Lordship, but I have someone waiting for me."

This was certainly not the answer the Earl had expected.

He glanced round, finding there was no other vehicle in the street except a passing dray and only a few pedestrians.

"I think you are mistaken," he said, "and I can only repeat my invitation. I am very anxious, Miss Carver, to drive you home in style."

"It is not an invitation I can accept, My Lord," Thalia said and the Earl thought there was a deliberately repressive note in her voice.

She stepped to one side of him and before he could make any effort to stop her, she was walking quickly down the street. He stared after her, not quite certain what he should do.

Then as he watched he saw the figure of an elderly woman dressed in black, move towards her.

They stopped, spoke for a moment, then hurried around the corner.

The Earl climbed back into his Phaeton. He drove in the direction in which Thalia had gone and was just in time to see her turning another corner into Hay Hill.

Again he followed, but this time he encountered a coach-and-four coming down Dover Street and by the time he had allowed it to precede him he merely had a glimpse of Thalia's grey gown disappearing into Lansdowne Passage.

This at any rate told him in which direction she was

going because Lansdowne Passage was a short cut to Curzon Street.

By the time the Earl had driven through Berkeley Square passing Lansdowne House and into Curzon Street, Thalia and her elderly companion were far ahead.

However skilfully he drove, the Earl was brought to the irritating conclusion that he had been out-witted when he saw Thalia turn under the archway which led into Shepherd's Market.

Here it was impossible for his Phaeton to follow her, but at least he told himself, as he drove on up Curzon Street, he knew whereabouts she lived.

He had almost reached the top of the street before he came to a decision.

"Get down, Henry," he said, to his groom. "Go to Shepherd's Market and find out all you can about Miss Carver. The place is so small that I cannot believe there will not be someone to give you her address. Discover if she lives alone or has a family. I want every possible detail, but make your enquiries with discretion. I know I can trust you."

"Oi'll be as quick as Oi can, M'Lord," Henry replied.

It was not the first time he had been sent on strange missions for his employer, and as he was usually the conveyor of notes, flowers and presents to the ladies in whom the Earl was interested, he referred to himself jokingly when he was among the other servants as "Eros."

"Get along with ye!" the housemaids would say. "Ye ain't got no wings, 'Enry, an' never likely to 'ave!"

"Ye've got no idea what Oi can do with me bow and arrow," Henry would boast.

They would scream with laughter as he chased them round the passages at the back of Hellington House, only to be reproved by the Butler or the Housekeeper for making a noise.

Now he jumped down from the Phaeton and made his way back towards Shepherd's Market.

Like all His Lordship's staff he admired the Earl whole-heartedly not only for his appearance but also because he was an outstanding sportsman, and it was, therefore, a very enviable position to be in his employment.

The Earl was not aware that the servants who had been with him since he returned from the war all preferred service with a bachelor.

Most of them had found that in a position where their employer had a wife, life was far more arduous, far more difficult and there was inevitably much less freedom.

The Earl expected everything to be perfect where he was concerned, but he was never niggardly or petty.

There was no one amongst his servants who had not tales to tell of how difficult their lives could be when there was a nagging mistress, or worse still, a cheese-paring one, in contrast with the tolerance of a good master.

Of one thing Henry was sure, that the Earl would not be looking for a wife in Shepherd's Market, in fact, he assumed he had altogether another position in mind for the girl in grey.

There had been bets in the stables for some time as to how soon the place left empty by the last "bit o'muslin" would be filled.

Bet her jumps at the chance, Henry said to himself.

It was after six o'clock when the Earl, reading the newspapers in the Library at Hellington House was interrupted by the Butler to say that Henry wished to speak to him.

"Show him in!" the Earl ordered.

Henry came into the room and there was a smile on

his face which told the Earl before he spoke, that his mission had been successful.

He was a very small and wiry little man who looked far younger than he actually was, and had, as the Earl was well aware, an exceptional way with horses.

He was also completely honest but he had an adventurous streak which, the Earl thought, complemented his own.

He put down the *Morning Post.*

"Well, Henry?"

"Oi've found out all about 'er, M'Lord. 'Er lives at Number 82, a tidy little 'ouse it be."

"Alone?"

"No, M'Lord. 'Er mother lives with 'er an' they tells me 'er's always ill. A physician comes regular. An' th' women 'er were with, be a servant, M'Lord, name of Hannah—a regular old battle-axe they tell Oi 'er can be when it comes t' shoppin'. Expects th' best cuts for as little as 'er can get 'em."

The Earl smiled.

He was aware that Henry would have made enquiries at the butchers of which there were traditionally a number in Shepherd's Market.

"Anything more, Henry?" he enquired.

"Everyone speaks well o' the young lidy, M'Lord. Said as 'er were having a 'ard time 'til 'er got a job in Bond Street, since then 'as paid on the' nail an' never asks for favours like some they could mention!"

The Earl had learned what he wished to know.

"Thank you, Henry."

"Pleasure, M'Lord!" Henry said cheekily.

With a grin that was an impertinence in itself, he went from the room.

The Earl, who would have permitted no familiarity from any other member of his household, was particulary lenient where Henry was concerned.

He supposed it was because Henry was such a little man. At the same time, he was not only useful but trustworthy and that was something the Earl had found in the war was more important than spit and polish and an unbending conventionality.

Without hurrying himself the Earl rose to his feet and walking into the Hall, took his hat and cane from the footman on duty.

"Do you require a carriage, M'Lord?" one of the lackeys enquired.

"No, I am walking," the Earl replied.

He left the house. The south end of Berkeley Square was only a short distance from Shepherd's Market and the Earl knew he would anyway, have to proceed on foot in the market itself.

Although it was late in the afternoon, the small shops were still open as the majority of them catered for those who worked and were so individualistic they had no wish to copy the more important shops who had certain closing hours, but remained a law unto themselves.

It was obvious that those who shopped in the market were friendly and in most cases as familiar with each other as if it was really the small country village it had been throughout the centuries.

It was not difficult for the Earl to find amongst the modest little dwellings which he suspected were occupied mostly by craftsmen, Number 82.

As he approached it, he liked what he could see of the curtains that hung at the windows, the cleanliness of the windows themselves and the way the ancient knocker on the door had been polished until it reflected its surroundings like a mirror.

The Earl raised the knocker with his hand and waited.

There was a pause before he heard footsteps coming down an uncarpeted passage and a moment later the door opened.

The elderly woman dressed like a respectable servant who he knew had accompanied Thalia home, was looking at him in what was quite obviously a hostile manner.

"I wish to see Miss Carver," the Earl said in a commanding manner which intimidated most people.

"Miss Carver is not at Home, M'Lord."

The Earl noted immediately the way he was addressed, and knew that Thalia must have told the servant who he was, when she had seen him speaking to her in the street.

"I think that is not true."

"Miss Carver is not receiving, M'Lord."

There was no doubt now of the aggressive note in the woman's voice and she was making it clear in case the Earl was very obtuse what 'not at Home' meant.

"I think she will see me," the Earl said firmly.

He stepped forward as he spoke and because he was so large there was nothing Hannah could do but move backwards.

For a moment she was discomfited. Then, perhaps afraid of being rude to so distinguished a visitor, she opened a door on the left-hand side of the passage, saying:

"If Your Lordship will wait in here."

The Earl moved into a small Sitting-Room. It was, he saw, decorated in good taste although there was nothing of any value in the room. But he noted immediately the desk piled with papers and wondered if Thalia drew designs before she trimmed her bonnets so skilfully.

He stood waiting with his back to the fireplace, wondering with a faint smile on his lips, what consternation his arrival was causing upstairs.

Then the door opened and Thalia came in.

She had changed her gown, he noticed, for a simple muslin which became her and seemed to accentuate the lights in her hair and the clearness of her skin.

There was no doubt, the Earl thought as he looked at her, that she was lovely, lovelier than anyone he had seen for a long time, and he knew with a sensation almost of triumph that his persistence in finding her had been well worth while.

He was not prepared however for the way that she shut the door behind her and came quite near to him before she spoke. Then she said in a low voice that was hardly above a whisper:

"You must not come here! Please leave at once!"

"Leave?" the Earl enquired. "But why?"

"Because my mother must not know that you have called."

The Earl raised his eyebrows.

"Does your mother's disapproval apply only to me?" he enquired, "or are your other male acquaintances equally unwelcome?"

"I have no male acquaintances," Thalia said. "But Mama would be horrified if she knew you were here."

"Why?" the Earl asked again.

"Because . . ." Thalia began, then stopped. "There is no need for me to make explanations, My Lord. As Hannah told you I am not at home, and I must ask you to leave."

"I have no wish to do so," the Earl said. "I want to talk to you, Miss Carver."

"We have nothing to say to each other."

"That is for me to decide, and quite frankly I have a great deal to say."

Thalia looked up to the ceiling as if she was afraid his voice would be overheard. Then again she was pleading with him:

"Please go! It will upset Mama and she is not well. She has so many troubles already, and if she knew . . . you were . . . here it would perturb her . . . greatly."

"Then of course I must leave," the Earl said, "but as you will understand, as we cannot talk here, we must meet somewhere."

"That is impossible!" Thalia said quickly.

"Then I must insist upon staying."

She made what was a stifled cry of annoyance.

"You cannot be so . . . unfeeling when I have told you that my mother is . . . ill."

"Then where can we talk?" the Earl persisted.

There was a sound upstairs and again Thalia looked up at the ceiling saying frantically:

"Anywhere . . . anywhere but . . . here!"

"Very well," the Earl said, "I will collect you at half-after-eight o'clock, and we will dine somewhere quiet and discreet where we can talk without being overheard."

Thalia opened her eyes in sheer surprise until they seemed so large they almost filled her face.

"D—dine with you alone?"

"I was not thinking of inviting anybody else."

"But of course I . . . cannot do such a thing. It would be . . . wrong."

"Then let us talk here," the Earl said genially. "You are well chaperoned, even though your mother is on another floor."

"You are blackmailing me," Thalia said after a moment.

"Yes I am!" the Earl replied, "and let me tell you, I always get what I want, so it would be easier to give in at the beginning and allow me to have my way."

"What can you . . . possibly have to . . . say to me?"

"That will take time," the Earl said, "but as I have told you, I am ready to say what must be said now, if you will permit me to do so."

He knew that she was agitated, apprehensive and a little afraid, not of him, but of the effect his presence would have on her mother.

He knew she was considering, thinking, trying to find a way out of the position in which she found herself.

Then once again a slight noise overhead seemed to make up her mind for her.

"Very well," she said at length, "you have forced my hand and I hate you for doing so. But because I cannot have Mama upset at this . . . moment, I will dine with you. But not until after nine o'clock when she goes to sleep."

"I will call at fifteen minutes past nine," the Earl replied.

"Do not knock on the door," Thalia instructed him. "Just wait outside until I can join you."

He smiled in acknowledgement of her instructions. Then as if she was extremely anxious to get rid of him, she moved to the door and stepped into the small passage outside, to open the front-door.

"Nine-fifteen," the Earl said. "I am prepared to wait quite patiently, Miss Carver, if you are unexpectedly delayed."

Thalia did not answer but merely shut the door, and the Earl had the feeling that if she had been able to act naturally she would have slammed it.

He was smiling as he walked away.

He thought that he had won what had been quite a skirmish—not a battle, that would come later—but definitely a trial of strength in which, as was to be expected, he was the conqueror.

When the Earl had gone, Thalia had stood for a moment in the passage composing herself before she went upstairs.

She was so incensed with the Earl that she felt her mother might easily be aware of the vibrations of anger which she was sure she was sending out almost like sparks of fire.

How dare he follow her here! How dare a man she had seen only once—twice if one counted his coming to the shop to buy a bonnet for some woman he fancied—force himself upon her in such a ungentlemanly manner?

And to blackmail her into dining with him, when

she knew it was something she should not do, and would doubtless give her mother a heart attack if she ever learned of it!

"What can I do?" Thalia asked herself.

She had an uncomfortable feeling that if she refused to join him when he came to fetch her, he might easily knock on the door until either she or Hannah opened it, and make a scene if she refused to join him.

"It is impossible! He is behaving in a most ungentlemanly manner!" she stormed.

Then she realised it was because he was not treating her as a lady.

She supposed this was the type of difficulty shop-assistants often encountered, and perhaps for the first time, she understood a little of her mother's apprehension that she should pretend to belong to a class inferior to her own.

She took several deep breaths as if to calm herself, then walked slowly up the stairs.

Lady Caversham watched her enter the room.

"Who was it, dearest?" she asked. "Hannah said there was somebody at the door who wished to see you."

There was a note in her mother's voice which told Thalia that she was already worried and a little apprehensive.

Just for a moment she thought of telling her the truth and asking her advice, but she saw how frail her mother looked and knew that any more anxiety, any more worry, might prove disastrous.

It was enough for her to lie awake night after night crying helplessly for her husband, without adding yet another problem to the ones with which they were already beset.

Any further aggravation might be enough to prove fatal.

Thalia made up her mind.

"Actually, Mama, I have had a secret for a long

time," she said, "but now I am going to tell you what I have been keeping from you."

"Keeping from me?" Lady Caversham repeated.

"I hope it will make you feel proud of me," Thalia said. "I have written a book!"

"Written a book!" Lady Caversham replied in sheer astonishment.

"Only a very small one," Thalia said. "I was going to wait until your birthday on Friday and give it to you as a present, but as I cannot bottle it up any longer, you must have it now. Wait, Mama, while I fetch it."

Thalia rose as she spoke, to cross the passage from her mother's room to her own.

The author's copies of her book which she had collected yesterday from Hatchards after she had been with Mademoiselle Genevieve were in a little pile on her dressing-table.

One had already been wrapped in tissue paper and tied with a bow of pink ribbon.

She had intended to give it with a number of other small presents, to her mother on her birthday, but she knew now she must at all costs, divert her attention from the Earl's intrusion and she could think of no better way to do so.

She carried the wrapped book back to the bedroom and put it into her mother's hands.

"There you are, Mama," she said, "your daughter's debut into the literary world, and I am praying, as you must, that it will be a success and make us a lot of money."

"I cannot believe it!" Lady Caversham exclaimed.

She undid the ribbon with fingers that trembled and pulled the book out of its wrapping.

" *'Gentlemen, by a Person of Quality',* " she read aloud. "Thalia what have you written?"

"It was a book I saw in the Library at home that made me think of it," Thalia replied. "It was in French and it was called simply: *Les Femmes.* It was a book of sayings which a Frenchman had collected about women all through the ages."

"I think I remember it," Lady Caversham said.

"I showed it to Papa. He laughed and said he could add a great deal to it if he chose and perhaps one day he would write a book about all the women he had known, none of whom were as beautiful as you, Mama."

"Darling Denzil, did he really say that?" Lady Caversham asked.

"He was always saying it," Thalia said. "When I was wondering how I could possibly make money I remembered *Les Femmes* and thought I would do the same about gentlemen."

"You have written this all yourself?"

"It is not very long," Thalia said modestly.

"How did you get it published?"

"I went to see Mr. John Hatchard at his shop in Piccadilly. I knew he published George Crabbe and although my work is very different, I asked him if he would read my manuscript. He said he would and was so kind to me, Mama. But do you know what he told me about himself?"

"What did he say?" Lady Caversham asked.

"He said that when he opened his bookshop he wrote in his diary: *'This day, by the grace of God, the goodwill of my friends and £5 in my pocket, I have opened my bookshop in Piccadilly.'* Just think of it, Mama. He took such a gamble on his shop being a success."

"It was certainly a brave action," Lady Caversham agreed.

"When I told him how very important it was for me to make some money," Thalia went on. "I think he thought of his own struggles and wanted to help me."

"It was very kind of him to publish it when you are unknown," Lady Caversham said. "But this book does not really seem like you, dearest, and I should have thought you might have written a novel."

"I am no Jane Austen," Thalia laughed, "and Mr.

Hatchard said he was sure this book would amuse the *Beau Monde.* I am keeping my fingers crossed, Mama, hoping that it makes a lot of money and I become a success overnight like Lord Byron."

Lady Caversham was staring at the book she held in her hand.

"I can hardly believe it," she said. "It seems only the other day that I was teaching you the alphabet and you were trying to read the words of two syllables. Now you have written a book, but I wish you could have put your name on it."

"I would have liked that too," Thalia said, "but Mr. Hatchard said he thought a lot of people would think it impertinent for a woman to criticise gentlemen, and he also thought it would sell better if it had an air of mystery about it."

"I shall read every word," Lady Caversham promised, "and think as I do so, what a clever daughter I have."

She looked down at the book again, then asked:

"How could you know so much about men?"

"I suppose the answer is that I know very little, but I remember the things Papa used to say and the witty sayings in many books I have read. Then the idea came to me when I was listening to what the customers said about their husbands and their young men."

"You mean, they actually discuss such things in front of you?" Lady Caversham said in a shocked voice.

"Of course, Mama," Thalia answered. "You know people always behave as if servants were deaf. Well, in the eyes of those who buy bonnets, I am only a servant."

She was not listening as her mother started once again to say how much she disliked her being in such an inferior position and working for a living.

Instead she was wondering what the Earl thought of her or why he was so insistent that he must see her.

She thought when he had come into Mademoiselle

Genevieve's bedroom looking so tall and elegant that it was quite obvious why he was there, and from what Genevieve had said before he arrived, Thalia had known she was expecting an important gentleman to call on her.

Then surprisingly this afternoon the Earl had come into the shop with Lady Adelaide, who according to Mrs. Burton was one of the beauties of Society and whatever she wore, set a fashion amongst the other ladies who all envied her.

When he could have such gorgeous creatures to engage his attention, why on earth should the Earl want to talk to her?

Thalia suddenly had a terrifying idea that he might have discovered who she was, then she told herself that was absurd.

Why should anyone ever connect Thalia Carver, a Milliner in Bond Street, with Sir Denzil Caversham?

No—that was not the explanation, and she supposed she would learn what it was when she dined with him.

Although she told herself the Earl was utterly despicable in forcing her to do something which she knew would shock and horrify her mother, she could not help but feel slightly excited at going out to dinner.

Ever since they had come to London Thalia had become so used to playing the part she had set herself, that she was not expecting to have any social life.

She knew her mother was right in saying they must avoid all the friends they had ever known, not only because it was impossible to give an explanation as to why Sir Denzil had disappeared, but also because they had no wish for sympathy or pity.

"When your Papa returns," Lady Caversham had said often enough, "we will first go to the country and live quietly until all the gossip has died down, then we will take up our lives where they left off."

"How will we pay for it, Mama?" Thalia asked.

"Perhaps your father will have some money when he comes home," Lady Caversham replied weakly.

Thalia had thought it very unlikely, knowing her father had a genius for spending money but none for acquiring it.

She did not, however, wish to make her mother more depressed than she was already, but merely said:

"I am sure Papa is clever enough to put everything to . . . rights, even our finances."

Lady Caversham ate her supper brought up to her on a tray and managed because she was so interested in Thalia's book, to eat more than usual.

"You have been very good this evening, Mama," Thalia said with satisfaction, "and you must not forget to tell Hannah how much you enjoyed the new way she cooked the chicken."

"Was it chicken?" Lady Caversham asked vaguely, then said quickly: "Of course I will. Dear Hannah tries so hard to tempt my appetite. I feel so ashamed that I am never hungry."

"Perhaps the book will bring in lots of money," Thalia said, "then we can tempt you with all sorts of exquisite delicacies. You might even like the Romans fancy peacock tongues."

Lady Caversham gave a little cry of horror.

"How could they be so cruel?"

"I was only teasing, Mama," Thalia said quickly. "You are feeling much better this evening, but I want you to try and go to sleep and not read my book, as I know you are longing to do."

"I would be much happier for us to read it together."

"We will do that tomorrow," Thalia murmured, "but now I am going to help you into bed. Then I will just read you a few extracts to make you laugh."

By the time Lady Caversham was in bed having laughed over some of the things Thalia had written, it was past nine o'clock.

After kissing her mother goodnight Thalia went to her own bedroom. She told herself if His Lordship was expecting her to be wearing evening-dress he was going to be disappointed.

She did not possess one.

She had been fifteen when her father had left England and since then the only new gown she had had was one which she and Hannah had made together.

Recently they had found some cheap but attractive muslin in the market and there were ribbons too, not the expensive satin ones which during the war were smuggled in from France, but in pretty colours, although they creased easily.

Thalia washed and changed into her latest gown simply because the rest were almost in rags.

It was a sprigged muslin with two frills on the bottom of the skirt and a frill round the neck which made her look very young.

"If he expects someone sophisticated," Thalia told her reflection, "he should take out Lady Adelaide!"

Then she told herself that she was presuming very much on the idea that the Earl was asking her to dine because he thought of her as a woman.

She could not help feeling that he had a very different reason and again Thalia asked herself a little apprehensively what it would be.

As she arranged her hair she realised it was already twenty-minutes past nine and doubtless the Earl was waiting.

"Let him wait!" she told herself savagely, then was afraid he might put his threat into operation and knock loudly on the door disturbing her mother.

Like many people who are ill Lady Caversham had a habit of dropping off almost immediately when she went to bed, only to awaken two or three hours later, and find it impossible to sleep again.

To be disturbed early in the evening was disastrous, for that meant she would often have what was described as a "white night" and in the morning would seem so frail that Thalia would be afraid.

I must go down to him, she thought.

She took from the wardrobe a long cloak which her mother had worn in the days when they were more affluent.

It was of velvet in a deep madonna blue, and had once been trimmed with sable before Thalia had sold the fur because it had provided them with something to eat.

It was simple and hung over her shoulders making her with the strange colour of her hair, appear as if she had stepped out of a stained-glass window.

To herself she merely looked somewhat under-dressed, but she thought if the Earl was ashamed of her, there was nothing she could do about it.

She tip-toed very quietly down the stairs and went into the kitchen.

Hannah looked at her and her face darkened.

"What's the world coming to, that's what I'd like to know!" she said. "He's no right to ask you out alone. You know that!"

"I do know it, Hannah," Thalia answered, "but what else could I do? I could not have him upset Mama."

"I suppose you could have insisted I came with you." Hannah said grudgingly.

Just for a moment Thalia thought it would be amusing to see the Earl's reaction to this request. Then she said aloud:

"That is what I would like to do, but supposing Mama should wake and find nobody in the house?"

"I only hopes as you can manage a man like His Lordship," Hannah said grimly, "but I doubts it."

Thalia rather doubted it too, but she asked herself what was the alternative.

Hannah gave a sudden cry.

"What is it?" Thalia asked.

"I've an idea! I've an idea, Miss Thalia! Just you wait here."

As she spoke she went from the kitchen down the stairs which led to the cellar.

Thalia look after her in perplexity.

There was nothing in the cellar she knew except for the trunks they had brought with them from the country, a number of which belonged to her father and contained his clothes.

When they had unpacked there had been nowhere to put his things in so small a house and Hannah therefore put them in the cellar to unpack them from time to time to make certain they were not being spoilt by damp or moth.

Thalia waited, aware that the Earl was waiting too and doubtless growing more and more impatient.

Then Hannah came heavily up the narrow staircase from the cellar.

"Here's what I was looking for," she said. "You take it with you, Miss Thalia. You might find it useful."

She held out her hand as she spoke and when Thalia saw what was in it, she gave a little gasp.

"A pistol, Hannah!"

"It's your Papa's, and it's loaded. I could only find one bullet, so if you have to use it, you have only one chance."

"I cannot! I cannot take it!" Thalia said. "It was because Papa shot a man, that we are in this situation now."

"I know that," Hannah said stolidly, "but there's worse things to be afraid of than fire-arms, and you take this pistol with you, Miss Thalia, in case you need it."

Thalia knew she was talking sense.

She also realised that the pistol was a very small one which she remembered now her father carried in the evening when he drove some distance to a party.

There were always Highwaymen and footpads to be wary of in every part of the country.

Although Thalia never remembered their being held up or robbed, there were always stories of other people who had unpleasant experiences when, with nothing with which to defend themselves, they had been obliged meekly to hand over their valuables.

It struck her that she might be in the same position —obliged to do anything the Earl demanded of her because she would be quite unable to fight him . . . if that was how their evening ended.

"Perhaps you are right, Hannah," she said. "It is always wise to be prepared."

She took the pistol from the maid and put it in the satin bag she carried which was attached to her arm by ribbons.

It was heavy, but at least she thought it unlikely that the Earl would be aware of it and she thought she must be careful if she opened the bag to obtain her handkerchief that he did not see what was inside.

"Now I must go," she said.

Hannah did not reply. She merely walked stolidly and slowly ahead of her as if, Thalia thought with a hint of amusement, she was taking her to her execution instead of to the front-door.

It was just beginning to grow dark but it was quite easy to see the Earl standing a little way up the road.

As Thalia walked towards him she was aware that he was looking particularly resplendent in an evening cloak thrown back over one shoulder.

Beneath it he was wearing full evening-dress with the exception that instead of knee-breeches, he had on the long "drain-pipe" trousers which had just been introduced as a new fashion.

As Thalia reached him, she was aware how insignificant and nondescript she must appear in contrast.

"You are late!" the Earl said without any more formal acknowledgement of her presence. "I was just beginning to wonder if I should have to remind you I was outside by knocking on the door."

"I was afraid you might do that. That is why I am here."

"Your mother is not aware that you have left the house?"

"No."

He stood looking at her, and Thalia said suddenly:

"You have won your bet, My Lord, or perhaps it was just a challenge you set yourself. Now may I go back? There is no point in your giving me dinner for, as you can well see, I am unable even to dress the part."

"You look charming!" the Earl said in a voice that was impersonal. "But if you are afraid of who might see you, we are going somewhere very quiet, where I can talk to you as I wish to do."

Thalia did not reply and he said:

"My carriage is waiting in Curzon Street. I think this is the quickest way to join it."

He put his hand under her elbow as he spoke and started to move in the direction he wished to go, and Thalia feeling there was no point in arguing any further, went with him.

Many of the shops in Shepherd's Market were still open and there were a few customers mostly chatting with the shop-keepers rather than buying.

But otherwise the place seemed almost deserted and Thalia had the feeling that she was walking in a dream as they came from the shadows of the archway into the bright gas lights of Curzon Street.

There was a closed carriage waiting embellished with the Earl's crest and drawn by two horses with a coachman and a footman in attendance.

She stepped inside and as the Earl joined her, she thought for a moment that she had moved back into the past.

It was her father's carriage in which she was riding, and there was no tragedy, no years of worry and privation, no heart-searching as to where the next meal would come from.

She was for the moment so deep in thought that she did not realise the Earl, leaning back comfortably in the corner of the carriage, was watching her with a look of amusement until he asked:

"What are you thinking about so seriously?"

"Myself." Thalia answered. "Forgive me for being inattentive, but for the moment I find it an absorbing subject."

It struck the Earl that any other woman would have told him that she had been thinking of him.

"At least you are honest, Miss Carver," he said. "Most people think incessantly about themselves, but are not frank enough to say so."

"I always tell the truth if it is possible," Thalia replied, "it is so much less of a struggle. I am ashamed tonight that I am deceiving my mother, who I love very deeply, by being here with you."

"As she will not know you are deceiving her," the Earl said, "I cannot feel that there is any very great damage, and if we are going to have a pleasant evening, Miss Carver, I suggest we omit any recriminations which invariably bore me."

"I was not aware that my duty this evening is to prevent you from being bored or to keep you entertained, My Lord."

"You are doing that already," the Earl said, "by not telling me as effusively as I expect, how much you are looking forward to being in my company."

"As I have already said, I try always to tell the truth," Thalia replied, "and you know without my saying so, that I have no wish for your company but would much rather be at home in bed with a good book."

"Is that what you do every night?"

"Yes."

"That is certainly extremely wasteful of your youth and of course, your looks."

"But not my brain?"

"You consider that of more importance than your more obvious assets?"

"Naturally, and more lasting."

The Earl laughed.

"You are certainly original in that contention, if it is indeed the truth, but perhaps spending your time with women who think only of their outward appearance has caused you personally to concentrate on something different."

"I feel sorry for a lot of them."

"Why?" the Earl enquired.

"Because they have been brought up to believe that the only thing that matters is to attract men. That is why they buy bonnets, why they spend hours choosing materials; ribbons, face-creams, shoes, stockings, sun-shades. There is no end to what they believe will be the bait to catch a fish."

"Like myself?" the Earl asked.

"But of course!" Thalia agreed. "The Earl of Hellington would be a very large catch if they could land him!"

"I assure you I fight ferociously never to be netted."

"That I can well believe," Thalia said, "but shall I be prophetic and tell Your Lordship you will be caught in the end and once you are in the net there will be no escape?"

"That is exactly what I am afraid of," the Earl said. "At the same time perhaps you are right. It is nature's way that a man should be caught and captured, and made a fool of by some determined woman. Think how Adam suffered through Eve!"

"And from all I have heard he has never stopped whining about it ever since!" Thalia added.

She spoke with a little stringent note in her voice which made the Earl laugh.

"When you take off your grey disguise, Miss Carver, I see you are very different from the demure creature who spoke softly and almost ingratiatingly to your client."

"Do I sound like that?" Thalia asked. "That is interesting."

"Why?"

"Because the Egyptians believed in the power of the voice, and I have often wondered how much a voice counts in the modern world."

She thought for a moment, then she said:

"In the Army it obviously galvanises a soldier into action because he has been trained to obey, but perhaps used more hypnotically it can control ordinary people not trained to listen."

"It is certainly an interesting contention," the Earl said, "and one we must certainly pursue further. But as you see, we have now arrived at our destination."

Thalia looked out of the window to see that the horses had drawn up outside a large building lit by gas-lamps which gave it a garish appearance.

At first she could only stare, then she said in a small, rather frightened voice:

"N—no . . . I cannot go . . . there!"

"It is all right," the Earl said soothingly, "you will not be seen. We are dining in a private room."

It struck Thalia that was certainly not the sort of place she should go alone with a man.

She had read of private rooms. Casanova and the Marquise de Sade, and all sorts of other rapacious creatures in history had taken the woman they wished to seduce to private rooms in different parts of Europe, but she did not know they existed in London.

But if it was not a private room here it was, she told herself practically, sure to be a private room somewhere else, and she was no more likely to be safe in the Earl's house in which she had somehow expected they might dine than she would be anywhere else.

The footman opened the door and the Earl stepped out to help her alight.

Just for a moment she hesitated, then as she moved her arm, she felt the heaviness of her bag and found it extremely reassuring.

Chapter Four

As the waiters withdrew the Earl sat back in his chair with a glass of brandy in his hand.

He thought as he looked at Thalia sitting opposite him that the dinner had been unexpectedly stimulating and interesting. In fact he could not remember when he had last had such an intelligent conversation with a man and never with a woman.

Their conversation had ranged over a great number of subjects and he had become aware that Thalia was exceedingly well-read and also had an original turn of mind.

She looked very young, but he thought he might, in fact, have been talking to Lady Melbourne, or Lady Holland, very much older women who were noted in the *Beau Monde* for their intelligence.

For Thalia it had been a fascinating experience to talk with a man who she realised was very unlike the empty-headed *Beaux* who came into Mrs. Burton's shop and chattered inanely while their Ladies fitted on bonnets.

She had often wondered what it would be like to dine with a man alone, and to find herself free to express the opinions which she had kept very much to herself these last three years.

Many of the tutors under whom she had studied in London, and there had been several, had told her almost reproachfully that she had a man's brain and it was not what they expected to find in a woman.

With her father she had been able to talk about a great number of things, subject to the handicap that Sir Denzil was not a good listener and preferred his own opinions to other people's.

Her mother on the other hand, was an excellent listener, but although Thalia adored her, she had to be honest and admit that her mother was not interested in anything that did not particularly touch her personal life.

Perhaps one of the reasons why she and her husband had been so happy together was the fact that while he talked she was completely content to listen and think that everything he said was wonderful.

But the Earl was undoubtedly a much cleverer man, though Thalia thought he was somewhat dogmatic in what he asserted and was obviously surprised if ever she disagreed with him.

They had several spirited arguments, but it was only now when there were no longer any servants in the room that she looked around her and was conscious of her surroundings.

She had, in fact, when she first entered the place where the Earl was giving her dinner, been apprehensive.

There was the sound of music and of voices and there were a number of servants standing about in crimson uniforms heavily over-trimmed with gold braid.

Then to her relief they were escorted up a staircase which led to the first floor and shown into a room where there was a table laid only for two.

If this is a Private Room, Thalia thought, *then it is not what I expected.*

She had always had a picture in her mind of something gaudy and rather vulgar, but this room was decorated in the French fashion in discreet good taste.

There were a number of French prints on the wall, a sofa and several chairs covered in brocade, and at one end of the room where Thalia thought there must be windows, turquoise blue curtains were hanging, of a very attractive hue.

She thought to herself that it was the blue that François Boucher used in his pictures, and somehow, because it was so different from what she had anticipated, it was reassuring.

The Earl took her cloak from her shoulders and she was tense because he was touching her. Then because he did it in a manner which had nothing but politeness about it, she felt at ease as she sat down on the sofa.

"A glass of champagne, or would you prefer Madeira?" the Earl enquired.

Thalia hesitated.

"It is a very long time since I tasted either."

"Then I think it should be champagne," the Earl suggested.

The waiter handed Thalia a glass from which she took only a tiny sip, knowing that it would be a very great mistake if she became muddle-minded from alcohol and remembering that it was hours since she had eaten anything.

Hannah always packed her a light luncheon to take with her to eat in the workroom at Mrs. Burton's shop.

Some of the women would go out for a little while at midday to buy themselves food from the stalls that were always to be found in side-streets, or just to stretch their legs.

But Thalia had promised her mother that she would go nowhere alone and had no wish to do so. Besides which, there was always far too much to do in the work-room.

Because she was so skilful at trimming the bonnets she was well aware that Mrs. Burton made her do the work of two people and she not only trimmed herself the fashionable creations she made so skilfully, but also sold them.

The dinner she had eaten with the Earl had been rich and delicious, and Thalia was now wondering how she could explain what had been on the menu to Hannah so that she could copy some of the things she had enjoyed for her mother.

"Is there anything else you would like?" the Earl asked.

"It would be impossible to eat any more!" Thalia replied. "I only wish I were a camel, then I would not have to eat for at least a week after such a delicious dinner."

"You are too thin," the Earl said. "Is that because you wish to be fashionable, or because you usually do not have enough to eat?"

"I have enough now that I am fortunate in being able to earn the money with which to buy the food."

"I cannot believe that Mrs. Burton is over-generous."

Thalia smiled.

"I am told she is typical of all the Bond Street shopkeepers who extract astronomical sums from their clients, but pay their work-people as little as possible."

"That is what I thought," the Earl said, "and I have another proposition to put to you."

"Proposition?" Thalia asked.

He looked at her for a long moment before he said:

"You must be aware that a Milliner's is not the right background for anyone as lovely as yourself."

He saw Thalia's eyes widen in surprise and went on:

"Are you going to be so mock-modest as to tell me you are not aware of your beauty?"

"Of course I should like to think I am beautiful,"

Thalia answered, "but when I compare myself with the acknowledged beauties who come to the shop like the one you were with today, or indeed, with Mademoiselle Genevieve, I am well aware of my deficiencies."

"If you have any, I cannot see them."

Because the Earl spoke with that cynical note in his voice that was characteristic of him, it was difficult to take what he was saying as a compliment.

Thalia gave a little laugh as she said:

"Anyway, I have learnt it is a handicap to be thought too attractive when one is only a shop-assistant. As Your Lordship might have been aware, I am only allowed to wait on the old and the plain, but not on the Ladies of Quality who bring their admirers with them."

"And yet you were permitted to visit a ballet dancer."

"That was different," Thalia replied. "A person like Mademoiselle Genevieve is not likely to notice somebody as insignificant as myself. But actually it was the first time I had been sent on such an errand, and I hope it will be the last."

She spoke so positively that the Earl questioned in surprise:

"Why do you say that?"

"Because although a ballet-dancer may not notice me, the gentlemen who frequent her dressing-room undoubtedly do so, like yourself, My Lord," Thalia answered. "If I had not gone to Fletcher's Hotel, I would not be here at this moment."

"Then I am glad you did so," the Earl said.

There was a little pause, which for some reason she did not understand, made Thalia feel embarrassed.

It might have been because of the way the Earl was looking at her, scrutinising her, she thought, as a man might scrutinise a picture or a horse, almost as if he appraised and valued her points.

"I think, My Lord," she said, "while I must thank you for that delicious dinner it is now time for me to go home."

"Not yet," the Earl said sharply. "I have not yet told you of my proposition."

"I will of course, listen to what you have to say, but I would remind you that it is getting late."

"Not as far as I am concerned."

"But you do not have to get up as early as I do," Thalia remarked.

"Very well then, you have made your point," the Earl said. "Listen carefully . . ."

Thalia bent forward, put her arms on the table and rested her chin in her hands.

Her bag was in her lap and she thought she must remember not to rise quickly, otherwise it would fall to the floor with a clatter.

"I think we agree," the Earl said, "that you are in the wrong environment. What I am going to suggest is that you move to a larger house in a quieter locality and you will allow me to make you very much more comfortable than you are at the moment.

"You will not have to make the bonnets you wear, you can have your own carriage and two horses to drive you, and you will certainly need one, if not two servants to wait on you."

He spoke in the same voice that he had used all the evening, quiet and clear, with just a faint note of cynicism which made everything he said seem somehow impersonal.

He stopped speaking and realised that Thalia was looking at him incredulously, then she said:

"Is that . . . all?"

"All?" the Earl questioned. "What else would you like me to add? Jewels? A box at Covent Garden?"

"I did not mean it like that," Thalia said. "It is just impossible to believe that what Your Lordship is saying is not some strange jest."

The Earl frowned.

"Jest! Why should you think that?"

Thalia linked her fingers together and sitting up very straight looked at him.

"Unless I am mistaken, My Lord . . . and perhaps I am . . . I think, although it seems highly . . . improbable, that you are inviting me to become your . . . mistress."

"That was my intention," the Earl said.

"Do gentlemen really make such suggestions in the same business-like way that you have approached me?"

"Did you expect something different?"

"But of course!" Thalia answered. "I imagined that a man would burn with a fiery passion and address the object of his fancy with heart-rending eloquence."

She paused to say:

"Alternatively he could threaten her with a closure of the mortgage or whatever else is traditionally held over women on such occasions."

Looking at Thalia the Earl saw the two dimples he had noticed before at the corners of her mouth and was aware that she was laughing at him.

"I have a feeling," he said, "that you are not taking me seriously."

"How could I?" she asked. "I have never heard such a ridiculous proposition in my life! If that is the reason you brought me out to dinner, My Lord, all I can say is that Hannah need not have been afraid of what might happen to me."

"I thought, perhaps wrongly," the Earl said, "that before we entered into an agreement together you would wish to know what to expect."

"I have told you what I expect."

"A fiery passion?" the Earl questioned. "That, of course, comes later."

"I am glad you have warned me," Thalia replied, "but now, My Lord, I really must go home."

"You have not yet given me my answer."

"Do you expect one?"

"But of course. I am not in the habit of asking questions and receiving no answers."

"Then let me make it plain, My Lord, so that it is impossible for you to misunderstand me—the answer is an unqualified 'No!' "

"Can you really be so foolish?" the Earl asked. "Have you thought of the advantages I can offer you?"

"It may come as a surprise to Your Lordship, but nothing you have said so far seems to offer me in any way, an advantage over what I have already."

"And what is that?" the Earl asked.

"My self-respect," Thalia replied, "and that, My Lord, is something it is not in your power to give."

The Earl put down his glass.

"Shall I approach you in another way?" he said after a moment, "and tell you how very desirable I find you and how much I would like to look after you and do everything within my power to make you happy."

"That you can do now."

"How?"

He had the feeling as he spoke, that her reply would not be what he wished to hear.

"By leaving me alone," Thalia said. "You are well aware you have blackmailed me into coming here tonight, simply because I could not upset my mother. That is something which must not happen again."

She saw an expression that she thought was one of annoyance on the Earl's face and could not resist adding:

"As for your house, your carriage, your horses and your jewels, I am certain Mademoiselle Genevieve will accept all those and a great deal more with pleasure!"

"I am not interested in Genevieve but in you!"

"For which you obviously think I should be flattered and grateful. I am neither! When I think it over

I shall find your proposition, My Lord . . . insulting!"

"It was not meant to be that."

Thalia made a little gesture with her hands.

"How can you expect me to think anything else?"

The Earl did not reply and after a moment she said:

"I know exactly what you are thinking, My Lord. You are wondering how anyone so inferior, so unimportant as an underpaid Milliner, can refuse the Earl of Hellington. Well, I am not only refusing you but making it very clear that I consider, despite your intelligence, that you are a very bad judge of character."

If she had tried she could not have said anything to annoy the Earl more.

If there was one thing on which he had always prided himself it was that he could sum up a man the moment he talked to him.

He did not require references for his servants, and when people came to him with an appeal for help he could tell the moment he met them whether or not they were genuine.

Now that this chit of a girl, with no background and nothing to distinguish her except her beauty from thousands of women like her, should consider that he had insulted her, and at the same time accuse him of bad judgement in making his offer in the first place, almost took his breath away.

"Now listen to me, Thalia . . ." he began, only to be interrupted as Thalia replied:

"I have listened to you, My Lord, and really there is nothing more to say on the subject. If you want the truth I find it extremely boring to go on discussing it."

As she spoke she picked up her bag and rose to her feet looking, although she was unaware of it, alluring and at the same time, very young and untouched in the candlelight.

Thalia had been so intent on talking to the Earl that she had not realised when the waiters left the room that they had extinguished all the lights except for the four candles on the dining-table.

There was however another light and only as Thalia turned from the table did she become aware of it.

She had been sitting with her back to the curtains at the end of the room which she supposed concealed a window. Now they were slightly drawn back and she saw no window but another room in which was a bed.

There was a small chandelier containing three candles at the side of one of the curtains which draped it. There were lace-edged pillows and on the bed a cover of frilly pink, also a Boucher colour, decorated with love-knots and turquoise blue ribbons.

For a moment Thalia stood as if turned to stone. Then she moved towards her cloak which was lying on a chair beside the sofa.

Only as she reached it did she realise that while she had left the table the Earl had not moved.

He was watching her from the high-backed chair in which he had sat at dinner and once again he held his glass in his hand.

"I wish to go, My Lord."

"Supposing I do not let you?"

"I think you would find it . . . difficult to . . . prevent me."

"Do you really believe that?"

"Yes. At the same time I should be very disappointed."

"Disappointed?" the Earl questioned.

"When I was talking to you at dinner I thought you were not only intelligent, but also a gentleman in the correct sense of the word. I would not wish to be disillusioned."

"That sounds very plausible, Thalia, and what I might have expected from you," the Earl said. "At the same time, since you have made it clear that you have no wish to see me again, what you feel about me after tonight can hardly be of any particular consequence."

As Thalia sought for a reply she thought that once

again they were arguing as they had at dinner, almost as if they fought a duel with clever words.

Because she could find no ready answer she bent down and picked up her cloak and put it over her shoulders.

"I intend to leave, My Lord," she said. "Are you going to stop me by brute force? That as you must know, is the last resort of an animal without brains."

"No, I will not make that sort of attempt to stop you," the Earl replied, "but shall I say instead that I will call on you tomorrow and if you are not back from the shop where you enjoy working, then perhaps I will discuss the alternative situation I have offered you with your mother."

Thalia gave a little gasp, then with her eyes blazing with anger she walked back towards the table.

"That is the most underhand, dirty, caddish type of blackmail any man could stoop to use!"

She stood at the table almost spitting the words at him and the Earl laughed.

"You look very lovely when you are angry," he said, "and I could not resist your eyes flashing as I assure you they do, and hearing you denounce me!"

"You were not . . . really . . . threatening me?"

"No. I would not sink to that level."

"Then why did you frighten me?" Thalia asked. "You know how vulnerable I am where Mama is concerned."

"Just as I am vulnerable where you are concerned."

"You can hardly expect me to believe that after the way you have behaved."

"How have I behaved?" the Earl asked, "except when just a few minutes ago I obeyed an irresistible impulse to make you angry."

Thalia did not reply and he said:

"I merely offered you something I thought you would find more enjoyable than struggling as you are now to keep yourself, your mother and doubtless your maid, Hannah alive. You have refused me! Very well, we must start again. I must find something that you will accept."

He was aware that Thalia was looking at him uncertainly, not understanding his change of mood, and he went on reflectively:

"Perhaps it would be special treatment for your mother and the very best doctors in London to diagnose her condition."

"That is also unfair . . . and you know it!" Thalia cried.

" 'All is fair in love and war'," the Earl quoted.

"Love!" Thalia exclaimed derisively. "That is the first time you have mentioned love! But you cannot use that word in connection with your . . . proposition."

"So that is what you want."

"Of course I want love," Thalia retorted, "but that is something you could never give me, My Lord, and so there is no point in our talking about it."

"I see I have been, as you so rightly point out, extremely stupid," the Earl said.

There was a twist on his lips as he added:

"How could I have forgotten that a woman always wants to be wooed?"

"That is the last thing I want," Thalia said sharply. "If you mean by wooing an attempt to persuade me by some . . . devious method to accept the . . . things I have just . . . refused."

"But if they were yours you would appreciate them all the same," the Earl said shrewdly.

"I have always heard one should beware of Greeks when they come bearing gifts," Thalia said, "and forewarned is forearmed My Lord. Whatever you offer me now, I shall be well aware of the ulterior motive behind it."

"Then I shall have to think out my campaign from another angle."

Thalia gave a little laugh.

"So that is what I am—a campaign! The battle that must be won at all costs in case you lose face. Well, this time, My Lord, you have met an implacable enemy who will not be intimidated or taken by surprise."

"You sound very sure of yourself."

"And you are not as frightening as I thought you were."

The Earl raised his eyebrows.

"What makes you say that?"

"Because you have just reassured me, although you may not be aware of it, that you are a gentleman and that, whatever you might do to me, you will not hurt . . . Mama."

The Earl did not reply and after a moment Thalia took a step nearer to him.

"I am right?" she questioned. "I am right about . . . that?"

It was a plea and after a moment he said ruefully:

"I concede that, but nothing more."

He saw the relief in her eyes and it touched him.

There was something very valiant in the way she fought for her mother.

He put down his glass of brandy and rose to his feet.

"I will take you home."

"Thank you," Thalia said simply.

As they went downstairs she had the feeling that she was escaping from something menacing which strangely had not frightened her as much as it should have done.

The noise of music and voices as they reached the Hall were louder than they had been before.

The Earl's carriage was waiting outside and as they stepped into it it struck Thalia that she had just been through an experience which might at some time prove useful if she could write about it.

It would be interesting to be able to describe what a Private Room really looked like.

As the horses moved off, the Earl asked:

"Will you give me your hand?"

It would seem petty and childish, Thalia thought, to refuse to do what he asked.

She put out her hand towards him and he took it in both of his.

She felt the warm strength of his fingers and it gave her a rather strange sensation that she had never known before.

"Will you believe me," the Earl said in his deep voice, "if I tell you that although our dinner together was not in the least what I expected, I have enjoyed every minute we have been together, and that I want more than I can tell you, to see you again."

"It is too . . . difficult, My Lord," Thalia replied, "and . . . something we should not do."

"It is something I want to do," the Earl said, "which is a very different matter. I think, Thalia, when you go to bed tonight, it would be rather disappointing having read the first chapter of a book to find there was no more to come and you had reached the end."

What he was saying was very reasonable and she had to admit true. At the same time she was afraid.

She could not ignore him as a man, as she had been able to do for the first part of the evening, because she was acutely conscious of his hand holding hers and that they were sitting very near to each other.

"Because I enjoy . . . talking to you, My Lord, when you are not . . . blackmailing me," Thalia said after a moment in a rather small voice, "I would like to . . . see you again, but I know it is . . . wrong and too difficult for me so . . . please do not ask me! It would be much easier if you would just . . . disappear out of my life."

"That is something I have no intention of doing," the Earl said. "Will you believe me, Thalia, if I tell you I find you so fascinating that I shall in fact, be counting the hours until I can see you again."

He saw Thalia turn her head to look at him swiftly.

Then as she was unable to see the expression on his face, she said:

"I think, My Lord, you have changed your tactics and are now . . . wooing me. I have said that I like talking to you, but it depends on what we talk about."

"I want to talk about you."

"That subject is barred and out of bounds."

"Then I will talk about myself."

"It depends in what connection."

The Earl gave a little laugh.

"If you are going to make all the rules I shall have to make some too. That would only be fair, and let me add that every intelligent man and woman knows that rules are made to be broken."

As he spoke he lifted her hand and she felt his lips first on the back of it, then he turned it over and kissed the palm.

Thalia could not think what to do or say and as she felt the warm pressure of his mouth she quivered as something strange streaked through her whole body.

It was like lightning, and yet there was a pleasure and excitement about it she could not describe.

She wanted to protest, she wanted to speak, but she could not find the words.

Then as she tried to take her hand from his, the horses came to a standstill and she realised they had reached the entrance to Shepherd's Market.

The Earl set her free and as the footman opened the door, he stepped out.

Thalia knew that he was waiting for her to give him her hand and help her alight, but she managed to do so without his touching her and walked quickly into the darkness of the arch leading into Sheperd's Market.

The market was quiet. There were only a very few flickering gaslights and the stars overhead to help them find their way to Number 82, but before they reached it, Thalia stopped.

"Do not come any nearer, My Lord," she said.

"Hannah will be watching from the window to let me in so that Mama will not hear me."

"Then we must say goodnight, Thalia," the Earl said. "When shall I see you tomorrow?"

"I have told you that is impossible."

"You know there is not such a word in my vocabulary."

"Please . . . you know I have to think . . . over what you said about . . . talking to each other . . . and it will not be . . . easy."

"Then dine with me tomorrow night."

"I . . . should not do so."

"But you will."

"I do not . . . know . . . I cannot think at this moment . . . please . . . let me think or the decision I make might be . . . wrong."

She was pleading with him, her head thrown back because he was so much taller than she was, her eyes looking up into his.

He looked down at her, then he said quietly:

"You know that I want more than I have ever wanted anything before, to kiss you goodnight. Yet because, whatever you may say, I am wooing you, Thalia, gently and, as you would say, like a gentleman, I would not do anything you would not want me to do."

Thalia drew in her breath.

Something in the way he spoke, the quietness of his voice, the fact that there was no cynicism or mockery in it, made her heart beat in a very strange way.

"Thank . . . you," she said, in a whisper he could hardly hear.

Then she ran away from him almost as if she would find protection and shelter waiting for her at the door of Number 82.

The Earl stood watching until, noting that she did not look back at him, he wondered if she was aware how much he wanted her to do so.

Then the door opened and she disappeared inside.

Out riding the following morning before the majority of the fashionable world was awake, the Earl turned over in his mind what had happened the previous night and thought he had never spent a more interesting or intriguing two hours.

Nothing that he had expected had happened, and he knew he should be feeling frustrated and perhaps angry that his plans had gone awry.

Instead he found himself fascinated in a manner that made him know that Thalia was different from anyone he had ever met before.

Then he told himself cynically that he was only thinking that because she had refused to accept his protection—which was something that was certainly unique in his experience.

He supposed when he had decided to make her his mistress, that he had not taken into account that she was decidedly of a different class from any of the women who had enjoyed his protection in the past.

I suppose one could say she is a lady, the Earl told himself as he rode into Rotten Row.

The question was how was it possible that the term "Lady" in the way it was conventionally used could apply to a woman who was a shop-assistant and lived in a workman's house in Shepherd's Market. And who apparently had no relatives or background with the exception of an ailing mother.

It struck the Earl that perhaps she was the love-child of some nobleman who had callously omitted to provide adequately for the baby he had fathered.

There were plenty of love-children about and they commonly were both beautiful and talented.

That, he thought, must be the explanation.

But those he had met in the past had always been acutely conscious of their position and certainly had not the pride or the self-possession which was, he thought, characteristic of Thalia.

She had certainly been brought up in genteel circumstances. There had been no mistakes in her behaviour at dinner last night, and the way she ate, moved and behaved would have been acceptable at Carlton House and would have borne the scrutiny of the most critical of the great London hostesses.

She was certainly well-bred, the Earl decided, and there was nothing she had done or said that he could fault.

Going over their conversation he found there was no other lady of his acquaintance who could equal the sharpness of her brain or the manner in which she could fence with him so that he had to use all his ingenuity not to leave her the victor.

She was well-bred at least on one side of her parentage, intelligent, well-educated, and yet, if Henry was to be believed, at one time so impoverished that she had not enough to eat.

It was all an enigma that preoccupied the Earl's mind until several acquaintances who raised their hats to him were astonished when he rode by, without even glancing in their direction.

The difficulty, he was thinking, was what he was to do about Thalia.

Her "rules" were certainly going to make it very difficult for him to see her as much as he wished to do, although he had no intention of moving out of her life as she had suggested.

It suddenly struck him that this was what he had been looking for—someone who kept him guessing, who had to be pursued as cleverly as any fox, and who would certainly make the chase an adventure such as he had never enjoyed before.

This was, however, not the reason he had returned to London from Hellington Park, where he had decided to look for a wife.

But marriage could wait while his pursuit of Thalia could not, and he began to plan the type of house in which he would instal her which would be very different from the one in Chelsea which had been occupied by his last mistress.

He would not insult her by putting her where he had kept any previous woman, and as he considered the houses he had seen, and what vicinity would be most suitable, he suddenly thought that perhaps after all, he would not be able to persuade her to accept his proposition.

Defeat was a word which never entered the Earl's mind and in war he had always told himself that if he was not ultimately the victor, then he would die in the attempt to achieve it.

The war with Napoleon was over, but he was now engaged in another campaign.

He would never give up and yet the doubt that he might not win it was there insidiously in his mind, although he tried to shake it off impatiently.

It would be better, he thought as he rode on, if she had been shocked or shy as he had half-expected her to be at what he suggested because she was so young.

But that she should first of all criticise the way he had suggested he should become her protector, and then should find it amusing was yet another experience that he had not expected.

Now, because she had almost goaded him into saying he would win her she would be suspicious of every move he made.

Because he was very experienced where women were concerned, he was aware that she had quivered when he had kissed the palm of her hand and he thought it was the one encouraging thing about the whole evening.

And yet she had not swayed towards him as any other woman would have done, when he said he wanted to kiss her.

That she had run away meant that perhaps she was not only running away from him, but from herself.

The trouble was he did not know with any certainty the answer to any of his own questions.

What did she feel about him?

When she was alone did she really feel shocked, perhaps disgusted because he wished her to be his mistress?

If she was the lady she appeared to be, that was understandable, but surely she must have known other men who had complimented her and perhaps because she was so lovely, had attempted, if not to seduce her, at least to arouse her interest.

She had said there was no one, but was it likely that a girl in her position would admit to anything?

And yet she appeared to be truthful. Except that she would tell him nothing about herself, the Earl was certain she had not lied to him.

He had learnt to recognise a liar almost before they opened their mouths. He had known that strong men trembled when he asked to see them in his tent or more usually in some dirty peasant's house that had been commandeered for the few nights they had rested somewhere on their advance into France.

A soldier would always try to lie his way out of having looted or of raping some wretched woman. But the Earl, while he forced himself to listen to what the man had to say, knew instinctively whether or not he told the truth.

Thalia did not lie, he would stake his life on that.

He rode back towards Berkeley Square and as he passed Shepherd's Market, deliberately riding down Curzon Street so that he could do so, he had an almost insane desire to go and look at the house where she lived, almost as if it might tell him something about her.

Perhaps he would see her setting off for work escorted by Hannah in the same way as she was taken home in the evening to guard her from being molested by gentlemen like himself.

Then he told himself that to do this, would not only embarrass her, but he would gain nothing by it.

He had already planned that he would send a groom, preferably Henry because he was discreet, to the shop with a letter saying that he would be waiting for her tonight at the same time and the same place.

Henry would bring back an answer and he knew, at least he was almost sure he knew, what Thalia's reply would be. He had a sudden vision of her dressed as he intended to dress her in the most expensive and beautiful gowns that could be purchased in London.

He would give her jewellery too, not the flashy, gawdy pieces which most of the "Fashionable Impures" thought embellished their appearance, but the very best gems like those in the Hellington collection which had been in the Bank since his mother died, and must remain there until they were required for his wife.

That will be many years ahead, the Earl thought. *If I have Thalia, I shall certainly not have any time to spend looking for a wife.*

He thought how much he would like to take her to Hellington Park and show her the house which was his home, and which he had loved perhaps more than anything else in his life.

There was so much he would like her to see and watch her reaction—so much that he knew would interest her.

There was no reason why she should not go there. After all, most of his friends had what were called "Bachelor Parties", but the guests included attractive young women who needed no chaperon and certainly made the evenings after they had been hunting or shooting amusing.

But that was not the sort of party he wanted to give for Thalia.

The answer to that was that he wanted her alone, not in some "private room" but seated at his dining-table in Berkeley Square, or in the great Banqueting Hall at Hellington, which designed by Adam was one of the finest Dining-Rooms to be found anywhere in the country.

I wonder what we would talk about? he thought with a smile.

Then he remembered that even if he invited her to Hellington Park she would most certainly refuse the invitation. It was as if the thought was like a dash of cold water in his face.

Damn that girl! She is more trouble than she is worth! he told himself angrily, as he reached Berkeley Square.

But he knew, even as he spoke the words beneath his breath, that he lied and he would never give up until he had won her, as he intended to do.

CHAPTER FIVE

The Earl opened the note which Henry had brought back to him and read it with a rueful expression on his face.

It was what he thought he might have expected, and yet he had been optimistic because never in the past, had any woman in whom he had shown an interest turned him down.

But the note he held in his hand was very explicit and he read it again.

"I regret, My Lord, it is impossible for Me to meet Your Lordship tonight as You suggest. I thank You for a very interesting Evening.

I remain, My Lord,
Yours sincerely,
Thalia Carver."

The writing, he thought, was what he had expected, elegant, educated and with a distinct personality about it.

He realised the servant who had brought him the note after Henry had returned with it to his house was waiting.

"That will be all," the Earl said.

When he was alone carrying the note in his hand he walked across the room to the window to look out at the garden in the centre of Berkeley Square.

He, however, did not see the trees, the flowers, but only Thalia's lovely face with its wide eyes, two irrepressible dimples and firm little chin.

He wondered what he could do to persuade her to dine with him.

He had the very unpleasant feeling that she had decided that they should not see each other again, and he was at a loss as to how he could break down that decision and force her to do as he wished.

He walked from the window across the room and back again.

Was it possible that after all these years of getting his own way too easily where women were concerned, he had found the one woman who was not interested in him as a man?

Then he remembered the little quiver that had passed through Thalia when he had kissed her hand and knew that she was interested even if it was only slightly, and perhaps that more than anything else was the reason why she was determined to have nothing to do with him.

"What shall I do?" he asked.

He found himself thinking of what should be his next approach almost as if in fact, as she had said, it was a battle between them.

The door opened and Richard, without being announced, came into the room.

"What are you up to, Vargus?" he asked. "I have been waiting for you at the Club."

"I am sorry, Richard," the Earl replied. "I had actually forgotten that we were to have luncheon together."

Richard looked at him sharply.

"Forgotten?" he repeated. "What is on your mind, Vargus? It is unlike you to be forgetful."

That was indeed the truth, for the Earl was extremely punctilious and Richard knew that for him to forget an engagement must mean that he was deeply preoccupied.

"You must forgive me," the Earl said quickly as if he had no wish for Richard to search for an explanation. "As a matter of fact I have not yet eaten and we can go to the Club or have luncheon here, whichever you prefer."

"Let us eat here," Richard said, "because I have something extremely interesting to tell you, something which will astound you, and I want your advice as to whether I shall tell the others, or keep it to ourselves."

As he was talking the Earl had rung the bell. The door opened and he said to the Butler:

"Mr. Rowlands and I will be having luncheon here. Ask the Chef to have something ready as soon as possible."

"Very good, My Lord."

As soon as the door closed Richard went on excitedly:

"I will give you three guesses what I have discovered."

"Why not just tell me?"

"You do not seem particularly interested."

"I am—of course I am," the Earl answered, forcing himself to concentrate on what his friend was saying.

"Then be prepared for a surprise," Richard said and added triumphantly, "I have discovered the identity of 'The Person of Quality'!"

It took the Earl a second to remember what he was speaking about. Then he recalled the book which had both amused and annoyed the members of White's the last time he had been in the Club.

"How could you do that?" he asked as he knew Richard was waiting for his reaction. "And who is it?"

"A woman," Richard replied.

The Earl raised his eyebrows.

"That is certainly a surprise! At least the members of the Club are off the hook."

"Some will be relieved, some merely annoyed," Richard replied. "Sefton was screaming only yesterday when he found one maxim which he was certain referred to him, and Toby considered himself insulted by another."

"It is obvious that they think themselves to be of more consequence than they are," the Earl said dryly, "unless of course, the author knows them and is deliberately putting their idiosyncracies in print."

"I do not know her," Richard said. "In fact I never heard of her until I discovered who 'The Person of Quality' was."

"How did you do that?" the Earl asked, forcing himself to sound attentive.

"Everybody was making such a commotion about the book that I thought I would go along to see Hatchard and find out what he had to say. After all, he published it."

"It seems quite a simple solution to the mystery," the Earl smiled.

"It was not as easy as that," Richard explained. "Hatchard himself refused to tell me anything. In fact, I thought he was delighted to hear that people were interested in the identity of 'The Person of Quality'."

" 'The book is selling well, Mr. Rowlands,' he said, 'so as far as I am concerned the more curious everyone is, as to who is the author, the better!'

"I argued with him but he would not listen, and having talked to one or two of the people I knew in the shop, I walked back into Piccadilly."

Richard paused to make sure that he held the Earl's attention, then continued:

"I had only proceeded a few paces towards St. James's Street when a man sidled up to me and said:

" 'I heard you talking to Mr. Hatchard, Sir, and saying you wanted to know who wrote the book called *'Gentlemen'*."

" 'You mean you know who it is?' I asked in surprise.

"Then I saw he was in his shirt-sleeves and wearing a large holland apron, and I guessed he was a packer or something of that sort, from the shop.

" 'Are you prepared to tell me what I want to know?' I asked.

" 'Times are hard, Sir, and I've a sickly wife and three children.' "

"So he was ready to sell the information," the Earl remarked.

"I hesitated as to whether I should tell him he should be loyal to his employer or pay him to find out what I wanted to know."

"I need not ask the choice you made."

"I must admit I was too curious to resist the temptation. It cost me two guineas, but I think it was well worth it."

"What did he say?" the Earl enquired.

"He told me that 'The Person of Quality' was a woman and he had seen her when she brought the manuscript to Mr. Hatchard.

" 'A pretty piece, she were, Sir,' he said, 'all dressed

in grey, and I hears the Guv'nor call her 'Miss Carver'."

The Earl had already stiffened when Richard had mentioned what Thalia was wearing. Now he stared at his friend incredulously before he asked:

"You are quite certain that is what the man said?"

"Quite!" Richard replied. "In fact I made him repeat it."

"I cannot believe it!" the Earl said beneath his breath.

He walked across the room to the grog-tray and poured himself a drink.

"I thought you would be surprised that it was a woman," Richard said, "but I wonder who she can be, and how she can know so much about men. I would have been prepared to wager a hundred pounds, if I had it, that every word had been written by a man, and a gentleman at that!"

The Earl did not reply. He still had his back to his friend and appeared to be busy.

Then he turned to say:

"Forgive me one moment, Richard, before we continue with our conversation. I have a note I have to send without delay. It will not take me long."

He walked towards the writing-desk as he spoke.

Thalia trimming a bonnet automatically but with her usual skill, found it impossible to keep her mind on anything but the Earl.

She had gone to bed thinking of him and had been a long time going to sleep and when she awakened it was to think of him again.

She found herself going over their conversation of the night before.

First of all she kept remembering the note in his voice when he bade her goodnight and the strange feelings he had aroused when he had kissed the palm of her hand.

Even to recall what she had felt created an echo of it within her, and she wondered how she could have lived so long without experiencing that particular feeling and why it was like no other emotion she had ever known.

I cannot see him again . . . I cannot! she told herself as she walked with Hannah to work.

When Henry had arrived later in the morning with a letter from the Earl she had known even before she opened it, what her answer must be.

He had forced her into dining with him last night—blackmailing her was the right word—but it must not happen again and she was sure, because she could appeal to his finer instincts, that he would not in revenge do anything to hurt her mother.

That was all that mattered.

At the same time, having sent Henry away with a note that she had written hastily at the desk where Mrs. Burton did her accounts, she had told herself despairingly that the conversation that had taken place the night before between herself and the Earl would be the last intelligent one in which she was likely to participate until her father's return to England.

Being with the Earl had made her realise that for the last three years her brain had been starved, just as her body had been, only to a greater degree.

Sir Denzil had played such a large part in Thalia's life that it was only when he was gone that she realised what a huge void he had left and how desperately she missed him.

She loved him because he was her father, but his place as a companion had, she thought looking back, been an almost unique relationship between a father and daughter.

Because their minds were attuned and Thalia was so advanced for her age, they had talked as though they were equals and Sir Denzil had found in his daughter the only thing that was lacking in the perfection of his wife whom he adored.

Last night, Thalia thought, despite the many emotions that had been evoked within her, had been an intellectual delight that she would never know again.

"It is too . . . dangerous . . . and I cannot go on . . . deceiving Mama," she told herself.

At the same time she knew there was a deeper reason for her decision and one that she did not wish to express in words even to herself.

The morning passed slowly. Thalia waited on two customers who as usual, bought more bonnets than they had intended, and Mrs. Burton smiled at her approvingly as she returned to the workroom.

She continued with the trimming of a bonnet on which she had been engaged before she was called to the front of the shop.

"Ye've used up all th' roses, Thalia!" one of the work-girls exclaimed.

Thalia was suddenly aware that she had in fact over-decorated the bonnet to the point of absurdity.

It was pretty and at the same time, sensationally theatrical. It could only have been worn by someone like Genevieve or perhaps Lady Adelaide.

"It is too much," she admitted.

She was aware she had been working with her fingers but using her mind in a very different way.

"Pretty though," the work-girl said. "Why don't you put it in th' window? Bet it's snapped up so quick yer'll be sitting here half the night making 'nother."

Perhaps it would be better to do that, Thalia thought, than to go home and think where she might have been instead of alone in bed with a book.

She had actually risen to take the bonnet and put it in the window as had been suggested, when there was a knock on the back-door and one of the young matchers who opened it, said:

"Another note for yer, Thalia! Yer're certainly a success today."

All the work-women looked at Thalia curiously.

Ever since she had been at Mrs. Burton's she had never received as far as they knew, any attention from the outside world. Now there had been two notes in the same morning which set everyone whispering to each other as she opened it.

It was written in the Earl's forceful hand on his crested parchment paper.

"I have discovered your secret. It is something we must discuss. I shall therefore expect you to dine with me. Hellington."

Thalia stared down at what she had read almost as if she was turned to stone.

It could not be true. How could he have found out? And if he knew—who else?

She felt a sudden terror of what this might mean at this particular moment. She would have to give up her work at Mrs. Burton's and take her mother somewhere else.

They would have to find another house and perhaps change their name again, in which case when her father returned there would be another alteration to the address and he might be unable to find them.

She felt for the moment as if the ceiling had caved in and hit her on the head. Then with her usual practical common sense she thought that even if the Earl had discovered who she was, that might not mean that many other people knew.

She could persuade him, of course she could persuade him, to keep her secret to himself.

Because for the moment she was so agitated she could not think clearly, she only knew that the Earl was right. They must discuss it and she must plead with him not to say anything, so that perhaps she would not have to take her mother away.

She felt when she had read what he had written, that her heart had stopped beating, but now she felt as if it was functioning again more normally and she forced herself to walk slowly to the back-door to where Henry was waiting.

"Please . . . carry a message to your Master," she said remembering not to mention the Earl's name.

He doffed his cap respectfully and she realised the Earl with his usual consideration had sent his groom dressed in ordinary clothes and not wearing the Hellington Livery.

"Just tell him . . . I agree," Thalia finished.

"Very good, Miss."

Thalia shut the door on him quickly, hoping that the work-girls had not overheard what she had said as she had spoken in so low a voice. At the same time, she knew if they had, they would have learnt little.

She felt weak about the knees as she walked back to her usual seat at the work-table, feeling as if the world was whirling around her and it was impossible to know how she could stop it.

Thalia thought that evening as she helped her mother to bed, tidied the room, pulled the curtains, and finally blew out the candles, that it had been the longest day she had ever spent in the whole of her life.

She had see-sawed between believing that the Earl would help her by keeping silent and planning what to do if he would not.

When her father had been forced into exile he had not realised how humiliated his wife and daughter would be.

They had not only to keep what had actually happened secret, but they had to make plausible explanations for his absence.

When Lady Caversham discovered that it was first believed he had run away from his creditors, then later from far more heinous crimes, she had not only been affronted, that such aspersions should be cast on her beloved husband, but also ashamed that they should have to lie on his behalf and of course their own.

It was, Thalia realised, the only thing possible to disappear from the County where they were so well known and certainly from their fashionable, pleasure-seeking friends in London.

She thought there were some who would have stood by them in trouble, but she was too young to know who they were and she was aware that for her mother to be snubbed by any of those who had entertained her in the past, would be intolerable.

When finally she realised she would have to exist on the proverbial "shoe string" until her father's return, she had thought that the best hiding-place was London, because their neighbours would not be interested in them and it was always easier to be anonymous among a crowd.

She had grown used as the years passed, to living in the present, just as her mother lived only for the future when her husband would return.

There was no point in looking back into the past. To Thalia, because she was young, it seemed to recede month by month until she seldom thought of the days when they had been able to enjoy the luxury of carriages, servants and the freedom of being in the country.

She felt that the only thing she had to fight was her mother's weakness and her ever-increasing fear that she might never see her husband again.

Thalia grew used to telling herself day after day that her mother must not be upset, must not be perturbed, must not lose faith.

And she knew now that the upheaval of moving house again or the fear of disclosure would definitely injure her to the point where she might relinquish her always precarious hold on life.

I must make the Earl understand, Thalia kept thinking.

When finally her mother was settled for the night she hurried into her own bedroom to change hastily into the gown she had worn the evening before, and throwing the velvet cloak over her shoulders, she tiptoed down the stairs to the kitchen.

"You are playing with fire, that's what you are doing!" Hannah said uncompromisingly from the other side of the kitchen-table.

"I have to see His Lordship," Thalia said. "I refused to dine with him again, but then I learned something that makes it imperative that I should . . . talk to him."

There was a note of desperation in her voice that made Hannah ask sharply:

"What's he been saying to upset you?"

"I will tell you about it tomorrow," Thalia replied. "There is no time now. Oh, Hannah, when you say your prayers tonight, pray that he will do what I ask of him."

"If my prayers had been heard," Hannah said tartly, "he would not have been coming here in the first place."

"Goodnight, Hannah."

Now as she turned to leave the kitchen, the old maid gave a little cry.

"Have you got your pistol with you?"

"I have forgotten it, but I will not need it," Thalia answered.

"How can you be sure of that?" Hannah asked.

"I am not quite certain why, but I am."

Then without waiting for Hannah to open the front-door for her, she sped towards it knowing that if she left it open Hannah would close it quietly behind her, so that it would not disturb her mother.

The Earl was waiting in the same place as he had been the night before, and as Thalia ran towards him she had the strange feeling that in a way she could not explain, he stood not for disruption resulting from the discovery she feared, but for security.

She reached him and he took her hand in his.

"You are cold," he said.

"I am . . . frightened."

"Of me?"

"No, of what you are going to tell me. How . . . could you have . . . found out?"

"Shall we talk about it over dinner?" he suggested.

Thalia wanted to reply that she could not wait until dinner-time to know the worst, but after the anxiety of waiting all day for this moment, now that he was here, the urgency did not seem quite so intense.

They walked to where the Earl's carriage was waiting and as they drove away the Earl said:

"Let me look at you. You are even lovelier than I remember, and I have been thinking about you ever since we said goodnight."

Thalia forced a wry little smile to her lips, but she had no ready reply.

He had again taken her hand in his, but he did not kiss it as she half-expected he would, but instead held it close so that she could feel the warmth coming back into it.

At the same time she felt as if in some way she did not understand she was drawing on his strength and absorbing it into herself.

The carriage came to a standstill and she looked out in surprise.

It had only been a few minutes since they had left Shepherd's Market.

"Tonight I thought we would dine at my house," the Earl said. "There are a number of things in it which I would like to show you, and I realise that where we went last night is not the right place for you."

Thalia stepped out and she followed him feeling as she entered the large Hall with its beautiful wrought-iron staircase twisting upwards to a painted dome, that she had stepped into another world.

The Butler opened the door of the Salon, and Thalia thought it was exactly the type of room she imagined the Earl would possess.

It was decorated sumptuously, at the same time in a manner which made it appear to achieve a perfection of design and furnishing that was like listening to great music, or seeing a picture painted by a great master.

But for the moment she had no interest in anything but what the Earl had to tell her, and having accepted the glass of champagne she was profferred without even realising what she was doing, she waited until the servants left the room before she said:

"Tell me . . . tell me what you have discovered . . . and how?"

"I should like you to have trusted me with your secret," the Earl said.

"How could I," Thalia replied, "when I was not the only person involved?"

"You mean somebody helped you?"

"Helped me?"

"Was it a man?"

The Earl's voice was sharp and as Thalia looked at him in surprise, not understanding what he was saying, he said:

"I suppose I might have guessed that it could not be entirely the work of a woman. After all, only a man could have managed to put the innuendoes in such a way that each gentleman who read it, would think it was referring to himself."

"Read . . . it?" Thalia said beneath her breath.

Then in a voice that was very different from the way she had spoken before, she said:

"Y—you . . . are talking about . . . my book!"

"Of course," the Earl replied. "What else did you think I was speaking of?"

He saw the look of relief spread over her face which

brought the color back to her cheeks and the light to her eyes.

Then she made a little sound that was half a laugh and half a sob and put her glass down on the table as if it was too heavy for her to hold.

"My . . . book, of course . . . that is what you have discovered about me!"

"I cannot actually claim the credit," the Earl said. "It was a friend of mine who found a man in Hatchard's employment who was prepared to sell him the truth in exchange for two guineas."

"Why should he be interested?"

There was now a touch of Thalia's old spirit not only in her voice, but in the look in her eyes.

The Earl laughed.

"You are obviously not aware that you have set the whole of White's by the ears. They suspected it was one of their members who was holding them up to ridicule and they were determined when they discovered who he was, he should be expelled from the Club."

"You mean . . . they were . . . annoyed?"

"Quite a number of them were very annoyed."

"How many copies do you think they have bought?"

There was no doubt she was eager to know, but the Earl had not missed the transformation that had taken place since she had discovered that it was her book he was talking about, and not something which to her, was infinitely more sinister.

What can she be hiding? he asked himself. *What crime could she have possibly committed?*

Then he remembered she had said that her secret involved other people besides herself.

If it was not her mother who was in trouble it could only be her father.

The Earl turned over in his mind how he could broach the subject. At the same time he had no wish to frighten Thalia as she had been frightened when she met him that evening.

He could still feel the coldness of her hand when he had touched it, and the way her fingers had trembled beneath his.

"Drink a little more champagne," he said. "I think you need it."

Thalia obeyed him. At the same time she felt such a surge of relief sweeping over her that she had no need of champagne, and after the anxiety and misery of the day it was as if she was suddenly enveloped in sunshine.

"Tell me about your book," the Earl said.

"Who else knows that I am the . . . author of it?" Thalia asked.

"Only my friend Richard Rowlands," the Earl replied, "who discovered your identity."

"Please . . . can he be . . . persuaded not to tell . . . anybody else?"

"I am sure he will do that if I ask him to. But, as you can imagine, he is longing to confront the members of White's with the information that they have been made to look fools by a mere woman."

"I . . . did not intend them to feel . . . like that," Thalia said, "it was just when the idea came to me I remembered some of the things I had read and I suppose heard and I . . . jotted them down."

"And used your clever little brain to invent a number of others," the Earl smiled.

"Yes . . . that is true, but if it sells a lot of copies . . . then I shall make some money . . . and perhaps be able to write another book."

"On the same subject?" the Earl asked. "How can you be so knowledgeable about men when you tell me you know none?"

"Mama asked me the same thing," Thalia replied. "I think the answer is that people are kind enough to find more in what I have said than what I meant in the first place."

"Now you are being modest," the Earl remarked. "You know as well as I do that your book is both witty and provocative, and uncomfortably for some people, it hits the nail on the head!"

"Perhaps the Dandies will feel like that."

"If they do, it serves them right," the Earl answered. "They deserve everything that is said about them."

"You do not consider yourself to be a Dandy?" she asked provocatively.

"I do not!" the Earl replied firmly, "and if you call me one I shall prove very forcefully that I am a very different type of character entirely!"

Thalia laughed, and it swept the last vestige of anxiety and fear from her face.

"Now you are offering me a challenge," she said. "Be careful in case I find it irresistible!"

"There are so many challenges between us," the Earl said, "the most important still being what I am to do about you."

"The answer to that is . . . nothing, that is why I refused your invitation in the first place."

"I am aware of that," he said, "but Fate in the shape of Richard Rowlands stepped in on my side and you are here."

He paused before he added very quietly:

"And that is all that matters for the moment."

They dined in the oval Dining-Room, where the polished table, clothless in the fashion set by the Regent and decorated with gold candelabra and magnificent gold plate, was to Thalia as fascinating as if she was watching a performance at Covent Garden.

The servants moved silently dressed in their livery coats with crested buttons, serving them with exotic dishes on what she knew was extremely rare and beautiful Sèvres china.

To Thalia it was an enchantment that until now had existed only in her books of fairy-stories, but she knew the centrepiece of what was almost a pageant being unfurled before her eyes was the Earl himself.

If last night he had seemed imposing in the private room where they had dined, tonight sitting against the crimson velvet background of his chair at the top of the table, he was magnificent.

His cravat was tied in an intricate design she had never seen before, and as his eyes searched her face in the light of the candles she felt as if she was playing the leading role in a drama.

They talked not exactly as they had done the night before, because there were often pauses in the conversation, yet although they were silent, it was as if they were still communicating without words.

Thalia felt a strange excitement, and there was also a shyness for which she did not understand the reason.

She told herself it was because she had never before been in such grand surroundings or alone with a man who was so splendid in his appearance.

As soon as the dinner was over they left the Dining-Room, the Earl walking beside her towards the Salon, and she said:

"I would like to look at your treasures."

"That, before you arrived, was what I wanted you to do," he answered. "I wished to see if you appreciated them, but now they are unimportant beside you."

"You are . . . flattering me."

"I am speaking the truth."

As they walked into the Salon and she seated herself on the sofa he said, looking down at her:

"I keep wondering what you have done to me. Ever since I have known you I find it hard to think of anything but you. When I went riding this morning, I felt that you were riding beside me, and when I came back to find your note saying that you would not meet me this evening, I felt an emotion I have never encountered before. It was one of despair."

The way he spoke made it impossible for Thalia to answer him lightly.

For a moment she did not speak. Then she said:

"I think what you are feeling is simply irritation because having been . . . spoilt all your life, for once you are . . . unable to have your own . . . way."

"Why should you think me spoilt?" the Earl asked aggressively.

"How can you be anything else?" she replied. "Look at this house, the things you possess, and of course . . . yourself."

"Tell me about myself."

He spoke almost as if he was a child eager for praise.

"What can I say about the Earl of Hellington?" she asked. "He is a noted sportsman, he is at the top of the social pinnacle of fame, he is handsome and wealthy! There must be a snag somewhere, but I have not yet found it."

"The snag is," the Earl said, "that I cannot persuade one small, extremely determined young woman to give me her heart."

"If I did," Thalia asked, "what would you do with it? Add it to all the others you have accumulated? You must have quite a valuable collection by now."

"You are not to speak to me like that," the Earl retorted.

"Why not? And because you are angry I have the feeling that I have touched you on a raw nerve which doubtless is the truth!"

"If there was ever an infuriating, irritating young woman, it is you!" the Earl exclaimed. "Stop jeering at me, and talk to me sensibly for a change."

"If by sensibly you mean you are going to persuade me to do what I have no intention of doing now or ever, then you can save your breath!"

Thalia rose from the sofa on which she had been sitting.

"I intend to look now at all the lovely things you have in this room."

She walked resolutely towards one picture.

"A Rubens!" she exclaimed. "If you only knew how much I have always wanted to see one. The colours are superb! Just as I thought they would be. In a book I once read it said that he always painted his second wife whom he adored into each of his pictures."

"I have no wish to put you in a picture," the Earl said, "I want you in my arms."

Thalia turned from her contemplation of the Rubens.

"That is a very banal statement," she said, "and not really worthy of you."

"Damn you!" the Earl exclaimed. "One day you will make me lose my temper, then there will be no use your complaining of the consequences!"

Thalia laughed.

"You do not frighten me," she said. "And now that I know what you are really like, I will let you into another secret. Last night Hannah made me bring a pistol with me when I dined with you."

"A pistol?"

There was no doubting the Earl's astonishment.

"I carried it in my satin bag. It was a very small pistol, but it could still do a lot of damage."

"Is that why you were not afraid when I said I might keep you by force?"

"Actually I doubted from the very beginning that you would behave in such a manner. The truth is, as I said last night, you are too much of a gentleman!"

"You certainly make me feel it is a severe handicap."

"I would prefer you to think of it as a state of mind of which you can be justly proud."

"I shall not feel that, if it prevents me from getting my own way."

The Earl took a step nearer to Thalia as he said:

"Let us stop fencing. I want you, Thalia, and at the moment I cannot contemplate my life without you."

There was a note in his voice which she had found difficult to resist last night and although he had not touched her, she put out her hands as if to protect herself.

"Please . . . please," she said. "I do not want you to talk to me like this. I prefer it when we are arguing and confronting each other."

"I have no wish to confront you," the Earl said. "All I want is for you to be mine."

He saw what he thought was a little quiver go through her and he went on:

"I think you know already, even though you will not admit it, that we mean something to each other; something which neither of us can dismiss lightly, or lose without suffering in consequence."

Thalia was again studying the Rubens and the Earl said softly:

"Look at me, Thalia."

She shook her head.

"I must go home. You know I cannot stay long."

"Not if I ask you to do so?"

"You know the answer to that."

"That is not really an answer. You are just relying on the rules you made yourself which have no real sense where we are concerned."

"Nevertheless they are what you have to obey."

"Why?"

"Because . . ." Thalia began, then stopped. "Please . . . take me home."

"I desperately want you to stay. Does that mean nothing to you?"

Again there was that note of appeal which she found very difficult to resist.

"Please . . ." she said.

Now she raised her eyes to his and was lost.

They gazed at each other without moving, and it

seemed to Thalia that the whole world had vanished into two steel grey eyes and there was nothing else.

They filled her heart, her body, and were part of the very breath she breathed.

She was never certain afterwards whether she moved or the Earl did.

She only knew that without thought, almost unconsciously, she was in his arms and he was holding her against him.

She did not even think that she ought to struggle. It was as if her mind would no longer work, and there was only his eyes, then his lips, and as they held hers captive there was only him.

She felt that his mouth took possession of her and she was no longer herself, and it was almost as if her body melted into his and they became one person which they had been once long ago at the beginning of time.

His arms tightened and his lips became more insistent, demanding, and she felt that strange streak that was both pleasure and pain flash through her, moving from her lips to her breast until she knew it touched her heart and again it became part of his heart and there was no escape.

She knew what she was feeling was love; love, not as she had imagined it would be, but far more poignant, more wonderful and more glorious.

It was not a question of fighting against anything, because she now belonged to it and she was no longer herself but his.

She felt as if he annihilated and captured completely the last semblance of herself alone.

This was the mystery of love, the wonder to which she could only surrender completely and absolutely.

Then at last, when she felt as if she was no longer human but part of the divine, the Earl raised his head.

"My darling, my sweet! How can you fight against

this?" he asked. "You are mine—mine as you were always meant to be."

It was then that Thalia came back to reality, as if she fell from the sky down to the roughness of the earth beneath.

"Please . . ." she whispered.

As if he knew what she was feeling, he said:

"I will take you home. We will talk about what we shall do tomorrow. It is late now, and you are very tired."

With his arm around her, he drew her across the Salon and into the Hall.

The footman on duty hurried to fetch her cloak and when the front door was open she saw the Earl's carriage was waiting outside.

She stepped into it, too bemused for the moment even to think, and as if he understood what she was feeling, the Earl put his arm around her and her head turned naturally against his shoulder, but he merely pressed his lips against her forehead.

They drove in silence towards Shepherd's Market. Then as they walked through the quiet streets towards Number 82, the Earl said:

"Do not worry about anything. Leave everything to me. When we meet tomorrow night I shall have a plan for you which will make everything easy, and you will never have to worry again."

He stopped at the same place they had parted the night before. The Earl looked down at her.

"Goodnight, my precious darling," he said tenderly. "I shall be thinking of you. Just trust me, that is all you have to do."

Thalia looked up at him.

She could see his eyes and she felt as if she was still held captive by them.

Then because her voice had died in her throat she turned and walked away from him towards the house.

Only as she waited for Hannah to open the door, did she look back.

The Earl was standing where she had left him, and she felt as if he grew taller and taller until his head touched the stars.

Chapter Six

"Are yer all right, Thalia?"

The voice broke in on Thalia's thoughts and she turned to look down at the young matcher who was staring at her in surprise.

"I am sorry," she said. "Did you speak to me?"

"I've asked yer three times if yer think this velvet's what yer want for Lady Standish's bonnet."

With an effort Thalia forced herself to look at the piece of material the matcher held up in her hand.

"Yes, I think that will do very well. Thank you Emily."

The matcher walked away and Thalia tried to remember that she must work and think of what she was doing.

It was difficult as, ever since she had awoken this morning, she had felt as if her heart was singing and she had been carried into a world where nothing seemed real and everything was dazzling with sunshine.

This is love, she had told herself, *and everything is different. Nothing is the same as it was before.*

Then some critical part of her mind asked her if

love, to the Earl, meant the same thing as it did to her?

Because she was afraid of the answer, she could not risk depressing herself by being introspective.

The fact that she loved him presented a whole number of new problems—problems that sooner or later would have to be faced—but, just for the moment, the dazzling glory of it was all that mattered.

She had gone to bed feeling as if his kiss had carried her up to the stars and left her there suspended high above the earth where nothing frightening could encroach upon her.

Now I have to face reality, she told herself severely.

She picked up the bonnet on which she was working and tried to remember how she had intended to decorate it and who it was for.

Just as she was starting to thread her needle, Mrs. Burton came hurrying from the front of the shop.

"Lord Dervish's here," she whispered, "with that tiresome sister of his, Lady Wentmore. Don't forget to put ten per cent on his bill, so that he can take it off."

This would have been an incomprehensible instruction to anyone outside the shop but Thalia knew exactly what Mrs. Burton meant.

There were a certain number of her clients who argued about the price of everything they bought and insisted on a reduction. To those Mrs. Burton always asked more to begin with than she expected to obtain.

There were also those like Lord Dervish who automatically cut ten per cent off the bill when he paid it.

The same adjustment to the price therefore applied to him.

Without hurrying Thalia walked gracefully into the front of the shop to find, as she anticipated, Mrs. Burton was serving one of the petulant, temperamental Beauties who was determined to try on every bonnet available before she decided which one she would buy.

In front of another mirror Lord Dervish and his sister were waiting.

Thalia curtsied respectfully.

"Good morning, My Lady," she said to Lady Wentmore whom she had served on several other occasions.

Her Ladyship wasted no time in the courtesies.

"I want to see your prettiest and newest bonnets, and those that are most original," she said sharply, "and I shall be extremely annoyed if I see anyone in a replica of what I am wearing myself."

"You will not do that, My Lady," Thalia promised, "we pride ourselves on never turning out the same model twice."

Lady Wentmore sniffed as if she did not believe what Thalia was saying, but she sat down in front of the mirror patting her skilfully dyed hair into place.

Fifteen years ago she had been an outstanding beauty, but now she was fading a little while striving with every known artiface to keep her looks and a semblance of youth.

Lord Dervish who was almost a Dandy in his appearance was obviously intent on his own thoughts and took no notice of Thalia.

"As I was telling you, my dear," he said to his sister, "I said to the Chancellor of the Exchequer, things need to be tightened up. If nobody pays their taxes as they should, how can we ever expect to afford an Army, a Navy and all the other responsibilities which have to be met?"

"I am sure you are right," Lady Wentmore murmured.

She was turning her head from side to side to see the effect of a very attractive bonnet that Thalia had just placed on her head.

"That reminds me," Lord Dervish went on, "I had a surprise last evening."

He waited for his sister to ask what it was and as she did not do so, he continued:

"Lawson has just returned from America, and who do you think he saw there?"

"I have no idea," Lady Wentmore murmured.

"Caversham! Denzil Caversham strutting about, Lawson said, as if he owned the place!"

"Sir Denzil?" Lady Wentmore exclaimed. "I thought he was dead!"

"Very much alive from what Lawson was saying," Lord Dervish answered. "And if he comes back to this country I have a surprise waiting for him."

At the mention of her father's name Thalia felt as if she was turned to stone. Then when Lord Dervish said he was alive and apparently well, her relief was so overwhelming that she felt as if it might physically sweep her off her feet.

"I am waiting to try on another bonnet!" Lady Wentmore said sharply.

Hardly realising what she was doing, Thalia picked up the nearest to her hand and placed it on Her Ladyship's head. "You were saying you had a surprise for Sir Denzil," Lady Wentmore prompted as Thalia tied the ribbons under her chin. "What sort of surprise?"

"It is one he will not relish, or forget in a hurry," Lord Dervish answered.

There was an unpleasant note in his voice which made Thalia hold her breath.

"Do tell me what it is, Arthur, and stop being so mysterious," Lady Wentmore said. "I always had rather a partiality for Sir Denzil. He was so attractive and danced exceedingly well."

"When he comes back to England you will not be dancing with him for a long time," Lord Dervish replied.

"Why not?" Lady Wentmore enquired.

"Because, my dear, he will be in the Fleet!"

"In prison? What do you mean, Arthur, and why should he go to prison?"

"Because that is where I intend to send him," Lord

Dervish said. "You could hardly believe it, but the damned fellow slipped out of the country owing me £1,000!"

There was no doubt that he had aroused his sister's interest, for she turned from the mirror to face him.

"£1,000, Arthur? How did he come to owe you so much?"

"A debt of honour, my dear, at least it is to those who are honourable!"

"Oh, you mean cards!"

"Yes, I mean cards," Lord Dervish snapped. "Caversham gave me his IOU but I learnt it was as worthless as the paper on which it was written."

"Are you telling me that was why he went abroad?" Lady Wentmore asked.

"Mine was not the only debt he owed. I hear he was heavily indebted to his tradesmen and decided to vanish. Damned unsporting, if you ask me. No gentleman would behave in such a manner!"

"It sounds very unlike Sir Denzil to me," Lady Wentmore said, turning back to the mirror, "and doubtless when he returns he will repay you."

"I am making sure of that," Lord Dervish said, "by taking out a warrant for his arrest."

Lady Wentmore gave a little cry.

"Oh, Arthur, that would be too cruel! I cannot bear to think of someone of Sir Denzil's elegance incarcerated in that horrible debtor's prison at the Fleet. I hear the conditions there are intolerable!"

"It will teach him a lesson," Lord Dervish said with satisfaction, "and personally, I never cared for the fellow myself, despite the fact that you and your friends fluttered around him like a lot of stupid moths round a candle!"

He paused to add:

"You did not get your wings burnt—I did! I intend to make him suffer, if it is the last thing I do!"

Lord Dervish spoke with a vindictive spitefulness; and listening with a kind of sick horror, Thalia realised the stories about his meanness and his avarice were all too true.

Mrs. Burton had always said he was the one person among her customers whom she dreaded seeing in the shop, knowing he would beat her down to the very last penny, then deduct his inevitable ten per cent from the bill.

"A thousand pounds!"

For her father to owe so much to a man like Lord Dervish was as terrifying as being faced with the National Debt, or a bill for the entertainment at Carlton House.

Everything that could be sold had gone from the Manor in the country, and living only on what she earned Thalia thought she would find it impossible to produce a thousand pennies, let alone the same number of sovereigns.

Her father would receive no mercy from Lord Dervish.

At the same time he had been seen in America. He was well and, she thought, perhaps making plans to return home now that the three years of his exile was over.

She felt as if there was a conflict within her that tore her in pieces: gladness that her mother's fears that her father was dead were wrong, and horror at the idea that once he set foot on English soil, he would be arrested and taken to the Fleet.

Lady Wentmore was not the only person who had heard of the terrors of the prison where men who could not pay their bills languished amongst the criminals, pickpockets and prostitutes for years on end.

How could she contemplate her father being in such a place?

And yet she knew that Lord Dervish would make good his threat and, what was more, enjoy humiliating a man who had not only lost to him at cards, but in his opinion, had deliberately defrauded him.

It was difficult for the moment, to realise the full

horror of what she had just heard, but of one thing she was quite certain, that if as Lord Dervish intended her father was arrested the moment he arrived, it would kill her mother.

She would not be able to stand the shock or the humiliation after what she had suffered already.

I must do something! I must do something immediately! Thalia thought frantically.

Vaguely as if from the end of a very long tunnel she heard Lady Wentmore say:

"I will take the blue bonnet. I think I look better in that than in any of the others. Do you not agree, Arthur?"

"Yes, the blue suits you admirably, my dear."

"And it was very sweet of you to say you would give it to me as a present," Lady Wentmore said. "Thank you very much."

"Wait a minute! Wait a minute!" Lord Dervish cautioned. "You are going too fast! I have to find out the price. I do not intend to be taken for a greenhorn."

Lady Wentmore laughed a tinkling little laugh that somebody had once told her sounded like bells.

"Nobody would ever suspect you of being a greenhorn, Arthur! You are far too astute, far too clever in every way."

"I hope so," Lord Dervish said complacently.

Thalia looked across the shop to Mrs. Burton, who seeing that Lady Wentmore had replaced her own bonnet, made her excuse to her client and came to Lord Dervish's side.

"I understand Her Ladyship is satisfied," she said, "and I hope you too, My Lord. As an old and valued customer we always do our best to give you satisfaction."

"That depends on one thing and one thing only," Lord Dervish began.

Carrying the blue bonnet in her hand Thalia escaped to the back of the shop.

"Pack this up," she said to one of the work-women,

"and tell Mrs. Burton if she asks where I am, that I have just gone out for a breath of air."

"A breath o' air?" the work-woman repeated. "That's not like ye, Thalia. I thought ye never left th' place 'til 'twas time to go home."

Thalia did not even bother to answer. She was slipping on her grey bonnet.

Then without saying any more, she opened the back-door and stepped out into the street.

She stood for one moment irresolute, then lifting her skirts in both hands, she started to run.

If it was a surprise to the passers-by to see anybody running down Hay Hill into Berkeley Square, Thalia did not notice them.

Still running, swerving to avoid anybody walking in the opposite direction, she was breathless by the time she reached the imposing entrance to Hellington House.

Only then did she stop to draw in a deep breath which she hoped would ease the frantic beating of her heart.

As she did so, the front-door opened and two footmen wearing the Earl's livery came out to start laying a red carpet which would cover the steps and run out over the pavement.

A second later Thalia saw the Earl's Phaeton being driven around the corner.

She realised she was only just in time.

She walked up the steps and as she reached the front door she saw standing in the Hall the Butler who had waited at dinner last night.

"I wish to speak to His Lordship," she said.

"Good morning, Miss," the Butler replied politely. "I'll tell His Lordship you're here."

Thalia followed him and he led her across the Hall and showed her into an attractive room that she thought from its appearance must be the Morning Room or used perhaps only for a caller like herself who arrived without an appointment.

But she could not think of anything except her father and the trap he would walk into the moment he arrived in England.

It seemed to her she waited for a long time before the door opened again and the Butler said:

"Will you come this way, Miss? His Lordship's in the Library."

Feeling as if it was impossible to think of what she would say, conscious only that her mother's life as well as her father's freedom rested on what happened in the next few minutes, Thalia followed the Butler across the Hall.

He opened the door of a room where the walls were lined with books.

She could however, see only the Earl moving towards her and was aware with one glance at his face, of his surprise at seeing her.

He waited until the door had shut behind the Butler, then he asked:

"What has happened? Why are you here?"

She raised her eyes to his and when he saw her eyes, he looked at her for a long moment before he said quietly:

"You have had a shock. Come and sit down and tell me about it."

It flashed through his mind that perhaps her mother had died. Then because of her expression he knew that something unexpectedly traumatic had happened, otherwise she would not have come to him.

The Earl had, in fact, been astonished when just as he was about to leave the house the Butler had come into the Library to say:

"There is a lady to see you, My Lord."

"A lady?" the Earl had asked sharply, thinking it might be Lady Adelaide and having no wish for her to delay his departure.

"It is the young lady who dined here last night, My Lord."

For a moment the Earl thought he could not have heard aright, then he said quickly:

"Show her in here."

"Very good, My Lord."

When the Butler left the room to fetch Thalia, the Earl told himself that something very strange indeed must have occured for her not only to communicate with him so early in the day, but to come in person.

He had been worrying ever since he awoke this morning as to whether Thalia would once again refuse to dine with him unless he could find a very reasonable excuse to force her into doing so.

She had certainly not said last night when he left her, that she was not prepared to listen to the plan of which he had spoken, or that they could not meet as he intended, but he had been afraid that when she left him she would once again be making difficulties.

Only because she was afraid of what he had discovered about her—and Heaven knows what her secret was—had she dined with him last night.

Even though he wanted to believe that the magical kiss they had exchanged had changed everything, he could not be sure of it.

Yet, inexplicably, almost unbelievably, she was here to see him and he knew without being told, it would not be just for the pleasure of his company.

Now as he looked at her, he realised how upset she was and he wanted to allay her fears and take away her unhappiness whatever might be the reason.

"I will . . . not sit down," Thalia said inaudibly, "there is . . . just something I want to . . . ask you . . . but it is . . difficult to put it . . . into words."

"I can see you are upset," the Earl said, "and I think too, you have been hurrying to get here. Let me send for some coffee, or perhaps it would be better for you to have a glass of wine."

"I . . . want . . . nothing, just for you to . . . listen to me."

"You know I will do that," the Earl said. "But I hate to see you like this. Give me your hand, darling."

"No . . . no!" Thalia cried. "You must not . . . touch me . . . please . . . do not . . . touch me . . . not until you have heard what I have to . . . say."

The Earl was surprised, but because it was what she wanted he stood waiting, while he knew she was feeling for words.

It was difficult to see her face for she bent her head and her grey bonnet obscured everything but her small, determined chin.

The Earl waited, curious, at the same time feeling any questions he might ask would only make it more difficult.

At last, it seemed that Thalia controlled herself enough to raise her eyes to his.

"You . . . asked me," she began in a very small voice, little above a whisper, "if I would be . . . your mistress."

"A harsh word," the Earl said, "for something which, where we are concerned, would be something very different, something which I believe, Thalia, would make us both very happy."

"I cannot . . . do what you . . . want . . . the way you want," Thalia said, "because Mama must . . . never know . . . but if . . ."

She stopped for a moment as if it was impossible to say any more. Then with what was a superhuman effort, she went on:

"If I . . . stay with you as I could . . . have done last . . . night or the night before . . . would you give me . . . one thousand . . . p—pounds?"

The last word came out in a rush almost as if she found it impossible to say, until it burst from her lips.

Now she could no longer look at him, but he saw the burning flush that swept over her face before she bent her head.

"A thousand pounds!" the Earl said slowly.

"P—please . . ." Thalia began, "I must have it now . . . at once . . . I cannot . . . wait!"

Once again she had raised her face to his and her eyes were searching his frantically, as if her very life depended on his answer.

"Who is blackmailing you?"

"Nobody . . . it is not . . . like that . . . it is something . . . very different."

"Will you tell me the reason why you need this money?"

"I cannot do that . . . although I want to . . . but it is a secret."

"The secret you thought I had discovered last night?"

"Y—yes."

"And, as you said, it concerns someone else?"

"Y—yes."

For a moment the Earl did not speak and Thalia said desperately:

"Please . . . do not ask questions . . . I cannot answer them. It is impossible . . . but I have to have the money . . . and if you will not give it to me . . . I do not know to whom I can . . . turn or . . . where I can . . . go."

The Earl looked down at her and now her eyes were beseeching his and he saw too that there was a terror in their depths that had not been there before, the terror of fear that he might refuse her.

"I will give you the money," the Earl said quietly.

He knew by the way Thalia drew in her breath how afraid she had been that he would not.

"I suppose," he went on, "you do not wish for a cheque because it would bear my name."

"No, no! It must be in . . . notes!"

"Very well," the Earl replied. "Just wait here."

He walked from the room as he spoke, and Thalia, as if her legs would no longer hold her, sank down in a chair and put her hands up to her face.

He would help her and her father would be safe!

For a moment she could think of nothing else, not even of what she had promised in order to obtain the money.

All that mattered was that her mother must never know, and her father could come home safely.

She realised how petrified she had been that the Earl would refuse to give her the money immediately, and say instead that she could earn it as time passed.

Had he done that, it would have been like hanging on a cliff's edge, wondering every moment of the day whether her father would arrive in England before the debt was paid only to be arrested as he stepped off the ship.

"He will be safe now . . . safe," she told herself and tried not to think of anything else except of her mother's happiness and that soon they would all be together again.

The door opened and the Earl came back into the room.

He held nothing in his hands and for the moment, almost like a stab of a dagger, Thalia wondered if he had changed his mind and perhaps would tell her that it was impossible to give her the money after all.

Almost as if he sensed what she was feeling, he said:

"My secretary is getting what you require. Fortunately we always keep quite a considerable sum of money here in the safe. While we are waiting, I am going to insist that you have a glass of wine."

He did not wait for her answer but went to the grog-tray which stood in a corner of the room and poured from a bottle which he took from a silver wine-cooler.

He brought the glass to her and put it in her hand.

"I do not . . . want it," Thalia said.

"But you will drink it to please me."

"Yes . . . of course."

There was a note of humility in her voice and it suddenly struck her that she had now committed herself to do what he required of her, whatever it might be.

I am grateful . . . very, very grateful, she thought.

At the same time, she felt as if already she had lost what she told him she prized so highly—her self-respect.

Now she would take her place with women like Genevieve who would entertain gentlemen in their nightgowns and expect the man to whom she had just been introduced to pay for the pleasure of looking at her.

I must not think of it, Thalia told herself.

Nevertheless, the thoughts were there, crowding in on her and making her feel as if she had ceased to be herself, but instead was the type of woman she had despised even while she waited on them as a humble shop-assistant.

The Earl did not speak and neither did she.

She sipped her wine because he had ordered her to do so, aware although she did not look up at him, that his eyes were on her face.

The door opened and the Earl's secretary came into the room.

He held a large, bulky envelope in his hand.

The Earl walked across the room towards him.

"I have included notes of the highest value we have, My Lord," the secretary said.

"Thank you," the Earl replied.

He took the package and as the door closed he reached Thalia's side and held it out to her.

"This is what you require," he said, "and because I do not think you should walk about with such a large sum of money on you, may I leave it anywhere you wish? Or take you there in my Phaeton?"

"Will you . . . take me . . . back to the shop?"

"If that is what you want," the Earl agreed.

She put down her glass and now, holding the envelope in her hand, she rose to her feet.

She looked at him, her eyes very wide and a little frightened in her pale face.

"I want to say . . . thank you."

"Shall we leave that until this evening?" the Earl asked.

"Y—yes . . . of course."

There was an apprehensive note in the words which he did not miss.

"Before we leave," the Earl said, "there is something I want to say."

Thalia looked up at him and he thought she was trembling.

"It is this," he said. "The money I have given you is a gift that has no strings attached, and I do not want your gratitude in any way that you have not shown me already."

"You mean . . . ?" Thalia began incredulously.

"I mean, my darling," the Earl said, "that nothing has changed as far as I am concerned from the way it was when we left each other last night. What you have asked me for, is something quite different from what we have discussed previously or intend to discuss tonight, or at any other time."

As if she understood what he was saying, he saw the tears come into her eyes making them seem larger and even more beautiful than they were before.

"How can you . . . be so . . . different from what I . . . expected?" she asked, "and so much more . . . understanding?"

The tears overflowed and ran down her cheeks.

"That is another question I will answer tonight," he said, "when we have more time. I have a feeling now that you should be back at your work. I would not wish you to get into trouble on my account."

Thalia's lips quivered but she could not speak and the Earl took his handkerchief from his breast-pocket and very gently wiped away the tears on her cheeks.

"I am sure everything will be all right," he said, "and better still if you trust me as I want you to do. I just want you to realise I am there to help you in any way I can."

"I . . . love . . . you!"

The words were hardly audible but the Earl heard them.

"I have a lot to tell you about my love for you," he said, "but it is going to take a very long time. Now, since the Regent is waiting for me and he very much dislikes being kept waiting, I suggest we leave all the things we have to say to each other until tonight."

Thalia thought that from the expression in his eyes and the feeling, although he was no longer touching her, that she was really in his arms, there was no need for words.

She knew they were close to each other as they had been when he had kissed her and she was sure he felt the same.

They walked across the room side by side and the Earl helped her into the Phaeton.

As they drove away down Berkeley Square she thought the sunshine was more golden and glittering than she had ever seen it before, in her whole life.

Only as the horses moved a little slower up Hay Hill the Earl asked:

"Shall I take you to the back-door?"

"Yes . . . please," Thalia replied.

As she spoke she thought it would be always the back-door in his life where she was concerned, and yet he was treating her not only as a woman he could possess, but something infinitely more precious. It reminded her of the way her father had always treated her mother.

"I love you, I love you!" she wanted to say to him, over and over again.

But she remembered that the groom was sitting behind them and might hear what she said.

The Earl drew up his horses outside the back-door of the shop.

"You are quite certain I cannot help you further?" he asked.

"No . . . I am all . right," Thalia replied.

She put out her hand and as he took it in his, she felt herself quiver because he was touching her.

The groom helped her to step down from the Phaeton and she slipped in through the back-door, hoping that none of the work-women would be aware of the way in which she had returned.

Fortunately when she got inside, it was to find that Mrs. Burton was still serving in the front of the shop.

It was easy for Thalia to go to the desk where the bills were made out and procure a plain sheet of paper.

On it she wrote:

"The Trustees of Sir Denzil Caversham's Estate enclose the sum of £1,000 owed to Lord Dervish, and deeply regret that this sum has been overlooked and was not paid three years ago, as it should have been."

She took an envelope from the desk, slipped the one containing the money inside and also the letter.

Then she folded the top of the envelope down and sealed it with sealing-wax which Mrs. Burton kept to use when money had to be taken to the Bank.

Thalia then addressed the envelope to:

"The Rt. Hon. Lord Dervish,
White's Club,
St. James's Street."

When she had finished she asked:

"Is Bill here?"

"Yes, Thalia," one of the work-women replied. " 'E's just agoing ter take this bonnet round ter Lady Wentmore. She said at first she'd take it with 'er then 'er changed 'er mind."

"I will give it to Bill," Thalia said.

She picked up the box from the work-table and went down to the basement where Bill sat when he was not delivering packages containing the purchases the customers had made.

He was not idle, for Mrs. Burton found innumerable things to occupy him.

There were parcels and crates from Paris to be unpacked. There were things to be mended and a great deal of his time was spent in cleaning and polishing. Mrs. Burton saw no reason to engage anyone else to do the work that he could do.

He was a man of over forty with grey hair who was terrified of losing his job and when Thalia called him, he said quickly:

"Oi be comin'," as if he was half-expecting to be reproved for tardiness.

"There is a box to take to Lady Wentmore who lives in Curzon Street, Bill," Thalia said, "and would you be very obliging and leave this letter for me at White's Club? It is not very much out of your way."

" 'Twouldn't matter if it were," Bill replied. "Oi'd do anythin' to 'elp yer, Miss. Yer knows that."

"Thank you, Bill, it is very kind of you, but be careful of this envelope. It is rather valuable."

" 'Ave yer ever known me lose anythin', Miss Thalia?"

"There is always a first time, Bill."

"Not when I be lookin' after somethin' as belongs to yer, Miss."

"Thank you, Bill. I am very grateful."

Thalia went upstairs thinking as she did so that Lord Dervish with his spite and hatred for her father, would have a surprise when he found what the letter contained.

The rest of the day seemed to pass more slowly than usual except when Thalia thought of the Earl and found in those moments she had no idea of time or anything else.

How can he be so kind, so marvellous to me, she asked.

And yet she told herself perhaps it was wrong and dishonest of her to accept such overwhelming generosity and give nothing in exchange.

She was not absolutely certain what happened when a man and a woman made love to each other. She only knew that she had always believed it was wrong and wicked unless their union was blessed by the Church.

Now she could not help feeling that perhaps if the Earl made love to her it would be as wonderful as his kiss had been.

Then she was shocked by her own thoughts.

Of course it would be wrong, and most of all because she would then become, as she had sworn she never would be his mistress, whatever he might call it.

That would be in her mother's eyes, something so degrading and appalling that she knew Lady Caversham must never, never learn of it.

Walking home with Hannah, Thalia knew that if she told Hannah what the Earl had suggested she should become when they first dined together, the maid would not be surprised.

It was the way she had expected a gentleman of the Earl's standing would behave with those he considered his inferiors. The only thing that would have shocked her, was that his invitation was given to someone who had been born a lady and was therefore, in Hannah's eyes, his equal.

That is something he will never consider me to be, Thalia thought and felt suddenly as if the sun had gone down and darkness already covered the eart.

Thinking of herself, she felt ashamed because they were nearly home before she asked Hannah:

"How has Mama been today?"

"Rather depressed," Hannah replied. "Her Ladyship had a little weep after luncheon when we talked about your father. She thinks perhaps he'll never come home, since it's nearly a week now since his three years were over."

"Is it really that?" Thalia asked. "I suppose I had lost count."

Then she told herself that she had good tidings for her mother. After all, she need not explain in what context she had heard it, but at least she could say that her father was alive, well, and had been seen in America.

"I have news for Mama," she said with a lilt in her voice. "She will not be depressed tonight when she hears what I have to tell her."

"News?" Hannah questioned instinctively walking quicker.

"I must first tell it to Mama," Thalia said.

Hannah opened the door and she ran upstairs.

Lady Caversham was lying on the chaise-longue as usual.

"There you are, my dearest!" she exclaimed. "I have been lying here reading your book and thinking how amusing it is. I had no idea I had such a clever daughter."

"That is what I wanted you to say, Mama," Thalia answered, "and I have something to tell you; something you have been waiting to hear."

She saw the sudden alertness in her mother's eyes, then even as she opened her lips to speak, she heard Hannah's voice sounding curiously like a scream downstairs.

Lady Caversham was startled.

"What is it?" she asked.

"I will go and see," Thalia replied.

Even as she turned she heard a man's voice answering Hannah and footsteps coming up the stairs.

For a moment she could hardly believe it was true, then she gave a cry which seemed to echo and re-echo around the room.

"It is Papa! I know it is Papa!"

"So you were expecting me," Sir Denzil said.

Then he was in the room, looking for his wife and a second later she was in his arms.

"Papa, how could you arrive just when you are wanted most?" Thalia asked.

He could not answer her but as she kissed his cheek he put his arm round her and held her as close to him as he could.

Lady Caversham was crying helplessly against his shoulder.

"It is all right, my darling, I am back. Everything is going to be all right now, with no more worries, no more troubles. How could I have guessed, how could I have known, that you would not have enough money?"

"It does not matter," Lady Caversham sobbed, "but I thought you might be dead!"

"Dead!" Sir Denzil cried. "I am very much alive! Listen, my precious! Listen, Thalia! I am rich! Immensely, enormously rich!"

Thalia moved in his arms to stare at him.

"Rich, Papa?"

"A millionaire several times over."

"But, how? How is it possible?"

"It is a long story, but shall I tell you simply that I now own a Gold Mine and a very successful one at that!"

"Denzil, why did you not write to me?" Lady Caversham asked.

"Write?" Sir Denzil exclaimed. "I wrote the first month."

"I never received the letters," his wife murmured.

"Then," Sir Denzil went on, "I could hardly write, my darling, when I was living in the back of beyond!"

"And you really own a Gold Mine, Papa?" Thalia asked.

"I not only own it, but I have floated a Company on the Stock Market which will make me even richer than I am already!"

"I cannot believe it!" Thalia exclaimed.

"I will tell you all about it," he said, "but first I must tell your mother how much I love her and apologise for not letting her know sooner that I can now give her everything in the world she has ever wanted."

"All I want is . . . you Denzil," Lady Caversham murmured, tearfully.

Her husband smiled over her head at his daughter in a conspiratorial fashion.

"That is what you have got," he said, "and I would have been here sooner, my darling, if I had not thought it expedient to call on Lord Eldon first."

Thalia looked at him apprehensively.

"It is all right? You are allowed to return?" she asked in a low voice.

"The Lord Chancellor was exceedingly kind," Sir Denzil replied. "He did suggest, and I think he is right, that we should leave for the country immediately and stay there, until it is generally accepted that I am back and all my affairs are in order."

"That is what Mama has always planned we would do," Thalia said.

"And that is what we will do," her father replied. "I do not suppose you have much to pack? There are two carriages waiting for us."

"You intend we should leave now?"

"What is there to keep us?" Sir Denzil replied. "We will not require any of this rubbish in the future."

He waved a disparaging hand towards the furniture in the room, then he looked down at his wife with an expression of love and consternation in his eyes.

"I will make up to you, my precious, for everything you have suffered while I have been away," he promised, "and now you shall have all the things you gave up for me, diamonds, jewels, horses, and we will do all the repairs to the Manor that we always planned we would do when my 'ship' came in."

He gave a laugh with a triumphant note in it.

"Well, my ship is in and a very large one it is."

It is like old times, Thalia thought, to have her father boasting of his triumphs, elated by some success and seeming to make everything he said an excitement in itself.

He bent and kissed his wife again before he said:

"Get your cloak and your bonnet, my beloved. We are leaving at once, and if we hurry we will be home in time for a late dinner."

"But, Denzil, there are no servants."

"That is where you will get a surprise," her husband said. "I went home first expecting to find you there. Then I heard what had happened, and I told nearly everyone in the village to come and look after us, until we get things organised. They will do it, you can be sure of that."

"Oh, Denzil, it does not seem true that you are here, and I need be unhappy about you—no longer."

There was a note in Lady Caversham's voice as she spoke, which Thalia knew was not tiredness or lassitude but an overwhelming happiness.

It would be a long journey home, but she had a feeling it would not tire her mother half so much as sitting being miserable as she had these last three years.

The mere fact that her father was back made her look radiant and there was a flush on her cheeks and her eyes were shining as if she was a young woman again.

"Come along," Sir Denzil said firmly. "Hurry, Thalia. I have no intention of spending a night in this poky little hole."

They were being swept along in the flood tide of her father's vitality, Thalia thought.

But while it was wonderful to have him there, thrilling to know he was alive and well, there was nevertheless a nagging feeling in her heart that told her his return could not be as perfect for her as it was for her mother.

I must tell the Earl . . . I must let him know what has . . . occurred, she thought.

Even as she thought of it she knew it was something she must not do.

If he learnt who she really was, then he would feel obliged after all that had passed between them, to offer her marriage.

She would have caught him, as he had said he had avoided being caught all these years.

She remembered only too clearly how she had told him that the women she waited on bought their clothes as . . . a bait to catch a fish, and had laughingly added that the Earl of Hellington would be a very large catch if they could land him.

She could still hear the note in the Earl's voice as he had said:

"I assure you I fight ferociously never to be netted!"

She had told him she spoke prophetically and that in the end he would be caught and once he was in the net, there would be no escape.

"That is exactly what I am afraid of," the Earl had said.

He had no wish to be married, that was obvious, not even to someone he loved.

That is why, Thalia told herself, as she reached for the cloak she had worn when she dined with the Earl, to put over her thin gown, *he must never know who I really am.*

Her whole being cried out in an agony at the thought of going away, of disappearing and never letting him know what had happened to her.

Then suddenly she remembered what had happened today.

Strangely, it was the first time it had occurred to her since her father's return that she had tried to save him from being arrested by repaying the money he owed, which the Earl had given her at luncheontime.

His arrival had swept everything from her mind except of course, her love for the Earl.

She went back into the Drawing-Room.

Hannah was there wrapping her mother in shawls so that she would not be cold on the journey.

"I want to speak to you, Papa," Thalia said.

"What is it, my dearest?" he asked. "Now I look at you I see you have grown extremely attractive while I have been away."

"Thank you, Papa, but this is important."

She drew him out of the Drawing-Room and into her own tiny bedroom.

"Listen, Papa, there is no time to explain now, although I will tell you later, but I need to have £1,000 immediately. Is that possible?"

"£1,000?" her father asked. "Whatever for?"

"It is a debt of honour. Something you owed and which you forgot to pay before you left England."

"£1,000?"

He put his hand up to his forehead.

"My God! It is the money I lost to Dervish!"

"Yes, I know. He has threatened to have you arrested the moment you arrived in England."

"Well, I will soon put that right," Sir Denzil said.

"I have done so already," Thalia replied, "but I must repay the money now you are here, and at once!"

"But of course," Sir Denzil agreed. "Who was kind enough to rescue me from the heavy hand of the Law?"

He spoke jokingly and Thalia answered:

"There is no time for questions, and I do not want Mama to know what has happened. It would upset her. Can you give me the £1,000 now?"

"If you had told me earlier it might have been easier," Sir Denzil said, "but, wait a minute! I have a Bearer Bond with me."

"Does it bear your name?" Thalia asked quickly.

"No. As a matter of fact I called the issue after the place where I found the Gold Mine."

"Then that is all right," Thalia said, "as I do not

wish the person to whom I am sending it, to know who you are."

Her father looked at her with a puzzled expression on his face, then as he was about to speak, Lady Cav-ersham called from the Drawing-Room:

"I am ready, Denzil!"

"I will be with you in a second, my dearest," he answered. "I have something to do for Thalia first."

He ran down the stairs saying as he did so:

"Tell Hannah to get your mother into the carriage. You wait here!"

A few minutes passed, then for the second time that day Thalia put a thousand pounds into an envelope.

As she did so, she thought of something else.

She picked up one of her own books which were still lying on the Dressing-Table and opened it to write inside:

"To a Gentleman who is kind, gentle, understanding and very, very wonderful, and whom I will never forget.

Thalia."

She put it with the bearer bond, into an envelope and addressed it to the Earl of Hellington.

As her father and Hannah tucked her mother up into the big, comfortable carriage drawn by four horses that was waiting for them on the road by the side of the market, Thalia ran to the nearest Butcher.

"Good evening, Miss Carver," he said. "You're later than usual!"

"I want you to do me a great favour," Thalia said. "Will you send your son, or someone trustworthy, with this letter to the Earl of Hellington in Berkeley Square?"

"Yes, of course, Miss Carver," the Butcher agreed. "It'll be no trouble—no trouble at all!"

"You will ensure that it is delivered safely?"

"You need have no fears on that score. It'll be in

His Lordship's hands within ten minutes o' your giving it to me."

"Thank you very much," Thalia said, "and thank you also for all your kindness to me and my mother since we have been living in the Market."

"You're leaving?"

"Yes . . . we are leaving," Thalia answered. "We are . . . going home!"

Chapter Seven

The Earl walked into the Coffee Room at White's and threw himself down in a chair beside Richard.

One glance at his friend's face was enough to tell him that he had been unsuccessful in his search.

"Will you have a drink?" Richard enquired.

The Earl hesitated as if it was difficult to concentrate on the question. Then he replied:

"Order me a brandy."

The waiter took the order and Richard asked in a low voice:

"No luck?"

"None at all," the Earl replied.

As he spoke he was thinking despairingly that it was now ten days since Thalia had disappeared.

He thought he had known from the moment he received the £1,000 Bearer Bond and read the inscription in her book that she was determined never to see him again.

"Whom I will never forget."

He was sure that the words were written on his heart and would haunt him all his life.

"It seems extraordinary that anybody can disappear so completely!" Richard exclaimed.

It was the same remark he had made a hundred times before, in fact, ever since the third day of his search when the Earl had confided in him as if he could not bear being alone with his anxiety any longer.

As the waiter brought the brandy to the Earl, both men were thinking of the steps they had taken to trace one elusive young woman about whom they knew so little that it had made the difficulty of finding her almost insuperable from the beginning.

Investigations by Henry in Shepherd's Market had told the Earl that a gentleman had arrived late in the evening with two expensive carriages, each drawn by four horses.

It had not escaped the notice of curious neighbours that he had not been at Number 82 for very long before he left together with the whole household—Mrs. Carver, the servant Hannah and Thalia.

They had driven away without luggage, without returning as the Earl had at first thought they must do, to collect anything the small house contained.

It seemed to Richard even more incredible than it did to the Earl.

"Why should they have taken nothing with them?" he asked.

"Presumably because it was no further use to them," the Earl replied. "I know that Thalia was very poor. Carriages and horses cost money. Obviously the man who called for her and her mother could afford to pay for them."

When the Earl had first been informed of the circumstances of their leaving, he had thought with a fury which he had later recognised as jealousy, that

Thalia had been swept away from him by some ardent lover.

Then commonsense told him, when he could think about it more sanely, that it was unlikely if she was going on a romantic journey that she would have been accompanied by her mother and Hannah.

The only information the Earl had not communicated to Richard was that he had given Thalia £1,000 and she had returned it to him within a few hours.

That was a secret between himself and Thalia, and it merely contributed to his theory that whoever she had left with must be a rich man.

At night when he could not sleep, which he had failed dismally to do ever since he had lost Thalia, he would go over their conversations together word by word, trying to discover a clue, even the slightest hint, which might give him some idea of where she had gone.

Without this, he asked himself, how could he even begin to search the length and breadth of England for a young woman who had intrigued and mystified him ever since he had first known her.

Intent on his own problem, he was not aware that Richard regarded his behaviour first with astonishment, then with compassion.

Never in all the years he had known the Earl had he ever seen him in such a state about anything or anybody, least of all a woman.

Always in the past he had accepted them as necessities in that they could amuse and entertain him.

Never, and this was the truth, had he ever become involved so that he actively suffered from the need of one of them.

"He is in love!" Richard told himself.

But he did not say it out loud because he felt that it would only contribute further to the Earl's obvious unhappiness.

As the Earl sipped his brandy, to change the subject he asked:

"How are your horses?"

"I have no idea."

"I thought you might have been running one at Epsom."

"I believe my trainer did enquire if I wished to do so," the Earl answered vaguely.

It was obvious that his mind was elsewhere, but at that moment a member who was passing said:

"Hello, Hellington! I expected to see you at Epsom yesterday."

The Earl merely nodded his head in recognition of the greeting, but Richard, in an effort to be polite, enquired:

"Did you have a winner?"

"Only as regards my bets," was the reply. "I withdrew my own horse."

This was obviously a sore point and the speaker moved on to sit down in a chair behind the Earl and Richard, obviously not wishing to talk any further of what had occurred.

There was a rustle of paper and then someone said:

"Good morning, Dervish. I have not seen you for some time."

"I have been staying at Epsom," Lord Dervish replied, then in a louder tone than he had used before, he exclaimed: "Good God!"

"What has happened?"

"You will hardly believe it, but Caversham has returned the £1,000 he owed me. It has taken him three years, and I can hardly credit it is not a joke!"

"Sir Denzil Caversham? I thought he was abroad."

"He is, but here is the £1,000 he owed me from his Trustees."

The Earl, who had been sitting in what Richard called to himself "the darkest gloom," suddenly sat upright.

Then to his friend's astonishment he sprang to his feet and walked to where Lord Dervish was sitting behind him.

"Forgive my intrusion, Dervish," he said, "but I could not help overhearing you saying you had received £1,000 from somebody after a lapse of three years."

"That is true," Lord Dervish replied. "I can tell you it is quite a shock! I never expected to see the money again. In fact, I intended to take out a warrant for Caversham's arrest if he ever returned to this country."

"Would you permit me to see the £1,000 you have received?" the Earl asked.

Lord Dervish looked at him in surprise. Then he said:

"I cannot see why you are interested, Hellington, unless he owes you money too. As a matter of fact, his Trustees have sent me £1,000 in notes. I could not think what it was when I picked up the envelope just now, when I came into the Club."

He held out the opened envelope as he spoke and with it the letter that Thalia had written.

One glance at the writing told the Earl what he wished to know.

"Thank you," he said. "Do you happen to know Caversham's address?"

"I cannot remember it," Lord Dervish replied, "but I expect the porter can tell you. If not, he will doubtless be listed in Debrett."

"Yes, of course," the Earl said.

He turned without another word and went from the Coffee-Room leaving Lord Dervish and Richard staring after him in perplexity.

"I do not mind betting," Lord Dervish remarked as he closed the envelope which contained the notes, "that Caversham owes Hellington a packet!"

Thalia stepped through the French window which opened on to the lawn.

As it was growing late in the afternoon the sun had lost its strength and she did not need a sunshade to prevent its rays from spoiling the whiteness of her skin.

The gardeners her father had engaged to cut away the wild growth of three years neglect were beginning to make the garden look almost as she remembered it.

It had been a shock to see the green velvet lawns which had been there for centuries turned, as her father had said contemptuously, "into hay-fields" and the shrubs and flower-beds overgrown until they had almost a jungle-like appearance.

The house seemed to have suffered less from neglect through the years, especially as on Sir Denzil's instructions the women of the village had already removed the worst of the cobwebs and dust before they arrived.

Like a Commander directing operations in the field, Sir Denzil had begun to redecorate and refurnish the house as he and his wife had always longed to do.

Thalia lost count of the items he ordered from tradesmen who flocked to the Manor eagerly, once it was known that he required their services.

It was not only that he wanted everything around him to be as fine and grand as he had always wished it to be, it was also, Thalia knew, an almost childish delight in being able to spend, spend, spend as he had never been able to do before, in the whole of his life.

The story of his adventures in America left his wife and his daughter breathless, and because he was so excited about them himself, it was hard for Thalia at times not to believe that she was listening to some boys' adventure story rather than a tale of persistence and sheer good luck.

It had been lucky that Sir Denzil had become friends on board the ship that carried him away from England, with a man who was a prospector for gold and was, in fact, an expert in the field.

Sir Denzil had gone with him to Arizona and it was due to his new-found friend that he staked the small amount of money he had with him in a prospective gold field that was not yet developed.

With a determination that his friends would not have expected of him, Sir Denzil worked harder, he said, than any navvy in panning gold, and was astute enough to invest every nugget he found in buying more land.

Besides the prospectors in the field, there were the riff-raff who were always looking for a "strike."

Most of them were interested in what they found only so that they could drink more with the bawdy women who were to be found in the hastily erected bars that were too sordid to attract any man who was in the least fastidious.

Gradually Sir Denzil and his partner acquired all the land that was worthwhile and when finally they struck the deep vein they hoped for, there was no question of their ownership being in dispute.

The moment he had gained everything he required, knowing the years of his exile were coming to an end, Sir Denzil was ready to return to New York on the first step of his journey back to England.

The mine by this time, was being worked by experts and there was nothing he and his partner could do personally but collect their profits and make sure that they would continue to flow in.

Everything was tied up extremely satisfactorily by the best lawyers and financial experts in New York.

Then Sir Denzil's partner was shot by a man who believed many years earlier, he had defrauded him of his claim.

The accusation was untrue, but the fact that the man was arrested did not save his victim's life.

He only just had time to make a will in Sir Denzil's favour, before he died.

"I've had the greatest fun in my life these last three years that we've been together," he said to Sir Denzil.

"In fact, I'd never known what it was to laugh before."

He gasped for air before he added:

"Spend my money for me, Denzil, and laugh as you do so. I shall be listening to hear you."

There were tears in Sir Denzil's eyes as he related this part of the story, and his wife held tightly onto his hand to show she understood and wanted to comfort him.

Although the sound of her father's laughter filled the Manor and brought his wife such happiness that every day she seemed to glow with a new beauty, Thalia knew there was one part of herself that no laughter could reach.

Every night when she was alone she found herself crying helplessly for the Earl, wondering if he had forgotten her already, and whether somebody like Lady Adelaide or Genevieve had taken her place in his affections.

She was certain she had done the right thing in running away without telling him where she was going, or who she was.

Although it was an agony to think there were only a few hours' fast driving between them, she could not have borne the knowledge that the Earl might believe he must behave in an honourable manner and offer her marriage.

It was not just marriage she wanted from him, but something very different, and to have trapped him, for that was what it would have amounted to, into losing his freedom would, she told herself with a wry smile, have been definitely "unsporting."

"He will forget me . . . of course he will forget me," she kept saying, "but I will never, never forget him!"

She faced the fact that she would never love anybody else and therefore it was unlikely that she would ever marry.

It did not trouble her particularly except that it was

hard to think of the Earl without crying, and she was well aware that in some ways she was *de trop* in her own home.

Always before, she and her father had been so close and she had never wanted other companions of her own age, being utterly content to be with him.

Now something was missing between them, something she recognised as being as much his fault as hers, if fault was the right word.

His experiences in America, the tremendous effort he had to make in an entirely different world from his own, had changed Sir Denzil from the light-hearted, rather irresponsible man he had been, into a much older and wiser person.

He still retained his gift of laughter and *joie de vivre* but he was content as he had never been before with his home, his estate and his wife who adored him.

In the past he had talked to Thalia of subjects which interested him and which were outside his immediate home-life.

Now she realised almost in surprise, that her father was middle-aged and wanted to settle down.

"Eldon was right," he said several times to his wife and daughter, "as soon as people have begun to accept me, I shall take my rightful place in County affairs. Perhaps, who knows, one day the King might appoint me to be Lord Lieutenant!"

"I hope so, darling," Lady Caversham said, "and how handsome you will look in your special uniform."

"I shall have to 'play myself in'," Sir Denzil said. "There are a great number of charitable boards I must sit on first, and I must join the Yeomanry, which I should have done years ago."

He paused before he said to please his wife:

"We must entertain, my dearest, and who will look lovelier than you at the head of the table? And of course, presiding over the Ball we must give every year."

There is really no place here for me now, Thalia thought sadly.

She put on one of the beautiful gowns that her father had ordered for her and her mother before he bought anything else, and she could not help wondering what the Earl would think if he could see her in it.

She knew it was very different from the grey gown she had worn in the shop or the simple muslin in which she had dined with him.

Her new gown accentuated the perfection of her figure, the whiteness of her skin and was a frame for the shining glory of her hair with its touches of fire.

A fire, Thalia thought miserably, that would never burn in her again whatever compliments she might receive, whatever man's eyes looked into hers.

She walked slowly across the lawn, thinking as she smelt the fragrance of the rose-garden that it was still, with its weather-beaten Elizabethan brick walls and water-lily pool, one of the most beautiful places she had ever seen.

It is a place for lovers, she thought instinctively.

Then she drew in her breath, as if the thought stabbed her physically, like a sharp dagger.

She walked between the beds, crimson, white and pink with their roses in bloom, to stand looking down into the water-lily pool thinking she must remind her father to replace the goldfish that had been there when she was a child.

Then she asked herself what did it matter?

Goldfish were what children loved, and she would never have any children to try with their small fat hands, to capture the elusive little fish, or to bring her as she had brought her mother, the first primrose of the spring.

She knew what she wanted more than anything else was a child who would resemble the Earl because he was his father.

Then as the tears, never far from the surface, came to her eyes, she felt ashamed of her own weakness.

"I will go back to the house and find something useful to do," she told herself severely.

As she turned she heard the footsteps of somebody walking into the rose-garden and thought it must be her father.

Because she knew it would upset him if he saw her in tears, she blinked her eyes to prevent them from falling, and turned her head aside as she sought for a handkerchief in the sash of her gown.

Several tears fell before she found it and a voice she had not expected to hear, asked:

"You are not crying, Thalia?"

She gave a little gasp of astonishment. Then her eyes, wide and shining with tears, looked in amazement to see the Earl standing beside her.

For a moment she thought she must be dreaming, but there were his grey eyes holding hers captive as he had done before, and she could only stare up at him, feeling as if her whole body had come alive simply because he was there when she had never thought to see him again.

"You are . . . here!" she exclaimed wonderingly.

"I am here!" he repeated. "I had almost given up hope of ever finding you. How could you behave in such a cruel, wicked manner? What have I ever done to deserve such punishment?"

He spoke so sternly that her hands fluttered to her breasts as if to control the violent beating of her heart.

Then as she knew he was waiting for an answer, she said hesitatingly:

"I . . . I thought it was . . . best."

"For me? You have nearly destroyed me by making me suffer in thinking I had lost you for ever!"

"I did not . . . mean to upset you."

"What did you expect me to feel?" he asked sharply, "when you just vanished, and I was left trying to imagine what had happened."

"I . . . am . . . sorry . . . terribly sorry," Thalia whispered.

She spoke humbly, yet at the same time there was music in the air and the Earl seemed to be surrounded by an aura of light which was dazzling.

He was here! He was beside her and he appeared to mind because she had gone away.

She knew too, that while he looked amazingly handsome, he seemed thinner and his face was more sharply drawn.

"You might at least," the Earl was saying, "have told me your real name."

"I . . . did not . . . wish you to . . . know it."

"Why not?"

She could not tell him the real reason and as Thalia was silent he said:

"I think you must be the only woman who would not have been curious to know what my plans for you were, the plans I told you we would talk about at dinner that night."

Thalia looked away from him as the colour rose in her cheeks.

The Earl's eyes were watching her and he thought that her little straight nose and the curve of her lips silhouetted against the roses were the loveliest things he had ever seen in his whole life.

"Have you thought about me?" he asked unexpectedly.

"O—of course I . . . have!"

"And have you wondered what I was going to suggest to you when we dined together?"

It was impossible to answer and after a moment he said:

"I had a present for you."

"You . . . know I would not have accepted a . . . present after what you had . . . given me already."

"I told you the £1,000, which I know now was for your father, did not concern us. The present I was going to give you was something very different."

"I am . . . sorry I had to . . . miss . . . receiving it."

"I will give it to you now."

She turned her head to look up at him.

There was an expression in his eyes which made her heart beat even more violently than it was already.

"I am afraid since I have taken so long in finding you that it is somewhat out of date."

The Earl drew something from the inside pocket of his closely fitting coat as he spoke.

It was a piece of paper and as Thalia took it from him, she wondered what it could be.

It was difficult to think of anything except the Earl himself, but because he was waiting she opened the paper, then stared at it astounded.

It was a Marriage Certificate made out in the name of Vargus Alexander Mark, 5th Earl of Hellington, bachelor, and Thalia Carver, spinster!

For a moment she could hardly believe what she saw, then an inexpressible joy swept over her.

He wanted to marry her! He loved her enough to want her not as his mistress, but as his wife, even though she had been nothing more than a shop assistant!

The Marriage Certificate trembled in her hand and she was aware that the Earl had drawn a little closer, so close that their bodies were almost touching as he said:

"Perhaps Miss Caversham feels different from Miss Thalia Carver, whom I very distinctly remember saying that she loved me."

"I . . . did not wish you to . . . feel that I was . . . trying to . . . catch you," Thalia stammered.

"I was caught already," the Earl replied, "caught, and completely hooked for all time."

He took the Marriage Certificate from her and threw it on to the ground. Then he pulled her into his arms, holding her so close against him that it was hard to breathe.

"Will you marry me, my darling, for I cannot live without you?"

He did not wait for her answer, but his lips sought hers.

As he kissed her, Thalia knew again that wonder and glory he had given her before when he had carried her up to the stars and they hung suspended there with all the problems of the world far away from them.

She felt as if the Earl made her his and they were indivisible, and yet it was something they had been since they first knew each other.

They belonged, they were one and she had never thought that what he felt for her could be the same as she felt for him.

Now she knew how much he wanted and needed her and she felt her whole mind and body respond in a manner which told her they could never be divided.

Their love was greater than time or space or any man-made divisions of class or status.

"I love . . . you! I love . . . you!" she whispered as the Earl released her lips.

She was trembling with the ecstasy he had evoked in her and she thought he was trembling too.

"I love you and you will never leave me again!" he replied. "I could not bear it."

Then he was kissing her wildly, passionately, demandingly, and a fire leapt within them both until Thalia seemed to break under the strain of it and she hid her face against his shoulder.

"How soon will you marry me?" he asked, and his voice was deep and unsteady.

"As soon as . . . you . . . want me to . . . do so."

"That is now—this moment!"

She gave a little cry of sheer happiness.

"I was so . . . certain that you had no wish to . . . marry anybody."

"I only want to marry you. There has never been another woman who made me feel as you do, or made me realise I could never be happy without her."

"And . . . suppose you find . . . once we are married . . . that you are . . . bored with me, as you have . . . been with so many . . . other women?"

The Earl's arms tightened around her.

"I became bored with other women because they were not you," he said. "This is different, my precious love, and it will take me a very long time to tell you how different."

He looked down at her, then held her from him at arms' length.

"I have never seen you fashionably gowned before."

"Do you . . . like me like . . . this?"

"I love you whatever you wear," he replied, "but I am disappointed."

"D—disappointed?" Thalia asked anxiously.

"I wanted to give you the right background for your beauty and I used to imagine how different you would look without that little grey gown. But now your father has had the fun that I had promised myself."

"It has not . . . spoilt things for . . . you?"

The Earl smiled.

"Nothing would do that. It is just that I wanted you to belong to me so completely and absolutely, and to know there was nobody in your life except me."

"There is . . . no one in my life . . . except you."

She saw the delight her words brought to his eyes.

Then as if she felt she must reassure him, she moved closer to him.

"It is . . . hard to believe you are . . . here," she said. "I have . . . missed you so . . . desperately . . . I have been so terribly . . . unhappy without you . . . and I thought I should be . . . alone for the rest of my life."

She knew he understood what she meant by the word "alone" and he said with his lips touching the softness of her cheek:

"That is what I felt. It was as if you took part of me away with you and I knew I would never be complete again until I had found you."

He made a sound that was half a laugh and half a groan.

"I never knew that love could be so painful, such excruciating misery."

"And . . . now?"

"Now it is a wonder beyond words, a happiness which I believe, my darling, will grow every day and every year that we are together."

He drew her closer still before he said:

"There is no end to our love—yours and mine—it is something which Fate brought to us and Fate will never take away. I will love you, my beautiful one, from now until eternity, and that will not be long enough for me."

"That is . . . how I . . . love you."

Thalia gave a little cry as she raised her lips to his.

"Make me . . . sure this is . . . true! Make me . . . sure I am not . . . dreaming," she begged. "It is so wonderful . . . so absolutely . . . wonderful . . . as you are."

It was impossible for her to say any more, for the Earl's lips were on hers.

She knew that everything they were trying to put into words was expressed in his kiss that came from the sun itself and enveloped them with the dazzling, blinding light that was Divine.

Gift of the Gods

Author's Note

The Gunning Sisters, Maria and Elizabeth, arrived in London from Ireland in 1751. They were immediately pronounced "the most beautiful women alive," but they were so poor that for some time they used to share one gown between them.

In 1752, Elizabeth, the younger, married the sixth Duke of Hamilton at half-past-twelve at night at the Mayfair Chapel, with "a ring of the bed-curtain."

She had two sons who both became Dukes of Hamilton, and when her husband died in 1758 she married the Marquis of Lorne, who became the Duke of Argyll.

The elder sister, Maria, married the sixth Earl of Coventry. Because for her beauty she was mobbed in Hyde Park, the King insisted she should have a guard of fourteen soldiers to protect her.

She had five children, but she was only twenty-seven when she died of consumption after her health was upset by using cosmetics containing white lead.

The fascinating little Madame Vestris, the pet of the Regency Bucks and Beaux, was notorious for her amorous interests as well as for her professional accomplishments. She blazed a trail of new attitudes and practises on the stage, and her exquisite legs and her laughter were like a gleam of sunshine.

Chapter One

1821

As Sir Hadrian Wynton was driven away down the unkept drive, which was a complete contrast to the smart carriage in which he was travelling, his daughters gave a sigh of relief.

They had been hustling and bustling from morning until evening during the last few days, getting their father packed up and ready to set off for Scotland.

Sir Hadrian's hobby was geology and he had written erudite but rather dull books on the rocks and stones of Britain.

Therefore, when he received an invitation from an old friend to visit him in Scotland, with the promise that he could not only explore the mountains of Perthshire but also journey to the Shetland Islands, he was as excited as a schoolboy at the idea.

"I have always wanted to research, for one thing, the Pictish forts," he said, "and see what type of stones they used, and I should not be surprised if the Vikings brought with them stones from the other side of the North Sea which up to date have not been discovered."

Penelope, his youngest daughter, made no pretence of listening to her father talk on subjects in which she had no interest.

But Alisa, who loved her father, tried to understand

what he was saying, and she knew that, now that her mother was dead, his whole interest was concentrated on what he termed his "work."

She offered to copy out his manuscripts for him in her neat, elegant handwriting before they went to the publishers, and he would even read to her aloud a long chapter when Penelope was either in bed or trying to improve her very scanty wardrobe.

Now as they turned from the front door, having waved their father out of sight, Penelope said:

"I have an idea to tell you about."

Alisa did not answer, and Penelope said insistently:

"Did you hear me, Alisa?"

"I was just wondering if Papa has taken enough warm clothing with him," Alisa answered. "I am sure it is much colder in the North than it is here, and he will go out in all weathers and forget that he is getting older and more prone to coughs and colds."

"Stop fussing over Papa as if you were a hen with only one chick!" Penelope exclaimed. "And come into the Sitting-Room. I really have something very serious to talk to you about."

She had by now alerted her sister, and Alisa looked at her with startled eyes as she followed Penelope from the Hall into the untidy but comfortable Sitting-Room which in her mother's time had been called the Morning-Room.

Now it was where Alisa and Penelope pursued their special hobbies, and in consequence there was a half-finished gown thrown over one chair with a work-basket open beside it, and on the small easel by the window a picture which Alisa was painting of some primroses in a china vase.

There were a great number of books in the room, too many to find places in the large Chippendale bookcase which was already full.

Many therefore stood rather untidily in one corner, and there were also little piles of two or three on most of the tables.

Alisa was the "reader" and Penelope the "do-er," and they were very different in character, although in looks they were not unalike.

At the same time, there was a difference.

Both were lovely, almost outstandingly beautiful, but Penelope was undoubtedly the more spectacular.

It was impossible to think that any girl could present such an ideal of prettiness.

Her hair was the gold of ripening corn, her eyes as blue as a summer sky, her complexion the pink-and-white that was to be found more often in poems than in actual fact.

People when they saw Penelope thought she could not be real, then when they looked at Alisa and looked again, they realised that she was as lovely as her sister, and yet it was not so obvious.

It was their father who, in one of his more perceptive moods, had christened them "the Rose and the Violet," and it actually was an extremely apt title, which he then forgot because he seldom had time to think about his daughters.

In fact it was only two days before he left for Scotland that he said to Alisa:

"Oh, by the way, Alisa, I have written to your Aunt Harriet and asked her to have you to stay."

"Aunt Harriet? Oh, no, Papa!" Alisa exclaimed involuntarily.

"What do you mean by that?" her father enquired.

There was a pause, then Alisa said:

"I suppose we . . . could not . . . stay here? We would be quite . . . safe, as you well know, with the Brigstocks to look after us."

"The Brigstocks are servants," her father replied, "and although it has been all right for me to leave you with them for a night or two, it is quite a different thing to be away for two or perhaps three months."

Alisa did not reply.

She was racking her brains to think of somebody they could invite to stay with them instead of having to leave the country she loved and stay with their aunt in London.

They had been to her twice before for short visits and had found it incredibly boring, and she knew that Penelope found the atmosphere of the house in Islington unbearable.

Sir Hadrian's elder sister had married, long before he had, an Army Officer.

General Ledbury had had a long career in the Army, being what her father called scornfully "an armchair soldier," which meant that he spent his time at the War Office and never saw active service.

On his retirement he was awarded the K.C.B., then died, leaving his wife with little money and no children.

This was perhaps the reason why Lady Ledbury took up good works and spent her time working to raise money either for Missionaries, crippled soldiers or orphaned children.

Whenever her nieces stayed with her they were forced to spend their time either making ugly garments for natives in far-off places who found it much more convenient to go naked, or copying out tracts which the Society concerned found too expensive to have printed.

The idea of spending two or three months on such activities was appalling, but as her father was adamant that they could not stay at home, Alisa, who disliked arguing with him, accepted that there was nothing they could do but hope that he would return as quickly as possible.

Now, looking around their Sitting-Room, she thought despondently that her aunt would never allow her to waste time in painting, and if Penelope wished to sew for herself she would have to do it secretly after she was supposed to be in bed.

Penelope, however, was smiling and there was a look of excitement in her large eyes that made Alisa ask in surprise:

"What is it? What has happened?"

"I have a wonderful idea!" Penelope replied. "And it is all because of something Eloise said to me yesterday."

Eloise Kingston was the daughter of the local Squire, with whom the girls had shared lessons until she had been sent away a year ago to a smart Seminary for Young Ladies.

She had come home a week ago and Penelope had seen her, while Alisa had been too busy packing for her father to be able to visit The Hall.

"I am longing to see Eloise," Alisa said now. "Is she excited at having left School?"

"She is going to be presented at a 'Drawing-Room' at the end of this month," Penelope replied.

For a moment the light had gone from her eyes and there was a bitter note in her voice.

Only Alisa knew how much Penelope resented that Eloise could have the chance to go to Court, to attend Balls, Receptions, and Assemblies in London, while she had to stay at home.

"It is unfair!" she had said over and over again. "Why should Papa not do something for us?"

"The answer is that he cannot afford to," Alisa had replied. "As you well know, Penelope, it is a struggle for us to live here as it is."

"Then why cannot Papa write a book which would make money, instead of producing those dreary old tomes that nobody wants to read?"

Alisa had smiled.

"I do not think it has ever struck Papa that he should be a wage-earner. I am sure he would think it beneath his dignity."

"We cannot eat the family tree, nor does the fact that Papa is the seventh Baronet buy me a new gown!" Penelope snapped crossly.

Things might not have been so boring if Eloise, who was extremely fond of both of them, had not spent every moment, when she was at home, telling them of the people she had met and the entertainments planned for her in the coming Season.

At Christmas the Squire and his wife had settled down to consider how they could launch their only daughter into the *Beau Monde*.

The Squire was well known in Hertfordshire and was a large landowner, but London was different, and the famous hostesses would not be likely to include Eloise among their guests unless her parents contrived to be socially recognised.

They had been partly successful, for Eloise, according to Penelope, had already received invitations to various Balls that were to take place next month, and the reason she had delayed coming home after her time at the Seminary was finished was that her mother was buying her new gowns.

"I have never seen anything so beautiful!" Penelope had explained in awestruck tones when she had described them to her sister. "The latest fashions are quite, quite different from anything we have been wearing."

Her voice was lyrical as she went on:

"Skirts are fuller round the hem and very elaborately trimmed with lace, flowers, and embroidery, and although the waist is still high, the sleeves are full, while the bonnets are so beautiful that they are indescribable."

Alisa could not help thinking that it was a mistake for Eloise to make Penelope so jealous of her possessions, but she knew it would be wrong to say so.

She thought it would be a good thing when the Squire, his wife, and their daughter left the country for London.

Now thinking that she would have to listen to another rapturous description of Eloise's clothes, Alisa sat down on the sofa and waited for Penelope to tell her what was on her mind.

"Eloise was talking about two girls called the Gunning Sisters," Penelope said. "When they were eighteen they arrived in London from Ireland, and although they were both exceedingly beautiful they had no money."

Alisa smiled.

"I know the story," she said. "I read it ages ago and I told you about it."

"I suppose I was not listening," Penelope replied. "The younger sister married two Dukes, Hamilton and Argyll, and the elder married the Earl of Coventry."

"And she died when she was very young," Alisa added, "from using a face-cream to improve her skin that contained white lead."

"There is no need for you to do that."

Alisa's eyes widened.

"Why should I want to?" she enquired.

"Because we are going to be the Gunning Sisters!" Penelope answered. "I have thought it all out, and I know, however modest you may try to be, that we are just as beautiful as they were."

Alisa laughed.

"I am quite prepared to agree with you, dearest, but it is very improbable that two Dukes will drop down the chimney or an Earl come through the window!"

"Have you forgotten," Penelope asked, "that we are going to London?"

"To be honest, I am depressed at the thought," Alisa answered. "The only men Aunt Harriet entertains, as you are well aware, are Parsons and Missionaries."

"Nevertheless, Aunt Harriet lives in London."

"But how does that help us?"

Penelope was silent for a moment, then she said:

"I am absolutely certain that if you and I had a chance to appear at any of the parties to which Eloise has been invited, we should have the same sensational success as the Gunning Sisters."

Alisa laughed again.

"I think that is unlikely. And we would look like

beggars at a Ball, dressed as we are now, with everybody else wearing the new gowns which you have described so eloquently."

"The Gunning Sisters had one gown," Penelope said, "so when one went out, the other one had to stay in bed. We are going to have two gowns, one for you and one for me!"

She saw that her sister looked surprised and went on:

"Mrs. Kingston said something to me the other day which made me realise that, unlike the Gunning Sisters, being together is important."

Alisa looked puzzled and Penelope continued:

"She was talking about the vases on the mantelpiece —you know, the Sèvres china ones in the Drawing-Room. As I have known them for years, I suddenly realised there was only one there instead of two.

" 'What has happened to the other Sèvres vase, Ma'am?' I enquired.

"Mrs. Kingston sighed and answered:

" 'One of the housemaids smashed it last week. I was very angry with the tiresome woman, because you know as well as I do that Sèvres china is valuable, but a pair are worth far more than just one by itself.' "

"I have an idea what you are trying to say," Alisa said. "But I am still wondering how, even if we were invited to a Ball, we could afford one gown, let alone two."

She got up from the sofa on which she had been sitting and said:

"Oh, dearest, I know you mind so much not being able to come out and do the things that Eloise can. But as it says in the Bible, it is no good 'kicking against the pricks'! We just have to accept things as they are and make the best of them."

As she spoke, she put her arm round her younger sister and kissed her cheek.

To her surprise, instead of responding as Penelope

usually did to any expression of affection, she merely moved away, saying in a hard, determined little voice:

"I have every intention of 'kicking against the pricks,' as you put it, and what is more, I will not lie down and let fate, or rather poverty, trample all over me!"

She looked so lovely, even when she was irritated, that Alisa could understand her frustrations.

She knew that Penelope was rather like her father, determined to the point of obstinacy when he wished to do something, while she was like her mother, compliant, gentle, and ready to accept the inevitable.

"We have to have money for new gowns," Penelope said, speaking as much to herself as to Alisa.

Then suddenly she gave a scream that seemed to echo round the room.

"I have thought of what we can do!"

"To obtain money?" Alisa asked.

"Yes," Penelope replied. "I remember now something Mrs. Kingston said at tea yesterday when she was gossipping about people who have already asked Eloise to their parties. One woman was a Lady Harrison, whom Mrs. Kingston had known when she was at School.

" 'She is very smart these days,' Mrs. Kingston said, 'because her husband is permanently in attendance on the new King.'

"She drivelled on for some time," Penelope went on, "you know how she does. Then she said something that I have just remembered."

"What is it?" Alisa asked.

"She said: 'Of course, Lady Harrison tries to keep young by using salves and lotions, dozens of them, which she tells me she buys in Bond Street from Mrs. Lulworth, and do you know that even the smallest pot of cream to restore the roses in her cheeks costs as much as a pound?' "

Penelope stopped speaking and looked at Alisa.

Then, as if she knew she was expected to say something, Alisa remarked:

"It seems a terrible lot of money. I wonder if it does any good."

"If it does not, then that is exactly what we want."

"What are you saying?" Alisa enquired. "I do not understand."

"Oh, dearest, you are being very thick-headed!" Penelope exclaimed. "Suppose you and I sell the creams that Mama used and which we now have to make for ourselves and which do improve the skin? Remember we gave some to that ugly Cosnet child two months ago, who had sores and blemishes on her cheeks, and they healed in four days?"

"Are you saying . . . are you suggesting . . . ?" Alisa started.

"I am telling you," Penelope interrupted, "that that is how we are going to make enough money to buy four gowns—one each for the morning and one each for the evening!"

"You are crazy!" Alisa exclaimed. "Nobody would pay us a pound for our creams, good though they are. All Mrs. Cosnet gave us for our trouble was a bunch of daffodils from her garden!"

"I was not thinking of selling them to Mrs. Cosnet or people like her, stupid!" Penelope said impatiently. "We are going to make the creams and sell them to women like Lady Harrison, who would pay anything to try to look as beautiful as they did when they were young."

"It is an impossible idea! Besides, what would Papa say?"

"Papa will not know for at least two months, by which time the Season will be over. And you know as well as I do that as it is Coronation Year, it is going to be the most exciting, glamorous summer that has ever happened!"

Alisa knew that was true.

The Regent, who had waited so long to become

King and was now at fifty-eight an old man, was to be crowned in July.

If the newspapers were to be believed, already London was filling up not only with the English nobility coming in from the country for the festivities, but with foreigners from all over Europe.

"If we make quite a number of Mama's creams," Penelope was saying, "and think up wonderful names for them so that they will sound attractive, it will make people eager to buy them."

"Are you really suggesting," Alisa asked, "that we should take them to London to Mrs. Lulworth and sell them as if we were pedlars?"

"I am prepared to sell anything so that we can buy gowns, and what does it matter what Mrs. Lulworth thinks? She has never seen us before, and unless we have money she is never likely to see us again!"

This was unanswerable, and as Penelope went on pleading and persuading, Alisa found herself weakening.

There was no doubt that her mother's herbal products, which she had made from the flowers, herbs, and plants in their garden, had been a success locally.

People with sores and abrasions of every sort had begged her help, and they also found that the tisanes she made could soothe and reduce a fever and remove a cough far more effectively than anything the Doctors could prescribe.

Her two daughters had always helped her in the Still-Room, but not until this moment had Alisa thought that anything they might make could be saleable.

"If we sell twenty pots at ten shillings each," Penelope said in a practical way, "which Mrs. Lulworth could then sell for a pound, that would be enough for one gown."

"We are not even certain that this Mrs. Lulworth will take them."

"At least we can try, and I am not going to London

dressed as I am now. I refuse! I shall stay here all by myself until Papa returns."

"What does it matter what we look like in Islington?" Alisa asked almost beneath her breath.

This was undoubtedly true, and it made Penelope more determined than ever that they would have to get some money by hook or by crook so that, like the Gunning Sisters, they could dazzle Society.

"In any case," Alisa went on, "even if we do make a little money, that will not get us invitations to the Balls or even to the Receptions of anybody of importance."

"I have thought of that too," Penelope said.

Alisa waited apprehensively.

The ideas that Penelope had already expressed were frightening her.

"Do you remember how Mama used to talk about a friend of hers she used to stay with when she was young, a woman by the name of Elizabeth Denison?" Penelope asked.

She did not wait for Alisa to answer, but went on:

"I realised only the other day that she is now the Marchioness of Conyngham, whose name often appears in the newspapers."

"The Marchioness did not pay much attention to Mama after she married," Alisa commented.

"How could she, when Mama was buried down here with Papa? And Elizabeth Denison, who was older than Mama, was very rich."

Alisa was silent, knowing that her mother had been far too proud ever to ask favours of anybody.

If her friend had drifted away into a higher social circle, she would never have tried to cling to her for old times' sake.

"What we are going to do," Penelope went on, "and I thought this out last night, is to write to the Marchioness of Conyngham when we reach London, telling her that Mama is dead and that we have a little memento of her when she was a girl which we are sure she would like to have."

"How could we do such a thing?" Alisa asked indignantly.

"It is something I have every intention of doing," Penelope declared. "Oh, Alisa, do stop being stuffy and realise that the one thing Mama would have hated would be for us to be incarcerated here as if we were shut up in a tomb, seeing nobody, going nowhere, and just wasting our beauty!"

Penelope spoke so passionately that Alisa was silent.

She knew it was true that her mother, who had been completely happy living in the country because she loved her husband, would have wanted them to enjoy the life she had known when she was a girl.

Her parents had been important in Hampshire, where her father had a large Estate, and they had always gone to London for the Season.

When their only daughter grew up, she had been presented at Court to the King and Queen and had a Season whose gaieties had been described over and over again to her daughters when they were old enough to understand.

However, three months after their mother had made her debut, she became engaged to Sir Hadrian, and they had been married in the autumn, to live, as Alisa had often said with a smile, "happily ever after."

Unfortunately, during the long-drawn-out war, Sir Hadrian's fortune had dwindled year by year, and when his wife's father died he left everything he possessed to his son.

Then, soon after he came into his inheritance, their uncle had been killed fighting with Wellington's Armies and the Estate went not to his sister but to a distant cousin of the same name.

Alisa knew that Penelope was speaking the truth when she said it would have upset her mother if she had known how dull it was for them these days, and how seldom her father entertained, with the consequence that they were rarely invited to other houses in the neighbourhood.

Another reason for this was obvious.

"We are too pretty and attractive, that is what is wrong with us," Penelope had said last week. "I heard from Mrs. Kingston that the Hartmans are giving a small dance next month but there will be no invitation for us."

"I think it is rather unkind of them not to invite us." Alisa agreed.

"Unkind? They are just taking precautions against our taking away any young man who might be interested in that plain, tongue-tied Alice, or that spotty-faced Charlotte!"

"You should not say such unkind things!"

"It is true! You know it is true!" Penelope insisted. "What man, if he could dance with you or me, would want to trundle round a dance-floor with them? They are both as heavy as a sack of coals!"

Alisa laughed as if she could not help it.

Although she hesitated to agree with Penelope, she had seen the expression on Mrs. Hartman's face the last time they had been there, when Colonel Hartman had told them how pretty they were and made them sit one on either side of him at luncheon.

Because she felt agitated, Alisa went to the window. The lawn was unkept, but there was a carpet of golden daffodils under the trees and the almond-blossoms were pink and white against the sky.

"It is so lovely here!" she said. "We ought to be content."

"Well, I am not!" Penelope replied positively. "So please, please, Alisa, help me! I have nobody else to turn to but you."

It was a cry that went straight to Alisa's soft heart and it was impossible for her to refuse.

Ten minutes later, she agreed to what she thought was the wildest, most ridiculous scheme Penelope had ever suggested.

"We will try to sell Mama's face-creams," she agreed, "but I will take them to London alone."

"You will never sell them as well as I could," Penelope said.

"Yes, I will, if they are saleable," Alisa answered, "and you have convinced me that they are. What I think would be a mistake, dearest, would be for you to be seen selling in the shops in Bond Street where, if we are successful, we shall have to buy our clothes."

She saw that she had made a point, and as Penelope was silent she went on:

"As you well know, I am not half as striking as you are, and I think the wise thing to do would be to take just two or three pots to Mrs. Lulworth and ask if she thinks they are saleable. If she says 'yes,' then we can go ahead and make her many more."

She hesitated a moment, then she said:

"Perhaps we could then swear her to secrecy, and instead of giving us money she might let us have the gowns now and pay for them month by month as the demand for the creams increases."

Penelope clapped her hands together, then flung her arms round Alisa.

"Dearest, you are so clever!" she said. "I knew you would be sensible about my idea, once I had convinced you that it was necessary."

"Of course it is necessary," Alisa agreed. "It is just that I am not certain that this method will obtain the gowns we need."

"Right or wrong, there is no alternative," Penelope said. "Even if we wanted to sell a picture or a mirror off the walls, we would not know how to go about it."

"We could not do that!" Alisa exclaimed in horror. "That would be stealing from Papa!"

Penelope smiled.

"I was sure that was what you would feel. But if you ask me, I do not believe that Papa, if he had his nose in one of his books, would notice if we took down half the house."

This was indisputable, but Alisa was not prepared to go further in that direction.

"We will sell only what is ours," she said firmly, "and the first thing is to prove that face-creams are saleable."

Two days later, Penelope saw Alisa off on the Stage-Coach which stopped at the crossroads in the centre of the village.

They had been hurrying about since dawn, for it was important that Alisa should have time to sell the creams and return on the Coach which passed through the village at six o'clock in the evening.

"If you miss it," Penelope said warningly, "you will have to stay the night with Aunt Harriet, and she will think it very strange that you should go to London by yourself."

"I shall have masses of time," Alisa answered. "In fact I shall find it rather frightening to be alone in London unless I go to the waiting-room at the Two-Headed Swan and just sit there until the Stage-Coach arrives."

"That would be a sensible thing to do," Penelope approved, "but I think really I should come with you."

"No, no," Alisa answered.

She knew only too well that whatever Penelope wore she would attract attention. Although she knew it was wrong for either of them to go to London alone, it was impossible to ask Mrs. Brigstock to accompany her, because she was too old.

Emily, the girl who came in to scrub the floors, was too uncouth, and what was more she was certain to talk of what happened to everybody in the village.

"I must go alone," she told herself, "and as I shall be dressed quietly, nobody will notice me."

Because she was not only nervous but more than a little frightened, she picked out a very plain dark-blue gown and a plain straight cape that had belonged to her mother to wear over it.

Although her bonnet was cheap, it had been trimmed skilfully with flowers. These Alisa removed, leaving only the ribbons round the crown and those under her chin.

"You look like a Puritan," Penelope said as they walked up to the crossroads.

"Perhaps I should hold one of Aunt Harriet's tracts in my hand," Alisa said with a note of laughter in her voice. "Then I would be quite certain that nobody will pay any attention to me!"

"If I have to sit night after night in that gloomy house in Islington," Penelope argued, "listening to Aunt Harriet talking about 'the poor people in Africa,' I shall throw myself into the Serpentine!"

"Then I hope some dashing young gentleman would dive in and save you!" Alisa laughed.

"I expect I would simply be fished out by some old man with a boat-hook!" Penelope retorted. "So save me by selling those creams."

They had both taken the greatest trouble in mixing the creams exactly as their mother had done. One contained fresh cucumbers from the garden, herbs, and a number of other ingredients of which fortunately they had quite a large supply.

Before Sir Hadrian had left, he had given Alisa ten pounds.

"If you take the Coach to London," he had said, "it will leave you enough to tip your aunt's servants and to pay for anything that is absolutely necessary. I have given the Brigstocks their wages for two months, and I cannot afford any more."

"No, I understand, Papa," Alisa had said.

She knew that although he was being driven to Scotland with his friend, he would still have quite a number of expenses when he was there.

Leaving so early in the morning, the Stage-Coach

contained inside only two farmers' wives journeying as far as the next market-town.

The men, who were mostly farmers, preferred to sit on the box, but Alisa noticed that young or old they all turned to stare at Penelope as she kissed her good-bye.

It is a good thing she is not coming with me, she thought.

As soon as the Stage-Coach started off, she waved to her sister, then sat comfortably in a corner-seat and soon got into conversation with the farmers' wives.

All they wanted to talk about was the coming Coronation and the village festivities which would take place to celebrate the occasion.

"Well, all Oi can say is 'e's had a good time, one way or another," one woman said, "an' at least 'e's given us all somethin' to talk about."

"Not the sort of talk Oi cares for," another answered. "Debts an' women are a bad example, that's wot Oi says to me lads. Ye pays yer way as ye goes, Oi tells 'em, or Oi'll have somethin' to say about it."

That is what we will have to do, Alisa thought to herself, and she felt despondently that the sale of a few pots of cream could not possibly pay for all the things that Penelope wanted.

It was still early in the morning when she reached London, and because she had plenty of time she started to walk from Islington to Bond Street.

It was no hardship, because Alisa was used to walking long distances, since although she preferred to ride they had been too hard up these last years to afford more than two horses. This meant that she and Penelope had been forced to take it in turns to go out hunting with their father or to ride wherever they wished to go.

"It has been rather like sharing a gown!" she told herself now.

She found herself thinking of the huge success which the Gunning Sisters had achieved entirely because they were beautiful.

She was not sure that she herself was beautiful, although she was not so foolish as not to acknowledge that she was pretty. But she thought nobody could be lovelier than Penelope.

She now decided that she had been remiss in not speaking to her father, before he left for Scotland, about Penelope having a chance to meet the type of young man she should eventually marry.

"After all, it was my duty to do that," Alisa chided herself. "I am the elder."

She was actually eighteen months older than Penelope, who had just celebrated her seventeenth birthday.

Alisa knew that things would not have come to such a pass if her father had not gone away or Eloise Kingston had not made Penelope envious by talking so much about her own prospects.

What chance have we. Alisa asked herself, *of meeting, as Mama did, somebody like Papa?*

She knew that her father must have looked very handsome in his uniform.

He had been in the Grenadier Guards, and in his red coat, white breeches, and bear-skin, she could understand that her mother had found him irresistible.

And Papa loved her, Alisa thought.

It was the sort of marriage she herself would like to make, for while Penelope wanted to have an important social position and wear a tiara and glittering jewels at Carlton House and the Royal Pavilion at Brighton, she would be quite content to be anywhere as long as she was with the man whom she loved and who loved her.

I suppose I am not ambitious, she thought with a sigh.

Then she told herself, although it was something she would not say to anybody, not even to Penelope, that love, if one found it, would be so wonderful, so glorious, that there was nothing else with which to compare it.

Walking through the streets, she found herself fascinated by the pedlars who were already crying their wares.

There were men carrying pails of milk fresh from the cow, women with baskets of primroses and daffodils, and others with country produce like butter and new-laid eggs.

Having been in London before, she knew the way to Bond Street, and when she finally reached that most fascinating shopping street in the city, she could not help staring in the shop-windows and finding them extremely inviting after having been in the country for so long.

She saw at once, as Penelope had said, that the clothes they were wearing were out-of-fashion. The new bonnets had crowns that were raised in front and were covered with ostrich-feathers or a profusion of silk flowers.

Alisa stood for some time outside one window, trying to see if it was possible to transform their outdated head-gear into something that at least reflected, if indecisively, the vogue.

She decided it was just possible that she might be able to do something with what they already possessed, when a man stopped beside her and she knew in a sudden panic that he was about to speak to her.

Quickly she walked away, just as his lips began to move, and she told herself that it was entirely her own fault for loitering.

With her heart beating rather quickly, she hurried down the street to where she thought Mrs. Lulworth's shop would be situated.

It was a large Emporium that sold quite a number of things besides gowns, and already there were a few customers fingering some very attractive and doubtless extremely expensive silks at a counter near the door.

Not daring to stop and stare into the window, she had, however, noted at a quick glance that elegantly displayed on a silk cushion were several glass bottles and what looked like a pot of face-cream.

"Can I assist you, Madam?"

It was a supercilious shop-assistant who spoke, and for a moment Alisa thought it was impossible to tell him the reason why she was there. Then she forced herself to say:

"Could I . . . please see . . . Mrs. Lulworth?"

She thought that the shop-assistant looked her up and down and took in her shabby appearance before he replied:

"Could I enquire as to your requirements?"

Alisa lifted her chin a little.

"It is a private matter, and I would ask you to take me to her immediately!" she replied, speaking in what she hoped was a commanding and dignified manner.

As it happened, her voice was so musical, and when he looked under her bonnet her face was so pretty, that the shop-assistant, who was more perceptive than he looked, decided to do what was asked without further argument.

"If you will come this way, Madam," he said, and swept ahead to where farther in the shop were a number of gowns and bonnets on display.

Standing in front of a cowed-looking shop-girl was a large woman dressed in black.

She was obviously complaining about something very volubly, until Alisa appeared, and when the assistant said: "Someone to see you, Madam," she turned, and there was a smile on her lips that was obviously put on for effect.

The assistant she had been berating hurried away as if relieved at being released, and the shop-assistant also disappeared, as if he was sure he had made a mistake.

"What can I do for you—*Madame?*"

There was a little pause before the last word, which made it quite clear that Mrs. Lulworth thought she was not entitled to it.

For a moment Alisa felt as if her courage failed her. It was impossible for her to speak, and it would have been far easier to leave without attempting to sell anything.

Then she thought of Penelope's disappointment, and she steeled herself.

She also remembered what Penelope had told her to say because she was certain it would make an impression.

"I understand . . . Mrs. Lulworth . . ." Alisa began, with only a slight tremor in her voice, "that Lady Harrison purchases from you some excellent face-creams."

"That is true, and Her Ladyship has been very satisfied."

"I have here some . . . face-creams that are far . . . superior to anything Lady Harrison has . . . tried so far. I have brought them hoping you might be . . . interested in . . . selling them."

There was a little pause before Mrs. Lulworth asked:

"You are saying that you make face-creams?"

"Yes."

"And they are good?"

"Very, very good! Everybody near where we live in the country begs us to help them when they have any sort of trouble with their skin. And after they have used these creams, the trouble vanishes almost at once!"

Mrs. Lulworth looked sceptical, but while she had been talking Alisa had opened the silk bag she carried, which contained three pots of cream.

"Will you please look at the creams, Mrs. Lulworth?" she begged. "The one with the green ribbon round it is called *The Freshness of Spring.*"

Mrs. Lulworth made a sound that was untranslatable but might have indicated either approval or disgust.

Alisa drew out the other pots. One, called *Golden*

Wonder, contained cowslips, and the other, which had been made from the first carrots that had appeared in the garden, was *Red Sunrise.*

Mrs. Lulworth tested each one by rubbing it into the skin of her left hand. It was an old hand with the veins showing prominently, the skin darkened by what the country-folk called "sun-spots" but which Alisa knew always appeared with old age.

Then sharply, so that Alisa almost jumped, Mrs. Lulworth asked:

"Do you use these creams yourself?"

"Yes, always," Alisa answered.

"You swear that is true?" Mrs. Lulworth persisted, staring at Alisa's smooth and flawless cheeks, which had just a touch of color in them because she was agitated.

"I swear it!" Alisa answered. "And my sister also uses them."

She knew as she spoke that it was quite unnecessary to involve Penelope, but Mrs. Lulworth appeared to be thinking.

Then she asked:

"How much do you expect me to pay you for this cream?"

Alisa hesitated.

"I . . . understand that Lady Harrison pays over . . . a pound for a pot of your cream . . . and I thought . . . if I sell mine to you at ten shillings a pot . . . that would be fair."

Mrs. Lulworth gave a scornful laugh.

"And how, young woman," she asked, "do you think I should pay the rent and the services of my staff and stock my shelves and cupboards without getting into debt, if I took so small a profit?"

Alisa felt her spirits sink.

She might have guessed, she thought, that Penelope had been too optimistic in anticipating that they would be paid so much.

Then, perhaps because she looked so crestfallen

and at the same time so young, while her skin in the morning light coming through the window had a translucence about it, like a pearl that had just been raised from its oyster-bed, Mrs. Lulworth said:

"I tell you what I'll do—I will send you to a very good customer of mine who has, as it happens, just sent a message asking for something new for her skin. When you arrived, I was wondering what I should reply."

Alisa's eyes were bright again with hope as Mrs. Lulworth went on:

"I am going to tell you now to go to this important customer and show her these creams. If she takes them, and if she likes them, then I'll buy from you quite a number of pots, because half of London will follow her example. Is that clear?"

"Oh, thank you . . . thank you!" Alisa cried. "I am sure she will like them."

Mrs. Lulworth shrugged her shoulders.

"She may, or she may not. She's unpredictable, and if she's in one of her tantrums she'll be more likely to throw the pots at you than to buy them!"

Alisa looked apprehensive, and involuntarily her fingers tightened on the bag she was still holding in her hand.

"Are you willing to test your luck?" Mrs. Lulworth asked. "If you can't sell your wares where they are most needed, then they are of no use to me."

Her shrewd eyes were still looking at Alisa's flawless skin, as if she could not believe it was real and not some trick of the light.

Then she said:

"Well, be off with you. I'll be interested to hear *Madame* Vestris's opinion of what you have to sell, so come back here after you have seen her."

"*Madame* . . . Vestris?" Alisa questioned, thinking she could not have heard the name aright.

"*Madame* Vestris at the King's Theatre. She tells me they're having a rehearsal there this morning, and so whether she'll be in a good temper or a bad one depends on how it is going. You'll just have to take your chance."

"*Madame* Vestris—the King's Theatre!" Alisa repeated, as if she was afraid she might forget.

"What are you waiting for?" Mrs. Lulworth asked. "Go there and don't bother to come back unless the 'Prima Donna,' as she fancies herself, has made a purchase."

"Thank you," Alisa said.

She put the pots back into her silk bag, then walked through the shop and out into Bond Street.

CHAPTER TWO

*I*t was not a very long way from Bond Street to the King's Theatre in the Haymarket, but Alisa hurried along, frightened that if she was late, *Madame* Vestris would have left and she would not be able to see her.

As she went, she was trying to remember all she knew about the actress, which was actually a good deal.

Penelope was extremely interested in anything that concerned the Theatre, simply because they very seldom were able to go to one.

When their mother was alive she had insisted that their father take them to the Opera, which she thought was good for their education, and they had several times been to a Shakespearean Play.

It was Penelope who talked about *Madame* Vestris, who had, according to the newspapers, captivated the town when she first appeared in London five weeks after the Battle of Waterloo.

Alisa remembered Penelope telling her that Lucy Vestris, who was the daughter of an artist, was then married to an Italian who was also an actor.

The newspapers always described her as being vivacious, extremely pretty, and having, although it sounded rather improper, the most exquisite legs on the stage.

For some years her success appeared to have been due to her dancing, then last year the newspapers had made the sensational announcement that *Madame* Vestris was to appear as a man in a new Operetta called *Giovanni in London.*

This was something which for an actress was sensational, and it was said that *Madame* Vestris accepted the part with much reluctance.

Thinking back over what she had read herself and what Penelope had read aloud, Alisa remembered that *Madame* had had an overwhelmingly favourable reception and the Theatre had been packed night after night to see her famous legs.

"I think it is very brave of her," Penelope had said.

"But . . . surely it is somewhat . . . immodest?" Alisa had replied hesitatingly.

They had argued about it until Alisa had for once got the better of her sister by producing a notice which criticised *Madame* Vestris by saying:

> *It is the part which no female should assume until she has discarded every delicate scruple by which her mind or her person can be distinguished.*

"Well, I refuse to agree to that until I have seen her for myself," Penelope had answered, "and I think it would be rather fun to dress as a man."

"Really, Penelope, what will you think of next?" Alisa had cried.

At the same time, she could not help feeling it would be very exciting to see *Giovanni in London,* but when Penelope suggested it to her father, he said it was certainly not the type of entertainment for young girls.

"What a pity Penelope is not with me now," Alisa thought as she walked towards the King's Theatre.

Then she reflected that it would have been a great mistake, because undoubtedly Penelope would have got a new idea: that they should both go on the stage to make money.

It made her laugh to think of anything so ridiculous.

When she reached the King's Theatre she was aware that an actress would go in through the stage-door, and she was relieved when she saw that it was open and knew that therefore the rehearsal could not be over.

However, there was always the chance that *Madame* Vestris might have left early.

Apprehensively she hurried to where an elderly man with white hair sat just inside the door in what looked like a glass box.

"I would like, please, to see *Madame* Vestris."

"That's not very likely, Miss, unless ye've got an appointment!"

"I have brought something *Madame* requires from Mrs. Lulworth," Alisa answered.

"The shop in Bond Street?"

"That is right."

"Then I expect her'll see ye."

He came out of his box and started to hurry along a dark passage with a stone floor which made Alisa aware that the back of the stage was certainly not as attractive as the Auditorium.

She followed the old man for quite some way until she saw several doors with names painted on them, from behind which came the sounds of voices and laughter.

It made her more nervous than she was already. The old man stopped and said:

"Wait here!"

Holding tightly to the bag that contained the pots of cream, Alisa sent up a little prayer that she might be successful in selling them.

She was quite certain that if *Madame* Vestris tried any of the creams, she would be delighted with them.

Nobody had ever failed to find them healing, and people returned year after year for more of her mother's herbs in whatever form they appeared.

The old man had knocked on the door ahead, which she saw was marked in large white letters: *MADAME VESTRIS*.

As he did so, a door on the other side of the corridor opened and three women dressed in gowns which they obviously wore on the stage came out laughing and talking to one another.

Close up, their gowns looked tawdry and to Alisa's eyes were cut so low as to be indecent.

She moved to one side to let them pass, and there was a strong fragrance of a musty perfume that was overpowering and lingered on the air even after the women were out of sight.

Then she could hear the voice of the old man speaking to somebody, and again she was afraid that *Madame* Vestris might be, as Mrs. Lulworth had warned her, in one of her tantrums.

There had been some rather unkind references in the newspapers to her temperament, and Penelope had said, although how she knew was a mystery, that all great actresses and Prima Donnas made scenes and flounced about the stage, upsetting the other actors just to show their superiority.

After what seemed a long time, although it was only a few minutes, Alisa saw the old man returning.

" 'Er'll see ye," he said laconically, jerking his

thumb at the door he had left open behind him, before he limped away down the corridor.

Alisa moved to the open door, wishing that she had not come, but at the same time determined that for Penelope's sake she would do everything in her power to make *Madame* Vestris buy their creams.

The dressing-room was exactly as she had expected it to be, except that it was larger and there were more flowers. But for the moment it was impossible to look at anything except a small figure standing in the centre of it—a woman wearing breeches!

Everything Alisa had been going to say went out of her head and she could only stare at *Madame* Vestris, dressed for her part in *Giovanni in London,* wearing revealing, tight-fitting breeches on her famous legs.

She also wore a red coat, embroidered and glittering, which reached down on her hips, although somehow it did not make her appearance any more respectable.

It was with an effort that Alisa managed to stare at *Madame*'s face rather than the lower part of her body.

She was certainly very pretty, with large sparkling dark eyes and curly black hair. She looked Italian, but when she spoke it was with a French accent, and Alisa remembered that she had only returned to England from Paris the previous year.

"You'ave brought me somethEEng from Mrs. Lulworth?" she asked.

Somewhat belatedly Alisa remembered that as a pedlar she should have curtseyed.

Hastily she replied:

"Yes, *Madame*. Mrs. Lulworth informed me that you require some new face-creams, and I have some very exceptional ones which have never been sold in London before."

"Can that be true?" *Madame* Vestris enquired.

Quickly Alisa opened her bag, and as she did so she looked round for something on which to stand it while she took out the contents.

Every available table in the dressing-room was piled with flowers, which were also ranged against the walls.

But as she looked behind her Alisa was aware that *Madame* was not alone, for there was a Gentleman she had not at first noticed, seated in a comfortable chair with his legs stretched out in front of him.

She only had a quick glance at him, and then, intent on what she had come for, she drew out the first pot.

"This is called *The Freshness of Spring,*" she said. "All the ingredients come from our garden, and it really does make the skin soft and removes all blemishes."

"I verry much doubt zat!" *Madame* Vestris replied cynically. "And who could 'elp haveeng a dry skeen in thees terrible climate?"

Feeling a little braver, Alisa said:

"May I suggest, *Madame,* that you use *The Freshness of Spring* at night, and once or twice a week use *Red Sunrise,* which contains carrots which clear the skin of any impurities."

Madame Vestris opened the pots and sniffed them.

Then, as if she looked at Alisa for the first time, she said:

"You speak as eef you know wat you talk about, but do you use these creams or are you just 'ired to sell them?"

Because what she said sounded rude, Alisa stiffened. Then she said:

"I promise you, *Madame,* I not only use them myself but I also make them. It was my mother who taught me how to mix the ingredients."

"Your skeen is certainly verry clear," *Madame* Vestris said grudgingly.

Now Alisa thought she was looking at her in a hostile manner, and she said quickly:

"In a month's time I shall be able to make a wonderful cream from fresh strawberries. It is extremely efficacious for very bad eruptions or spots."

"I do not 'ave the spots!" *Madame* Vestris said

sharply, and for the moment Alisa thought she had offended her.

Holding the pots of *The Freshness of Spring* and *Red Sunrise* in her hands, *Madame* took them to the dressing-table on which Alisa could see a huge array of bottles and pots.

There was also a hare's foot, rouge, brushes and pencils for the eye-brows, as well as innumerable sticks of grease-paint.

She could not help looking at everything with interest.

Then she forced herself to watch *Madame* Vestris, who, sitting down, had begun to smooth some *Red Sunrise* on one cheek and *The Freshness of Spring* on the other.

"I wonder eef these are any different from the ones I 'ave tried before?" she remarked.

"I promise you they are," Alisa insisted, "and after using them for one night you will notice an improvement."

"Eet ees not the creams that impress me so much as your skeen," *Madame* Vestris said. "I cannot 'elp thinking that either you are the best recommendation a product ever 'ad, or else you are such a good actress that you should be on the boards!"

"Perhaps she is both!" a drawling voice said from behind them.

For the moment Alisa had forgotten that there was someone else there, and, as if *Madame* Vestris had forgotten too, she turned a laughing face towards the Gentleman.

"Advise me, *Milor'*," she said. "Shall I try something new?"

"It is something you have never been backward in doing in the past," the Gentleman replied, and *Madame* Vestris laughed again.

"C'est vrai, and when I'm daring, I 'ave never regretted it."

"Why should you, when you have taken London by storm?" the Gentleman asked.

Alisa was aware that they were speaking of *Madame*'s daring act of appearing as a man in the very debatable breeches.

She glanced down at them and thought it was in fact very brave of any woman to appear on stage in such outrageous garb.

Then as *Madame* rubbed the cream into her cheeks and powdered them she asked:

"How much is that charlatan Mrs. Lulworth expecting me to pay for thees? I'm quite certain 'twill be somethееng *extraordinaire!*"

Alisa drew in her breath, but before she could speak, *Madame* Vestris went on:

"I'm quite aware that eef I use them, by tomorrow all London will follow my example, so really I should be paid for introducing a new fashion and not 'ave to put my 'and into my own pocket!"

Alisa felt with a sudden stab of horror that if *Madame* refused to pay, Mrs. Lulworth would certainly not buy them from her.

Then the drawling voice said:

"I suggest you leave that to me. As you are well aware, Lucy, I am quite prepared to be your Banker."

Madame Vestris laughed.

"It would certainly be an original present, and very much cheaper than a diamond bracelet."

"Is that what you want?"

Madame Vestris shrugged her shoulders in a typically French gesture.

"What woman ever has enough diamonds?" she asked softly.

"I will not forget," the Gentleman said. "Now, regrettably, I must leave you, but tonight I will collect you after the Show, and I promise you will not be disappointed with the party that has been arranged in your honour."

"In which case I must certainly use your latest present, *Milor'*."

The Gentleman walked to the dressing-table and Alisa was aware that he was tall and broad-shouldered.

He was also extremely elegantly dressed, and she appreciated the high polish on his Hessian boots and the intricate way in which his crisp white cravat was tied.

She knew only too well how difficult it was to achieve such perfection, for she had helped her father with his cravats. He was always too impatient and kept saying: "That will do! That will do!" long before she was satisfied.

She moved her eyes from the Gentleman's cravat to his face, and she thought he was extremely handsome if somewhat overpowering.

Something in his firm features, strongly marked eyebrows, and square chin made Alisa aware that he had a dominating character and perhaps even an aggressive one.

At the same time, she looked at him curiously, thinking that perhaps he was the type of gentleman whom Penelope might meet in London.

Then she told herself that he was too old for Penelope and anyway she had no wish for her sister to be pursued by the type of men who were enamoured of actresses and Opera-dancers.

Although they lived very quietly in the country, reports of the excesses introduced by the Prince Regent had gradually percolated through to the village, and they talked with bated breath of the Prince of Wales's association with Mrs. Fitzherbert and then with Lady Jersey, who was followed in turn by Lady Hertford.

They were only names to Alisa, but when she listened to the conversation of her father and some of his friends, they kept cropping up, and Eloise and her mother, Mrs. Kingston, were always full of the latest gossip whenever they returned from a visit to London.

The Bucks and Beaux, Alisa learnt, pursued pretty actresses and women whom no lady would condescend to know.

Now as the Gentleman raised *Madame* Vestris's hand to his lips, Alisa told herself that she would have to take great care that Penelope did not become involved in any way with Rakes or the sort of men who would flirt with her without intending to offer marriage.

"Until tonight," the Gentleman said.

Then, looking at Alisa, he said:

"Come with me, I will settle your account."

Alisa was just about to ask why she should go with him when there was a sudden loud knock on the door and a voice called:

"On stage, *Madame!*"

Madame Vestris gave a little cry, and, snatching up a plumed hat that was lying on a chair near some flowers, said:

"*Au revoir, Milor'*. I look forward to—*tonight.*"

She accentuated the last word and gave him what Alisa felt was a very intimate glance from under her mascaraed eye-lashes.

Then she was gone and they could hear her footsteps hurrying along the passage towards the stage.

Alisa looked up and found that the Gentleman was staring at her in a penetrating manner which made her feel shy.

"As I imagine you have no carriage," he said in the dry, somewhat drawling manner in which apparently he always spoke, "I will convey you wherever you wish to go."

"There is no need," Alisa said quickly. "I walked here . . . and I can walk back."

"From where?"

"From Bond Street."

"As I live in Berkeley Square, we go in the same

direction, and I think you will find my Phaeton quicker than your feet."

It seemed rather foolish to protest, and Alisa therefore said quietly:

"Thank you."

She walked out through the door first, and as she did so she was conscious that beside the Gentleman's elegant appearance she must look very shabby and insignificant.

They reached the old man who was seated once more in his glass box, and as they passed him Alisa thought he smiled at her.

"Thank you very much!" she said, and then she and the Gentleman went out through the door.

Outside the stage-door, which was in a side-street, there was a magnificent pair of horses and a Phaeton which was higher and more splendid than any vehicle Alisa had ever seen before in her life.

Yellow and black, it seemed to shine like its owner's Hessian boots.

She stood staring first at the horses, then at the Phaeton, until the Gentleman said with a slight smile:

"I am waiting to help you!"

"I am sorry," she said humbly, and put her hand in his.

He helped her up onto the seat, then went round to the other side to take the reins from his groom, who climbed into the small seat at the back behind the hood.

As the horses moved away, Alisa thought that never again in her whole life would she drive in anything so smart and so impressive.

Penelope will be very envious! she thought.

"I am interested to know what you are thinking," a voice said beside her.

"I was thinking how magnificent your horses are." Alisa replied, "and your Phaeton is finer than any vehicle I have ever seen!"

She wondered if she should add that she had never

before driven behind horses which wore a harness of real silver.

"I am gratified by your appreciation," the Gentleman said, "but at the same time I am mortified that you have not referred to the driver of such a turn-out."

For a moment Alisa did not know what he meant. Then quickly, without thinking, she replied:

"Mama always said it was very rude to make personal remarks."

The Gentleman laughed.

"You are not as demure as you appear."

"I hope not," Alisa replied, thinking how shabby and nondescript she looked.

"What do you mean by that?"

For a moment she wondered if she should tell him the truth, then decided that there was no reason not to do so.

"I had to come to London . . . alone, and I had no wish to be . . . noticed."

There was just a little tremor on the last word, as she remembered the man who had tried to speak to her in Bond Street.

"That was certainly wise," the Gentleman replied. "I gather you live in the country, where you make these miraculous products to sell to famous actresses."

He made it sound rather a dreary pursuit, Alisa thought, and she decided it would be a mistake to answer, so she merely looked ahead of her, holding her chin a little higher than she had done before.

"I was just thinking," the Gentleman went on, "that as I have to drive first to my house to write a cheque to pay you for your wares, perhaps you would like to join me for luncheon before you continue your sales or return to the country."

As he finished speaking, Alisa was aware that she was in fact very hungry.

She was quite certain that by now it was past noon, which was the hour Mrs. Brigstock usually gave them luncheon, and it was a long time since she had eaten an egg for her breakfast.

She had in fact been too excited and too afraid of missing the Stage-Coach to eat any more even if it had been provided.

Now she was conscious of what was an emptiness inside her, and the idea of luncheon of any sort was very attractive.

"It is very . . . kind of you to suggest it," she said hesitatingly, "but I do not . . . wish to be a . . . bother in any . . . way."

"You will certainly not be that," the Gentleman answered. "And I imagine that you would not wish to spend much of the money I am paying you on food, which in London is quite expensive."

"No, indeed not!" Alisa said quickly. "The money is for . . . something very . . . special. But perhaps it would be . . . best for me to wait to eat until I arrive home."

As she spoke, she thought that if she had to do that, she would be ravenously hungry.

But she had no idea where she could buy anything to eat and she was sure that her father would be very angry at the idea of her eating alone in a public place.

"You will have luncheon with me," the Gentleman said firmly, "and you can tell me about yourself. I am interested in how you make your creams, and why."

It flashed through Alisa's mind that he might be thinking of buying some himself. Then she thought that was a ridiculous idea.

There was a lot of traffic about and the Gentleman did not speak again until they were driving down Albemarle Street.

"Do you often come to London?" he asked.

Alisa shook her head.

"I have not been here for two years," she replied, "and there appear to be more carriages on the roads than there was then. But of course it is Coronation Year."

"That is undoubtedly the explanation," the Gentleman replied, "and at this rate of increase, the whole of the traffic in London will inevitably come to a standstill!"

Alisa laughed, for it seemed a funny idea. Then the horses were drawn up outside a very large and impressive house at the end of the Square.

She remembered seeing it once before and thinking how attractive it looked.

Over the front door was a portico supported by two pillars, and the moment the horses came to a stop, footmen in powdered wigs laid down a red carpet so that Alisa stepped from the Phaeton onto it.

She waited until the Gentleman had walked round from the other side of the Phaeton to join her. Then they walked into a large, cool Hall in which there was an impressive staircase and a number of paintings in gilded frames.

"We have a guest for luncheon, Dawkins," the Gentleman said to the Butler, "and I expect the young lady would like to go upstairs."

"Yes, M'Lord."

A gesture of the Butler's hand made a footman come to Alisa's side to say:

"Will you please follow me, Miss."

Obediently she went up the staircase, feeling that because the carpet was so thick and soft her feet sank into it.

This is an adventure! she thought. *I must notice and remember everything so that I can tell Penelope.*

She was shown into a bedroom on the first floor which was more magnificent than any other room she had ever seen.

There was brocade on the walls, a draped bed, fringed curtains, and a dressing-table with a muslin flounce trimmed with lace. She looked round wide-eyed until a housemaid came hurrying into the room.

"I've come to help you, Miss," she said.

Alisa took off her cloak, then sat down at the pretty dressing-table to remove her bonnet.

There were gold-backed hair-brushes and a comb, also edged with gold, with which to tidy her hair.

She was glad that she had washed it only yesterday, so that its natural wave fell gracefully on each side of her face, and she knew that while she might not look smart, she was certainly tidy.

Her gown of deep blue seemed to accentuate the whiteness of her skin, and she thought gratefully that it was that which had really sold the pots of cream first to Mrs. Lulworth and then to *Madame* Vestris.

She remembered excitedly that both these women had said there would be a demand for more, and she began to calculate how many pots she and Penelope could make before they went to stay with Aunt Harriet.

She hoped that if *Madame* Vestris was pleased, Mrs. Lulworth would allow them at least one gown on credit, and although Penelope might say that two of them together were more impressive than one, Penelope must go to the first parties.

Only when they could afford a second gown would she, Alisa, be able to join her sister.

The housemaid was carrying across the room a shining brass can filled with hot water which somebody had handed through the door.

Now she poured the water into a basin which Alisa noticed was made of very pretty flowered china with a ewer to match, which stood in the corner.

She washed her hands and face and felt fresher and free of the dust which had blown out behind the Stage-Coach in a huge cloud.

Then as she dried her hands she said:

"Thank you very much for helping me. When I go downstairs, will there be somebody to show me where I am to go?"

"Yes, of course, Miss," the maid replied. "Mr. Dawkins, the Butler, will be waiting for you."

She spoke as if for him to fail to do so would be a social error, and Alisa smiled.

She tried to remember all the things her mother had told her about grand houses and what happened when one stayed in them.

She hoped she would not make a lot of mistakes when, as Penelope hoped and prayed, they were invited to parties of any consequence.

She wondered if the Gentleman who was being so kind as to give her luncheon would be of any help, then once again she felt certain that he was not the type of person with whom she would wish her sister to associate.

The Butler, waiting at the foot of the stairs, led her without speaking to a door at the end of the Hall.

When she entered the room, Alisa saw that it was a Library painted a deep shade of green and picked out in gold with books set into every wall.

There was shelf after shelf of them, and she could not help giving a little exclamation of excitement before she turned her eyes to her host, who was standing in front of the fireplace waiting for her.

"What a beautiful Library!" she said. "You are lucky to have so many books!"

There was a faint smile on his rather hard mouth before he replied:

"It is a possession on which I do not usually receive many congratulations."

"Why not?" Alisa asked in surprise, as she moved towards him.

"I find that few people have time to read, and women are certainly not among them."

"How extraordinary!" Alisa exclaimed.

She was genuinely surprised. Her father was always reading and so was she, and in the Library at home her mother had had a whole section in which she kept her favourite books.

"I suppose from that remark I must assume you are a reader?" the Gentleman asked.

"But of course!" Alisa replied.

"Before we express our opinions on this or any other subject, let me offer you a glass of champagne, or would you prefer madeira?"

Alisa hesitated.

She was very tempted to accept champagne, which she had drunk only a few times in her life on special occasions, such as a birthday or Christmas, but then she remembered that she had eaten nothing for a long time.

"I think," she said after a little pause, "I should say 'no.' "

"Why?"

His monosyllabic question, spoken in a dry, abrupt manner, was, Alisa thought, almost intimidating.

"I had breakfast a long time ago."

"So you are being sensible. Is that something you invariably are? Or do you just consider it advisable on this particular occasion?"

Alisa considered the question for a moment.

"I hope I am always sensible."

"Then as this is the exception rather than the rule, I suggest I give you a very little champagne just to celebrate our first meeting."

Alisa thought it was rather a strange thing to say.

At the same time, because he spoke so impersonally and in the same tone of voice he had used before, she thought it was just a manner of speaking, rather than that they actually had anything to celebrate.

He took the champagne bottle from the gold ice-bucket and poured her a small glass of it, which he then handed to her.

As she took it she said:

"It may seem rather a belated question . . . but could you please . . . tell me . . . your name?"

"I forgot we had not introduced ourselves. I am the Earl of Keswick.* Now inform me who you are."

* (pronounced Kes-ick)

"I am Alisa Wyn . . ."

As she spoke, Alisa suddenly remembered that if they were to be coming to London and, as Penelope hoped, be acclaimed for their beauty, it would be a great mistake for anybody to know how they had been able to buy their gowns, least of all this cynical and imperious man.

". . . Winter," she finished. "Alisa Winter."

"The name does not suit you," the Earl replied, "at least not the second part of it. But 'Alisa' is charming, and I do not think I have ever known anybody by that name before."

"It is Greek."

"Who told you that?"

"I have always known it, I imagine because my mother was very interested in Greek Mythology."

She thought the Earl raised his eye-brows, but at that moment the Butler announced:

"Luncheon is served, M'Lord."

Alisa took another sip of the champagne, then because she thought it was wise not to drink any more she put it down on a table.

Then she walked ahead of the Earl and as she stepped into the Hall she saw that the maid who had looked after her upstairs was putting her cloak and bonnet on a chair, together with the black bag which had contained her pots.

It made Alisa remember that she must not take too long over luncheon. She must give herself time to go back to Bond Street to tell Mrs. Lulworth what had occurred, and then she must hurry to the Two-Headed Swan in Islington.

If she missed the Coach it would be disastrous!

The Dining-Room was a delightful room, oval in shape and painted in what Alisa knew was a pale Adam green, with alcoves in which stood statues of Greek gods and goddesses.

As she sat down in the place indicated to her, she looked at them excitedly and said:

"I wonder if I can guess who each statue represents. I am sure the one opposite me is Apollo."

"You are right," the Earl said. "But before we start talking once again of my possessions, I suggest you tell me about yourself, Miss Winter."

He frowned, then he said:

"No! 'Winter' is wrong! You must be 'Alisa.' It is a lovely name and it suits you."

Alisa was hardly attending to what he was saying, knowing that it would be a great mistake for him to know too much about her.

Then she thought that her fears were probably groundless.

Contrary to Penelope's plan of getting in touch with the Marchioness of Conyngham, she had the unhappy feeling they would end up sewing for the natives in Africa and copying out tracts. And Aunt Harriet's complaints about the wickedness of the world would force them to go to Church at least half-a-dozen times a week.

If only we could stay in a house like this! she thought wistfully.

Then as she started to eat she realised how hungry she was, and she knew that the food was more delicious than anything she had ever tasted before.

The Earl sent away the red wine which the Butler had offered and had it replaced by white. By the time he spoke, Alisa had eaten half of what was on her place.

"I am waiting!" he remarked.

"There is . . . nothing to tell," Alisa said quickly, "unless you want to hear about country life, like the arrival of the cuckoo, the first baby lamb born in the field next to the garden, and the loveliness of the daffodils which of course grow wild."

She spoke in the teasing way that she would have spoken to Penelope, and after a moment the Earl said:

"What *Madame* Vestris said about you is right. You

are in fact a consummate and extremely skilful actress."

"If I were, I would then be able to make a great deal of money," Alisa replied. "I remember reading in a newspaper that *Madame* Vestris receives an enormous salary every week, and her benefits exceed everybody else's."

"So that is what you want," the Earl remarked. "Money!"

"Not much," Alisa answered, "just enough for something very, very special which would make my sister very happy."

"And what is that?"

Alisa realised she had been indiscreet and wondered if in fact the champagne was making her talk too much.

"It is a secret, My Lord," she said. "And now please tell me about yourself. I have never seen such a beautiful house or so many treasures."

"Especially my books?"

"I noticed your paintings also as I went up the stairs."

"Then what shall we talk about?" the Earl enquired.

"It is difficult to decide what is the most important. When I look at the books we have at home, I shall think of those here, and the same applies to your paintings."

"And where is home?"

"It is just a small village in Hertfordshire. I do not think you will have heard of it."

"In other words, you are reluctant to tell me. Why should you be so secretive?"

"May I, in turn, My Lord, ask you why you are so inquisitive?"

"I should have thought the answer to that was obvious."

He realised that she looked puzzled, and he said:

"I have been looking at you and wondering how

you make your skin so clear that it is almost transparent, and yet it seems to have the texture of a rose-petal."

Again, the dry way in which he spoke made it sound like something he was reading out of a book, rather than like a compliment, and Alisa laughed.

"Why are you laughing?" he demanded.

"Because I have never been told I am like a rose before. It is my sister who is always compared with a rose. I am a violet . . . an unimportant, quite unobtrusive little violet."

"For which one must search amongst the green leaves," the Earl said.

"You sound almost poetical. My Lord!"

"You will find quite a number of books of poetry in my Library."

Alisa gave a little sigh.

"I wish I could read every one of them, but Papa does not care for poetry and so we have very few at home."

The Earl helped himself to another course before he asked:

"You say you do not often stay in London?"

"Only very occasionally, although we may do so in the near future."

"To sell your creams?"

"Yes . . . of course," Alisa agreed quickly.

"It seems rather a dreary existence for a young girl to live in the country where nature is the only entertainment and to produce creams in order to make other women beautiful."

"I do hope that *Madame* Vestris will . . . like them."

Now there was a note of anxiety in Alisa's voice, as she thought how disappointed Penelope would be if after all their plans they had to come to London in the gowns they had made themselves and nobody would take any interest in them.

It flashed through her mind that just one of the silver ornaments that decorated the table, just one of the silver dishes in which the food was served, would buy them half-a-dozen beautiful gowns in which, like the Misses Gunning, they would be a sensation.

Oh, please . . . please God, she prayed silently, *let* Madame *Vestris find that the creams improve her skin.*

She was praying with such intensity that she was startled when the Earl asked:

"Who are you thinking about?"

"*Madame* Vestris."

"You admire her?"

"I am . . . told she is a very . . . successful . . . actress."

"That is not what I asked you. When you first came into her dressing-room I thought that you were shocked by her appearance."

"I am . . . sure it was . . . presumptuous of me," Alisa said in a low voice, "but I did . . . think it was rather . . . immodest."

"Of course it is," the Earl agreed, "and that is why *Giovanni in London,* which is a very poor Show, is packed night after night."

"*Madame* Vestris has, I believe . . . a good . . . contralto voice."

"The public is more interested in her legs."

As the Earl spoke somewhat scathingly, Alisa blushed.

It seemed improper to be openly discussing another woman's legs.

"When you come to London," he said, "you will find that you have to move with the times. So perhaps it would be a mistake for you to come."

"A . . . mistake?" Alisa repeated.

"You would doubtless soon have your pretty head turned and become conceited, pleased with yourself, and ready to show off."

"I think that is a very unkind thing to say," Alisa replied. "I am sure I would become nothing of the sort! Anyway, I am not likely to receive any compliments."

As she spoke, she thought that the Missionaries and Parsons with whom Aunt Harriet concerned herself would certainly not be complimentary, if they noticed her at all.

"If you are not listening to compliments," the Earl said, "what will you be doing?"

"Sewing clothes for the natives for the Missionaries to take with them to Africa."

The Earl stared at her as if he could hardly believe what she was saying.

Then, as if she felt she had been wrong to be so frank, Alisa said quickly:

"There is no reason for you to be interested, My Lord. And please . . . as I must leave in a very short time, may I have one more look at your books?"

"Of course," the Earl agreed.

Alisa realised that the Butler was bringing a decanter of port to the table, and she said quickly:

"Forgive me! You have not finished, and it is very impolite of me to hurry you away when you have been so kind."

"I have finished," the Earl said, "and as I have no wish for any port, we will go to the Library and look at my books."

Feeling that she had been rather rude, Alisa rose and walked a little nervously ahead of him towards the Dining-Room door.

She remembered the way back to the Library, and as she entered the room the sunshine was coming through the windows, seeming to envelop everything with its golden light and make it part of a fairy-story.

The books in their leather covers tooled with gold against the green walls made a picture which she wished she could paint on canvass.

Over the mantelpiece, instead of the usual mirror, there was a very fine picture of horses which, although she was too shy to say so, she thought had been painted by Stubbs.

She stood looking round and realised that the Earl

had walked to the desk that was in front of one of the windows and had sat down.

She thought he would not mind her roaming round, and as she read the titles of the books she realised that they were far more recent in publication than anything in her father's Library. His books were mostly historical and dealt with such ancient times that the peoples and nations they described were now extinct.

The Earl had a number of books on fascinating subjects which she wished she had time to read, but she moved on quickly, not wanting to miss anything, and saw that there was one shelf filled with books of poems, many of them by Lord Byron.

"Do you know Lord Byron?" she asked.

"Of course!" the Earl replied.

"I would love to have met him when he was in England."

"All women found him irresistibly attractive," the Earl replied, and she thought he spoke cynically.

"I was thinking not of his looks but of the way he wrote. There seems to be a feeling of life and excitement in his poetry which is irresistibly infectious. It makes me want to dance and sing and express myself in verse."

"I am sure George Byron would be very flattered by your appraisal of him," the Earl remarked.

He rose from the desk and Alisa turned from the book-shelves.

"Thank you for letting me look at your books," she said. "I feel almost as if I have stepped inside some of them, and listened to music."

The Earl held out an envelope, then he said:

"Here is the money I owe you."

"But . . . I have not told you how much the pots . . . cost."

"I think you will find the sum adequate, and now before you go I have something to suggest to you."

Alisa looked up at him and thought there was a

rather strange expression in the Earl's eyes as he looked at her.

"I learnt, from all you have told me," he said, "that you are wasting your youth and certainly your beauty on the birds, the lambs, and the flowers, and I have a suggestion to make which I hope you will consider when you return home."

"A . . . suggestion?"

"It is that you let me look after you and give you all the things which will make you even lovelier than you are at the moment."

Alisa looked at him in a puzzled fashion, and he went on:

"Perhaps we could arrange it so that you can come to London without your family asking too many questions, but being content to know that you will be comfortable and well off."

"How . . . could I be? I do not know . . . what you are . . . suggesting."

The Earl smiled.

"I am suggesting that I will make you very happy and provide you with a fitting background. Or, should I say, a violet should not be hidden away so completely—at least not from me!"

As Alisa tried to understand what he was saying, thinking that she must be very stupid to find it so difficult, the Earl's arms went round her.

Then before she could understand or realise what was happening, he had pulled her close to him, and as she looked up in astonishment his lips came down on hers.

For a moment she was paralysed into immobility by sheer surprise.

Then as she knew that she was being kissed for the first time in her life and that she should be horrified and shocked that anything so appalling should happen, she was aware of the strength of the Earl's arms, and the insistence of his lips, and a feeling that was different from anything she had ever felt before.

It was as if a wave of sunlight moved up through her body and into her breasts, to her throat, and then to her lips.

It was strange, yet at the same time, in a way she could not even grasp, it was so wonderful and rapturous that it was impossible to do anything but let it happen.

Her mind had ceased to function and all she was aware of was an ecstasy she had never known before in her whole life.

Then, as if suddenly she came out of a dream, she realised that she was in a strange man's arms and he was kissing her!

She knew it was the most shocking and reprehensible thing that could possibly happen!

She came back to reality and pressed her hands against the Earl's chest, and as his arms slackened she fought herself free with a sudden strength that he had not expected.

Then with a cry that echoed round the room she ran away from him, pulled open the door, and rushed across the Hall.

With a detached part of her mind she was aware that her bonnet, cloak and bag were lying on a chair and she picked them up.

The front door was open, as a footman was taking a note from a groom in a livery.

As quickly as her legs could carry her, Alisa ran past them and up the Square until she saw a turning, then ran down another street to turn again into a Mews.

Only when with some detached part of her mind she knew it would be difficult for anybody to follow her did she stop running, breathless and with her heart pounding, beside the blank wall of a house.

She propped herself against it, shut her eyes, and told herself that it could not have happened and she must have been dreaming.

Chapter Three

"And after you had luncheon, what happened?" Penelope insisted.

As she spoke, she thought that her sister looked very pale and the long day in London had been too much for her.

Penelope had met her sister at the crossroads, and Alisa had been silent all the time they were walking back through the village.

Only now, after she had washed and changed, was she able to tell Penelope what had happened when she visited Mrs. Lulworth's shop in Bond Street.

Penelope had listened entranced as Alisa described how she had gone to the dressing-Room at the King's Theatre to show *Madame* Vestris the pots of cream and how the Gentleman she was entertaining had said he would pay for them and had taken her back to his house in Berkeley Square.

She had described the Dining-Room and the Library, but now her voice trailed away into silence. . . .

Alisa had decided on the way home in the Stage-Coach that she must never, never tell Penelope that she had been kissed.

It was something so reprehensible, so immodest on her part, that she was desperately ashamed of her own behaviour.

Yet, she was aware that she had to make some explanation as to why, instead of returning to Mrs. Lulworth's shop as she should have done, she had gone directly, almost running, to the Two-Headed Swan in Islington. When she got there she had sat in the Waiting-Room, feeling that she must make herself invisible until she could board the Stage-Coach for her return journey.

In the Coach it had been difficult to think of anything but her own misbehaviour, and as she thought of it she felt again that strange feeling of rapture and wonder that the Earl's lips had evoked in her.

I had no idea that being kissed could make me feel like that, she thought, and blushed because it was impossible not to be shocked at herself.

What would her mother have said if she had known that Alisa had allowed a strange man whom she had met for the first time to put his arms round her and touch her?

But she had to make some explanation to Penelope, and, apart from the kiss, she thought she must tell the truth.

"What happened, Alisa?" Penelope asked again.

"I hardly . . . like to . . . tell you."

"Are you trying to say that he made love to you?"

"N—not . . . exactly."

"Then what did happen?"

Alisa looked down at her clasped hands.

"He suggested that he should . . . look after me so that I should . . . not have to . . . work and sell . . . face-creams."

To her surprise, Penelope gave a cry that was not exactly one of disapproval.

"Oh, poor Alisa!" she exclaimed. "But of course it is what you might have expected from going to luncheon alone with a man in his house."

Alisa raised her head to look at her sister wide-eyed.

"Do you . . . think it was . . . wrong of me?"

"It is what I would have done in the circumstances,

rather than go hungry, but of course it made him think you were not a lady."

Alisa groaned.

"How could I have been so . . . foolish? But he seemed so . . . aloof and not the . . . type of man who would . . . behave in such an . . . ungentlemanly fashion."

Penelope laughed.

"It has nothing to do with being a gentleman, and Eloise says that all the gentlemen in London have mistresses who are either actresses, dancers, or pretty Cyprians. For them it is much the same as owning good horse-flesh."

Alisa jumped to her feet.

"How can you know such . . . things?" she demanded. "And if you do . . . why have you not . . . told me?"

"Because, dearest, you would have been horrified, you know you would! No lady would speak of such women, but it proves how lovely we both are, and even in your drab, old-fashioned clothes the Earl was attracted to you."

Alisa drew in her breath and hoped that Penelope would not guess that because he was attracted to her he had kissed her.

Aloud she said:

"It is . . . something I do not take as a . . . compliment, and I have no . . . wish to . . . speak about it again."

"No, of course not," Penelope said soothingly. "You must just forget, dearest, that you were frightened, and remember that your visit to London has been completely and overwhelmingly successful."

Alisa looked at her in a startled fashion.

"You mean we must go . . . back to . . . Mrs. Lulworth and sell her . . . more face-creams?"

"But of course!" Penelope said. "If, as you say, the mere fact that *Madame* Vestris is using them will make everybody demand the same creams, then the sooner we get to work, the better!"

Alisa wanted to cry out that she could not do it and never again would she go to Mrs. Lulworth's shop or anywhere else where she might meet the Earl.

Before she could speak, Penelope said:

"Dearest, do you not see how wonderful this is? We can have the gowns we wanted, and then we can write to the Marchioness of Conyngham. I know in my very bones that we are going to be just as successful as Maria and Elizabeth Gunning."

It flashed through Alisa's mind that Maria had married an Earl, but she told herself that marriage was the very last thing the Earl of Keswick was likely to offer her.

I must forget him, she thought to herself, and tried to listen to Penelope as she went on excitedly:

"I am sure you were right when you said Mrs. Lulworth might give us credit to have the four essential gowns we need before we can pay for them completely. How much did the Earl give you?"

"Three pounds, I suppose."

"Where is it?" Penelope asked, as if she wished to look at it and make sure there was no mistake.

"He wrote a cheque," Alisa replied. "It is in my silk bag in which I took the pots to London. I left it in the Hall."

"I will fetch it."

Penelope left the Sitting-Room and came back a moment later with the bag in her hand.

"We must start work first thing tomorrow," she was saying. "I noticed there were three cucumbers ready for picking in the garden this morning, and I will send one of the village boys to collect some watercress down by the mill."

As she was speaking she had taken the envelope out of Alisa's bag, and now as she opened it she gave a shrill scream.

"What is it? What is the matter?" Alisa asked.

Her sister was staring at the cheque she held in her hand as if she could not believe her eyes.

"What is wrong, Penelope?"

"Nothing is wrong," Penelope answered, and her voice suddenly sounded hoarse. "Do you know how much this cheque is for?"

"I thought it would be for three pounds."

"It is for fifty!"

"I do not believe it!"

Alisa walked to her sister's side and took the cheque from her hands.

Penelope was right. The cheque, made out to "Miss Alisa Winter" in a strong, upright hand, was for fifty pounds.

"There must be some . . . mistake," she said in a whisper. "I will tear it up."

Penelope snatched the cheque from her.

"You will do nothing of the sort!"

"But we cannot keep it."

"Why not?"

"Because it would be stealing."

"He gave it to you."

Alisa thought for a moment. Then she said in a halting tone:

"I suppose . . . because he thought I would . . . agree to what he . . . suggested . . ."

"Well, he will be disappointed, but I for one am grateful to him."

"But we . . . cannot take the . . . money!"

"I do not see why not."

"Because it is . . . something nobody with any . . . breeding or . . . decency would do."

"He was not giving it to you because he thought you were well-bred or decent, but because he thought you were lovely, which you are, Alisa."

"I have no . . . intention of . . . behaving like the woman he . . . thought me to be," Alisa said proudly.

"Well, I have no such qualms," Penelope replied.

"Think, Alisa! This is the answer to our prayers. We can have the gowns we want, the bonnets to go with them, and there will be no difficulty now about obtaining everything else on credit."

"I will not . . . let you . . . keep it," Alisa said fiercely.

"Then you must write to the Earl, explain who you are, and ask him to apologise."

"You . . . know I . . . cannot do . . . that."

"Then why make such a fuss?"

Penelope, looking at her sister's face, realised that she was really upset, and she said in a very different tone of voice:

"Please, Alisa dearest, be sensible for my sake. This is a gift from the gods, and it is fate that we should receive it at this particular moment when we need it so badly. How can you be so ungrateful?"

"It is not a question of . . . gratitude," Alisa said, "but of . . . conscience."

Penelope paused for a moment, then in her most persuasive voice she said:

"You went to London to help me. How can you be so unkind and so cruel as to make me go and stay with Aunt Harriet looking like I am now? Nobody will be interested in me, unless of course I am so fortunate, as you were, to find unexpectedly a stranger who is prepared to spend a great deal of money on me."

Alisa looked at her sister in a startled fashion.

"You are not to . . . think of such . . . things!"

"It happened to you. Why should it not happen to me?" Penelope asked. "And I should certainly have no scruples about taking everything I could get."

She saw that she had horrified Alisa, but she went on:

"To the Earl, the loss of fifty pounds is like backing a horse which does not win. It is bad luck, but he will merely shrug his shoulders and not think of it again."

Alisa walked to the window but outside she did not see the daffodils and the almond-blossoms.

Instead, she saw Penelope growing more bitter and frustrated and perhaps in consequence getting into trouble. She did not try to explain to herself what that trouble might be.

But it was difficult not to remember the strength of the Earl's arms and how his lips had taken possession of her so that it was impossible to move and she could no longer think.

As if she knew that Alisa was weakening; Penelope got up and joined her at the window and put her arms round her.

"Please, please, Alisa," she begged, "do not spoil things for me. If we can have just a month or even two weeks in London wearing beautiful gowns, I am sure everything in our lives will somehow be changed."

"I do not . . . know what to . . . say," Alisa said unhappily.

"Then leave everything to me," Penelope said, "and if it worries you so very much, why do you not send the Earl a present?"

"A . . . present?"

"Well, there must be something in the house that he would like, and therefore you need not feel so guilty about taking his money."

Alisa thought of the Earl's paintings, his books, the silver on the table, and the gold ice-bucket from which he had poured her out a glass of champagne.

It was almost laughable to think that anything they possessed would have the slightest interest for him.

Then, almost as if something outside herself made her think of it, she remembered the painting which hung in her father's bedroom.

She had painted it after he had called Penelope and herself "The Rose and the Violet."

It had been spring, and she had gone out into the garden to pick a bunch of the first white violets peeping from between their green leaves.

It had taken a great deal of patience to paint them, but when she had finished the picture, both her mother and her father had said it was the best painting she had ever done.

"You must think of me whenever you look at it," Alisa had told her father.

"I would rather look at you, my darling," he had replied.

Nevertheless, her mother had found a pretty carved and gilded wooden frame for Alisa to put her painting in, and they had hung it on the wall in her father's bedroom.

She was sure her father would not miss it, but she told herself that she would paint him another exactly the same in case he should ask where the original had gone.

"If I send the Earl a . . . present," she said aloud, "he might know where it had come from."

"You can give it to Fred, the Carrier," Penelope replied. "He goes to London every week, and he is so stupid he is not likely to ask any questions."

There was a light in her eyes and a smile on her lips because she knew she had won and Alisa would now agree to keep the fifty pounds.

"We will put the money in the Bank when we get to London," she said aloud, "because we would not want Mrs. Lulworth to know that the Earl had given you the money to pay her."

"No, of course not," Alisa said quickly. Then she added:

"Supposing . . . because I would not do what he . . . suggested, that he . . . stops the . . . cheque?"

She remembered how once her father had stopped a cheque because he found he had paid the same bill twice.

"That would leave three pots of cream unpaid for," Penelope said quickly, "and I cannot believe that any gentleman would behave so meanly."

"No. I am . . . sure you are . . . right," Alisa agreed.

She was thinking that whatever she felt about his behaviour, at least the Earl was a man of honour.

She did not know why she was so sure, but she was, and she thought too that Penelope was right when she said that losing fifty pounds would be to him no more than backing a horse which lost a race.

Penelope kissed her cheek.

"Cheer up, dearest, you have been very, very clever. Now everything is going to be exciting and wonderful, and I am quite, quite sure that the Marchioness of Conyngham will help us."

She was so thrilled that she could talk of nothing else the whole evening, and she did not appear to notice that Alisa was very quiet.

When finally Alisa turned out the light and was alone in the darkness, she found it impossible to sleep.

All she could think of was the Earl, what they had said to each other at luncheon, and being held captive in a way which was more exciting and more marvellous than any dream she had ever had before.

How could a kiss from a man I did not even know be so wonderful? she asked herself not once but a dozen times before she finally fell asleep.

"Now that you are here," Lady Ledbury said, "I hope you are prepared to work. There is a great deal to be done."

"I am sorry, Aunt Harriet," Penelope replied, "but we will not be able to help you on this visit as much as we have been able to do in the past."

Lady Ledbury looked at her niece in astonishment.

Unlike her brother, even when she was young she had never been particularly good-looking, and with age she had grown gaunt and bony. With her greying hair dragged back from her forehead, and wearing an extremely ugly black gown, she looked rather like an aged raven.

"I do not know what you mean, Penelope!" she said sharply.

"Papa has given us instructions, now that we are grown up, as to how we are to employ our time in London," Penelope said airily. "And although we are very grateful to you for having us to stay, Aunt Harriet, Alisa and I will have to spend quite a lot of time on our own interests."

To say that Lady Ledbury was taken aback was to express it mildly.

She had, in fact, although she would never have admitted it, looked forward to having her two nieces to stay so that they could help her with her Charities, and at the same time she would have somebody to order about and bully.

The servants in the house, who had been with her for a long time, had learnt that when she told them to do anything they thought was unnecessary, it was best to agree, and then to forget it or find there was no time to carry out her commands.

Because she paid them little and they were as it happened well trained, Lady Ledbury was aware that it would be a great mistake to push them so far that they would leave.

In the past, the help that Alisa and Penelope had given her had received the approval of her pet beneficiaries, which had been like music in her ears.

Only this morning she had said to the Vicar of St. Mary's, Islington:

"I know you have had difficulty recently, Vicar, in finding somebody to repair your hymn-books, but my nieces are coming to stay and they are quite skilful with their fingers, so that if you bring to me tomorrow the books that need repairing, I will make that one of their tasks while they are with me."

"How very kind of you, Lady Ledbury," the Vicar had answered. "It will be a great help, and I must make a point of bringing it to the attention of the Church Wardens at the next Vestry Meeting."

Now Lady Ledbury saw that her authority was being undermined, and she said quickly:

"I must make it clear from the beginning, Penelope, that I expect both you and Alisa to repay my hospitality by making yourselves useful."

"Perhaps that will be possible a little later, Aunt," Penelope answered in what her aunt thought was a very impertinent manner.

Lady Ledbury decided that somehow she would prevent this independent nonsense from going too far.

"Do be careful!" Alisa warned Penelope when they went upstairs to the small and comfortable but dull bedroom they always occupied.

"I am not afraid of Aunt Harriet!" Penelope replied. "And I am only praying that Mrs. Lulworth can fit us out very quickly with our new gowns, and we can then call on the Marchioness."

Alisa made a sound, but she did not argue, and Penelope had once again won a battle when it came to carrying out her plan of writing to her mother's old friend and saying that they had a memento for her.

"How can we possibly find anything that will be good enough?" Alisa asked.

"There must be something," Penelope said confidently.

Only after a great deal of searching and argument did they find amongst her mother's things a pretty handkerchief-sachet that Lady Wynton had embroidered with her own monogram and trimmed with a piece of real lace from one of her gowns when she had been a girl.

"Do you not see!" Penelope exclaimed excitedly. "We can say that Mama told us that when she wore that particular gown she was staying with the Denisons, and we felt sure that was why the Marchioness would like to have it."

"How do you know that is true?" Alisa asked.

"I feel instinctively that it is," Penelope replied loftily.

Penelope was so excited at the idea of the new gowns that she found it difficult to sleep the night after they arrived at her aunt's house, while Alisa lay awake worrying.

Suppose, she asked herself, *the Marchioness does ask us to her house, or even to a party, and I meet the Earl. What will I say to him? How could I ever explain that I spent his money when really I should have returned it with a polite note saying that he made a mistake and the price of the creams was exactly three pounds?*

But, to do that, she would have to give him her name and address, and although she was quite certain he had forgotten her by now, there was just a chance, a very slim one, that he might have wanted to see her again.

I shall just have to pray, she thought finally, *that he is too busy with* Madame *Vestris to wish to go to respectable parties such as the Marchioness would give.*

The following morning, having breakfasted with their aunt, Penelope managed to evade her questions as to where they were going before they set off for Bond Street.

"I do not know that I really approve of you walking about London alone," Lady Ledbury had said in a last effort to extract from them their destination once they left her house.

"I always understood," Penelope replied, "that it was correct for two ladies to walk about together and only if a lady is alone should she be accompanied by a maid. But of course, Aunt Harriet, if you want us to take one of the housemaids, then we will do so."

Penelope knew as she spoke that not only were the housemaids too old to walk far, but also it would be difficult for her aunt to spare them from their usual duties.

"I suppose you will be all right," Lady Ledbury admitted grudgingly, and did not notice the glance of amusement Penelope gave to Alisa.

It was a sunny spring day, and the two girls, walking in what was actually a very countrified manner, reached Bond Street even more quickly than Alisa had done when she had come to London the previous week.

Because Penelope had for the moment no wish to stare at other shops, being intent on only one thing—for them to be elegantly dressed as swiftly as possible—she walked straight towards the Piccadilly end of Bond Street.

"Once we are well dressed," she said to Alisa, "we can start being débutantes."

Alisa felt that her sister was being over-optimistic, but, because she loved Penelope and wanted her to be happy, she had no wish to damp down her enthusiasm.

They reached Mrs. Lulworth's shop and Penelope's eyes were shining as just before they entered she pointed out a very elegant bonnet in the window that bore no resemblance whatsoever to those they had on their heads.

The high crown was encircled with a wreath of crimson roses and the pointed brim was edged with a row of delicate lace.

"That is what we want," Penelope said firmly, and walked into the shop.

She asked for Mrs. Lulworth in an authoritative manner and a moment later they were facing the large, rather frightening woman whom Alisa had met before.

"How can I help you, young ladies?" Mrs. Lulworth began, then she looked at Alisa and gave a cry.

"Where have you been?" she enquired. "Why did you not come back to me as I expected you to do? It was only when you left that I realised I had not asked your name and had no idea how I could get in touch with you."

"Why did you wish to do so?" Penelope enquired, realising that Alisa had lost her voice.

"*Madame* Vestris was absolutely delighted with the face-cream. A number of other actresses have asked for them, and already the rumour has spread round those in Society that I have something new!"

"I see . . ." Penelope said slowly, "and so you need some more creams!"

As if she felt she had been too enthusiastic, Mrs. Lulworth answered warily:

"I might consider taking some more, of course on sale-or-return."

"I am afraid that would not suit us," Penelope answered. "We have a proposition to put to you, and perhaps we could sit down while I tell you what my sister and I have in our minds."

She was aware that Alisa was looking at her apprehensively, as if she thought she was being very high-handed, but Mrs. Lulworth merely said:

"Perhaps you would come into my private office where we'll not be disturbed."

"I think that would be a good idea," Penelope agreed.

As they followed Mrs. Lulworth, she squeezed Alisa's hand to reassure her.

Half-an-hour later they came back into the shop, Mrs. Lulworth looking somewhat bewildered, at the same time treating what she now considered two customers in a very different manner.

Penelope had stated their terms very clearly:

They would give Mrs. Lulworth fifty pounds to provide them with gowns and other accessories which they needed immediately.

They had fifty pots of face-creams with them in London and would make more if necessary.

The fifty pots must be credited to them outright at ten shillings per pot.

There was a heated argument while Mrs. Lulworth insisted that seven shillings was all she could pay, while Penelope stuck to her figure of ten.

There was quite a battle before finally Penelope accepted nine shillings with the proviso that, if there was a sudden rush for more and they had to go to the country to make more cream, for the next batch they would receive ten shillings.

Alisa had taken no part in the discussion. She only thought that she would easily have been talked into accepting seven shillings with gratitude, and that she was hopeless in negotiations of this sort.

This was especially true when she thought that not only did the pots of cream not cost them anything like ten shillings to make, but it was in fact embarrassing to be in the position of having to sell anything.

It meant so much to Penelope that, despite her conscience, which pricked her all the time, they were spending the money which came from the Earl. Alisa tried to be happy about it.

When they finally got down to choosing their gowns, it was a thrill she had never enjoyed before to know how different she could look dressed in the height of fashion.

It was Penelope, of course, who contrived to make Mrs. Lulworth interested in them as social assets, by saying:

"We are staying with our aunt, Lady Ledbury, in Islington, and it is very important that my sister and I should have something fashionable to wear before we call on a very old friend of my mother's, the Marchioness of Conyngham."

Alisa thought that Mrs. Lulworth looked startled before she asked:

"Did you say—the Marchioness of Conyngham?"

"Yes, that is right. My mother used to visit the Marchioness's family when she was a girl, and my sister and I intend to get in touch with her as soon as we have something respectable to wear."

"That is certainly something I did not expect," Mrs. Lulworth said almost beneath her breath, and Alisa wondered why she should be so astonished.

"Her Ladyship," Mrs. Lulworth went on, "has bought some gowns from me in the past, and I should very much like to have the privilege of dressing her again."

"Then you must certainly make us gowns which she will admire when we call on her," Penelope said.

With her usual quickness, she realised that Mrs. Lulworth was extremely impressed by the Marchioness of Conyngham, and she went on:

"I am not being conceited, Mrs. Lulworth, but I do know that my sister and I will 'pay with dressing,' as the saying goes."

Mrs. Lulworth realised that she must supply them with gowns immediately, and she produced some that were already half-finished.

As Penelope and Alisa looked so lovely in them, she said she would finish them off, then start making others for the lady who had originally ordered them.

Mrs. Lulworth's assistants were sent running from one end of the shop to the other to produce materials which were so beautiful that Alisa knew they would be very expensive.

The moment she was able to do so, she whispered in Penelope's ear:

"Please, please . . . we cannot afford to . . . spend so . . . much."

"Leave everything to me," Penelope replied, undoing a roll of blue silk the exact colour of Alisa's eyes and holding it up against her.

"Look!" she exclaimed, and she did not have to put into words how lovely Alisa would look in it.

When finally they left the shop it was already luncheon-time and they knew their aunt would be annoyed with them for being late.

But nothing mattered except that Mrs. Lulworth had promised that by the next morning she would deliver two day-gowns to 43 Islington Square, and two evening-gowns would be ready by tomorrow night if they had a fitting during the afternoon.

Alisa had the uncomfortable impression that Penelope had ordered a number of other gowns as well.

She was quite certain that the fifty pounds that had come from the Earl and the twenty-two pounds for the new pots of cream would not cover the cost of the gowns, bonnets, gloves, shoes, stockings, and sunshades which Penelope had stipulated as being absolutely essential.

She tried to say as much as they hurried back to Islington, but they were walking so quickly that conversation was impossible, and they were in fact both breathless by the time they reached their aunt's house.

To put Aunt Harriet in a good mood after luncheon, which had been delayed for over half-an-hour, Alisa repaired one of the hymn-books while Penelope sewed up the seams of a grey gown in a cheap and ugly cotton for some poor unfortunate child who would undoubtedly look hideous in it.

"I have a treat for you tomorrow," Lady Ledbury said when she came into the room where they were working.

"What is that, Aunt Harriet?" Alisa asked.

"I am going to take you to St. Mary's to hear the Choir practise for the Coronation Service. We are very proud that our boys have been chosen to augment the Choir at Westminster Abbey, and I know you will enjoy hearing them."

"I am sorry, Aunt Harriet," Penelope said quickly, before Alisa could speak, "but tomorrow afternoon we have planned to call on the Marchioness of Conyngham."

There was silence while her aunt stared at her in sheer astonishment.

"Did you say the Marchioness of Conyngham?" she asked.

"Yes, Aunt," Penelope answered. "As I expect you know, she was a close friend of Mama's, and we have something to take her which we are sure she will be very pleased to have."

"I do not believe it!" Lady Ledbury said. "I have never heard of your mother associating with the Marchioness!"

"She was not the Marchioness when Mama was young," Penelope explained. "She was Elizabeth Denison, and Mama used to stay with them. But of course after she was married she lived in the country, so it was difficult for them to meet."

"I cannot credit that what you are telling me is true," Lady Ledbury said, "and I do not believe that at this present moment the Marchioness is somebody with whom you should be closely acquainted."

Penelope looked at her aunt in surprise.

"What do you mean by that, Aunt Harriet?"

There was silence. Then Lady Ledbury said:

"I do not intend to elaborate on this matter or discuss it with anybody as young as yourselves, but I think I should really prevent you from doing as you intend."

"I cannot understand what you are saying," Penelope said. "If there is something against the Marchioness, then it would be wiser for you to tell us what it is."

"It is something I cannot discuss with two young and innocent girls," Lady Ledbury replied.

As she spoke, she rose and walked with dignity from the room, while Penelope and Alisa stared at each other in astonishment.

"What can this be about?" Penelope asked.

"Perhaps we ought to obey her and not take the . . . letter to the . . . Marchioness," Alisa said nervously.

"Do not be ridiculous!" Penelope answered. "If

Aunt Harriet disapproves of her, it means she will be charming and just the sort of person to help us."

She saw that her sister looked worried, and put out her hand towards her.

"Stop making difficulties, Alisa," she said, "or when you grow old you will look exactly like Aunt Harriet!"

It sounded so ridiculous that Alisa began to laugh.

"I would do anything rather than that!"

"So would I," Penelope agreed, "and it makes me more determined than ever to call on the Marchioness."

Later that evening, Alisa had gone up to her bedroom and was wondering what was keeping Penelope downstairs. Then her sister burst into the room.

She shut the door behind her and said:

"Alisa, what do you think? You will never believe it! I have found out why Aunt Harriet disapproves of the Marchioness of Conyngham!"

Alisa, who was half-undressed, sat down on her bed.

"What has she done?" she asked.

"Hold your breath and listen!" Penelope replied.

Then slowly and dramatically she declared:

"The Marchioness is the new favourite of the King!"

Chapter Four

The Marchioness of Conyngham was fat, religious, kindly, rich, and rapacious.

At fifty-two, with four grown-up children, she could hardly believe that her new Beau should be the King of England.

After twenty-seven years of marriage her beauty was beginning to fade, and although she had been greatly admired, nobody had ever said she was particularly amusing or outstandingly intelligent.

However, she was more shrewd than most people gave her credit for, and the King adored her.

For some time now he had been seeing less and less of Lady Hertford, who was tearful and angry at losing the Monarch's attention and was exceedingly spiteful to all her friends about the Marchioness.

The one thing that Elizabeth Conyngham really enjoyed was jewellery. She was excessively fond of clothes and money, but jewellery was something which brought a sparkle to her eyes and made her effusively grateful.

The King had realised this, and he was incessantly heaping presents of diamonds, pearls, and sapphires on her.

Those in attendance on His Majesty had always been aware that, for some unexplained reason, he had all his life needed a motherly and affectionate woman to fuss over and fondle, and he had invariably been in love with women older than himself.

The Marchioness was in fact five years younger than he, but there was no doubt that by her contemporaries she was counted amongst the Dowagers, and the *Beau Monde* was laughing heartily at the remark made by Lady Hertford's grandson, Lord Beauchamp, who seeing the King riding with the Marchioness in the Park, had exclaimed:

"My God! Grandmother must learn to ride, or it is all over with us!"

The King found with the Marchioness something that the other women with whom he had been enamoured had been unable to give him, and that was a family.

He loved the Conyngham children deeply, and he wrote to the Marchioness's youngest granddaughter, Maria, the most affectionate and touching letters.

At first people were incredulous at this new amatory obsession displayed by the King, then they were amused by it.

The King was so much in love that he even went on a strict diet to try to make himself more attractive, and ways of pleasing the Marchioness were in his thoughts both day and night.

However, quite a number of people were scandalised and shocked by the association, including the Marchioness's brother and Alisa.

At first she scornfully dismissed the information brought to her by Penelope as being merely belowstairs gossip.

"How can you discuss such things with the servants, Penelope?" she asked. "You know Mama would not approve."

"They are the only human beings in this gloomy house!" Penelope retorted. "In fact, I asked Martha very tactfully why Aunt Harriet was so disapproving of somebody who sounded so respectable."

Martha was their aunt's lady's-maid, housekeeper,

and, because she usually had nobody else to talk to, confidante.

Martha had been with Lady Ledbury for thirty years, and although she was somewhat strait-laced and definitely Puritanical, Alisa liked her.

She had certainly been kind to them when they were younger and were sent early to bed with the sort of supper which Aunt Harriet considered good for children.

It was Martha who had brought them up jellies or grapes and sometimes a chocolate or two.

"Martha says," Penelope went on, "that the Marchioness of Conyngham is as fat as the King, and the Cartoonists are drawing scandalous pictures of them both. We must certainly look at them when we have the chance."

"Perhaps we had . . . better not . . . call on the . . . Marchioness," Alisa said in a hesitating voice.

"Not call on her?" Penelope exclaimed. "How can you be so foolish?"

"But if she is . . . improper . . ."

"If she has the King in her pocket, as Martha says she has," Penelope answered, "can you not see how advantageous it would be if she would ask us to only one party? We would meet everybody there—but everybody!"

It flashed through Alisa's mind that this could include the Earl, and she said quickly, without thinking:

"Please, Penelope . . . do not . . . insist on our taking her a . . . present and . . . trying to make her . . . help us."

"If you are going to be so stupid as to behave like Aunt Harriet," Penelope exclaimed, "then I will go and see the Marchioness alone!"

This was something which Alisa knew she could not allow her sister to do.

At the same time, she hoped fervently that what they had been told was untrue and that Martha had exaggerated what was being said.

After all, surely the Marchioness was too old for a flirtation with the King or anybody else, and perhaps it was only jealousy which made people say unkind things of a lady he wanted merely as a friend.

She prayed that this was the truth, but when they were going for their fittings at Mrs. Lulworth's the following afternoon, Penelope insisted on stopping outside the shop in Bond Street that sold the latest cartoons.

There in the window was one by Rowlandson depicting the King and the Marchioness, both looking grossly fat and extremely flirtatious.

Because Alisa felt it was degrading even to look at it, she took only one glance and then walked on, regardless of the fact that she was leaving Penelope behind her.

Only when her sister caught up with her did she say:

"I think it is . . . wrong for you to be . . . interested in such . . . things! And because you are young and a débutante, I do beg of you, if anybody . . . mentions, which I am sure they will not . . . the King's . . . association with the Marchioness, you will pretend you know . . . nothing about . . . it."

"Very well, Miss Prude," Penelope replied.

She would have said more, but she was determined to have her own way in calling on the Marchioness later in the afternoon, and she was afraid that if Alisa was too shocked she would definitely refuse to go with her.

The evening-gowns were so lovely that Penelope was in raptures over hers, and Alisa found it difficult to argue about the behaviour of two elderly strangers —which was really how she thought of them—when they had so much for which to be grateful.

Nor did she wish to think of the man to whom they owed their gratitude! But there was no doubt that it was an exhilaration she had never known before, to realise that both she and Penelope could look so completely different and indeed so lovely in the gowns which made them as ethereal and graceful as any Greek goddess.

We should wear these standing in one of the alcoves in the Earl's Dining-Room, Alisa thought involuntarily, then rebuked herself for thinking of him again.

Mrs. Lulworth promised that the gowns would be delivered the next day, then added:

"You do me great credit, and I hope that if anybody asks you from where you purchased your gowns, you will give them my name."

"You know we will do that," Penelope answered.

"We are very, very grateful to you," Alisa added. "You have been very kind."

Mrs. Lulworth smiled, which was a rare occurrence.

"I've sold ten pots of face-creams already this morning," she said, "and I've only twenty-nine left."

"That is splendid!" Penelope cried. "Sometime next week my sister and I will have to go back to the country to make some more."

"We'd better wait and see," Mrs. Lulworth said cautiously, "but they may quite likely be needed."

As they walked from Bond Street towards the Marchioness's house. Alisa found herself once again trying to think that Martha's story of the King's love for their mother's old friend was merely gossip.

She could not imagine that anybody of her mother's generation would indulge in love-affairs, even with a King, and although she admitted that she was very ignorant about such matters, she supposed that people in love would kiss each other in the same way that the Earl had kissed her.

But it was not love he was offering her!

At the same time, she realised how little she understood what a man felt for a woman or a woman for a man, and it was something she had no wish to discuss with Penelope.

If Mama were alive, she thought, *I would ask her.*

Then she admitted to herself that she could not

have told even her mother that she had been kissed, nor could she have described the strange feeling it had aroused in her.

They neared the very impressive mansion which Penelope had learnt again from Martha, was where the Marchioness of Conyngham resided with those of her children who were unmarried.

"I am praying, Alisa," she said in a low voice, "and I hope you are too, that the Marchioness will be at home."

Alisa felt that if the truth were told she was praying the opposite, so that they could just leave their letter and go away. But she was aware that most Ladies of Fashion entertained their friends on one particular day of the week, the most usual choice being Wednesday or Thursday.

This was Wednesday, and, as if once again luck was on Penelope's side, the two girls saw that there were a number of smart and expensive-looking carriages standing outside the house, which made it obvious that this was in fact the day when the Marchioness was "At Home."

Penelope, with a self-confidence that Alisa admired and felt should be hers rather than her younger sister's, said to the Butler:

"Is Her Ladyship at home?"

"Yes, Madam. Her Ladyship is receiving," the Butler replied.

"Then would you be kind enough to give Her Ladyship this note," Penelope enquired, "and ask her if she will allow Miss Alisa and Miss Penelope Wynton to call on her?"

The Butler took the note and sent a footman hurrying up the double staircase to the landing from which came the sound of voices.

As they waited in the Hall, a carriage drew up outside, and two ladies dressed exceedingly elegantly with exquisite high bonnets trimmed with ostrich-feathers and gowns in the new shape, entered the house and proceeded up the stairs.

Penelope watched them, then said to Alisa in a low voice:

"They are smart, but not nearly as smart or as beautiful as we are! Stop looking so frightened, dearest! This is the moment we have been waiting for, and I promise you will not be disappointed."

Alisa tried to smile in response.

At the same time, she was wishing she were back at home in her shabby gown, looking at the daffodils in the Park and making face-creams in the Still-Room from her mother's recipes.

Then, looking at her sister, she thought it would be impossible for anybody to be as beautiful as Penelope.

Mrs. Lulworth had been very insistent that their gowns should, while being distinctive, complement each other's with the whole ensemble in each case being of one colour.

"*Madame* Vestris," she chatted as they were being fitted, "has always said that a Leading Lady should stand out and that the eyes of those applauding her should not be distracted by a multitude of bits and pieces, and that applies particularly to colour."

Alisa thought of the red coat *Madame* Vestris had worn and remembered that her hat was also red, as were her short boots.

The only exception had been her white breeches, but that was something which certainly need not concern Penelope or herself.

Penelope's gown was pink, the colour, Alisa thought with a faint smile, of a rose. Her bonnet was trimmed with roses and satin ribbons of the same colour, and even her slippers, showing beneath the elaborately decorated hem of her skirt, were pink.

It said much for Mrs. Lulworth's skill that neither the colour nor the shape looked theatrical, while at the same time it would be impossible for Penelope to remain unnoticed.

With Alisa beside her, no-one with eyes in their head could fail to stare at the two girls.

Alisa was dressed in very pale blue, the colour of a spring sky, and her eyes, in contrast to her dazzlingly white skin, appeared to hold mysterious depths in them.

Mrs. Lulworth had trimmed her bonnet with forget-me-nots and there was a small border of blue veiling round the edge of the brim.

"You look as if you had stepped out of the mists in the early morning!" Penelope had remarked when she was dressed.

"You are being poetical," Alisa said with a smile, and instantly thought of the books of poetry in the Earl's Library.

The footman came hurrying down the stairs and both girls held their breath. He spoke to the Butler, and Alisa thought with a little throb of apprehension how disappointed Penelope would be if they were turned away.

The Butler moved towards them and spoke to Penelope.

"Her Ladyship will be delighted to receive you, Miss," he said in a courteous tone, then went up the stairs in front of them.

As they entered the large Drawing-Room, which covered the whole width of the house at the back and looked over the garden, Alisa felt that everything swam in front of her eyes and she could see nothing but a sea of faces.

However, there were not many people there, as she could see when her vision cleared, and it was not difficult to pick out the Marchioness, who looked exactly the way she had been portrayed in the cartoon.

"Miss Alisa and Miss Penelope Wynton, M'Lady!" the Butler boomed, and a large, Junoesque figure advanced towards them with outstretched hands.

"My dears! How delightful to meet you!" the Marchioness exclaimed. "I have often thought of your dear mother, and I am deeply grieved to hear that she is no longer with you."

Alisa curtseyed, then looked up into the Marchioness's face to see that there was a smile on her lips and she did in fact look kind and sincerely pleased to see them.

Alisa felt she would have known at once if what she was saying was merely polite, and the Marchioness continued:

"There is a distinct resemblance to your mother in both of you, and how very pretty you both are! I am sure you will have a most successful time now that you have come to London. Is your father here with you?"

"No, Ma'am, he is in Scotland," Penelope replied.

"He sent us to London to stay with his sister, Lady Ledbury, but it is very, very dull there and we did so hope you would remember Mama and be kind to us."

Alisa drew in her breath.

She had never imagined for one moment that Penelope would be so outspoken or make a plea for help immediately on meeting the Marchioness.

But a moment later she realised that Penelope, as usual, had been quick-witted enough to take advantage of an opportunity which might never come again,

While the Marchioness was talking to them no-one else happened to be trying to attract her attention, so, as Penelope would have said herself in the colloquial manner which Alisa always deplored, she was "striking while the iron was hot!"

"That, my dears," the Marchioness exclaimed, "is something I am certainly ready to do!"

"Mama always told us how kind you were to her when she was a girl," Penelope went on, "and that is why my sister Alisa and I have brought you something which belonged to Mama, and which we hoped you would like to have."

"How very sweet of you!" the Marchioness purred.

Alisa produced the present she was carrying, which

they had wrapped in the soft paper in which their gowns from Mrs. Lulworth had been packed, and had tied it up with a bow of blue ribbon.

It certainly looked an attractive gift as she handed it to the Marchioness.

"I am going to open this later, when I am not so busily engaged," she said, "and when we can talk about your dear mother and I can tell you how lovely she was and how fond we were of each other."

She smiled.

"But now I must introduce you to my friends. It happens we are having a small dinner-party here tomorrow night for my daughter Elizabeth. The young people will dance afterwards and you must certainly join us."

"Oh, thank you, Ma'am!" Penelope cried. "Alisa and I were so afraid we would never have the chance of dancing in London, and it is something I would love more than anything else."

"I will see that you have plenty of opportunities to dance and to meet some charming young men," the Marchioness promised.

Then she took them round the room to present them to the other callers.

They drove home in a hackney-carriage because Penelope said she was too exhausted to walk and also because it was getting too late for it to be proper for them to be on the streets alone.

"I cannot believe that what is happening is true!" she exclaimed.

"You were right and I was wrong," Alisa admitted. "Her Ladyship is exactly the sort of friend Mama would have, and I do not believe one word of all the wicked things which have been said about her and the King."

"No, of course not."

Alisa thought there was a note in Penelope's voice which did not ring true, but for her sister's sake she was in fact too glad, at what had happened to make any comment.

It would have been impossible for either of them not to realise that the Marchioness's manner towards them had impressed all her visitors.

They were mostly friends of her own age, but a few had brought their husbands, who had looked, Alisa thought, at Penelope and herself in a way that she was quite certain would discourage their wives from inviting them to any parties they were giving.

However, two or three ladies did say that they would ask the Marchioness for their address and promised to invite them to parties later in the Season, and it was only the younger women, Alisa thought, whose eyes had been undisguisedly hostile and who had obviously no wish to further an acquaintance with two undoubted potential rivals.

The mere fact that they were to dine at the Marchioness's house on Thursday night was to send Penelope into a transport of delight, about which she talked all the way home.

"We are launched, Alisa! Do you realise it? We are launched on the social scene! It is the most exciting thing that has ever happened to us."

"It is all due to you, dearest," Alisa replied "and I can only hope that our frail little boats will not sink."

"Why should they?" Penelope asked. "And we shall need more than one gown each."

"Oh, no!" Alisa cried. "We cannot afford any more!"

"With Mrs. Lulworth already asking for more pots? You really are chicken-hearted, Alisa! Besides, supposing we do get into difficulties, we can pay our bills the moment we are married."

"Do not go so fast, Penelope! We have only been invited to one dance, and already you are talking of being married, and doubtless to a Duke!"

"I was thinking of not less than a Prince!" Penelope retorted.

They both laughed so much that it was impossible to continue the conversation.

Walking in the garden at the back of the Marchioness's house, which was lit with Chinese lanterns hanging from the trees and tiny lights edging the paths, Alisa felt she had stepped into a dream.

It was difficult enough to believe that Penelope's outrageous plan of launching them into Society would succeed, without finding that there really was a distinct similarity between their story and that of the Gunning Sisters.

Certainly the invitation-card that had been delivered at Islington Square from the Marchioness the following morning surprised Lady Ledbury.

Strangely, it silenced any protests she might have made about accepting it, and the same morning there had been two other invitations from hostesses to whom they could not remember being introduced by the Marchioness and who may just have heard about them.

"Once we are talked about," Penelope said, "everybody will want us."

"How do you know such things, dearest?" Alisa enquired.

"I am still remembering the story of the Gunning Sisters. The moment people began to talk about them, they were asked everywhere. Hostesses always like to have the latest lion in tow."

"Is that what we are now?" Alisa enquired.

"I hope so," Penelope said fervently, but even she was a little apprehensive on their way to the dinner-party.

"This is the really crucial test," she said.

"Of what?"

"As to whether we are a sensation or not. After all, so far we have not been up agianst any competition, but tonight there will not only be girls of our own age but the fascinating, sophisticated beauties who are pursued relentlessly by the Bucks of St. James's, while their husbands are pursuing somebody else's wife."

Alisa stiffened.

"That is not the sort of thing, Penelope, that you should say?"

"I am only saying it to you." her sister answered. "If you will not listen, I shall have to find somebody else to talk to."

She was only teasing, but Alisa thought that one safe-guard in respect to Penelope's impetuosity was that they talked frankly with each other, and she hoped, although she was not sure, that she curbed her sister's tendency to act without thinking.

She did not like to think of Penelope knowing and inevitably talking about the improprieties committed by the King or anybody else.

Yet she knew that it was impossible to stop people from gossipping about such things, and whatever she might or might not say, excesses certainly did take place.

Then inevitably she thought of her own behaviour, and shied away from the memory of the Earl like a young horse frightened by a leaf blowing across the road.

The Marchioness's impressive house looked very attractive at night, with the flaming torches which the linkmen had already lit, the red carpet laid outside the door, and the carriages queueing up to drop off their occupants one by one.

Alisa felt that perhaps they had been rather rude in not ensuring that their aunt was included in the invitation, but she was not quite certain how she should go about it, even if she had wished for Lady Ledbury to accompany them.

When she had suggested to Penelope that it was impolite to leave her behind, her sister had exclaimed:

"For goodness' sake, Alisa, the last thing we want is Aunt Harriet looking like the skeleton at the feast, and doubtless handing the King a tract on immorality."

Alisa laughed because she could not help it. Then she said in a low voice:

"You do not think the . . . King will be . . . there?

"No, of course not," Penelope replied.

But again there had been a note in her voice which had made Alisa feel apprehensive.

As they entered the front door there seemed to be a whole army of servants in smart gold-braided uniforms and wearing white breeches and powdered wigs.

Having taken off their wraps, which matched their gowns and which Alisa was quite sure was another costly extra which would have to be paid for sooner or later, they proceeded up the stairs.

The Marchioness, looking more Junoesque than ever, and glittering with diamonds so that she looked, Alisa thought, as if she were enveloped in the whole Milky Way, received them with a smile and kissed them on both cheeks.

"Welcome, welcome, my dears!" she said effusively, nodding her head, on which there was a large white feather secured by a hugh diamond brooch.

"These are Lady Wynton's daughters, my dear," she added to the Marquis who was receiving beside her, and when he had shaken them by the hand they were introduced to his daughter, for whom the dance was being given.

At dinner Alisa found herself seated next to a middle-aged man who paid her several compliments. Then, finding that she came from the country and was interested in horses, he embarked on a long, rather uninteresting discourse on the merits and successes of various racing-stables.

On her other side was a vacant-looking man who,

from his appearance, she guessed to be a Dandy. His cravat was so high and so tight that he obviously found it difficult to eat and to talk.

She did her best, but she found him a bore and turned back to her racing-friend with relief.

She discovered that he was a widower and the father of a débutante who was, like Penelope, just seventeen, and this was only the second party to which she had been invited in London.

When she met the girl when dinner was over, Alisa felt sorry for her. She was obviously extremely shy, and, with few pretensions to good looks, she would in fact have made a far more handsome horse!

When dinner was finished and the ladies retired to leave the gentlemen to their port, they were with few exceptions very polite to Alisa and Penelope.

Then other guests began to arrive and Alisa found that far from being a small party, as the Marchioness had described it, it appeared to be quite a large one.

Downstairs there was a Ball-Room decorated with wreaths of flowers, its windows opening onto the garden, and a Band whose music transported her into a dream world which she thought existed only in books.

The gentlemen whom they had met at dinner seemed only too eager to dance with her and Penelope, and she knew by the expression on her sister's face how happy she was.

The garden was like a fairy land, Alisa thought, as she walked in it with her partner, who was the older gentleman who had sat next to her at dinner.

But she knew she must not go far from the lights of the house or be inveigled into sitting in the arbours which she could see arranged in the shadows amongst the flowering shrubs.

"I should have warned Penelope to be on her guard," Alisa told herself.

She could not help thinking that if the Earl had been prepared to kiss her in the Library after luncheon, to be alone with a man with stars in the sky above them and music playing softly in the distance was an invitation to indiscretion.

"I hope one day, Miss Wynton," her partner was saying, "you will come and see some of my race-horses that I keep at Epson. I am sure you would appreciate that they are outstanding."

"I am certain you are very successful," Alisa said with a smile.

"I hope to be even more so," he answered, "and especially to win the Gold Cup at Ascot this year."

"Which of your horses are you entering?" Alisa asked. "If you will tell me his name, I will send up a very special prayer that he will win."

"It is very properly named *Victorious,* and because I am certain that we shall meet a great deal before Ascot, I shall keep you to your promise."

"My father has told me that the Gold Cup at Ascot is one of the most coveted prizes that every owner longs to win," Alisa said.

"That is true enough," her companion replied, "but *Victorious* will have to beat a very outstanding horse which has unfortunately pipped him at the post at several race-meetings recently."

"And what is his name?" Alisa enquired.

"*Apollo.* I am sure you must have heard of him, because he belongs to the Earl of Keswick."

"The Earl of . . . Keswick?"

Alisa was not certain whether she had said the words aloud or in her mind.

"He has certainly been very lucky with *Apollo,* so you see, Miss Wynton, I shall certainly need your prayers."

As they were talking they had reached the end of the path lined with fairy-lights, and now they turned to walk back towards the house.

It was then, as they did so, that the owner of *Victorious* exclaimed:

"Talk of the Devil, as the saying goes—there is the Earl! I thought he would arrive with the King."

Alisa felt that it was impossible to breathe, for there, standing just inside the open windows of the Ball-Room, she could clearly see George IV, and beside him, tall and slim and equally resplendent, was the Earl of Keswick!.

For a moment she longed to run away, to hide, to escape.

It flashed through her mind that she should find Penelope and say she was ill.

Then she remembered that in that case she would be obliged to explain to her hostess why she wished to leave, and the Marchioness would be beside the King, with the Earl in attendance.

She felt as though everything was jumbled dizzily in her mind, and she could not sort out anything or make a decision.

And all the time she was walking towards the Ball-Room, while the gentleman beside her was talking.

"I hope you will dance with me again, Miss Wynton," he said. "In fact, when I have done my duty with two of the ladies with whom we had dinner, I shall come and look for you."

Thank . . . you," Alisa managed to say, but her voice did not sound like her own.

They stepped in through the window and as they did so she told herself that it was very unlikely the Earl would recognise her.

He had only seen her in the drab gown in which she had had luncheon with him, and she was certain that she looked entirely different in the beautiful, expensive one she wore now and with her hair arranged in the latest fashion.

"Besides," she asked herself, "why should he expect to see me with the Marchioness of Conyngham?"

She stole a quick glance at him and thought he was looking bored and at the same time awe-inspiring, as he had when she had first looked at him in *Madame* Vestris's dressing-room.

Then she turned her face away so that if he did

glance in her direction, all he would see would be the back of her head, and, still escorted by her racing-friend, she proceeded to the far end of the Ball-Room, where to her relief she caught sight of Penelope.

Her sister was talking animatedly to a good-looking young man who she noticed had been beside her at dinner.

As Alisa joined them, the gentleman who had escorted her bowed and moved away, and Penelope said:

"Oh, dearest, I want you to meet Major James Coombe. He is going to ask us both to the Trooping of the Colour, which he tells me is a brilliant spectacle!"

"Almost as spectacular as you and your sister, Miss Wynton," the Major said gallantly.

Penelope laughed.

"That is the sort of flattering thing he says, but I do not believe a word of it!"

"Now that is very unkind!" the Major expostulated. "I can swear that everything I have said to you tonight is completely true and would come from the very depths of my heart if I had one."

Alisa laughed, but she was sure he was completely bowled over by Penelope's loveliness, and she was not surprised.

She could not imagine that anybody could look more fascinating than her sister did at this moment.

Her eyes were shining like the stars overhead because she was so happy and excited.

The next dance was starting and now half-a-dozen young men rushed up to claim a dance either with Penelope or with Alisa.

Those who were disappointed said:

"Please promise me the next, promise! Promise!"

Alisa had been told by her mother that Balls were usually very formal and no gentleman would ask a girl to dance unless he was introduced to her by a hostess or a lady acting in that capacity.

Now she understood that this was an informal party and why the Marchioness had referred to it as being "little."

It was certainly much more fun, but now as her partner danced with her to the end of the room she saw the Earl.

He was still standing near the King, who was seated on a sofa, holding the Marchioness's hand in his and whispering in her ear in a very intimate manner.

There was no doubt, Alisa thought, that the Earl was looking even more bored than he had been when they had first arrived, and she thought too there was a frown between his eyes.

She turned her head away as they passed him, but she had the feeling that his thoughts were far away, and she wondered if perhaps *Madame* Vestris had been difficult or if he might be cross that he could not be with her tonight, taking her to supper after the Show.

She wondered where they would go and what they would talk about and if the conversation would be as interesting as she had found it when she and the Earl had had luncheon together.

She imagined them having supper, perhaps by candlelight, perhaps at *Madame*'s house or at his, and she wondered if he would kiss her in the Library as he had kissed her.

With a start, Alisa realised that the dance had come to an end and her partner was waiting for an answer to a question she had not heard.

"I am sorry . . . I did not hear what you . . . said," she explained.

As she spoke, she saw that the Earl had moved from where he had been standing and was only a few feet away from her.

Then as she looked into his eyes she saw a surprised look of recognition in his.

"I asked you if you would dine with my mother tomorrow night. She is giving a party for my sister," her partner was saying, "and I could arrange for you and your sister to be invited. Please tell me you will come."

"Thank you. Thank you . . . very much!" Alisa answered, hardly aware of what she was saying.

Then, as if she was compelled by some force over which she had no control, she moved away from him towards the Earl.

Only as she reached him did she know what she had to do, and it was imperative that she should do it at once.

She was too shy to look again at his face, fixing her eyes instead on his cravat, which vaguely at the back of her mind she thought was even more intricately tied than when she had first seen him, and she said:

"Please . . . could I . . . speak to . . . you?"

She could hardly hear her own voice, and yet he must have heard what she had said, for he replied:

"Of course. Shall we go into the garden?"

They walked down the room, Alisa taking two steps to his one, and she felt almost as if she were being taken to her execution.

It flashed through her mind that unless she could persuade him to do what she wanted, she and Penelope would have to refuse every invitation, and she knew that her sister would never forgive her.

The Earl walked not along the lighted path as Alisa had done before, but across to where under the trees and sheltered by the foliage there was an empty seat with cushions on it.

He waited for Alisa to sit down, then he sat beside her and, turning sideways, rested his arm across the back of the seat.

She was acutely conscious that his penetrating eyes were on her face and it was impossible to look at him.

She could only twist her fingers together in an effort to think wildly of what she should say.

Then at last, as he did not speak, she said:

"Please . . . forgive me . . . I know it was . . .

wrong and you must be . . . angry . . . but we . . . kept the money because it . . . meant so much . . ."

What she said sounded inadequate and very hesitant, and the Earl said:

"You said you wanted to do something special, and I presume that meant buying the gown you are wearing now."

Alisa thought it was clever of him to guess the reason so quickly, and she answered:

"I wanted to . . . send the cheque back . . . but if I had . . . done so, I think I would have . . . broken my sister's heart . . . She felt it was a . . . gift from the . . . gods."

There was a faint smile on the Earl's face as he said:

"The gods certainly look after their own, and when you ran away I had the idea that you might have fled back to Olympus."

She thought he was laughing at her, and she said:

"It may seem to . . . you that we . . . stole your money, but I . . . swear that I will . . . pay you back, even though it may . . . take a long . . . time."

"With the proceeds from your creams?"

"We have sold a lot of those already, and that is . . . another thing I . . . wanted to . . . speak to you . . . about."

As she spoke, she felt as if the words were almost strangled in her throat, and after a moment's silence, the Earl said:

"I am waiting."

"The Marchioness of Conyngham and my mother were friends when they were girls . . . and she asked us here . . . tonight, and we have had other . . . invitations as well . . ."

She looked up at the Earl pleadingly.

". . . But please . . . please," she went on bravely, "I beg of you . . . not to tell . . . anybody that we sell . . . face-creams or that I . . . kept the money you . . . gave me."

"Do you imagine I might do that?" the Earl enquired.

Alisa made a helpless little gesture with her hands.

"If you do, you . . . know that we will be ostracised and . . . nobody will . . . speak to us."

"Which means, of course, that you would have to revert to working for the Missionaries."

"Yes . . . that is . . . true," Alisa said with something suspiciously like a sob. "It is what my aunt . . . expected us to do when we . . . arrived in London . . . but instead . . ."

Her voice died away.

"You spent my fifty pounds on your clothes!"

Alisa nodded. Then she said, still in the pleading voice she had used before:

"How could we go . . . anywhere or . . . meet anybody . . . dressed in the gowns we had made . . . ourselves, and which were out of . . . fashion? You saw how I . . . looked when we . . . met."

"In *Madame* Vestris's dressing-room," the Earl said. "Hardly the place for a débutante!"

"I know it was . . . wrong, but we thought the only way we could obtain a little . . . money was to sell the . . . herbal creams which Mama taught us how to make, and Mrs. Lulworth said that if *Madame* Vestris . . . liked the creams . . . everybody would want to buy them . . . and they are . . . selling!"

"You do not think that Mrs. Lulworth will betray you?"

"No, she has . . . promised on her . . . honour that she will tell . . . nobody where the creams come . . . from, and I am not . . . likely to see . . . *Madame* Vestris again . . . no-one else but . . . you saw me there."

"You did not think when you came to the Theatre you were likely to meet men there?"

"No . . . but now I am . . . afraid."

"Afraid?"

"That you may tell people, and also . . ."

There was silence.

"I would like to hear the end of that sentence," the Earl said.

The colour rose in Alisa's face, as she remembered how he had kissed her and what she had felt, and because she found it impossible to speak of such things she looked away from him across the garden.

"I suppose," the Earl said after what seemed a long silence, "you were shocked at what I suggested to you?"

"Very . . . shocked!"

"I can hardly blame you, but I did not realise that a seller of face-creams was a Lady of Quality!"

He was speaking in the dry, mocking tone she had heard so often before, and she answered impulsively:

"You are . . . laughing at me . . . and I know it was wrong . . . very wrong to have . . . luncheon with you . . . alone . . . but I was . . . hungry and I knew that Papa would not . . . wish me to eat . . . in a . . . public place."

"When did you realise it was wrong?" the Earl asked. "You did not appear to think so at the time."

"Penelope told me I should not have gone to a . . . gentleman's house, and I realised that was true . . . when it was . . . too late."

"Too late to prevent me from kissing you!"

Alisa dropped her head.

"I am . . . very . . . ashamed," she whispered.

"There is nothing for which you need be ashamed," the Earl said quietly. "And I thought, although I might have been mistaken, that while I am aware it was the first time you had been kissed, you did not find it repulsive."

"No . . . of course . . . not! It was just . . . something I . . . should not have . . . allowed."

"I think you could not have prevented it from happening."

Alisa knew this was true. Then he said quietly:

"If it upsets you, forget that it happened."

It flashed through her mind that that was impossible. At the same time, his words made her ask:

"Will you . . . forget that you have . . . ever met me . . . before this . . . moment?"

"Shall I say that I will not speak of it to anybody?"

"Do you . . . really mean that? Do you . . . promise?" Alisa asked.

As she spoke she looked eagerly up at the Earl, and now as her eyes met his she felt as if he held her spellbound and as if once again she was in his arms.

Almost as if she were swept back into the past, she felt that strange and rapturous feeling within her, rising from her breasts to her throat and from her throat to her lips.

It was so perfect that it was like the music she could hear in the distance and the soft rustle of the trees overhead, while for the moment it was impossible to look away or even to breathe.

"I have given you my word, Alisa," the Earl said, "so now enjoy yourself and believe that what the gods have given the gods will not take away."

As she opened her lips to thank him, he rose to his feet.

"Come," he said. "I will take you back to the Ball-Room. We must not have the gossips talking about you, as they will undoubtedly do if we stay here any longer."

The dry, cynical note was back in his voice, but as Alisa walked beside him towards the lights, her heart was singing.

Chapter Five

There was a loud rat-tat on the front door which echoed through the house, and Penelope looked at Alisa and smiled.

"More flowers?" she exclaimed.

The room certainly did not look as though it needed any more, and the two girls were overcome every day with the bouquets which kept arriving at their aunt's house and the invitations which poured in.

The servants had already complained that their feet were giving out from running up and down from the basement to answer the front door, and even Lady Ledbury was astonished at the commotion her nieces were causing.

What was more, the more traditional hostesses had included her in their invitations, and while at first Lady Ledbury wished to refuse, it was Alisa who persuaded her to attend one or two of the Assemblies and Receptions to which they were asked.

For the first time Lady Ledbury became feminine and exclaimed:

"How can I possibly go anywhere? I have no clothes for that sort of thing."

It was Alisa who persuaded her to buy a new gown and bonnet which were in blue rather than black, and when she had her hair arranged by the same hairdresser who attended the house almost daily for the two girls, she really looked rather handsome.

"Why do you bother with the old thing?" Penelope asked when she and Alisa were alone.

"I am sorry for her."

"She is quite happy with her Missionaries and her tracts."

"I think she was drawn to good works," Alisa said, "because she had nothing else."

Penelope looked at her sister in surprise as she went on:

"Can you imagine how empty her life must be when she has only those dreary Missionaries fussing all the time about children being naked and the Vicar who can talk of nothing but raising money for his Church?"

Impulsively, Penelope kissed her sister.

"You always have something nice to say about everybody, dearest," she said. "Whoever you marry will be a very lucky man."

Penelope had already had one proposal of marriage, but it was from a rather stupid young man and she would not have thought of accepting him.

At the same time, it was encouraging, and now as the two girls hurried down the stairs to the Drawing-Room, they found, as they had expected, the old parlour-maid taking in a bouquet, a basket filled with orchids, and a long flower box.

"More flowers, Henderson!" Penelope remarked.

"As ye says, Miss," Henderson replied tartly, "an' I hopes it's the last! I'm too old to keep coming up and down them stairs!"

She set the basket of orchids down on the floor at Penelope's feet, then shuffled away as if her legs were too tired to carry her.

"Perhaps we could persuade Aunt Harriet to have a young footman temporarily, now that we are here," Alisa said.

Penelope did not answer.

She was looking at the note which was attached to the basket of orchids, and when she saw there was a crest on it, she exclaimed with a note of triumph:

"It is from your Duke."

Alisa frowned.

"He is not *my* Duke."

"Of course he is!" Penelope replied. "And judging by the size of the basket and the expense of the orchids, it will not be long before he asks you to become his Duchess."

Alisa took the note which her sister held out to her and saw written on it the words:

To thank you for two very enjoyable dances.
Exminster.

She had been surprised when she found that the gentleman she had sat next to at the dinner-party that first night at the Marchioness's house was the Duke of Exminster.

She had learnt that he was a widower and she knew from their conversation that he was a racing enthusiast.

It was Penelope who had learnt that he owned the best racing-stable in the country, and his only rival was the Earl of Keswick.

The Duke had attached himself to Alisa at every party since, and because she realised that he was growing more possessive in his attitude, she had last night deliberately danced with him only twice and managed to avoid a quiet *tête-a-tête* that he obviously wished to have with her.

It was difficult to explain to Penelope why she did not want him to come to the point of proposing marriage, which she sensed instinctively was in his mind.

She knew only that the idea of marriage to somebody so much older than herself frightened her, and now that she was actually confronted with what had only been a fantasy, she wished to avoid committing herself in any way.

As she could not discuss her feelings for the Duke of Exminster with Penelope, she put down his note and said quickly:

"What flowers have you received, dearest?"

Penelope had in her hand the long flower-box. She opened it and inside Alisa could see that there was just one pink rose.

"What a strange gift!" she exclaimed. "Who sent you that?"

Her sister held out the card that was in the box and on it Alisa read:

From a rose to its twin.

She laughed.

"You can never get away from being described as a rose, dearest, and of course in your pink gown you look exactly like one."

"I am sick of being told so," Penelope said sharply, "and that tiresome Major Coombe keeps teasing me about it."

"It is really a compliment."

"It is one I do not want from him!"

She picked up the bouquet and said:

"This is better! I have a wonderful idea, dearest, that you and I will beat the Gunning Sisters."

"In what way?"

"You will marry a Duke and so shall I."

Alisa looked at Penelope wide-eyed.

"Do you mean the Duke you were dancing with last night?"

"Of course I do!" Penelope replied. "And I can assure you he is very ardent."

She watched the expression on Alisa's face as she went on:

"If we both become Duchesses, I am sure we will be in the history books."

Alisa was silent.

When she had been introduced to the Duke of Hawkeshead, she had thought him an extremely unprepossessing man.

He had a red face and was not in the least good-looking. Moreover, she had not liked the manner in which he was looking at Penelope, which somehow, although she could not explain it exactly, seemed an impertinence.

He had also been somewhat untidily dressed, and towards the end of the evening she had noticed that he got even redder in the face and talked over-loudly as if he had been drinking a great deal.

She wanted to say to Penelope that the Duke was the last sort of man she wanted her to marry.

Then she thought it would be a mistake to sound too critical, and she merely said:

"You are such a success, dearest, there is no hurry for you to make up your mind. I think Aunt Harriet is quite resigned to having us here. In fact, although she wouldn't admit it, she is enjoying the excitement of it all."

"Of course she is," Penelope agreed. "And that reminds me, I forgot to tell you there was a note last night from Mrs. Lulworth, saying that she wants some more creams immediately and is leaving two hundred empty pots here for us today."

"Two hundred!" Alisa exclaimed. "How splendid! Now perhaps we can afford one more gown each."

"I want a great deal more than that," Penelope answered. "I cannot bear to be seen again in pink, and my evening-gown is in tatters!"

Alisa knew this was almost true.

She and Penelope had both had to repair their gowns, and although they had tried to add different coloured ribbons, they were quite certain the women in the parties they attended were not deceived and knew that in fact they were each wearing the same gown night after night.

Alisa was mentally counting up how much money they would receive for two hundred pots, but they were already in debt to Mrs. Lulworth and she was very much against asking her for more credit.

She did not have to speak for Penelope to know what she was thinking.

"Oh, for Heaven's sake, Alisa!" she said. "Let us enjoy ourselves while we have the chance, and if both our future husbands are enormously rich, why should we have to pinch and scrape to please nothing but your tiresome conscience?"

"I wish you would not talk as if I had agreed to . . . marry the Duke, who has not even . . . asked me," Alisa said.

"But he intends to do so, and you will accept him, so why pretend?"

"I have not decided . . . whether I will or . . . not," Alisa replied in a small voice.

"How can you be so ridiculous?" Penelope asked. "Have you forgotten the alternative to being a Duchess? To go back to the country and sit, seeing nobody and doing nothing but copying out Papa's manuscripts."

"I had you, and I was very happy," Alisa said.

The way she spoke made Penelope immediately contrite.

"Forgive me, dearest, for being so horrid, but you know that what is happening now will never happen again."

She felt that Alisa did not understand, and she explained:

"We are a success because we are new and the *Beau Monde* is always intrigued by something new and sensational. But in a few months, perhaps sooner, they will be used to us. Then there will be other sisters, perhaps even triplets, to take our place, and we shall be forgotten."

Alisa laughed.

"I do not think that is likely to happen, but I understand what you are saying."

"We must be like the farmers at home," Penelope said, "who always say: 'Make hay while the sun shines,' and that is what we have to do. So thank your Duke very prettily for the flowers and promise to dance with him at my Duke's Ball the night after next."

"He is giving a Ball?" Alisa exclaimed in surprise.

"He says it is for me," Penelope replied, "and I have the feeling that he intends to propose to me that evening, then announce it. He likes to cause a sensation."

It flashed through Alisa's mind that that was the last way in which she would wish to proclaim her engagement, for she was sure it would be very embarrassing. But again she thought it would be a mistake to say so, and instead she asked:

"When do you plan that we shall go to the country to make the face-creams?"

"I suppose we shall have to go tomorrow," Penelope answered. "The only invitation we shall have to chuck is with that boring friend of Aunt Harriet's who is giving a luncheon simply because we are fashionable."

"Perhaps it would be unkind to behave like that to her," Alisa suggested.

"I am not concerned with her feelings," Penelope replied, "but it is a terrible bore to have to waste a whole day by going home."

"There is no need for you to come," Alisa said. "I can catch an early Stage-Coach and I am sure there will be one returning late in the afternoon."

"I have a better idea!" Penelope exclaimed.

There was another rat-tat on the door and another bouquet of flowers, and Alisa forgot to ask Penelope what it was she had been about to say.

She learnt what her sister was planning late that evening after they had been to a very grand Reception at the French Embassy at which both the King and the Earl had been present.

Alisa had not spoken to the Earl alone, but she had been vividly aware that he was there and also that while she was talking to the Duke of Exminster his eyes were watching her.

She thought he looked more bored and cynical than usual, until she noticed him talking to a very attractive lady with dark hair and flashing eyes, who was not unlike *Madame* Vestris.

"I suppose he only admires brunettes," she told herself, and wondered why the thought was curiously depressing.

It was when they got home just before midnight that Penelope said:

"I have fixed everything for tomorrow."

"What do you mean?" Alisa enquired.

"We are going to the country with four horses, which means it will not only be quicker but far less tiring."

Alisa looked at her in surprise, and Penelope exclaimed:

"You can guess whose carriage will be taking us! After all, there is only one person to whom our cream-making is no secret."

"You cannot mean . . . the Earl?"

"Of course it is the Earl," Penelope replied. "When I told him tonight what we had to do, he said at once that his horses will be at our disposal."

"How could you do such a thing?" Alisa asked almost angrily. "We are under an . . . obligation to him already, and I have no desire to make it . . . worse!"

"You became involved with him in the first place," Penelope said, "and actually there was no need for me to plead with him. I merely said that we had to leave the Reception early because we would have such a tiring day tomorrow. And when he asked me why and I told him that our creams were in such demand that

Mrs. Lulworth wanted more, he said at once that he would arrange for us to travel in comfort."

"I wish you had discussed it with me first," Alisa said.

Penelope laughed.

"You would only have said 'no,' and I should have asked him anyway, so what was the point?"

When Penelope had left her and Alisa was alone, she thought of quite a number of arguments she might have put forward to show that they should not accept any more favours from the Earl.

Then she told herself that there was no use trying to prevent Penelope from doing anything she wished to do.

"He must . . . think we are very . . . forward," she told herself before she went to sleep.

The following morning, she was just putting on her bonnet when Penelope burst into her room.

"Who do you think is waiting for us downstairs?" she asked.

The way she spoke made Alisa's heart miss a beat, but Penelope did not wait for her to reply.

"The Earl is driving us himself," she said, "and as the horses are fresh, he says we are not to keep him waiting!"

She slipped out of the room before Alisa could say anything, so she merely picked up the small case in which she had packed her old gown and an apron and ran down the stairs.

Outside the front door, looking magnificent and wearing his top-hat at a slightly raffish angle, was the Earl.

He was driving a different Phaeton from the High-Perched one in which Alisa had travelled the first time she had met him.

This one was lower and drawn by a team of four

perfectly matched jet-black stallions. As he had rightly said, they were fresh and difficult to hold.

The two girls got in beside him, and, having stowed away the box that contained the pots from Mrs. Lulworth, the coachman jumped up behind and they were off.

It was only as they drove out of the Square that Alisa realised that having stepped into the Phaeton first, she was sitting next to the Earl, with Penelope on her other side.

He was concentrating on his horses, and Alisa thought that, perhaps because he was doing something he enjoyed, he did not look so bored as he did at the evening parties.

In fact as he glanced at her there was a faint smile on his lips as he said:

"You look surprised to see me."

"I am more than surprised . . . I am . . . apologetic," Alisa answered. "I had no idea . . . that you would put yourself to the trouble of driving us . . . yourself."

"I thought you would travel quicker, and I am also interested to see where you live, after you were so secretive about it."

Alisa remembered how she had avoided his questions the first time when she had had luncheon with him, and she replied:

"I do not think . . . you will find it very . . . exciting."

As the horses were travelling very fast, it was not possible to have much conversation during the journey, which they achieved in record time.

When they turned in at the ill-kept moss-covered drive and had their first glimpse of the Manor House, Alisa felt that for the moment it looked smaller than it had ever done before.

At the same time, its weather-beaten bricks and gabled roofs were beautiful because it was home.

It was then that the Earl told them what he intended to do.

"I have a friend not far from here who possesses some horses I want to see," he said. "What I suggest is that you do your work and I will return to have a late luncheon with you, after which I hope we shall be able to return to London."

"A . . . late . . . luncheon?" Alisa faltered.

She was thinking that there would be nothing in the house to eat, except possibly some eggs from the chickens which were often very erratic in their laying.

The Earl smiled.

"I have taken the precaution," he said, "of bringing my luncheon and yours with us."

Alisa drew in her breath.

Somehow she felt it was an insult that he should provide his own food. But then she told herself that he was only being practical, and there was nothing she could do but accept gracefully.

"It . . . is very kind of . . . you to be so . . . considerate," she said.

As she spoke, she thought that he knew her feelings, because there was a twinkle she disliked in his eyes and a distinct twist to his lips.

As soon as they were in the house and the Brigstocks had exclaimed with excitement at seeing them, Alisa and Penelope rushed upstairs to change their gowns for the old muslins they had made themselves, then hurried to the Still-Room.

Fortunately, Emily was there, and they sent her into the garden to pick the cucumbers and the lettuce-leaves, while Alisa started mixing the preparations which her mother had left behind her, and Penelope fetched the pots of honey they required.

They worked at a feverish pace.

Alisa was frightened that they would not have finished by the time the Earl returned and he would resent not being able to leave for London as soon as he wished to do.

Gradually, one by one, the pots were filled, and there were only eleven left empty for which they had not enough ingredients.

"They will have to wait for another day," Penelope said firmly. "Mrs. Lulworth is certain to want the strawberry-cream, but when I looked in the garden just now I saw it will be at least three weeks before they are ready."

"I hope we will have to come back to make more cream before that," Alisa replied.

"Actually, I feel in my bones that this will be the last batch we will ever make," Penelope said. "When we are Duchesses we will sweep into Mrs. Lulworth's shop and complain if she does not have a new and different sort of face-cream to offer us!"

Alisa laughed at the idea.

Yet, every time Penelope spoke about their being Duchesses, she had a strange sensation that was almost like a feeling of repugnance.

However, there was no time to think now, and when finally the pots were ready and she had changed her gown again and hurried downstairs, it was to find the Earl in their Sitting-Room, looking at her unfinished painting of the primroses.

"I am . . . sorry if we have . . . kept you . . . waiting," Alisa said breathlessly.

"I was thinking that this would make an excellent pair to the one you have already given me," he replied.

It was the first time he had mentioned the painting she had sent him, and she blushed as she said:

"I thought . . . perhaps you would think it very poor . . . recompence for the very large . . . cheque you gave me . . . but there was . . . nothing in the house which would not look . . . ridiculous beside your . . . treasures."

"I was delighted to have it."

Alisa looked at him, wondering if he was speaking politely or if he meant what he said.

Then Penelope came into the room, crying:

"How could you have brought us such delicious things to eat? Mrs. Brigstock has set them all out in the Dining-Room, and I am so hungry that I cannot wait another moment!"

The Earl had certainly been very considerate, and as they sat down at the table where they had eaten for so many years, Alisa thought that because it was a picnic without servants to wait on them, it was the most enjoyable luncheon they had ever had.

Penelope chattered away, and the Earl, sitting between them in her father's chair, seemed relaxed and amused.

He had taken the precaution of bringing with him his own wines, and the only thing Mrs. Brigstock had to prepare was some hot coffee to end the meal.

"I could not eat another crumb!" Penelope exclaimed at length. "But I deserved every mouthful because Alisa and I have worked this morning at such a speed it would create a record anywhere in the world!"

"I am sure the women who benefit from your labours will appreciate it," the Earl said drily.

"The creams really are good!" Alisa said defiantly.

"I am aware of that," the Earl replied.

She thought he must have seen their beneficial effect on *Madame* Vestris, and she had a feeling that was almost one of pain, which she could not explain to herself.

"I think perhaps . . . you will want to be . . . returning to . . . London," she said.

She thought he might be planning to see *Madame* Vestris at the King's Theatre before her performance, or perhaps he was counting the hours until he could take her out to supper afterwards.

"There is no hurry," the Earl replied, "and Ben has to clear up what is left of our picnic, so I suggest you show me the rest of the house, which incidentally I find very attractive."

"You cannot mean . . . that!" Alisa exclaimed.

"Why not?" the Earl questioned. "Your home is Elizabethan, and it is a period which has always fascinated me."

Alisa's eyes widened.

"As it has me! I love to read about the way Queen Elizabeth lifted the heart of the nation and made us a great country."

"That is exactly what she did," the Earl agreed, "and we need another Queen to do the same thing today."

Alisa looked at him in surprise.

Then she remembered that since the death of Princess Charlotte, the heir to the throne, after the King's brothers who had no sons, would be the little daughter of the Duke of Kent, who was called Victoria.

"I think the Monarch should always be a man," Penelope said, "and the King I would like to have met is Charles II."

"Since he had an eye for a pretty woman, he would certainly have looked at you," the Earl said.

"Why not?" Penelope replied. "In which case I would have become a Duchess in my own right."

The Earl laughed.

"Is that what you are aiming for?"

"Of course!" Penelope replied. "You must have realised by now that Alisa and I are the Gunning Sisters up-to-date, and Elizabeth, the younger one, married two Dukes!"

The Earl lifted his glass and said with a twinkle in his eyes:

"May you succeed in your ambitions."

As he spoke, Alisa suddenly remembered that Maria, the elder sister, had married an Earl.

Quickly she pushed back her chair and rose from the table.

"If you will . . . excuse me," she said, "I have a . . . great many things to . . . see to . . . before we go back to . . . London."

Without looking at the Earl, she hurried from the room.

When they arrived home that evening, Penelope said:

"I must say, Alisa, the Earl was extremely helpful and far nicer than I thought he would be."

"He was very kind," Alisa murmured.

"It is a pity he is not a suitor for your hand," Penelope went on.

Her sister did not reply and she added:

"Major Coombe was telling me that the betting in White's Club is thirty-to-one against anybody catching the Earl as a husband."

"Why is he so . . . determined to remain . . . unmarried?" Alisa asked.

"Apparently he had an unfortunate love-affair when he was very young, and it made him swear that he would remain a bachelor in spite of the fact that his family have been on their knees for years begging him to produce an heir."

"I expect he has . . . plenty of . . . women in his . . . life," Alisa murmured, thinking of *Madame* Vestris.

"Of course there are hundreds of lovely ladies pursuing him!" Penelope agreed. "Major Coombe says they flutter round him like bees round a honey-pot, but the only things he is married to are his horses and his Estate in the country. Has he told you about his house?"

"No."

"It is said to be the most perfect example of Elizabethan architecture in England. That is why he was saying how much he admired Queen Elizabeth."

"I . . . did not . . . know."

"You are so stupid, Alisa!" Penelope complained. "You should ask people about their possessions. You know all men like to talk about themselves, and do not forget your Duke is interested in horses."

Alisa thought she was well aware of that and that she knew so much about the Duke of Exminster's stables that she might almost own them herself.

It was just a passing thought, but it made her feel again that strange repugnance which she could not explain.

She only knew that at the Ball tomorrow night she was quite certain he would be waiting not only to dance with her but to talk to her, and it was something she must avoid at all costs.

Because she and Penelope were so closely attuned to each other, her sister knew what she was thinking.

"Would it not be wonderful, dearest," she said, "if we both got engaged in the same night to a Duke? That would certainly startle the *Beau Monde,* and all those people who have refused to accept us would be falling over themselves."

"Are there such . . . people? I had no . . . idea."

"Oh, Alisa, your head is always in the clouds," Penelope complained. "You know quite well there are dozens of Balls to which we have not been invited, simply because we are either too pretty and put the hostess's plain daughters in the shade, or else because they do not consider us really grand enough to enter their exclusive, stuck-up circle."

Alisa merely looked surprised.

She had been so grateful to the hostesses who had invited them that she had never troubled to think there were others who deliberately refrained from doing so.

She could understand that Penelope, with her ambitions to be important, resented being left out, and if she did marry the Duke of Exminster there was no doubt that every door in London would be open to them both.

At the same time, when she thought of the redfaced Duke of Hawkeshead it seemed impossible to imagine him touching or kissing Penelope, but again she knew it was something she could not say.

"Nor do I want the . . . Duke of Exminster to . . . kiss me," she murmured beneath her breath.

The following day they took the pots to Mrs. Lulworth, who was delighted.

"I have a dozen ladies waiting for these to arrive," she said, "and I only hope they will be as good as the ones you made before."

"Of course they are!" Penelope answered.

"Well, you've fulfilled your obligation, Miss Penelope," Mrs. Lulworth said, "and now you will be delighted to hear that the two new evening-gowns are ready except for a few final touches."

Alisa looked at Penelope accusingly. She realised that her sister had not waited but had already ordered the gowns which she thought they both wanted.

"I should be angry with you, Penelope," she said when she thought Mrs. Lulworth was not listening.

"You ought to be grateful to me!" Penelope retorted. "You will have a new gown to wear tonight and another for the luncheon tomorrow which undoubtedly one of the Dukes will give for us."

It was impossible for Alisa to reply, because Mrs. Lulworth arrived back with two evening-gowns that were practically ready, and to Alisa's consternation two others that required a full fitting.

There were also two day-gowns for each of them. Although she wanted to protest, she felt it was hopeless and she just had to allow Penelope to have her own way.

There were bonnets to choose to wear with the day-gowns, and while they were being tried on she learnt the reason why Mrs. Lulworth was in such a good temper.

It transpired that quite a number of ladies had

come to the shop because they had learnt that Mrs. Lulworth had made the gowns which she and Penelope wore.

The shop-keeper reeled off a list of her new patrons, and added:

"The Marchioness of Conyngham has asked me to attend her tomorrow morning. I'm very grateful to you both."

"We are so glad you are pleased," Penelope replied, "but I hope, Mrs. Lulworth, that your gratitude will show itself in the account you render us."

Alisa knew she would never have been able to say such a thing, but Mrs. Lulworth merely smiled and said:

"I thought you wouldn't have missed saying something like that, Miss Penelope, and I'll remember what I owe to you."

"Good!" Penelope exclaimed. "In which case I will have another bonnet, but in a different colour, to go with that last gown!"

When they arrived back in Islington Square there were more bouquets of flowers and more invitations.

Only as they were going upstairs to their bedrooms to start changing for the evening did Alisa say:

"Have you written to the Earl to thank him for taking us to the country yesterday?"

"I have not had time," Penelope prevaricated, "and anyway, I thought that you could write for both of us."

"I wrote and Henderson posted the letter for me," Alisa said, "but as it was your idea in the first place, I think you ought to write too."

"I doubt if he will notice whether I do or I do not," Penelope replied, "and I expect anyway he would prefer a letter from *Madame* Vestris."

Alisa started.

"What have you . . . heard about *Madame* Vestris . . . and the . . . Earl?" she questioned.

"Somebody, I think it was Major Coombe, told me

that she had said at some party or another that she judged her success in London by the fact that she had captured the British public and, what was far more difficult, the Earl of Keswick!"

Alisa did not reply.

She merely went into her bedroom and wondered why her new gown lying waiting for her on her bed looked so unattractive that she might just as well wear one of her old muslins.

Penelope had arranged that as the Duke was giving a party for them, he should also convey them to Hawkeshead House in Park Lane.

By the time they were dressed, a very impressive-looking carriage with the Duke's coat-of-arms emblazoned on the doors was waiting for them outside.

"You look lovely, dearest," Alisa exclaimed when she saw Penelope wearing her new gown.

Once again it was white, but there were magnolias round the hem and round the top of the bodice which revealed Penelope's white shoulders.

She wore a wreath of the same flowers on her golden hair, and Alisa knew that no tiara, however valuable, could have been more becoming.

Penelope looked like a water-maiden stepping out from a silver stream, and there was something very young, spring-like, and lovely about her which Alisa did not realise was echoed in herself.

Her gown was also white, but instead of the rather exotic magnolias it was decorated with small bunches of snow-drops, and they nestled in the softness of the tulle that encircled her shoulders like a white cloud.

If Penelope looked spring-like, Alisa was like Persephone, bringing light back to the world after a dark winter.

She was certainly not as sensational as her sister, and yet it would be hard for any man who saw her not to look again and not to find it difficult afterwards to see anybody else.

She only thought that Penelope looked beautiful,

and she was content to follow behind her instead of leading the way as she should have done, being the elder.

"Be careful your wrap does not crush your gown," Penelope admonished her.

Then, having said good-night to their aunt, they hurried down the stairs to where the Duke's carriage was waiting.

Only as the horses moved off and they sat back against the comfortable, heavily padded seat did Alisa say hesitatingly:

"If the Duke does . . . ask you tonight to . . . marry him, dearest, please think . . . seriously before you . . . accept him."

"What is there to think about?" Penelope asked bluntly.

"Whether you will be . . . happy with him. After all, he will be your husband and you will be . . . together for the . . . rest of your . . . lives."

"Can you imagine always having a carriage like this to drive everywhere?" Penelope asked. "To be hostess of his house in Park Lane and his Castle in Kent? I believe too that he has half-a-dozen others in other parts of England."

"It is not . . . only what he . . . owns, but what he is."

"A Duke!" Penelope exclaimed irrepressibly.

It was hopeless, Alisa decided, to try to explain what she wanted to say.

She knew only that she wanted Penelope's happiness more than anything else in the world, but she could not help thinking it would be very difficult to be happy with the Duke of Hawkeshead.

Then she found herself thinking of the man Penelope called "her Duke" because she thought the same applied in her case.

What did it matter when they were alone together whether he was the Duke of Exminster or just plain

"Mr."? They would be husband and wife, and he would also be the father of her children.

Quite suddenly Alisa knew that she could not marry the Duke, whatever Penelope might say.

She felt, because she was nervous of seeing him again, that she wanted to stop the coach and get out and run back to Islington. Or, better still, to return to the country so that the Duke would not know where she was and would be unable to find her.

Then she told herself that she was being very stupid.

Perhaps he would not propose to her. Perhaps like the Earl, he had no intention of marrying anybody and was only being charming in sending her flowers because it was a fashionable thing to do.

But her intuition told her something else.

It was only a question of time before the Duke proposed, and unless she was to be faced with Penelope's reproaches and anger, she would have to accept him.

I cannot do so . . . I cannot! she thought despairingly.

She felt as if the comfortable carriage were taking her not to a Ball but to the guillotine.

CHAPTER SIX

Looking round the Ball-Room at Hawkeshead House, Alisa thought it was the most attractive of all those in which they had danced.

In fact, the whole house was extremely impressive, and from the moment they had entered through the front door she had felt that Penelope was thinking what a perfect background it would be for her as a Duchess.

She thought the double staircase was in itself like a stage-set for a woman to look her best, as she ascended to where the Duke was receiving his guests with his mother beside him.

The Dowager's jewels, including a huge tiara that was almost like a crown on her head, seemed to be a glittering inducement to every girl who saw it. But Alisa thought they would also have to include the Duke in their consideration.

The way His Grace received Penelope was extremely revealing.

He was looking, Alisa thought, even more red-faced and unprepossessing than usual.

She tried to feel charitable towards him because he might become her brother-in-law, but she noticed that his cravat was already wilting, one of his decorations was crooked, and his silk stocking had a run in it.

Perhaps he needs a wife to look after him, she thought, and was glad that it would not be her task.

The Reception-Room was decorated with orchids and lilies, but the Ball-Room, obviously as a compliment to Penelope, was a bower of pink roses.

All along one side of the house there were long French windows that opened out onto a garden which as usual was lit by Chinese lanterns and fairy-lights.

Tonight they were all pink, and Alisa thought the Duke was certainly declaring his intenions to all the world.

She did not say anything to Penelope but she saw that there was a gleam of excitement in her sister's eyes, and when the Duke invited her to be his partner for the first dance, she knew that the Dowagers seated round the Ball-Room were already aware who would be the new Duchess.

Alisa noticed too that there were many different faces from those she had seen at the other parties they had attended.

She had an idea that the Duke and his mother moved in a society loyal to the old King and Queen which was more sedate than the fashionable *Beau Monde* who had circled round the Prince Regent when he lived at Carlton House.

Now, Alisa thought, they would certainly wish to be in favour with George IV and undoubtedly would be only too eager to grace the Coronation in July.

"What are you thinking about?" asked the Duke of Exminster, who was partnering her in the dance.

"The Coronation."

He laughed.

"Does anybody think of anything else at the moment?"

"You are not looking forward to it?"

"Most certainly not! As far as I am concerned it will be a long-drawn-out bore! It is only women, and of course the King, who enjoy all that dressing up and the endless ceremonial."

As the Duke spoke, his eyes were on Alisa's hair, and it suddenly struck her that he might be thinking that the Exminster strawberry-leaves would become her.

Quickly she looked away from him, and as she did so, she saw the King arriving, accompanied by the Marchioness of Conyngham and behind them several younger men, one of whom was the Earl of Keswick.

She felt her heart leap in an uncomfortable manner, but she could not help staring at him, realising that as usual he was looking bored and cynical.

The King, however, was greeting the Duchess of Hawkeshead effusively, and with the Duchess on his right and the Marchioness on his left he sat down on a sofa which stood on a raised dais, from where he could watch the dancing.

The gentlemen in attendance ranged themselves behind him, and because Alisa had no wish for the Earl to see her, she said quickly to the Duke:

"It is very hot, shall we go into the garden?"

"I think that is a very sensible suggestion," he replied.

They walked through one of the open windows, and the pink lanterns glowed against the dark branches of the trees while the stars overhead were just coming out.

It was certainly very romantic, but as she thought of it Alisa remembered that she had no wish to be alone with the Duke.

However, it was too late to retrace her steps, and she realised that he was leading her away from the lights of the house. As usual when a Ball was given where there was a garden, there were little alcoves and secluded seats where two people could talk intimately.

Alisa stopped.

"We must not go too . . . far," she said. "I have not seen Penelope for . . . some time."

"I am certain your sister can look after herself."

"As my aunt is not with us this evening," Alisa replied, "I have to chaperone Penelope, who is younger than I."

"I can think of a better way for you to do that," the Duke replied.

As he spoke he took Alisa by the arm and led her from the lighted path over the lawn to where there was a seat under an ash tree.

Alisa was just about to say that she would like to go back to the Ball-Room when the music stopped, and those who had been dancing came pouring out through the lighted windows into the garden.

There was nothing she could do but sit down on the seat the Duke had chosen, and she saw apprehensively that there were no other seats near them. They were in the shadow of the boughs and to all intents and purposes alone.

Frantically she tried to think of how she could prevent him from saying what she was sure was in his mind, but while she was still trying to find the words, the Duke said:

"You are much too young, Alisa, to have to look after anybody, but if you wish to look after your sister more competently than you can do at the moment, I suggest the best way to do so would be to marry me!"

For a moment there was silence while Alisa tried to grasp the fact that she had received the proposal which she had been anticipating he might make, and which Penelope had been insistent she should accept.

Her head felt as if it were filled with cotton-wool, her throat seemed constricted, and she could do nothing but twist her fingers together.

"I know we have not known each other for very long," the Duke went on, "but from the first moment I sat beside you at dinner I knew you were not only beautiful but clever and everything I wanted in my wife. We will be very happy."

The way he spoke told Alisa that he had already assumed that she would accept his proposal. In fact, for him it was inconceivable that any woman would refuse him, let alone somebody of no social importance.

With an effort, and in a voice that did not sound like her own, Alisa said:

"I am deeply . . . honoured . . . Your Grace . . . that you should ask me to be your . . . wife . . . but as you say . . . we have known each other . . . only a very short . . . time."

"I have known you long enough to know that you will make me a very happy man," the Duke replied, "and as the King is here this evening, I would like him to be the very first to know of our engagement."

"Please . . . please," Alisa said frantically, "we are

. . . not engaged . . . not yet . . . you must let me . . . think. I have been in London only a short while . . . and could not . . . consider . . . marriage with anybody . . . unless I knew them . . . well."

She did not look at the Duke, but she was aware that he was surprised at what she had said and his eyes were on her face.

"I am sure," he said after a moment, "that you would wish to be married before the Coronation. The Duchess of Exminster has a traditional role to play in such ceremonies, and I know that no Duchess could be more beautiful than you."

"Thank you . . . Your Grace," Alisa said in a very small voice. "I am . . . deeply sensible of the . . . honour it is for me to receive such a . . . proposal . . . but I . . . must think about it . . . I must be sure . . . that I will be able to . . . make you happy."

"I am quite sure of that," the Duke said complacently.

"Then could we both . . . think it . . . over for a few . . . weeks?"

"I have nothing to think about," he replied. "I want you, Alisa, and although I know you are young and perhaps it frightens you to think you will have to play such an important part in the Social World, I will look after you and you need not be afraid of making mistakes."

"You are . . . very kind," Alisa said breathlessly, "but I must . . . think about it . . . I must . . . be sure before I give you my answer."

There was a pause before the Duke replied, and Alisa knew he was surprised that she should prevaricate and not accept him immediately as he had expected.

"I am sure enough for both of us," he said at length.

He put out his hand to take hers.

"I promise you we will be very happy together, and

tomorrow or the next day I will take you to meet some of my relatives."

The touch of his hand on hers gave Alisa again a feeling of repugnance that she had felt before.

Quickly she took her hand away and rose to her feet.

"I must go and . . . find Penelope . . . Your Grace," she said, and hurried away from him before he could follow her.

She sped across the lawn towards a different window from the one through which she had come with the Duke, and she found when she reached it that it did not lead into the Ball-Room but to a Sitting-Room at the side of it.

It was empty, but there was a door opening out of it into a room in which she could see card-tables and a number of gentlemen either playing or standing about with a glass in their hands.

She had discovered at the Balls they had already attended in London that there was always a room set aside where the older men who disliked dancing could gamble with one another and drink in comfort.

There was also a door which led to the passage, and as Alisa went towards it she heard a gentleman in the Card-Room say to another:

"Where's our host? I have not seen him for some time."

"Finding another bottle," a voice answered, "and I expect as usual he has lost count by now."

There was a burst of laughter at this, and just as Alisa was about to leave the Sitting-Room the gentleman who had spoken first said:

"I think he is more likely to be ravishing that attractive creature with whom he was dancing earlier in the evening!"

Alisa drew in her breath.

It was insulting that he should refer to Penelope in such a manner, and she thought, from the way he slightly slurred his words, that he also had been drinking.

Now she knew she must find Penelope and see if she was all right.

She did not know why, but when she had made Penelope an excuse for leaving the Duke, she had positively felt in some strange way she had often felt before that Penelope did need her.

Because they were so close, they often thought the same things and would laugh about it.

"We might be twins," Penelope had said more than once.

"I think really it is because we have always lived such a secluded life together in the countryside," Alisa had answered.

Now she was sure Penelope wanted her, and she walked down a corridor which contained some very fine pieces of furniture and a great number of valuable paintings.

Alisa had no idea where she was going, but she felt that if the Duke was proposing to Penelope, as was likely, he would not have taken her to the garden but to some quiet room where they could be alone.

There were a number of Sitting-Rooms on the ground floor, all of which were discreetly lit and decorated with flowers.

As she peeped into them, some were empty but in others there were couples, obviously talking intimately, and in one she saw two people kissing passionately, which made her hurriedly move away.

She had almost reached the end of the passage which seemed to run the whole length of the house when she saw somebody in white come through a door and realised that she had found whom she was seeking. It was Penelope.

She hurried towards her, seeing as she did so that there was a large notice on the door marked: PRIVATE, and Penelope was shutting it behind her.

Then as she turned and saw Alisa standing only a few feet away, she gave a little cry.

At the same time, Alisa saw the expression on her face and exclaimed:

"What is the matter? What has happened?"

She could see that Penelope was trembling.

"What has upset you, dearest?" she asked, as her sister did not speak.

"I—I have killed—the Duke!"

For a moment Alisa felt that she must have misunderstood, but there was a stricken look in Penelope's eyes and her face was so pale that it was obvious something terrifying had occurred.

"What do you . . . mean, dearest?" she managed to ask.

"I have—killed him!" Penelope answered. "He is—dead—in that—room!"

As she spoke she stretched out her hands blindly, and Alisa put her arm round her.

She saw an open door beside them and through it another Sitting-Room with shaded lights and decorated with flowers, and it was empty.

She gently pulled Penelope into the room and closed the door behind them.

"What are you saying?" she asked. "Did you . . . really say . . . you had . . . killed the Duke?"

"After he asked me to marry him—he tried to—kiss me," Penelope answered, "and when I resisted him—he forced me down on a—sofa."

She made a sound that was almost like that of an animal in pain as she said:

"He was—horrible—beastly—and I—hated him!"

"Then what happened?" Alisa asked, as Penelope seemed unable to say any more.

"I—escaped from him, but when I tried to—get out of the room he—stopped me."

She paused before she could go on:

"It was—then that I realised he had had too much to—drink, and he was—behaving like an—animal!"

"Oh, dearest!"

"I picked up the—poker, and when he—rushed at me—again—I pushed it—hard into his—stomach."

She held her breath as if it was frightening to remember what she had done. Then before Alisa could speak she continued:

"He—doubled up for a moment—then I hit him and hit him—on top of the head. He fell down and I went on—hitting him!"

"Oh . . . how . . . could you!" Alisa breathed.

"I wanted to—hurt him. Then I—realised that he was—dead!"

Alisa put her arms round her to hold her, and Penelope asked:

"What—shall we do? I—cannot tell—anybody about it but—you."

Because Penelope sounded so helpless and so unlike herself, Alisa found a strength that she had never had before.

"Somebody must help us," she said. "You stay here, dearest, until I come back."

She felt as if Penelope hardly heard her, and she added:

"I will lock you in. Then you will not be disturbed by anybody. Do not be frightened. I will be back in a few minutes!"

"I am—frightened!" Penelope said. "Oh, Alisa, I am—very—frightened!"

"I will be as quick as I can."

Penelope did not reply. She merely put her hands over her face, and because she seemed suddenly small and pathetic, Alisa moved to the door with a determination that was very unlike herself.

She closed and locked the door, then holding the key in her hand she ran down the passage.

She knew there was one person who could help her now, and as she went in search of the Earl it flashed through her mind that they might have to hide somewhere or perhaps even leave England.

She thought that the Earl would be with the King in the Ball-Room, but as the music grew louder she passed a room in which there were a number of people drinking champagne, and there she saw him.

He was standing talking to Major Coombe, and, as there was no sign of the King, he was apparently for the moment free of his duties.

Without thinking of anything except that he was there and he must help them, Alisa went to his side.

The Earl was just saying something to the Major when, seeing Alisa at his elbow, he stopped in the middle of a sentence and looked at her in surprise.

"I must . . . speak to . . . you," Alisa said in a voice that was barely above a whisper but with a distinct tremor in it.

The Earl realised at once that something untoward had happened, for her eyes were stricken as Penelope's had been.

He put down the glass he was holding in his hand and moved a few steps towards an empty corner of the room.

"What is it?" he asked.

For a moment Alisa felt it was impossible to tell him, impossible for the words to come to her lips. Then, so quietly he could only just hear, she said:

"P—Penelope has . . . killed the . . . D—Duke!"

The Earl was still for a moment, and there was a question in his eyes, as if he thought he had either misunderstood what Alisa had said or she was playing some joke on him.

Then, as if he was convinced not so much by her words as by the look on her face, he said quietly:

"We will walk slowly from the room as if nothing unusual has happened."

Then in a voice that could be heard by many of the people standing near them he said:

"I am finding, Miss Wynton, that it is extremely hot in here, and I am not surprised that some people are feeling faint. Let us try to find somewhere cooler."

Then as she took a few steps beside him to cross the room to the door, the Earl said to Major Coombe, whom they had left standing alone:

"Why do you not come with us, James? I have something interesting to tell you."

The Major put down his glass.

"Then I shall certainly accompany you," he replied.

They walked at what seemed to Alisa a funereal pace, and only when they were outside the room and had moved away from several groups of people talking in the passage did the Earl ask:

"Where is Penelope?"

"I have . . . locked her in a . . . room where she . . . will not be . . . disturbed."

"That was very sensible of you," he replied.

They walked back the way Alisa had come, and now when they were free of the guests and there was nobody within earshot, Major Coombe asked:

"What is the matter? Where are we going?"

"I want your help, James," the Earl replied, and the Major said no more.

They reached the end of the long passage, and as Alisa saw the Earl's eyes on the room marked PRIVATE, she knew there was no need to explain to him where the Duke was lying.

As they stopped she felt that her hands were trembling so violently that she would be unable to open the door of the room where she had left Penelope, and without speaking she held the key out to the Earl.

He opened the door and as she walked inside he shut it behind her and she heard the key turn in the lock.

Penelope was sitting where she had left her. She was not crying, only staring blindly ahead of her in a manner of utter despondency and despair.

She went to the sofa and took Penelope's hand in hers.

"I have brought the Earl," she said, "and I am sure he will help us. Perhaps we can hide somewhere or go abroad, but whatever it may be, he is the only person who can arrange it."

"I was—wrong to—hit him so—hard." Penelope said, "but I was—frightened."

"I can understand that," Alisa said, "but you say he asked you to marry him?"

"He said—he was *going* to marry me," Penelope corrected. "Then he—grabbed me, and his lips hurt my cheek—and I knew he was—horrible and I—could not let him—touch me!"

Alisa put her arms round her sister to hold her close against her.

"He was—rough and beastly!" Penelope was saying. "And I wanted to—get away—but he was big and—strong and I thought I—would not be able to—escape."

"You must not think about it," Alisa said. "It will not do any good."

"I am—sorry, Alisa, very sorry—I have spoilt—everything for you."

"There is no need to be sorry, not as far as I am concerned," Alisa answered. "I love you, Penelope, and it would not matter what you did, I should still go on loving you."

"Oh—Alisa—!"

Now the tears were in Penelope's eyes, and as she wiped them away Alisa thought she was suffering from shock and should have something to drink. But there was nothing in the room, and the only thing they could do was to sit and wait.

She could not think why the Earl was taking so long.

It would be impossible to conceal the Duke, and once he had confirmed that he was dead, he should be concerning himself with Penelope.

It was agonising to have to wait, not knowing what was happening, and Alisa in fact would have gone in search of the Earl if he had not locked her in.

Now Penelope was just staring in front of her, her

hands hanging limply at her sides, and Alisa could think of nothing more to say.

She could only sit listening and waiting for the door to open and the Earl to join them.

Then suddenly there was the sound of the key turning in the lock, and he was there.

He walked through the door and for a moment she could not look at his face and felt afraid.

Then as she rose a little unsteadily to her feet, Penelope also rose to hers and gave a cry that seemed to echo round the silent room.

"Jimmy!" she exclaimed. "Oh, Jimmy!"

To Alisa's amazement, she ran towards Major Coombe, who had followed the Earl in through the door.

She flung herself against him and his arms went round her, holding her close against him.

"It is all right, my darling," he said. "He is not dead."

Penelope burst into tears, and as she did so Major Coombe bent his head and his lips were against her cheek.

Alisa stood staring at them in sheer astonishment until the Earl said quietly:

"What James has just said is true and the Duke is not dead, although Penelope has certainly been very rough with him!"

To her surprise there was just a hint of laughter in his voice, and as she looked up at him in a bewildered fashion, he said in an authoritative tone:

"Now, all of you listen to me."

Penelope raised her head from Major Coombe's shoulder.

"I—I thought I would be—hanged," she whispered.

"Nobody will hang you," he said. "I will make sure of that."

There were tears on Penelope's face, but now there was a light in her eyes and she looked, Alisa thought, very different from the stricken helpless girl who a few seconds before had been sitting beside her on the sofa.

"I love you!" Major Coombe said. "I will look after you and see that nothing like this ever happens again."

As he finished speaking he kissed her on the lips and Penelope put her arm round his neck and held him close to her.

Alisa was aware that the Earl was watching them with an undoubted twinkle in his eye. Then the Major said:

"We will talk about ourselves a little later, but now we have to listen to what Landon has planned."

Obediently Penelope looked towards the Earl, and Alisa in surprise realised that she was not in the least embarrassed that he had watched her being kissed.

Instead, she groped for her handkerchief, and when the Major handed her his, she gave him a beguiling smile before she wiped her cheeks.

"Now, attend to what I have to say," the Earl remarked. "James and I have made it appear that while the Duke was alone in his private Sitting-Room, a thief broke in through the window and assaulted him, robbing him of his watch, his jewellery, and any money he might have had on him. So now none of us can be implicated in any way in any crime."

He paused before he went on:

"You, Penelope, and James will go back to the Ball-Room to dance so that everybody can see you, and Alisa and I will go into the garden to dispose of the Duke's possessions in a flower-bed where they will ultimately be recovered."

"That is a very—clever plan!" Penelope exclaimed. "But are you—quite certain he is not—dead?"

"He will undoubtedly live to enjoy a great many more bottles of wine!" the Earl said drily. "Now come along, we cannot waste time here when we should be seen in a different part of the house."

"I do not know how to thank you," Penelope said.

She looked at Major Coombe and asked:

"Do I—look all right? Is my hair tidy?"

"You look lovely!" he answered.

There was a deep note in his voice which Alisa thought revealed his feelings very clearly.

"Walk slowly and look happy," the Earl commanded.

He opened the door as he spoke, and Penelope went out first. She was holding Major Coombe by the hand, and as they walked down the passage ahead of Alisa and the Earl they made no attempt to release each other.

It was impossible for Alisa to speak, because she found that coming back from the depths of despair to find it was not as serious as she had feared had left her suspended, as it were, in mid-air.

She could only feel a surge of gratitude toward the Earl, and at the same time she felt as if she wanted to burst into tears and hide her face against his shoulder as Penelope had done with Major Coombe.

For a moment or two she could not adjust herself to the fact that Penelope had run to the Major as if she were a homing-pigeon returning to safety, that he had kissed her and that Penelope had put her arms round him to hold him close.

So that is whom she loves! Alisa thought, and found it impossible to understand why, loving James Coombe, she had been ready to accept the Duke.

However, she was not allowed to pursue her own thoughts, for the Earl was speaking to her so that as they mingled with the other people in the corridor it should appear that they were behaving in an entirely normal manner.

"I do not know whether Exminster told you earlier in the evening about his horse *Victorious?*" the Earl was saying.

"Y—yes . . . he did," Alisa managed to reply after a pause.

"*Victorious* is a very fine animal, but I would like to show you my *Apollo* who is his accredited rival," the Earl went on. "Whenever they run together they are always made equal favourites in the race, which is something that happens very rarely in the Racing World."

"No . . . I suppose it is . . . unusual!" Alisa forced herself to reply.

They reached the garden, and now as the Earl turned to walk towards the walls which were closest to the private Sitting-Room where the Duke lay injured, she knew what he was about to do.

She was not mistaken, for he took from his pocket a handkerchief which he had tied in a knot and which contained what the imagined robber was supposed to have stolen from the Duke.

He glanced over his shoulder to see that there were no people near, then tossed it at the foot of an outside wall.

Then he deliberately trampled down some of the flowers that filled the bed in front of it, and as soon as he had done so, he took Alisa by the arm and walked her away to another part of the garden.

"That was . . . very clever of . . . you," was all she could manage to say when she could speak.

"It was the most sensible thing to do in the circumstances."

"I am sure the . . . Duke should have . . . medical attention."

"You had better go back to the Ball-Room," the Earl replied. "I intend to deal with that now, and then I imagine you and Penelope will wish to go home."

"Yes, please . . . and as quickly as . . . possible," Alisa said, "I could . . . not dance any . . . more."

She spoke in a sudden panic, as if she was afraid she might have to dance with the Duke of Exminster again.

"Leave everything to me," the Earl said.

As they walked towards the Ball-Room they could

see Penelope and Major Coombe standing just inside the door.

The music had stopped and the dancers once again were moving into the garden or going in search of the Supper-Room.

The Earl walked into the room and up to Penelope.

"Your sister has a headache," he said loudly enough to be overheard, "and I think it would be a good idea if you two had an early night."

"Yes, of course," Penelope agreed, and turned to Alisa to say:

"I am sorry, dearest. It must be the heat."

"Yes . . . of course. It has been very . . . hot," Alisa agreed.

"I am just going to explain to His Majesty that I am escorting you home," the Earl said.

Then as a servant passed him he said:

"Will you find His Grace? I think His Majesty will soon wish to leave."

"I will tell His Grace," the servant replied.

The Earl walked away in a different direction, and Major Coombe said:

"Let us go into the Hall and send a footman to get your wraps."

They waited in the Hall for only a few minutes before the Earl joined them.

"I found the Duchess with His Majesty," he said, "and I explained, Alisa, that you were not feeling well and I made excuses for both of you."

Alisa started as he spoke, realising that she had forgotten that the Duchess was acting as hostess for her son and they should have thanked her for the Ball.

"It is all right," the Earl said before she could speak. "I made out that you were worse than you are, being sure that otherwise people would think it strange that you should wish to leave the dance which had obviously been given in Penelope's honour."

There was an undoubted touch of sarcasm in the last words, but Alisa realised that Penelope was not listening but was only looking at James Coombe with starry eyes.

Driving back in the Earl's comfortable carriage, Alisa thought it very strange that she and the Earl sat in the back seat side by side while Penelope and James sat opposite them.

Quite unashamedly the Major put his arm round Penelope and she laid her head against his shoulder, as if she felt that was where she wanted to be and there was no need to pretend in front of her sister or the Earl.

They had driven some way from Hawkeshead House before Major Coombe said:

"If we are to honeymoon before the Coronation, when I shall be on duty, we will have to get married immediately!"

Alisa gasped, but Penelope answered:

"I can be ready tomorrow."

Major Coombe laughed.

"I shall need just a little longer than that, my darling. And I think it would be polite for you to meet my mother before we are actually married."

"Yes, of course," Penelope agreed, "but nothing seems to matter except that you love me."

"I will make you sure of that when we are married," James Coombe said, "and it will not be in more than three or four days' time."

Penelope gave a sigh of happiness and moved a little nearer to him, while Alisa felt as if the world had turned upside-down and she could hardly believe what was happening.

As if to make sure she was not dreaming, she looked towards the Earl and saw that he was not looking at Penelope and James Coombe but at her.

It was impossible to see the expression on his face in the lights which occasionally flashed through the carriage-window, but even so, the mere fact that he was looking at her made Alisa feel shy.

Penelope was whispering something in James Coombe's ear, and as she did so he was holding her close against him with both his arms round her.

The fact that they had forgotten everybody except themselves made Alisa feel alone and a little lost.

She and Penelope had always been so close to each other that now she could hardly believe that while she had spoken of him scornfully, Penelope had really loved James Coombe without even telling her.

There was no doubt that she was in love, and Alisa knew her too well not to be aware that there was a new note in her voice that had never been there before.

She could feel too a vibration coming from Penelope which was also new, and which she knew was one of happiness and love.

That is how I want to feel, she thought, *and I will never, never marry anybody unless I do feel that way.*

She decided that tomorrow she would write to the Duke of Exminster and thank him for his proposal and say once again that she was deeply honoured that he should wish her to be his wife, but she would make it quite clear that it was something that would never happen.

I want to be in love, she thought.

She felt that only when she could cry out as Penelope had done at the sight of James, and run towards him knowing that he was everything she wanted in the whole world, would she accept a man as her husband.

The horses were slowing down and she was aware that they were turning into Islington Square.

It was then, as if he knew what she was feeling, that the Earl reached out and Alisa felt his hand take hers.

The strength and warmth of his fingers were comforting, and as they tightened they aroused in her the same feeling that she had felt when he had kissed her.

She could feel the rapture of it moving through her body, as it had done then, and she knew as it rose from her breast into her throat, then to her lips, that she was in love, completely and hopelessly in love, with the Earl of Keswick.

CHAPTER SEVEN

Alisa awoke early after spending most of the night lying awake and thinking about the Earl.

She realised that her love was hopeless for if he had made up his mind that he would remain a bachelor, nothing and nobody would change it.

She could understand now why the women he had in his life were like *Madame* Vestris or occupied a position such as he had offered her.

At all the parties at which she had seen him, he had never seemed to be interested in any particular woman, and although the sophisticated beauties who were married clustered round him, he continued to look bored and cynical in the way to which she had grown accustomed.

"I love him!" she whispered to herself.

She knew that it would bring her no happiness to stay in London and go to parties and Balls when all she wanted was to be alone with him.

When she was called, she rose and dressed before she went to her sister's room, hoping that after all the dramatic happenings of the night before, Penelope would sleep late.

But she was awake, sitting up in bed and looking exquisitely lovely with her fair hair falling over her shoulders and her eyes shining.

"I have had a letter from Jimmy!" she cried before Alisa could speak.

"What does he say?"

"That he loves me, and that we will be married just as quickly as he can arrange it. Oh, Alisa, I am so happy!"

"I am glad, dearest, but I had no idea that you even liked Major Coombe!"

"I tried to hate him because I felt differently about him than about any other man I had ever met, and I was determined to be a Duchess!"

Penelope laughed, and it was a very attractive sound.

"How could I have been so stupid? How could a Duchess's coronet be as thrilling as Jimmy's kisses?"

Alisa could understand only too well, and she sat down on the edge of the bed to say:

"I am so very very happy for you, dearest! But please, we cannot afford a great many expensive gowns for your trousseau, because it would take me a long time to pay for them."

"What does it matter what I wear?" Penelope asked. "Jimmy thinks I look lovely in anything!"

Alisa stared at her sister, remembering what a fuss she had made about having new gowns. At the same time, she was apprehensive as to how much they still owed to Mrs. Lulworth.

She was just about to mention it when Penelope said:

"Jimmy has arranged for us to have luncheon with the Earl today, then he and I are going alone to buy my engagement-ring."

"I am sure you must be careful not to choose anything very expensive," Alisa said warningly.

Penelope nodded.

"I have already thought of that. I know Jimmy finds it difficult as it is, being in such an expensive Regiment, and that is why, like the Earl, he decided he would never get married."

Alisa smiled.

"He certainly seemed very eager to do so last night."

"He loves me," Penelope said in a rapt little voice.

Then as if she forced herself to think sensibly she said:

"We may have to live in a cottage, but I know that you will always help me, and when you are married to the Duke, at least I can wear the gowns for which you have no further use."

Alisa stiffened.

"Jimmy says that he is one of the richest Dukes and spends thousands a year on his horses, so he is not likely to be cheese-paring where you are concerned."

It was impossible for Alisa to reply, and Penelope went on:

"Perhaps, dearest, if you ask him very, very nicely he will give me my wedding-gown. I would like that to be beautiful for Jimmy's sake."

Alisa looked at her sister and said in a faltering voice:

"I . . . I have no . . . wish to marry the . . . Duke."

Penelope stared at her for a moment. Then she asked:

"Are you crazy? Of course you must marry him! He is not a drunken brute like the Duke of Hawkeshead, and although he is a lot older than you, everybody speaks of him warmly and says he is kind and considerate to his family and those he employs."

Alisa got down off the bed to walk across the room to stand at the window.

Penelope watched her go with a puzzled expression. Then she said:

"Please, dearest Alisa, be sensible about this. I know you have been much more idealistic about love than I have been until now, but there is not another Jimmy! There could not be, and you will make such a beautiful Duchess of Exminster."

"I do not want to talk about it," Alisa said, and walked out of the room, leaving Penelope alone.

Driving in the Earl's comfortable carriage which he had sent to fetch them to Keswick House for luncheon, Alisa was aware that Penelope was longing to return to the subject of her marriage to the Duke of Exminster.

She knew her sister so well that she was aware that she was feeling a little embarrassed but at the same time was determined that Alisa's future should be settled as well as her own.

She began to speak of how fond Jimmy was of riding and how hard it was for him not to be able to afford fine horse-flesh of his own.

"The Earl is very kind to him and lends him his hunters and even his Phaeton," Penelope said, "but it would be far easier for him to borrow from a brother-in-law."

Alisa did not protest, and Penelope went on to speak of the many advantages there would be for both her and Jimmy if Alisa was married to the Duke.

Because Alisa had always allowed Penelope to take the lead in anything they did, she felt as if her will was being sapped away and she would not have the strength to go on fighting.

She had already written the letter she had planned to the Duke, and now she had it in her reticule, intending to post it after she had made it clear to Penelope that she would not accept him as her husband.

"The one thing I have always longed to do," Penelope was saying, "is to wear a tiara, and as the Exminster jewels are famous, I know, dearest, that you will sometimes let me borrow one of yours."

Alisa took a deep breath.

"Penelope," she said, "I cannot . . . I will . . . not . . ."

As she spoke the words, the carriage came to a standstill and she realized that they were outside the Earl's house in Berkeley Square.

"We are here!" Penelope cried excitedly. "And I am sure Jimmy will have come off parade by now."

The carriage-door was opened and she jumped out before Alisa and hurried up the steps as if she could not wait another moment before she saw the man she loved.

James Coombe was with the Earl in the Library, and as soon as the two sisters were announced, Penelope ran towards him with a little cry.

"Thank you for my lovely letter which I found when I woke up this morning!" she said. "I have read and read it until I know it by heart."

James Coombe smiled at her and raised her hand to his lips.

Alisa thought that Penelope in ignoring their host was being rude, and hastily she curtseyed to the Earl.

"Good-morning, Alisa!" he said. "I hope you slept well."

"Yes . . . thank . . . you."

She tried to speak calmly, but she felt as if he must be aware that her heart was beating violently in her breast, and it was difficult to look at him.

"I have good news for you."

"What is it?"

"I was informed this morning by several of my callers that our host last night had been savagely assaulted by a thief who entered his private Sitting-Room and, having knocked him unconscious, robbed him!"

Alisa clasped her hands together and found it difficult to breathe.

"Then an hour ago," the Earl went on, "I sent a servant to enquire as to how His Grace was faring, and I was informed that the doctors are satisfied with his condition, which is not dangerous, although he is heavily bruised."

Alisa gave a deep sigh of relief. Then she asked in a low voice:

"You do not . . . think that he will . . . tell anybody who . . . hit him?"

It was difficult to ask the question, and the Earl smiled before he replied:

"I think no man would admit to being knocked unconscious by a woman, especially one who is so delicately made and beautiful as your sister."

"You are . . . sure about . . . that?"

"Quite sure, so stop worrying!"

It was an order, and Alisa said meekly:

"I will . . . try."

Jimmy told Penelope the same news, and when they went in to luncheon, Alisa thought everybody seemed to be in extraordinarily good spirits.

There was champagne to celebrate Penelope and James's engagement, and as the meal finished the Earl lifted his glass and toasted them.

"To your happiness!" he said. "And may your future be as golden as it seems now!"

"That is a lovely toast!" Penelope cried. "And you know that everything that has happened to us is all thanks to you."

The Earl raised his eye-brows, and she said:

"I have told Jimmy that it was your fifty pounds that made us able to buy beautiful gowns in which we could call on the Marchioness of Conyngham."

As she spoke, Alisa made a little sound because she was upset, and Penelope said quickly:

"I am sorry, dearest, I should have asked you first if I might tell Jimmy, but I cannot have any secrets from him. Forgive me."

"It is all . . . right," Alisa answered.

It was impossible, however, for her to look at James Coombe, thinking that Penelope must have explained why the Earl had given her such a large sum of money, which was something she had hoped nobody would ever know.

As if to save her from being embarrassed, the Earl said:

"As I understand that Penelope said at the time it was a gift from the gods, and so we must therefore thank them, because in some obscure way of their own, which undoubtedly the Duke has found extremely regrettable, it has brought you two together."

"Of course, a gift from the gods!" Penelope exclaimed, "and the gift I have received is Jimmy."

"I shall always be extremely grateful," James Coombe said, "and we must, my darling, make a proper thank-offering, whatever that may be."

"I can think of quite a number I would accept," Penelope said, looking at him from under her eyelashes, and for the moment they both forgot there was anybody else in the room with them.

The Earl pushed back his chair.

"If you two are going shopping," he said, "I will order my carriage for you, and I suggest you leave immediately, before Bond Street becomes too crowded and your secret will be out before your relations have time to assimilate the good news."

"Yes, of course," James agreed, rising to his feet. "Come along, my beautiful. I intend to chain you to me with a ring that symbolizes that you will be mine for eternity!"

"That will not be long enough for me!" Penelope answered.

She linked her arm through Alisa's and they walked from the Dining-Room together.

"Did you hear from the Duke this morning?" she asked as they walked down the corridor.

"Some flowers . . . arrived just before we . . . left," Alisa replied hesitatingly.

"Good! That gives you an excuse to write to thank him and tell him about Jimmy and me. There is nothing more infectious than the engagement of somebody one knows, and I am quite certain he will call this evening and propose to you."

Alisa did not reply.

She knew that if she told Penelope that the Duke had already proposed and she had actually written a letter refusing him, there would be a scene.

They went to the Library, where Penelope had left her bonnet which she had taken off before luncheon.

She put it on in front of the mirror and James tied the ribbons under her chin.

As he did so, she looked so lovely that, as if he could not help himself, he kissed her on the lips. Then he said to the Earl:

"We will not be long. Look after Alisa until we come back!"

"Yes, do that," Penelope said. "And try to persuade her to be sensible, for at the moment she is being very foolish!"

"In what way?" the Earl enquired.

Penelope smiled.

"She has to make up for my short-comings where our plan is concerned."

She did not say any more but left the room with James, and the door shut behind them.

Now that she was alone with the Earl, Alisa felt shy, and at the same time, because he was near her and because he looked so handsome, she felt her heart begin to beat frantically.

She could not help remembering that it was in this room that he had kissed her.

It was in this room that she had realized that a kiss could give her a rapture that made her feel as if her feet no longer touched the ground and her head was among the stars.

Because she was frightened that he would guess what she was thinking, she walked to one of the bookcases to look at the books as she had done the first time she had come to his house.

"I presume the plan to which your sister was referring," he said behind her, "is that you should be, as she put it, 'the Gunning Sisters, up-to-date.' "

"That . . . was what . . . Penelope meant us to . . . do," Alisa agreed, "but she has fallen in . . . love."

There was silence. Then the Earl said:

"Are you telling me that neither of you are aware that Penelope is in fact following very closely in the footsteps of Elizabeth Gunning?"

Alisa turned round.

"She would have done so if, as she had intended, she had married the Duke," she replied. "But, having fallen in love with an ordinary soldier, she realizes that he can give her much . . . more than a coronet."

There was a faint smile on the Earl's lips as he said:

"James has been more astute than I gave him credit for. He has always hoped to be loved for himself, and that is what he has achieved."

"Of course," Alisa said, "and although they may be very poor, they have the only thing that . . . really . . . matters."

There was a little tremor in her voice as she said the last words. Then, looking puzzled, she said:

"I do not understand what you mean when you say that Penelope has followed in the footsteps of Elizabeth Gunning."

"That is something your sister will undoubtedly learn when she meets James's mother, but I will tell you what you obviously do not know," the Earl said, "which is that James is heir-presumptive to the Duke of Roehampton!"

Alisa stared at him as if she could not believe what she had heard. Then she asked:

"If that is true, why did James not tell Penelope?"

"The truth of the matter is that I do not think he is

particularly interested in his prospects," the Earl said. "The present Duke is very old and in ill health. He is unmarried, and his brothers produced only daughters, with the result that James's father, who was a distant cousin, had he lived would have come into the title. But now it will be James's in the not-too-far-distant future."

Alisa clasped her hands together and gave a little cry of delight.

"That will be wonderful for Penelope, and now . . . I need not . . ."

She stopped, realizing that what she had been about to say in her excitement was something about which she should remain silent.

"I should be interested to hear the end of that sentence," the Earl said.

Alisa turned round again to the book-case and her back was towards him.

"It was . . . not important."

"I think it was!"

She shook her head, then realized that he had come nearer to her before he said:

"Turn round, Alisa! I want to know what you were about to say."

"It is . . . nothing to do with . . . you."

Then she gave a little gasp as she felt the Earl's hands on her shoulders, turning her round.

He looked down at her and she was aware that his eyes were looking at her in that penetrating manner which always made her feel shy.

At the same time, because he was touching her, she felt a thrill go through her, and she thought wildly that if he would kiss her once again, it would be the most wonderful thing that could possibly happen.

"I want you to answer me truthfully," the Earl said. "Are you intending to accept Exminster?"

Because he sounded grim and his fingers tightened painfully on her shoulders, Alisa felt herself tremble.

"Penelope . . . told me I . . . had to . . . so that I could . . . help her."

"So you have said 'yes'!"

"No . . . no!" Alisa cried. "I . . . cannot . . . marry him, and I have . . . written to . . . tell him so."

The Earl's fingers relaxed and she was free.

"And when Penelope marries," he asked, "what do you intend to do with yourself?"

"I will . . . go home and be with . . . Papa."

"And that will make you happy? After all, Exminster is not the only man in the world, although I doubt if you will get a better offer."

"I could not . . . marry anybody unless I . . . loved him in the . . . same way that . . . Penelope loves Jimmy."

"And you think it might be impossible for you to find such a man?"

Alisa drew in her breath.

She wondered what the Earl would say if she told him she had found somebody she loved overwhelmingly, completely, with all her heart and with all her mind, and that it was impossible for any other man to mean the same.

"I . . . shall be . . . all right."

"That is not what I asked you."

She could not answer him, and after a moment he said:

"What has made you decide that you will not marry Exminster?"

That was an easy question to answer, Alisa thought, and she replied:

"I do not . . . love him!"

"How do you know that?"

She glanced up at him in surprise because the question seemed rather foolish.

Then, because he was looking at her in a strange way, she felt the blood rising in her cheeks.

"When I kissed you the first time you came here,"

the Earl said, "I realized you were very inexperienced and very innocent, I was quite sure you knew nothing about men and less about love."

"That . . . was . . . true," Alisa murmured.

"And yet now you know you do not love one of the most eligible men in the *Beau Monde.* How do you know that?"

Alisa made a helpless little gesture with her hand.

"Answer me!" the Earl insisted.

"It is . . . difficult to explain," she faltered, "but I do not . . . want him to touch me . . . and I know that if he . . . did, I would not . . . feel like I . . . did . . ."

She stopped, aware that what she was going to say would be very revealing.

". . . like you did when I kissed you," the Earl finished, and his arms went round her.

She made a little sound, but she did not struggle, and he said:

"Shall we find out if the second time we kiss each other is as wonderful as the first?"

He did not wait for her answer, but his lips were on hers and Alisa knew at the first touch of them that this was what she had been longing and yearning for and thought she would never know again.

The strength of his arms holding her against him and the wonder of his kiss brought the rapturous feeling that she had known before, moving through her breasts, up her throat, and onto her lips.

Then he was carrying her into the sky and they were one with the stars.

She felt thrill after thrill rippling through her until her whole body quivered with an ecstasy that was so intense that it was almost a physical pain.

He drew her closer and still closer until the feelings he was arousing in her were so glorious, so incredibly marvellous, that Alisa felt she must have died and reached Heaven.

Then he raised his head and said in a voice that sounded strange and a little hoarse:

"Is that the sort of love you want?"

Because she was bewildered, bemused, and radiantly happy, Alisa could no longer think but only stammer:

"I . . . love you . . . and I . . . could not . . . marry anybody . . . unless they could . . . make me feel . . . like this."

Then the Earl's mouth held hers captive again, and she wished she could remain in the Heaven to which he had taken her, and never return to earth.

A short time, or a long time, later—it was impossible to judge—the Earl looked down into her shining eyes and at her lips red and soft from his kisses.

"You are so ridiculously beautiful," he said unsteadily, "and somebody has to look after you."

It flashed through Alisa's mind that he was going to make the same proposition to her that he had made the first time he had kissed her, and she stiffened.

Knowing what she was thinking, he laughed gently before he said:

"You are aware that Maria Gunning married an Earl, and we must follow her story exactly."

"M—marry?"

It was hard to say the word, and she was not certain whether she said the word aloud or her lips only mouthed it.

"Must I ask you properly?" the Earl enquired. "Will you, my lovely little Alisa, marry me? It is the least you can do, after haunting me until it is impossible for me to exorcise you from my thoughts. You are always in my mind, my heart, and my eyes."

"Did you . . . try to . . . forget me?" Alisa whispered.

"You disappeared and I thought I would never find you again."

"But you . . . tried?"

"I sent half-a-dozen women to ask Mrs. Lulworth for the creams you had sold to *Madame* Vestris."

"She did not . . . know who . . . I was."

"Nor did I."

"And you . . . really minded?"

"I wanted you and I intended to have you!" the Earl said. "If you feel you cannot marry a Duke, I assure you that ever since we met I have been unable to see, hear, or realize that there is any other woman in the world."

His lips twisted for a moment in the mocking way she knew so well as he asked:

"What have you done to me, my darling? I would have bet my entire fortune that no woman would be able to make me feel as I do now."

"You . . . really . . . love me?"

"I adore you! I cannot live without you! Is that what you want me to say?"

"I cannot . . . believe it! I have . . . loved you ever since you first . . . kissed me, but I never . . . thought you would . . . love me."

The Earl did not answer. He merely kissed her again.

When finally he set her free, Alisa's cheeks were flushed and she felt as if her whole being had come alive, yet she was no longer herself but a part of him.

"How can . . . everything be so . . . wonderful?" she cried. "Penelope has found . . . somebody to love, and you . . . love me!"

"I am sure we can explain it as a gift from the gods," the Earl said, "but it is a gift that I shall treasure, protect, love, and be extremely jealous of for the rest of my life."

As he spoke he drew her almost roughly back into his arms and said:

"How dare you ever consider marrying the Duke? You are mine as you were meant to be since the beginning of time. If I had had any sense I would have kept you prisoner the first day you came into this room and never let you go!"

The masterfulness about the note in his voice and the way he was holding her made Alisa feel thrills like shafts of sunlight running through her.

The Earl was exactly as she had always dreamt a real man would be: authoritative, commanding, and yet at the same time kind and understanding, and when necessary a haven of security.

"You are so . . . wonderful!" she cried. "How can I have been so . . . lucky as to . . . find you?"

"In a very unlikely place," he replied a little drily.

She knew he was thinking of *Madame* Vestris's dressing-room, and she said:

"If it had not been for three pots of face-cream, I would never have gone . . . there, and I would never have found . . . you. How . . . extraordinary that such little things should lead to anything so . . . utterly and completely marvellous."

"I am deeply grateful to those three pots," the Earl answered, "but selling them and visiting actresses is something you will never do again."

"It is . . . all like a . . . fairy-story."

"Which one day we will tell our children."

He watched for the color that flooded into Alisa's cheeks. Then he smiled and with a note of unmistakable triumph in his voice said:

"A gift from the gods, and that, my precious one, is the love which we shall never lose and is ours today, tomorrow, and for the rest of eternity."

Then he was kissing her, fiercely, passionately, possessively, until Alisa knew they were no longer human but one with the gods themselves.

Music from the Heart

Author's Note

William IV and his prim little German wife, Queen Adelaide, raised the moral standard of England, which had fallen to a very low level during the raffish, extravagant reign of George IV.

Unfortunately, propriety at Court also meant boredom and evenings when the Gentlemen-in-Waiting yawned themselves to bed. In consequence, the parties and entertainments which the late Monarch had enjoyed took place in the private houses of noblemen.

Madame Vestris scandalised and delighted London during the Regency by appearing on the stage dressed in breeches. She continued to play male parts during the reigns of William IV and Queen Victoria and made a great success of the Royal Olympic Theatre.

Before the Season opened on January 3, 1831, Madame began to alter theatre practice in Britain. She paid salaries in advance and had a proper regulation of working hours and breaks.

Within an hour of the opening of the Season, Madame progressed another innovation—the design of a setting exclusively related to the matter of the play!

She ran the Olympic Theatre until 1839, appeared in New York at the Park Theatre, went on to manage the Theatre Royal Covent Garden, and to appear at the Haymarket and several other Theatres. She received an ovation at the Lyceum in 1854 at her final performance and died the following year.

Madame Vestris was undoubtedly one of the most fascinating personalities of the stage, and she made theatrical history as a Manageress and an Innovator.

Chapter One

1831

Sir James Armstrong read the letter he held in his hand, and when he had finished there was a smile of satisfaction on his face.

He looked across the breakfast-table at his wife and said:

"Denton is coming. I thought he would not be able to resist a Steeple-Chase!"

Before Lady Armstrong could reply, her step-daughter, Muriel, gave a cry of delight.

"Denton has really accepted, Papa?" she asked. "That is wonderful!"

"I thought it would please you," Sir James said.

"I am thrilled!" Muriel Armstrong replied. "He said he wanted to see me again."

She looked down a little coyly, then as she raised her eyes she looked at her step-sister and the expression on her face changed.

"I am not having Ilouka here," she said in a very different tone of voice.

Her father looked at his wife in surprise, raising his eye-brows, and there was an expression of concern on Lady Armstrong's beautiful face.

Ever since she had married for the second time, she had been upset by the animosity with which her stepchild regarded her daughter by her previous marriage.

It was creating an atmosphere of tension in the house, which she very much deprecated.

"Ilouka will have to go away!" Muriel said insistently. "I will not have her spoiling my chance of attracting Lord Denton as she did with Frederick Holder."

"That was not my fault," Ilouka said quickly. "I promise you it was not."

Her voice was soft and musical, very different from her step-sister's aggressive tone.

There was a frown between Sir James's eyes as he said slowly:

"I know my sister Agatha would be only too pleased to have Ilouka to stay."

"Then that is where she must go," Muriel said quickly.

Ilouka parted her lips as if to protest, but before she could speak she caught her mother's warning glance and the words died on her lips.

She knew her mother was pleading with her to be silent, and it was only when they had left the Breakfast-Room and mother and daughter walked up the stairs together that each knew without words what the other was thinking.

Lady Armstrong went into the Sitting-Room which led off her bedroom and as Ilouka closed the door she said pleadingly:

"Oh, please, Mama, I cannot go to stay with Mrs. Adolphus again. You know how terrible it was the last time. She never stopped saying nasty things about you in a rather subtle manner."

Lady Armstrong sighed.

"I am afraid your step-father's relations did not approve of his marrying a penniless widow who they thought would be too old to give him a son, or indeed any more children."

"How can they be so unkind when Step-Papa is so happy, if it were not for Muriel?"

"Yes, I know, dearest," Lady Armstrong agreed in a soft voice, "but perhaps she will marry Lord Denton, and then there will be no further problems. But you know as well as I do that if you are here when he arrives, you will spoil her chances."

Both mother and daughter were silent, knowing that Ilouka could not help attracting men, and it was only too true that when she was there Muriel had no chance of holding the attention of a man for long.

Muriel was in fact quite a good-looking girl, with clear skin and brown hair complemented by brown eyes which could, when she wanted something, be soft and appealing, but were as hard as iron if she was crossed.

It seemed from her point of view singularly unfair that her father, after years of apparently being content to be a widower pursued by a great number of attractive women, had fallen in love with the widow of a near neighbor.

When Colonel Compton had died, his wife was so miserable and bereft without him that it would not have occurred to her as possible that she should marry again.

But the Colonel, who had been a distinguished soldier and had, as someone had once said, "more charm in his little finger than most men have in the whole of their bodies," had never been a thrifty man.

His wife discovered a multitude of debts which she thought despairingly would take her years to pay off, and it meant that she and her daughter, Ilouka, would have to skimp and save every penny.

Of course there could be no new gowns, and certainly no London Season where Ilouka would shine as her mother had hoped for her in the Social World that she had known as a girl.

She was not at all interested in Sir James Armstrong, who, having called to commiserate with her on her bereavement, came again and again until it was quite obvious that he was courting her.

However, it was impossible not to realize how very different life would be if she became his wife.

His impressive country house with a large Estate was a focal point in the County for those who liked to be invited to his luncheons and dinner-parties.

They also enjoyed the garden-parties he gave in the summer and the two Hunt Balls which always took place at The Towers in the winter.

It was knowing the difference it would make to Ilouka which persuaded Mrs. Compton finally to accept Sir James's proposal, after he had grown more ardent and more insistent week by week and day by day.

Although she knew that nobody could ever take the place of her husband in her heart, she in fact grew very fond of Sir James.

Being a very feminine person, she longed once more to be protected and looked after and to feel that the burden of unpaid debts that her husband had left her, together with her memories of him, would no longer feel as if it was crushing her.

Finally, after a year of mourning, she allowed Sir James to announce their wedding after it had taken place very quietly and with nobody there except two of his closest friends.

When they came back from their honeymoon, the new Lady Armstrong looked not only radiant but exceedingly beautiful in expensive gowns such as she had never owned before, and with jewellery with which Sir James expressed his love more eloquently than he could put into words.

Ilouka joined her at The Towers, and then unfortunately a month later Muriel, Sir James's only child by his first marriage, also arrived.

It was impossible for anyone not to realize the contrast between the two girls, although they were almost the same age.

Ilouka was lovely with a beauty which owed a lot to her Hungarian great-grandmother, as did the color of her hair.

The very soft, dark red that the Hungarians all through the centuries have made their own was complemented by two enormous eyes, which dominated her face and which were green flecked with gold.

She was small and delicately made, and it was impossible for a man having once looked at her not to look again, and, unfortunately as far as Muriel was concerned, to forget there was any other woman in the room.

In some ways she resembled her mother, but it was her father who had told her stories of his grandmother after whom she had been named.

She had been a famous beauty in Hungary, and she run away with an obscure, unimportant young English Diplomat named Compton when it was all arranged that she should marry a rich aristocrat.

As a child Ilouka wanted to hear the story over and over again, and her father had said:

"Your name means: 'She who gives life,' and although I knew her only when she was very old, my grandmother still seemed to give life to everybody round her. It was nothing she specially did or said, it was just that she inspired people and gave them a vibration of the life-force just by being herself."

"How did she do that, Papa?" Ilouka had asked.

Her father had laughed and said that when she grew up she would have to read books on Hungary and visit the country to understand what he meant.

As Mrs. Compton watched her daughter grow up and become more and more beautiful every day and having, she thought, a quality about her which English girls did not possess, she realized it was unlikely that the more stolid and prosaic County people would appreciate the rare and un-English quality about her.

"We must see that she is presented to the King and Queen," she had said to her husband.

"I agree," he answered, "but God knows where the money is going to come from!"

Sir James was, of course, able to find the money, but unfortunately there was Muriel like a stumbling-block between Ilouka and her mother's ambitions.

"One cannot blame Muriel," Lady Armstrong said now with a sigh, "when you turn the head of every young man who comes to the house."

"I do not want them!" Ilouka replied. "As you know, Mama, most of them are dull and unimaginative and I could no more marry any of them than fly to the moon."

"I know, darling, but as things are, how are you to meet the right sort of man unless I can take you to London for a Season, and that would mean that Muriel would have to come too."

Ilouka gave a little cry.

"I could not bear it, Mama! She is so terribly jealous, and because she hates me it makes me feel not only unhappy but nervous and ill-at-ease."

She gave a little laugh but there was no humor in it as she said:

"In fact, I am afraid even to speak to a man if she is present."

Lady Armstrong knew without her adding it that any man present would want to speak to Ilouka.

Looking at her daughter now, she thought as she had so often thought before that it was not only her beauty that was so arresting, but the fact that there was something ethereal and almost supernatural about her.

"She is like a fairy-child," she had once said to Colonel Compton, and he had replied:

"Seeing how much we love each other and how happy we are together, my darling, is it surprising that we have produced something unusual who might actually have come out of a fairy-tale?"

He himself was very handsome, and wherever they went they were stared at.

It was unfortunate from their point of view that because of limited resources they were restricted to their small Manor House in Oxfordshire and it was only occasionally that they could afford a brief visit to London.

Mrs. Compton wanted so much more for her daughter, but now, when as Lady Armstrong she could afford it, there was Muriel.

"If I am to go away," Ilouka asked, "why should I have to stay with Mrs. Adolphus?"

Her mother made a helpless little gesture with her hands.

"She is the only member of your step-father's family who is willing to do exactly as he asks," she replied, "and I think too, although he would not admit it, he feels rather ashamed of having to send you away. He therefore wishes to send you where nobody would talk about it and in consequence disparage Muriel."

Ilouka drew in her breath but did not reply, and after a moment her mother went on:

"Actually your step-father is very fond of you, Ilouka dearest, but naturally his first thought must be for his own child, and you know as well as I do that Muriel has always resented him marrying again."

"How can she be so selfish, Mama, when you know how happy you have made Step-Papa? He loves you with all his heart."

"Yes, I know," Lady Armstrong agreed. "At the same time, he has a great sense of family, and he must do what is right and best for Muriel."

Ilouka pressed her soft lips together in case she should say anything to hurt her mother, but she was thinking how they both knew that Muriel had raged at her father furiously when she first learnt that he had married again.

Unfortunately, she had also written a lot of extremely derogatory and unkind letters, which Sir James very foolishly had shown to his wife after he had married her.

He had done so not to distress her but because he thought it was right that she should know the problems awaiting them both when their honeymoon was over.

Lady Armstrong had tried by every means in her power to make Muriel like her, and she might have succeeded if Muriel had not been eaten up with jealousy, spite, and malice from the moment she had first set eyes on Ilouka.

She had deliberately set out on what amounted to a campaign of spite against Ilouka and where possible to drive a wedge between her father and his new wife.

There she was completely unsuccessful, although she often made Lady Armstrong very unhappy.

But where Ilouka was concerned she managed to make her life a series of petty insults and slights that grew worse every day that they were in the same house together.

"It will be a relief, Mama, to go away," Ilouka said now. "At the same time, please, please do not let me stay away very long."

"You know, dearest, I have planned to present you at a 'Drawing-Room' in May," Lady Armstrong replied, "and your step-father wishes me to present Muriel at the same time. But now I cannot help feeling that it would be impossible to enjoy a London Season together."

"I do not mind missing the Season," Ilouka said, "but I do mind being away from you, especially with Mrs. Adolphus."

Lady Armstrong sighed.

She was well aware that her husband's sister hated her because she had set her heart on her brother marrying again and having several sons.

She was a demanding, elderly woman who her enemies said had driven her husband into the grave and then had transferred her ambitions to her only brother.

She lived in a bleak, ugly house in Bedfordshire,

where the flatness of the countryside seemed somehow to echo the deadly boredom of the neighborhood and of Mrs. Adolphus's household in particular.

The servants were old and crotchety and resented visitors because they made extra work.

The food was plain and dull, and even the horses which Ilouka was allowed to ride were slow and unspirited.

With her Hungarian blood she had all the talents that had made her great-grandmother so outstanding.

A magnificent rider, she could master any horse, however wild and unruly, and she was also extremely musical and with her fairy-like figure could dance in a way that made her father say once:

"We must put Ilouka on the stage at Covent Garden, and the money she obtains in 'Benefits' will keep us in comfort in our old age!"

His wife had protested laughingly.

"How can you say anything so outrageous, darling? For goodness' sake, do not put such ideas into Ilouka's head!"

"I was not serious," Colonel Compton had laughed.

Nevertheless, he would make Ilouka dance for him while her mother played the piano.

In the music was the wild dance of the Hungarian gypsies, and Ilouka would dance as if her feet never touched the ground and she flowed with a grace and an abandon that came from her instinct and not from anything she had ever seen.

"I tell you what I will do," Lady Armstrong said now, after a pause while she had been considering what her daughter had said. "You must go to Agatha before Lord Denton arrives, but I will write to your father's sister who lives not far away in Huntingdon and ask her if she will take you for a short while."

Ilouka's face lit up.

"I would like that," she said. "Aunt Alice is a sweet person, and I love her children."

"I know, dearest, but you do realize they are very poor, and although we could not insult them by offering money, even one extra would strain their resources even more than they are strained already."

As she spoke Lady Armstrong was thinking of how difficult it had been for her and Ilouka after her husband died.

"You know I understand," Ilouka said, "and perhaps you could give me some money to buy presents for the children; not toys or games which are really useless, but dresses for the little girls and perhaps a coat for each of the boys."

"Of course I will do that," her mother replied. "At the same time, you will have to be very, very careful not to let them feel it is an act of charity."

"Leave it to me, Mama. You know I would not do anything to hurt Aunt Alice."

"Then I will write to her at once."

"I suppose I could not go there first, and not to Mrs. Adolphus?"

Lady Armstrong shook her head.

"Your step-father thinks his sister is a delightful person."

"She always is, to him."

"It is only that she dislikes me, and in consequence you," her mother went on.

"Yes, I know," Ilouka said, "but it means that she will find fault every moment of the day, and will keep on telling me over and over again what wonderful chances her brother missed when he married you."

Lady Armstrong laughed.

"You will just have to remember that neither he nor I are complaining."

"I know, Mama, but she goes on and on, almost as if Step-Papa picked you up from the gutter, or you trapped him into marriage when he was least expecting it!"

Lady Armstrong laughed again, remembering how Sir James had pleaded with her and begged her to marry him so humbly that now in retrospect it seemed almost incredible how abject he had been at the time.

But she was in fact growing more fond of him all the time that they were together, and she prayed that for all their sakes Muriel would get married soon.

Then as far as she was concerned she could enjoy having a husband who adored her and who was prepared to give her all the money she needed for herself and her daughter.

At the same time, Sir James had his little meannesses, and one of these was that he did not like to send his own horses on long distances and he resented hiring conveyances when his stable was full.

"Ilouka will leave for your sister's early the day after tomorrow," Lady Armstrong said. "If she starts early in the morning, she will only have to stay for one night on the way, and you know I do not like her staying at Posting-Inns, even with a maid to look after her."

There was silence while both Sir James and his wife were thinking that Lord Denton was unlikely to arrive before tea-time, and by that time Ilouka would be far away.

"Lady Armstrong then said pleadingly:

"You will send her in a carriage, James?"

"That is impossible," Sir James replied. "I need all the coachmen and the grooms here to help with the Steeple-Chase, and it is also too far for our best horses."

Lady Armstrong stiffened. Then she asked:

"Then how are you suggesting that Ilouka should get to your sister's house?"

"She can go by Stage-Coach," Sir James replied. "After all, it will hardly be a new experience for her."

This was true, because before Lady Armstrong married Sir James she had during her widowhood been obliged to dispose of her horses, and she and

Ilouka had therefore had no option but to travel by Stage-Coach.

There was a little silence. Then Lady Armstrong said:

"I suppose if she is with Hannah she will be all right."

"Of course she will be all right," Sir James said sharply, "and very much safer than if she travelled by Post-Chaise, which is the only alternative."

"The Stage-Coaches are so slow," Lady Armstrong said, "and they do not always stop at the best Inns."

"I imagine, as it is a cross-country journey, there will not be much choice," Sir James replied drily.

Lady Armstrong was perturbed. At the same time, she knew that her husband would have made up his mind, and she thought that to plead with him to change it would be a mistake and might affect Ilouka.

He had already said that she should have a Season in London, and although they were both well aware that it would be difficult because of Muriel, so far he had not renounced his intention of opening his London House to give a Ball for both the girls.

Lady Armstrong was quite certain that behind her back Muriel was trying by every means she could to have Ilouka excluded.

But she was also confident that her husband would be too loyal to her to agree to what his daughter suggested.

At the same time, it would be a mistake to upset him in any way at this particular moment, and she could only pray more fervently than she was doing already that Muriel would marry Lord Denton, and Ilouka could then enjoy a Season alone.

Aloud she said:

"I will see that Ilouka is ready and that Hannah goes with her. Will you order a carriage to convey them to the cross-roads? And please ask whoever goes with them to see that she has a comfortable seat and to tip the Guard so that he will look after her."

"You know I will do that," Sir James said.

Then he put his hand on his wife's shoulder as he said:

"I am sorry to send Ilouka away, my darling, if it upsets you. At the same time, Denton is quite a catch, and I would welcome him as a son-in-law."

The tone of voice in which he spoke said far more than the words he used, and Lady Armstrong quickly put her hand over his as she said:

"You know, dearest, that I want Muriel's happiness just as I want yours."

Sir James bent his head to kiss her cheek and said no more, but Lady Armstrong knew by the expression in his eyes before he left the room how much he loved her.

At the same time, she could not help worrying about Ilouka.

Then she told herself that there was actually nothing to worry about except that her daughter would be exceedingly bored on the long journey across country.

The Stage-Coach would not be packed with dashing young men who might be beguiled by her beauty, but with farmers' wives journeying to a market-town, commercial travellers intent on what they could sell, and perhaps a few farm-boys returning home after taking a horse to sell at a Fair or driving a herd of cows to a new purchaser.

"And who could look after Ilouka more effectively than Hannah?" she thought with a smile.

Hannah had been their only maid after the Colonel's death, because they had been unable to afford any more servants.

She was a strict Presbyterian who thought the whole world was a wicked place filled with people who in her own words were "up to no good!"

Even the tradesmen who came to the Manor had been afraid of Hannah, and Lady Armstrong knew that any man who even attempted to talk to Ilouka without an introduction would be annihilated by Hannah's eyes before the first word had left his lips.

"I am afraid it will be a rather long and boring journey for you, Hannah," she said to the old maid in her sweet manner which every servant found irresistible.

"Duty is duty, M'Lady," Hannah replied, "and the Good Lord never said anything about it being a pleasure!"

"I know Miss Ilouka will be quite safe with you," Lady Armstrong went on.

"You can be sure of that, M'Lady."

"All the same," Lady Armstrong continued as if she spoke to herself, "I wish the Master could have spared a coach to take you to Bedfordshire."

Hannah's lips tightened, making her look very formidable.

Now that she was nearing seventy, the lines on her face were deeply ingrained, and when she was angry, as an impertinent footman once said, "She looks like an old gargoyle!"

Hannah had never really approved of Sir James from the time he came courting her mistress.

At the same time, she definitely appreciated the comforts of their new home, but she deeply resented it if "her ladies," as she thought of them in her mind, were insulted in any way.

"I am not so sorry for myself having to travel in the Stage-Coach," Ilouka said to her mother when they were alone, "but for the other travellers who will have to put up with Hannah! I cannot tell you, Mama, how intimidating she can be."

"I have seen her," Lady Armstrong replied, laughing.

The eyes of both mother and daughter twinkled at each other as they envisaged how Hannah, sitting bolt upright, would by her very presence seem to cast a gloom over the other occupants of the Stage-Coach.

Those who might have been talking gaily and vociferously before would lapse into an uneasy silence, and any man who dared to whistle beneath his breath would receive such a look of disapproval that he would hastily shut his eyes and pretend to go to sleep.

The cards with which men wiled away a long journey were frowned upon by Hannah to a point where a game lost its interest, and small children who otherwise might have been obstreperous hid their heads shyly against their mothers.

"I shall be perfectly all right," Ilouka siad. "Do not worry about me on the journey, Mama, but only when I reach Stone House, which is appropriately named!"

Both mother and daughter laughed, then Lady Armstrong said:

"Oh, dear, I wish worthy people were not always so dismal and dreary about it. I know Agatha Adolphus does a great deal of good one way and another, but I am sure as soon as she has bestowed her charity upon them it makes those who receive it long to go out and do something really wicked."

Ilouka put her arm round her mother's neck and kissed her.

"I love you, Mama! You always understand, and if after I have stayed with Mrs. Adolphus I do something really wicked, you must not blame me."

Lady Armstrong gave a little cry.

"Oh, Ilouka, I should not have said that, and please, darling, just do all the things I should want you to do in your usual adorable manner. Then perhaps even Agatha Adolphus will not seem so formidable."

"She will!" Ilouka said lightly. "She is like the Rock of Gilbraltar, and nothing, neither tempest nor earthquake, will change her, and certainly I will not."

They laughed again, but when the next morning Ilouka was ready to leave, she held on tightly to her mother.

"I love you, Mama!" she said. "I will hate being away from you."

"I shall miss you too, dearest," Lady Armstrong replied, "but there is nothing else either of us can do."

"Nothing," Ilouka agreed.

She would not upset her mother by telling her that last night when they had gone up to bed together Muriel had said to her:

"Surely there must be some men in Bedfordshire and you ought to be able to get your hands on one of them."

Ilouka had not replied and Muriel had gone on spitefully:

"You have certainly tried hard enough to encourage some idiots to propose to you, and now when they do so you only have to say 'yes.' "

As if she goaded Ilouka into a reply she said unwisely:

"I do not wish to marry anybody until I can find somebody I can love."

"That sounds very high and mighty," Muriel sneered, "and of course it will be very easy for you to fall in love with a man if he has a lot of money like my father!"

Ilouka stiffened, and Muriel went on:

"It was very convenient, was it not, your mother sitting wistfully on the door-step, so to speak, and looking so pathetic in a cheap black gown because she could not afford anything better."

The angry, spiteful note in Muriel's voice seemed to be reflected in her face, and Ilouka thought that when she spoke like that she looked ugly and it was unlikely that any man unless he was blind would want to marry her.

Because she would not demean herself to answer anything so untrue or so unkind, she merely said as they reached her bedroom door:

"Good-night, Muriel. You may not believe this, but I want you to be happy, and I hope and pray that Lord Denton will give it to you."

She did not wait for Muriel's answer, which she was

certain would be vindictive, but went into her own room and shut the door.

Only when she was alone did she feel as if she was trembling, as she always did when she heard her mother being abused.

After her father's death, her mother had thought it impossible for any man ever to mean anything to her, and she had said over and over again:

"Your father and I were so happy, so ideally, perfectly happy! All I want now is to die so that I can be with him."

Ilouka had looked at her in horror.

"You must not say such things, Mama. It is very selfish. After all, if you die I shall be all alone in the world, and you know I could not live without you."

Mrs. Compton had put her arms round her daughter and held her close.

"You are right, darling, I was being selfish. But I miss your Papa so much that I feel that the world has come to an end, because he is no longer with me."

However, for her daughter's sake, Mrs. Compton made a great effort.

She cried herself to sleep every night when she was alone in her own room, but in the day-time she tried to smile and to take an interest in what Ilouka was doing.

They went for long walks and talked of many things, both aware that while they did not mention it, Colonel Compton's name was uppermost in their minds.

Then gradually, as the first agony of grief passed and Sir James started to call, Mrs. Compton began to stop making excuses not to see him.

"It will do you good, Mama, to talk to Sir James," Ilouka would say. "Now tidy your hair and go down and make yourself pleasant to him."

"Oh, must I, Ilouka? I do not want to," Mrs. Compton would plead.

"He has brought us a huge basket of peaches from

his greenhouses, and some grapes," Ilouka would reply, "and even if you do not eat them, Mama, Hannah and I would find them a pleasant change from semolina pudding."

Because she felt too exhausted to argue, Mrs. Compton would do as her daughter suggested.

It was impossible to explain to Muriel that she had no wish to trap anybody or to put them in her beloved husband's place.

But now, as Ilouka knew, they were happy, very happy, except for Muriel.

I would go and stay with the Devil himself, she thought, *if it gave Muriel the chance to marry and go away!*

At the same time, she faced the fact that even if Muriel got engaged it might be the conventional long engagement.

That would mean that she would have to stay in hiding until the ring was actually on Muriel's finger and her fiancé could not change his mind at the last moment.

It was true that Ilouka had never made the slightest effort to attract any man's attention, but it was also true that she had not had much opportunity.

Nevertheless, her father's friends had looked at her with astonishment when they came to the Manor, and even when she was a School-girl with her long hair flowing over her shoulders she had heard the compliments that her mother received about her.

But she had known that while the men at any age looked at her with a certain glint in their eyes, the women on the other hand stiffened and looked down their noses, as if they thought her very appearance was somewhat reprehensible.

"I suppose I do look a little theatrical, Mama," she had said once.

Her mother had laughed.

"Nonsense! You are thinking about that ridiculous remark of your father's—that you could go on the stage because you dance well. Red hair is always supposed to be very theatrical, but actually, darling, you look very much a lady, and a very aristocratic one at that."

"Like my great-grandmother?"

"Exactly! We only have a miniature of her, but your father's father had a full-size portrait, although I do not know what happened to it."

"I never knew that before. Where is it?"

"At your grandfather's house, and when your father was away with the Regiment your grandfather died and the house was sold, and he never knew what happened to the contents."

"How disappointing!" Ilouka said. "I would love to have seen it."

"I expect it was very like the miniature we have, and the artist might in fact have been painting you."

The miniature, however, was rather faded, and although there was a distinct resemblance, Ilouka thought, she would have loved to see something of her great-grandmother which would have brought her more vividly to life than her imagination could do.

However it was only now, when she was eighteen, that Ilouka fully blossomed into what her mother knew was a beauty who would take the Social World by storm.

She had always been told how much the gentlemen of St. James appreciated a beautiful woman, and although she was her own child, she thought that it would be impossible to find anyone so lovely or so unusual as Ilouka.

Looking at her now in her travelling-clothes, which were simple enough but to which she gave a style and an elegance which could not be bought, she thought it was a terrible waste to send Ilouka off to dismal isolation in Bedfordshire.

She kissed her again and said:

"I will let you know the very moment you can come home. Take care of yourself, my precious one."

"I promise to do that, Mama."

Ilouka gave her a beguiling smile and went down the front-door steps to where her step-father's carriage was waiting.

Looking at the coachman on the box wearing his cockaded top-hat and the two horses with their silver harness, Lady Armstrong could not help wishing that her husband had been generous enough to send Ilouka all the way in it.

But they both had so much to thank him for that it would be stupid to resent his small meannesses.

There were not many of them, but as her first husband had said laughingly:

"Every man has a little of the miser and the spend-thrift in him. Unfortunately, as far as I am concerned, the balance is not very even and tips overwhelmingly towards the spend-thrift."

His wife had laughed.

"Darling, I have never known you to be miserly about anything," she had said.

"Only about the time I spend apart from you," the Colonel had replied. "Then I grudge every minute, every second we are not together."

He had kissed her and they forgot what they were talking about.

Now as the carriage carrying Ilouka drove away and Lady Armstrong waved until it was out of sight, she prayed:

"Please, God, let Ilouka find the love that her father gave to me and that I had with him."

It was a prayer that came from the very depths of her heart, and she knew that nothing she could wish for her daughter was more important than that she should find true love, which made everything else in the world vanish into insignificance.

Chapter Two

The Stage-Coach carrying Ilouka and Hannah was slow and uncomfortable.

It was a very old vehicle, as they had expected, because it was not on one of the main Highways where the quicker-moving, better-sprung ones plied for hire.

But on the twisting country lanes there was no choice, and the Coach which went by once a day carried passengers from one village to another so that in most cases it stopped practically every mile.

Ilouka, who was always interested in people, talked to the fat farmers' wives who carried baskets of baby chicks, or to their young daughters who were travelling to nearby towns to go into service for the first time.

Hannah made it obvious that she disapproved of her conversing so familiarly, but Ilouka paid no attention to her or to the manner in which she sat stiff and unbending, replying in monosyllables to anybody who addressed her.

They stopped for luncheon at a country Inn with the inevitable village green in front of it and a duck-pond in which there were no ducks.

Fortunately, the Inn-Keeper was wise enough not to try fancy dishes for his customers, but produced home-cured ham and a local cheese which to Ilouka's mind was far more palatable than anything more pretentious but badly cooked.

She accepted a glass of home-made cider with her meal, although Hannah insisted on having tea because the water was boiled.

As Hannah was so disapproving and critical of everything, Ilouka could not help wishing that she was with somebody young with whom she could laugh, or, better still, her mother, who when they were alone invariably saw the funny side of everything.

She planned that when she was at Stone House with her step-father's sister, whom she had been told to call "Aunt Agatha," she would write to her mother every day, making it like a diary and trying to find things to tell her which would sound amusing.

It is going to be difficult, Ilouka thought with a wry smile, knowing that at Stone House the days followed one another with monotonous regularity, and usually nothing happened which was worth recalling.

They stopped at Market Town where the other occupants of the inside of the Coach alighted and two newcomers came to join Ilouka and Hannah.

They were certainly more interesting than any of the passengers who had been in the Coach before.

The man was elderly but had about him a certain raffish air which for the moment Ilouka could not recognize.

He was obviously not rich, although his clothes were smartly cut, and his overcoat, which he carried over his arm, had a velvet collar.

At first she thought it strange that he should be travelling by Coach. Then because she was observant she saw that his shoes, although highly polished, were worn and the white cuffs at his wrists were frayed at the edges.

After she had looked at the woman who accompanied him she decided that they were probably an actor and actress.

The woman was small and very attractive, with dark

hair and flashing eyes made larger by the application of mascara on her eye-lashes.

Her lips were crimson, and Ilouka knew by the way Hannah's back became as stiff as a ramrod and she turned her face to look out the window that she disapproved.

As she and Hannah were sitting on the seat of the Coach which faced forward, the newcomers took possession of the seats opposite them, with their backs to the horses.

As the Coach began to move off again the actress, speaking for the first time, said:

"Well, thank the Lord we can rest our legs, and I personally am going to put mine up!"

As she spoke she seated herself sideways in her corner and put her legs up on her seat.

The man to whom she addressed her remark smiled.

"I think you're wise," he said. "You don't want to feel tired before you dance, although we'll have a night's rest before we get there tomorrow."

"In what sort of place?" the woman asked disparagingly.

"I hope it'll not be too uncomfortable," the man said apologetically, "but we'll certainly be in luxury tomorrow night."

The way he spoke with an unexpected lilt in his voice told Ilouka that he was looking forward to tomorrow and it meant something special to him.

She wondered where they were going and longed to ask them if they were in fact on the stage.

Then the man who was sitting opposite her looked at her for the first time, and she saw the expression of astonishment in his eyes.

It was something which often happened when men looked at her, and because it always made her shy she turned her face to look out the window at the passing countryside.

At the same time, she was well aware that the man

was still staring at her, and they had not gone far before he said, and Ilouka was certain it was merely an excuse to speak to her:

"Excuse me, Madam, but would you allow me to open the window a little?"

His voice was deep, somehow melodious, and also surprisingly well educated.

"Yes, of course," Ilouka replied. "It has grown much hotter this afternoon and it will be nice to have some air."

"Thank you."

He started to let down the window with difficulty because the sash was old, the leather which held it in place was worn, and it was quite hard to fix it in place on the hooks provided.

Finally he achieved it, and when he had finished the actress said:

"I hope there's not going to be a draught. I don't want to have a sore throat by tomorrow morning."

"If it is too draughty for you," the elderly actor replied courteously, "I'll of course close it again."

"Oh, leave it for the moment!"

The man settled himself back in his seat facing Ilouka.

"I'm afraid this Coach is very slow," he said. "We've been waiting for it for over an hour."

"The horses are tired," Ilouka replied. "They have come a long way, poor things."

"I feel sorry for them too," the actor agreed, "but at least this Coach isn't over-laden, although I should have thought it was too heavy a vehicle for only two horses."

Hannah fidgeted ostentatiously and Ilouka knew she was annoyed that she should be talking to a stranger but was not quite certain how she could end the conversation.

Because she thought it tiresome that Hannah should be so unfriendly, she said:

"It always distresses me to see how Stage-Coaches

wherever they are travelling usually carry far too many people and too much baggage for the horses which have to pull them. In fact, I have heard that the life of a horse drawing a Stage-Coach is little more than three years!"

"I agree with you, Madam, it's disgraceful!" replied the man to whom she was speaking. "And even though the service in most cases is lamentable, they still charge far too much for the fares."

"I told you we should have gone by Post-Chaise!" the young woman he was with said petulantly. "I can feel my bones rattling every time the wheels turn in this ramshackle old wheel-barrow!"

Ilouka laughed because the way she spoke was so funny, and it flashed through her mind that this would certainly be a conversation to relate to her mother.

As if she felt obliged to intervene, Hannah said:

"As we've still a long way to go, Miss Ilouka, I suggest you shut your eyes and rest. Otherwise, when we do get to the place we're staying you'll be too tired to sleep."

Ilouka smiled at her.

She was well aware that Hannah was trying to prevent her from talking to the man opposite, but she had no intention of being forced into silence until she had found out a little more about him.

"Will you tell me, Sir," she asked, "where you are going?"

"We're on our way, Miss Ganymede and I, to stay with the Earl of Lavenham!"

He spoke the name with a flourish as if he bowed while he did so.

"That's if we ever get there!" Miss Ganymede remarked. "And by the time we do I'll be rattled to bits, so it's very unlikely I'll be able to walk, let alone dance!"

"Are you a dancer?" Ilouka asked eagerly.

"I hope that's obvious," Miss Ganymede replied, "but you tell her, D'Arcy."

"Of course," the man answered. "Let me introduce myself, Madam—my name is D'Arcy Archer, at your service, and the lady beside me is Miss Lucille Ganymede from the Royal Olympic Theatre in London."

"How exciting!" Ilouka exclaimed. "I have heard of the Royal Olympic Theatre. In fact I read in one of the newspapers that they were performing a Play called *Mary, Queen of Scots,* and I longed to see it."

"That's indeed correct, Madam," Mr. Archer replied. "You're very well informed."

"Was the Play successful?" Ilouka asked.

Mr. Archer gave what sounded a very theatrical laugh.

"One of the newspapers said last week that Wych Street, where the Olympic Theatre is situated, should henceforth be called 'Witch Street,' for great is the enchantment of Vestris and Foote."

As he spoke he looked up to see if she understood, and in case she did not, he explained:

"Madame Vestris, of whom you must have heard, Madam, is the owner of the Royal Olympic Theatre, and Miss Foote, a great actress, plays the part of Mary Stuart, Queen of Scots."

"I have heard of Madame Vestris," Ilouka replied.

As she said the name she remembered that her mother had in fact been shocked by the publicity which Madame Vestris had acquired by appearing on the stage in Plays in which she played the part of a man and showed her legs.

Thinking back, Ilouka could remember how the newspapers had been full of the part she played first in a Play called *Giovanni in London.*

Then she had worn breeches, and although Ilouka had been very young at the time, she could remember her mother saying it was quite outrageous and improper and she was only astonished that anybody would go to see such a Play.

Her father, however, had laughed.

"It is not the Play they go to see, my darling," he had said, "but Lucy Vestris's extremely shapely legs!"

"Really!" Mrs. Compton had exclaimed. "While I am certain the Theatre is full of men, no lady could be expected to watch such an immodest exhibition!"

Her father had laughed again, but because it had intrigued Ilouka to think of a woman showing her legs, she had in the next few years read the notices that appeared about Madam Vestris in *The Beggar's Opera, The Duenna,* and *Artaxerxes,* where once again her legs were very much in prominence.

Because she knew it shocked her mother, she did not mention Madame Vestris to her, but some years later when she was with her father she asked:

"Have you seen this Madame Vestris, Papa, about whom the newspapers are always writing?"

"She is a very attractive woman," her father had answered, "but whether I was interested in her or not, she would be far too expensive for me."

He spoke without thinking, saw the puzzled expression on his daughter's face, and said quickly:

"Forget I said that. Your mother would not approve —what I was meaning was that the Bucks and Beaux of St. James's smother her with flowers, and the presents she receives are worth a very large sum of money."

After that Ilouka had watched the newspapers to learn more about Madame Vestris.

Three years ago she had seen sketches of her as "John of Paris" in skirts way above the knees, and as "Captain Macheath" dressed completely as a man in close-fitting pantaloons, a high cravat, and a top-hat on her head.

After her father's death, when her mother and she moved to Sir James's large and comfortable house, Ilouka had really forgotten Madame Vestris and the Theatres in London about which she had often talked to her father.

Now she found it absorbing to be actually speaking to an actor and an actress.

Because she was curious she asked:

"And do you also perform at the Royal Olympic Theatre, Mr. Archer?"

"Alas, I have not had that privilege," he replied, "but Miss Ganymede and I are on our way to give a private performance for the Earl of Lavenham and his friends, and I don't think His Lordship'll be disappointed."

As he spoke he looked towards Miss Ganymede and said:

"I know, Lucille, that His Lordship will appreciate the way you'll imitate Madame Vestris."

"I should jolly-well hope so," Miss Ganymede replied, "seeing the long way we've had to come to show what we can do!"

Ilouka noticed that while Mr. Archer's voice was cultivated, Miss Ganymede's had a common accent.

As if she wished to assert herself and prevent Mr. Archer from concentrating his attention on Ilouka, she said:

"I can feel a draught! For God's sake shut the window or I'll be hoarse tomorrow night and unable to sing a note!"

"Yes, of course, I'll close it at once," Mr. Archer said.

He bent forward and lifted the strap, but it was even more difficult to close the window than it had been to open it.

After a short struggle he put his top-hat down on the seat beside him and rose to his feet.

He gave the leather strap a mighty tug and it came away in his hand, with the result that instead of closing, the window slithered down and disappeared below the sill.

"Now see what you've done!" Miss Ganymede exclaimed.

"I'm sorry," Mr. Archer murmured, "but the strap

is rotten, although I daresay I can raise the window without it."

He started to try to pull the glass up from where it had settled deep inside the door.

As he did so the Stage-Coach turned a corner and lurched so that Mr. Archer had to hold on to the window with both hands.

There was a shout from the coachman as he pulled in his horses sharply and the Coach came suddenly to a halt.

It shook everybody inside so that Miss Ganymede gave a little scream, and Hannah, looking down her nose, said sharply:

"This is disgraceful! What's happening?"

The shouting outside went on although they could not hear what was said, but as the window was down Mr. Archer put his hand outside, opened the door, and stepped out into the road.

He stood staring ahead, then gave a sudden cry and came to the open door of the Coach to say:

"Get out! Get out quickly!"

Because Ilouka was nearest to him he took her hand in his and pulled her forward out of the Coach.

Even as she reached the road, wondering what on earth was happening, the Coach in which they had been travelling seemed to sway for a moment, then fell sideways at a strange angle.

As it did so, the coachman threw down the reins and jumped from the box, and as Ilouka looked on in horror the whole Coach, with the horses plunging to save themselves, turned over, falling over the side of the road and a second later disappearing out of sight.

For a moment Ilouka could not believe that what had happened was not some figment of her imagination.

Yet the Coach had gone and she realised that she, Mr. Archer, and the coachman were standing on the road which ended abruptly about two feet away from them.

As she stepped forward to see what had happened, she could see the Coach lying upside-down about twelve feet below them amongst the debris of the road, on which there had apparently been a landslide.

The horses were lying on their backs, their legs in the air, and neighing with fear, and she could see the Guard, who had been thrown clear in the fall, struggling to his feet and going towards the terrified animals.

Then as the coachman began to descend to where the Coach was lying, Ilouka was aware that she was still holding on tightly to Mr. Archer's hand.

"We must . . . help the . . . others," she gasped.

"Wait a minute," he replied. "I'm sure that even in this isolated spot, help'll come from somewhere."

As he spoke he looked over his shoulder in the direction from which they had come.

Sure enough, there were two men, obviously farm-labourers, running towards them.

"How can . . . this have . . . happened?" Ilouka asked. "Surely if the road had subsided they should have . . . prevented us from . . . coming this . . . way?"

"It may only just have occurred," Mr. Archer replied.

Ilouka thought this was very likely, but for the moment she could think only of Hannah trapped in the fallen vehicle and was at a loss as to what she could do about it.

She went to the edge of the road, saying:

"I think, Mr. Archer, we should climb down."

But he held her back, saying:

"Be careful! I doubt if it'd be possible to release the two women inside the Coach until there're enough men to lift it."

The coachman and the Guard were struggling with the horses, who were frightened to the point where it was difficult to go near them.

Then, almost by magic, people began to arrive seemingly from nowhere.

Afterwards Ilouka felt that they must have been working in the fields, or perhaps the people in the village they had just passed through instinctively became aware of the tragedy that had happened down the road.

Anyway, there were men starting to try to raise the Coach, men trying to release the horses, and others who carried the trunks and other pieces of luggage which had been stacked on the roof up onto the road.

"Now ye sit down, dearie, there's nought ye can do by going down there," a motherly old woman said to Ilouka when she tried to climb down the bank to where the Coach lay.

"I must see to my maid," she answered. "She is trapped inside!"

"Ye can't do no good," the woman replied. "Now sit ye down! It's hard, Oi know but women only gets in th' way at times like this."

Ilouka was obliged to admit that she was right, although she kept rising from the trunk on which she was seated to try to see what was happening.

She could see that the men were having great difficulty in moving the Coach, which seemed to have become embedded in two or three feet of mud.

It seemed to her that the methods by which they were working were uncoordinated, and while they kept shouting instructions to one another, nobody appeared to obey them.

Finally, after what seemed to Ilouka hours of anxiety when all she could think of was that Hannah must be suffering and was probably injured by the fall, the Vicar came to her side.

"I have been told that you are travelling with your maid, who is an elderly woman," he said.

"Is she all right?" Ilouka asked quickly.

"I am sorry to have to tell you that she is dead," the

Vicar replied quietly. "And so is the other lady in the Coach."

Ilouka sat in the shabby Sitting-Room in the Vicarage with Mr. Archer.

She was trying to realise that she would never see poor Hannah again, never hear her sharp, disapproving comments, which more often than not had amused her because they were so characteristic of Hannah herself.

The Vicar's Housekeeper had given her and Mr. Archer cups of strong tea and some sandwiches, which Ilouka had eaten mechanically without tasting them.

"I cannot believe it!" she said now.

"Nor can I," D'Arcy Archer replied quietly.

"I realise you saved . . . my life by pulling me out of the Coach," she said, "and I am very . . . grateful."

"It would have been better if I had died instead of that poor girl," Mr. Archer said. "I am an old man and I have lost my last chance, but there was no reason for her to die."

Because she thought it might be rude to seem unsympathetic, Ilouka asked:

"Why is it your last chance?"

"I don't suppose you would be interested," he said, "but I've been down in my luck of late."

"You mean you are not getting parts in the Theatre?"

"I think I have haunted the offices of every Theatrical Agent in London," D'Arcy Archer said bitterly, "but the only money I've been able to make was by singing and telling jokes in taverns, and the clientele of those places are not very generous."

"I am sorry," Ilouka said softly, as there seemed to be nothing else she could say.

"Then yesterday, out of the blue," D'Arcy Archer went on, "I had the chance of a lifetime."

"What was it?" Ilouka enquired.

"I was in an Agent's office, begging him almost on my knees to find me work. Even if it only brought in a few shillings I knew it would prevent me from starving."

He drew in his breath before he said:

"Yes, starving! The word may shock you, but it happens to be the truth."

"What happened?" Ilouka asked.

"He'd just told me that there was nothing and he was sick of seeing my ugly face," D'Arcy Archer answered, "when a letter was brought in to him by a groom in livery. The Agent, Solly Jacobs by name, took the note and opened it, and while he read it I waited.

" 'You can tell your Master,' he said to the groom, that I've no-one who will go to the country when there's plenty of work for them here in London.' "

Ilouka was listening now, interested in what Mr. Archer was saying, and as if her attention encouraged him, he continued:

"Because I was desperate I said:

" 'I'll go to the country!'

"Solly Jacobs laughed.

" 'Oh, you would, would you? Well, His Lordship wants something pretty and new to entertain his friends.'

" 'What does His Lordship want?' I asked quickly, in case the groom should leave.

"Solly Jacobs took the note and threw it across the desk at me.

" 'See for yourself,' he said.

"I picked up the note, and I think my hands were trembling. I had a feeling that was almost clairvoyant that this would mean something to me, and perhaps my luck would turn."

"What did the letter say?" Ilouka asked.

"It said that the Earl of Lavenham required two high-class entertainers for a party he was giving at his house in Hertfordshire tomorrow night. He was prepared to pay any sum that was reasonable, provided he had the best."

D'Arcy Archer paused as if to see what impression his story had made on Ilouka. Then, because she did not speak, he said:

"You must have heard of the Earl of Lavenham, the best-known sportsman on any race-course, rich as Croesus, and beautiful women surround him like moths round a flame."

"No, I have never heard of him . . . at least I do not think so," Ilouka mused.

"Then you can take my word for it, he's the tops in the Social World," D'Arcy Archer said.

"Do go on with your story."

As he continued, D'Arcy Archer's air of despondency seemed to lift and he sounded quite animated.

"I said to Solly Jacobs:

" 'If his Lordship wants the best, he can have it. You can leave that to me!'

" 'What are you talking about?' Solly Jacobs enquired.

" 'I'm telling you that I can supply the goods all right,' I replied.

" 'And how can you do that?' he asked.

" 'Well, I suppose you would think one of the leads from the *Olympic Revels* would please His Lordship and his friends?'

" 'If you're talking about trying to get Madame Vestris,' Solly Jacobs said, 'you can forget it. She wouldn't demean herself to go out of London for any man, not even Lavenham!'

" 'I wasn't thinking of Vestris herself I replied, 'but what about her understudy?' "

D'Arcy Archer paused and laughed.

"You should have seen Solly Jacobs' face!

" 'Are you certain you can get her?' he enquired.

" 'Quite certain,' I replied. 'She's been playing a small part in the *Revels* and she also understudies Madame Vestris. At it happens, she's a relative of mine.'

" 'I don't believe it!' Solly Jacobs said to me.

" 'It's true!' I answered. 'Lucille Ganymede is her name, and she'll not come for peanuts! But I'll fix it up.'

"I knew as I spoke from the expression on Jacobs' face that he only half-believed me, but he had no wish to refuse to do what the Earl wanted. He sent the groom away, telling him to come back for an answer in two hours' time, then he said to me:

" 'You've got two hours to fix it all up.'

" 'I'll fix it,' I said, 'but now I want to know how much you are soaking His Lordship for.'

" 'That's my business!' Jacobs said, 'But I'll make it worth your while, and the girl's. I'll give you fifty pounds all in. You pay the girl what she wants for her services, and I'll keep the rest.' "

D'Arcy Archer sighed.

"I knew 'the rest' would be a jolly heavy amount, but I was not disposed to argue. I knew that Lucille would not come cheap, but I also happened to know that she was hard up at the moment, had lost her Protector, and would at least listen to what I had to say."

"If she was acting at the Royal Olympic Theatre," Ilouka said, "how could she get away?"

"I can explain that," D'Arcy Archer said. "The last Season at the Royal Olympic has just ended. It started in January and finished in April, and Madame Vestris is having a rest, as is the rest of the cast, before they start up again."

"Oh, I understand!" Ilouka exclaimed. "So Miss Ganymede was free!"

"Exactly!" D'Arcy Archer replied. "And she jumped at the opportunity of meeting the Earl. There's not an actress in London who hasn't tried to catch his eye when he sits in his Box at the Theatre."

D'Arcy Archer chuckled before he said:

"Going down on their knees most of them are, hoping he'll ask them out to supper, but he's known to be very fastidious, and as one of them said to me:

" 'I'm more likely to be invited on a spree with the Man in the Moon than with the stuck-up Earl of Lavenham.' "

"Is he more important than any other gentleman?" Ilouka enquired.

"He is, and you would understand why if you saw him," D'Arcy Archer replied. "Top-lofty, an aristocrat to his finger-tips, and you're not likely to forget it."

He paused before he went on:

"And everything he touches turns to gold. His horses are nearly always first past the winning-post, gamblers go pale when they see him approaching the gaming-tables, and there is not a beautiful woman who doesn't fall into his arms like a ripe peach!"

Ilouka laughed because it sounded so funny.

"It is all very well to laugh," D'Arcy Archer said, and the despondent note was back in his voice, "but now you understand that without Miss Ganymede there is no point in my continuing my journey to the Earl's house."

His voice was bitter as he continued:

"I shall go back to London, tell Solly Jacobs I have failed, and you may be quite certain he'll want back what is left of his fifty pounds."

"It is not your fault," Ilouka said sympathetically.

"You tell that to Solly. He'll have his 'pound of flesh,' and I am the one who'll have to give it to him!"

D'Arcy Archer suddenly threw himself back in his chair and put his hands over his eyes.

"What is the point of going on?" he asked. "I'm old, finished, and the sooner I'm in the grave, the better!"

He spoke dramatically, but Ilouka knew that he meant it.

She could understand how bitter it was for him to lose the chance of making some money.

Through the Earl's influence, if he was pleased, Mr. Archer might have got other engagements of the same sort, but he had now, in her father's words, been "pipped at the post."

Poor man! she thought.

She knew it was as hard for him losing the little actress as it was for her losing Hannah.

She knew how upset her mother would be that Hannah was dead, and although she could not pretend that she was a particularly lovable person, she had been part of her childhood, and she knew that in many ways she would feel lost without Hannah, especially when she was at Stone House.

At least Hannah would have been a buffer between herself and Mrs. Adolphus, but now she would be alone there, with nothing to do but control herself from answering back when her mother's name was disparaged and everything she did was somehow wrong.

She gave a deep sigh and thought that when the Vicar returned she would have to ask him how soon there would be another Coach to carry them on to the next part of the journey.

Almost as if to think of him conjured him up, the Vicar came into the Sitting-Room.

He saw down beside Ilouka and said quietly:

"I have arranged, Miss Compton, for your maid and the young lady to be buried tomorrow morning. Our local carpenter is making the coffins for them at this moment, and I thought if you wish to continue your journey there would be no point in waiting any longer."

"No . . . of course not," Ilouka replied, "and thank you very much for all the trouble you have taken."

She paused, then she asked:

"Is there anywhere in the village where I can stay the night?"

"You can stay here," the Vicar said quickly. "I

thought I had already made that clear. I have told my Housekeeper to prepare a room for you and another for Mr. Archer."

"That is very kind of you, Sir," D'Arcy Archer said.

"I am afraid you will find my house is not very luxurious," the Vicar said with a faint smile, "but at least the rooms are clean, which I rather doubt they would be at The Green Man."

"I am very grateful."

As Ilouka spoke she knew that her mother would be horrified at the idea of her staying alone without Hannah to chaperone and look after her at a public Inn, however small and unimportant it might be.

"At what time will there be a Stage-Coach tomorrow?" D'Arcy Archer said. "Not to take me in the same direction in which I was travelling today, but back to London?"

"That is something I shall have to find out," the Vicar replied. "I think there is a man in the kitchen at the moment who will be able to answer that question."

He rose and left the room, and when he had gone Ilouka said:

"I am so sorry for you, Mr. Archer. I wish I could help."

"I wish you could too," he replied.

Then, as if she had suddenly put the idea into his head, he looked at her and his eyes seemed to take in for the first time since the accident the beauty of her face, the grace of her slim body, and her tiny feet which peeped beneath her travelling-gown.

He sat up, bending towards her.

"Tell me, Miss Compton, can you sing?" he asked.

"I have always sung at home," Ilouka answered, "and actually, now that I think of it, one of the songs which my mother has played for me is one which was made famous by Madame Vestris. It is the Bavarian Girls' song called *Bring My Broom.*"

D'Arcy Archer drew in his breath, and clasping his hands together so that he could control them, he said:

"And I am certain, almost certain, that you can dance."

Ilouka smiled at him and her eyes twinkled.

"Because that is something people often say to me," she answered, "I should now feel ashamed if I said 'no.' Actually, I love to dance!"

There was a little pause. Then D'Arcy Archer said in a voice which sounded strange:

"You know what I am asking you—no, not asking—begging, praying, pleading, beseeching you to do?"

Ilouka looked at him in surprise.

"What are you saying?"

"I am asking you save me—to give me the chance which I have just lost through fate, or perhaps by the intervention of the Devil!"

"I . . . I do not . . . understand."

"It is quite simple," D'Arcy Archer replied. "Would you, out of the charity of your heart, save a poor old man from starvation?"

"Are you asking me to . . . give you . . . money?" Ilouka enquired hesitatingly.

She felt it was rather embarrassing that Mr. Archer should plead with her in such a manner. But after what he had said she had in fact been wondering how, without offence, she could give him perhaps five pounds from the money she had with her for her travelling expenses.

"It is not a question of money," he said quickly in a low voice. "I want you to take Lucille's place. If you will do that, Miss Compton, you will literally and truly save my life!"

For a moment it seemed to Ilouka that she would not comprehend what he was asking her to do.

When he had enquired whether she could sing or dance she had thought he was just interested in acting, but it had never struck her for one moment that he was begging her to take an actress's place and go with him to fulfil an engagement he had with the Earl.

Now he had put it into words.

Her first instinct was to say it was something she could not possibly do. Then like a voice whispering insidiously in her ear she asked herself:

"Why not?"

It would undoubtedly be a kindness, and she was quite certain that the story Mr. Archer had told her was true and that his despair at losing Lucille was not assumed.

Then she thought how horrified and shocked her mother would be at such an idea.

At the same time, she could also see a picture of the bleak, ugly house waiting for her in Bedfordshire.

She could almost hear Mrs. Adolphus's scolding voice, and she knew she would feel that she was trapped in what was a particularly unpleasant prison for weeks, perhaps months, if Muriel could not wring a proposal out of Lord Denton quickly.

Now once again she realized how gloomy and lost she would be without Hannah.

At least the old maid was loyal to her mother and would in her own way somehow protect her from the worst unkindnesses that her step-father's sister would inflict upon her.

If I do what Mr. Archer wants, she thought, *it will at least take one day off the time I have to spend at Stone House; for even if Aunt Alice will have me, I cannot stay there long because they are so poor, and I might have to go back to Stone House.*

It all swept through her mind, not smoothly and rhythmically like something that was pleasant, but jerkily and disjointedly so that everything seemed worse.

I cannot go there without Hannah, Ilouka thought.

D'Arcy Archer was looking at her pleadingly, his hands clasped together, his eyes somehow like a spaniel dog's looking trustingly at its Master.

"I . . . I think . . . perhaps I rather exaggerated my . . . talents," Ilouka said hesitatingly. "I am sure

I am not . . . good enough to do anything . . . professional that you would . . . expect."

"I will be frank with you and say that while Lucille danced quite well and could sing with quite a pretty contralto voice—otherwise she would not have understudied Madame Vestris—she had little personality, and she certainly was not in any way as beautiful as you are."

He paused before he added impressively:

"I am not trying to flatter you, Miss Compton. I am merely telling you the truth when I say that I think you are the most beautiful girl I have ever seen in my whole life!"

"Thank you," Ilouka said. "But while I want to help you, Mr. Archer, you must realize that anything to do with the theatrical profession, even though this particular entertainment takes place in a private house, would seem very shocking to my mother."

"I think all mothers and Ladies of Quality treat the stage with suspicion," D'Arcy Archer remarked, "but I promise you, Miss Compton, I will look after you and make quite certain that everybody treats you with respect and propriety."

He paused before he continued:

"I happen to know that the Earl's interest is very much engaged at the moment with a very talented young actress who is appearing at Drury Lane, and in the Social World he has the pick of all the Beauties who are toasted from one end of St. James's Street to the other!"

"What you are saying, Mr. Archer, is that in no circumstances is he likely to be interested in me," Ilouka said.

"I am trying to reassure you, Miss Compton, that your visit will not involve you with His Lordship, nor, I hope, any of his friends. In fact I have always been told that the Earl is very fastidious as to whom he entertains."

"You certainly seem to know a lot about him," Ilouka said.

D'Arcy Archer laughed.

"Perhaps I am presuming on knowledge which comes from hearsay—the chatter in the Theater dressing-rooms and the gossip which occurs when men get together and discuss race-meetings and whose horses are most likely to win."

"I am sure I must have heard of the Earl in that connection," Ilouka said. "My father always followed the wins on the Turf, but I cannot remember the Earl winning either the Derby or the Gold Cup at Ascot."

"He did win the Derby three years ago," D'Arcy Archer contradicted, "but at that time his name was Hampton."

"Oh but of course!" Ilouka exclaimed. "Now I know whom you are talking about. He won with a horse called Apollo which my father said was the finest animal he had ever seen in his life."

"That is something I am sure the Earl would like you to tell him," D'Arcy Archer said.

Ilouka looked at him in a startled manner.

"I have not said that I will agree to your very strange and to me outrageous proposition."

"But you will, promise me you will? How can I tell you, Miss Compton, what it will mean to me? If you believe in answers to prayers, all I can tell you is that I'm praying fervently on my knees that you will not, like the Pharisees, pass by on the other side, but be a good Samaritan and save me."

Ilouka rose to her feet.

"You are making it very difficult for me to refuse you, Mr. Archer, although I ought to do so."

"If we always did exactly what we ought to do, the world would be a very dull place," D'Arcy Archer replied. "Put this down to an adventure, Miss Compton, something you will look back on and think that although it was rather daring, it was at least an act of courage and certainly one of most admirable Christian charity."

Ilouka walked to the window.

She looked out on the untidy, unkept garden, but she did not see the shadows growing longer as the last glimmer of the sun sank over the distant horizon.

Instead, she saw the flat fields of Bedfordshire stretching away towards a grey horizon, and she could hear the voice of Mrs. Adolphus, sharp as a needle, hurting her with every word she said.

An adventure! Something exciting, something new, something which would help a man who, through no fault of his own, had lost the chance of a lifetime.

How could she refuse? How could she be so hard-hearted as just to give him a few pounds and forget him?

She turned from the window.

"I agree to what you have asked me to do, Mr. Archer," she said quietly.

Chapter Three

Driving in a Post-Chaise, which D'Arcy Archer had found great difficulty in procuring, Ilouka thought it was certainly swifter and more comfortable than the Stage-Coach.

They had missed the latter because it passed through the village earlier in the day, when they were attending the Funerals of Hannah and Lucille Ganymede.

As they stood at the open graves in the small Churchyard where most of the tomb-stones were hundreds of years old, Ilouka felt that what was happening could not in fact be reality.

It seemed impossible that she had left home with Hannah, being her usual oppressive, rather disagreeable self, and now, by the mere chance of where she had sat in the Coach, she was dead.

If I had been sitting where she was, Ilouka thought, *I, like the young actress, would have died, and Hannah would still be alive.*

But one could only attribute what had happened to fate or to the direction of some Power which was beyond the comprehension of man and for which there was no intelligible explanation.

Whatever the reason for Hannah's death, Ilouka tried to pray fervently for her soul and that she would find peace and happiness in Heaven.

She was aware that Mr. Archer, standing beside her, was looking sad and very old.

It was as if with the death of the young actress he had brought from London he had lost not only his hopes and ambitions for the future but perhaps the last remnant of his youth.

Then Ilouka told herself that she was being imaginative, and what she must do was follow the Burial Service word by word and pray for the souls of those who had left this world.

When she had thanked the Vicar for his kindness and hospitality and had given his Housekeeper such a large tip for her services that she could hardly believe her eyes, Ilouka was glad to be able to leave.

She knew it was an episode in her life that she would want to forget, especially the terrifying moment when she had watched the Stage-Coach overturn and disappear down the small cliff where the road had collapsed.

She had learnt from the Vicar that one horse had broken its leg and had to be destroyed, and the other was very shaken by the accident and would have to rest for several days.

That is one good piece of news, at any rate, Ilouka thought.

She was quite certain that those who ran the Stage-Coach would hurry it back onto the road as quickly as possible.

D'Arcy Archer told her when he came down to breakfast that he had sent to the nearest Inn which could provide a Post-Chaise.

"It will take a little time to get here," he said, "but I could not ask you to travel in a Stage-Coach again, even if we had been able to catch the one that passed through here at eight o'clock this morning."

"I must admit it would make me nervous," Ilouka replied.

"What is more," D'Arcy Archer went on in a somewhat embarrassed tone, "I thought, Miss Compton, that as you are not a poor actress living on her earnings, you would not perhaps—require as large a—remuneration for your—services as Lucille demanded."

For the moment Ilouka found it difficult to reply. Then she said:

"I hope you will understand, Mr. Archer, that I am doing this entirely to help you, and I would not in any circumstances accept payment for what in your own words is an 'act of charity.' "

She saw by the smile which came to Mr. Archer's lips and the expression in his eyes that this was what he had hoped she would say and was delighted that he could keep all the money for himself.

"I can only hope," Ilouka went on, "that I am successful tonight, and that His Lordship and perhaps his friends will engage you for other parties, for which you can replace Miss Ganymede with an equally accomplished actress."

"One day, perhaps," D'Arcy Archer replied in a low

voice, "I shall be able to thank you for your kindness, but at the moment I find it difficult to express myself in words."

"Then please say nothing," Ilouka begged.

As soon as they set off in the Post-Chaise, the professional in D'Arcy Archer came to the surface and he began to explain to Ilouka exactly what he expected from her that evening.

"Usually on these occasions" he said, "the actors perform in the Dining-Room while the gentlemen are drinking their port and still sitting at the table."

Ilouka looked surprised.

"I suppose I somehow expected that anybody as rich as the Earl of Lavenham would have a private Theatre, or certainly a Music-Room where such performances would take place."

"I'm sure that His Lordship possesses both," D'Arcy Archer answered, "but this'll be far more informal and in fact a very *de luxe* and aristocratic version of the drinking-taverns where I've given my performances of late."

He spoke as if it had not been a very pleasurable experience, and Ilouka quickly changed the subject by asking him what the programme would be.

"First I'll play some spirited music . . ." he began.

"You are a pianist, Mr. Archer?" Ilouka interrupted.

"I started that way in an Orchestra at the Italian Opera House," he said, "but I soon wished to express myself as a person rather than as one of a team, so I struck out on my own."

"What did you do?"

"You name it, and I've done it!" D'Arcy Archer said. "I've taken parts in Plays by Shakespeare, I've travelled about the country, I've sung, danced, and at one time or another accompanied some very fine singers."

"It must have been very interesting," Ilouka said.

"Yes, but now I'm old," he remarked, "and nobody wants old men."

He spoke so sadly that Ilouka once again felt very sorry for him.

Then, as if he had no wish to depress her, he continued with his instructions on what they would do.

"I'll get them laughing," he said, "with jokes and songs at the piano which it'd be best for you not to listen to."

Ilouka looked surprised, and he explained:

"This is a party of gentlemen, Miss Compton, and I don't think there'll be any ladies present."

Ilouka felt as if he was a little doubtful on this score.

She did not realise that D'Arcy Archer was using "ladies" as the operative word and that the Earl might easily be entertaining a very different class of women, which would undoubtedly shock anyone as young as Ilouka.

Then he told himself that he was being needlessly apprehensive.

"Where we're going," he said aloud, "is the Earl's country seat, the home of the Hampton family, who are distinguished the length and breadth of England."

As he spoke he was quite certain that whatever the Earl might do in London, he would not bring women of doubtful virtue into his home.

Because he was silent, Ilouka prompted:

"And when you have finished singing, what happens then?"

"I announce you as somebody very talented and very original, and you'll come on and sing a song."

"What song?"

"That we'll have to sort out at rehearsal, which, incidentally, we should have as soon as we arrive."

D'Arcy Archer paused before he said:

"You told me that you know *Bring My Broom,* which Madame Vestris sings so brilliantly, but I'm not certain it's really suitable for you. Tell me what other popular songs you know."

"I was thinking about that last night," Ilouka replied. "I know *The Mountain Maid, The Month of Maying,* and a ballad from *The Beggar's Opera.*"

"Then we have a good choice," D'Arcy Archer said with a smile, "and we'll choose one which'll show you to your very best advantage."

"Thank you," Ilouka said.

"After that, you dance," he went on. "Now, what sort of music do you want for that? Without even having seen you perform, Miss Compton, I'm sure that you're a very light and graceful dancer."

"I hope so," Ilouka replied, "but you are well aware that I am not in the least professional."

"That is immaterial."

"Then if I have a choice, and you happen to know any," Ilouka said, "I would like to dance to gypsy music. I have Hungarian blood in my veins, and the mere sound of one of their melodies, which should really of course be played on the violin, makes me want to dance, and my feet feel as if they have wings."

She knew that Mr. Archer was pleased by what she had said.

As they drove on he hummed various pieces which seemed to her very melodious and which she was sure would inspire her to dance in the way she had danced for her father, which had always pleased him.

On the way they stopped for a glass of cider at a Posting-Inn where they also changed horses. Then they set off again at a good pace.

"At this rate we should arrive at four o'clock this afternoon," D'Arcy Archer said. "I hope, Miss Compton, you'll not be too tired for us to run over your song and also choose the music you desire for your dance?"

"I am not tired," Ilouka replied, "although I did stay awake rather a long time last night, thinking of poor Hannah."

"Try to forget it," D'Arcy Archer advised. "It was a terrible experience which I'm sure could only happen once in a lifetime and will never occur again."

"I hope not," Ilouka replied.

As they drove on she was in fact feeling guilty, not so much about Hannah but because she was going about with a stranger to stay in a private house to which she had not been invited personally.

However, she considered that the alternative of rumbling along in a Stage-Coach alone to Aunt Agatha's house in Bedfordshire was a far worse proposition.

"At least when I do get there," she told herself, "I shall have something to think about and remember, which will make the misery of that dismal house seem not so oppressive."

At the same time, she was well aware that she was behaving in a most reprehensible manner and that it would give Mrs. Adolphus a heart-attack if she ever learnt about it.

"Only Papa would understand that I have no wish to turn my back on an adventure," Ilouka told herself.

However, she was well aware that she was just making excuses for something she wished to do.

When she glanced at Mr. Archer she realised that he was indeed a very old man, and if he was not smiling and making himself agreeable, his face in repose looked almost like a mask.

The lines at the sides of his eyes and from his nose to his mouth were so prominent that she could understand why he found it so difficult now to obtain a part on the stage.

"At least with the money he will earn from this he will be comfortable for a short while," she told her conscience.

She thought that if she had refused him it would be something for which she would undoubtedly reproach herself for the rest of her life.

Then, when a little earlier than D'Arcy Archer had

expected the Post-Chaise turned in through a huge stone gateway surmounted by a coronet, Ilouka felt excited.

There was a long avenue of ancient oaks and at the end of it a magnificent house which she recognised as early Georgian with a lofty central block and two wings stretching out from it, making the whole a picture that was architecturally superb and of great beauty.

She was aware that Mr. Archer was impressed, but neither of them spoke as the Post-Chaise crossed a bridge at the narrow end of a large lake on which black and white swans moved serenely over the silver water.

They drew up outside a long flight of stone steps which led to the front door.

As they did so, footmen in green and yellow livery, which Ilouka recognised as the Earl's racing-colours, came hurrying down the steps to help them from the Post-Chaise and lift down the luggage from the back of it.

D'Arcy Archer paid their driver, then walked up the steps in a manner which told Ilouka he was acting the role of a lofty, authoritative Gentleman of Fashion.

The Butler greeted them, but not exactly with the kind of respect, Ilouka thought, that he would have done if she were arriving as herself.

"I think, Sir," he said to D'Arcy Archer, "you're the entertainers His Lordship told me to expect. Your bedrooms are ready for you, and on His Lordship's instructions there's a Sitting-Room adjoining them where there's a piano which His Lordship felt you might require."

"That is extremely considerate," D'Arcy Archer replied. "And is His Lordship at home at the moment?"

"No, Sir," the Butler replied. "His Lordship and his guests are at the races."

They were shown upstairs by a footman and taken along a corridor at the far end of which was a Suite consisting of two bedrooms with a Sitting-Room between them in which there was an upright piano.

Because it looked slightly out-of-place, Ilouka was sure it had been added as a concession to their profession.

She thought, as Mr. Archer had said, that it was considerate of the Earl to think it might be needed.

Then she remembered what Mr. Archer had told her about his being attached to a very talented actress who was appearing at Drury Lane, and thought he must have learnt from her what entertainers required.

Their luggage was brought upstairs and two housemaids appeared to unpack for Ilouka.

Because she had brought a great number of things with her for her stay in Bedfordshire, thinking perhaps it would mitigate her depression if she had the satisfaction of knowing she looked nice, she instructed them to unpack only the things she would need for the night.

Then she was puzzled for the moment by seeing that there were not only her own two trunks in the room but also another very shabby one which she did not recognise.

She was about to ask for it to be removed to Mr. Archer's room when she realised that it must have belonged to Lucille Ganymede.

Then she suddenly thought that if the actress had understudied Madame Vestris and sung the songs she had made so famous, she would undoubtedly dress in men's clothing.

It flashed through Ilouka's mind that Mr. Archer might expect her to do the same thing.

Then she told herself she was being needlessly apprehensive.

However, Lucille Ganymede's trunk in her room

made her feel uneasy, first because it belonged to a woman who was dead, and secondly because it contained clothes which she considered immodest and indecent.

She pointed it out to one of the housemaids, saying:

"This trunk contains 'props' which, as it happens, I shall not need for our act this evening. Will you remove it from here and place it either in the Sitting-Room or somewhere outside until we leave?"

"Very good, Miss," the housemaid replied.

As they unpacked, Ilouka realised they were looking at her with curious eyes, almost as if she were an unknown species of female.

It amused her, and when she changed her travelling-gown for one of the simple but expensive dresses which her mother had bought for her in London, she went into the Sitting-Room to find Mr. Archer already seated at the piano.

He went on playing and said without turning round:

"Is this the sort of music you like?"

He ran his fingers over the keyboard and began to play a melody which immediately conjured up pictures in Ilouka's mind of the gypsy musicians with their colourful clothes and painted caravans.

She listened with delight until D'Arcy Archer turned his head to say:

"I'm waiting to hear your verdict, Miss Compton."

"It is perfect!" Ilouka replied. "But if you will forgive me, I do not wish to practise my dance. I prefer to react spontaneously to the music when I hear it."

"There speaks the true professional!" he exclaimed. "At the same time, if I'm to accompany you for your songs, I think we should practise them."

"Yes, of course," Ilouka agreed.

However, they were interrupted when two footmen brought in a tray of delicious paper-thin sandwiches and a large selection of cakes which made Ilouka, after her simple luncheon, feel quite greedy.

She noticed that Mr. Archer ate hungrily, as if he was afraid the food would disappear before he had time to enjoy it.

Later thinking it over, she was certain he had at times been near to starvation and was afraid it would happen to him again.

If I have a chance, she thought, *I will ask the Earl to recommend him to his friends. If that happens, at least for a time he will not starve and will not be so afraid for the future.*

After tea they tried out two or three songs, then D'Arcy Archer said he preferred her singing of *The Mountain Maid* and insisted that she go to have a rest.

"I want you to be very good tonight," he said, "and look like Persephone herself coming down into the darkness of Hades."

Ilouka laughed.

"That would hardly be polite to our host, and anything less like Hades than this lovely and impressive house I could not imagine."

She spoke lightly, and she did not see the expression of apprehension in D'Arcy Archer's eyes, almost as if he was afraid for her in a way he had no wish to express.

Ilouka was in bed and almost asleep when she heard in the Sitting-Room an authoritative voice speaking to Mr. Archer.

At first it was just a sound that seemed to mingle with her thoughts, which had almost become dreams.

Then it became real and she was aware of it and was sure that their host had returned and was doubtless giving Mr. Archer his instructions for the evening.

As she listened to it she thought the voice was exactly what she had expected from what she had heard about the Earl of Lavenham—clear and authoritative, and yet cold, distant, and undoubtedly condescending as he spoke to an inferior.

I suppose, she thought, *that with all his possessions and the adoration he receives as a sportsman, and with all those beautiful women running after him, he is abominably conceited.*

She did not know why, but she felt at that moment almost hostile towards the Earl, although she had never seen him.

It was as if she were really a poor, aspiring actress hoping by his patronage to further her career and, like Mr. Archer, praying that the Earl's approval would somehow change her whole future.

After her father's death Ilouka had known what it was like to be very poor and be frightened of being entirely without money, so she had a kindred feeling for anybody in the same position.

She could hear Mr. Archer's voice, and although she could not hear what he said, she was aware that he was being humble and ingratiating.

It was almost as if he went down on his knees in front of the Earl.

It is wrong, she thought, *that one man should have so much and others so little, and I doubt if he has any sympathy for the under-dog.*

She told herself again that she would do everything in her power to make the Earl help Mr. Archer, and wondered if it would be possible to speak to him alone while she was staying here.

But she expected that when they had finished their act they would merely leave the Dining-Room, or wherever they were performing, and in the morning be sent away like unwanted baggage and never thought of again.

Then there was silence in the next room and she knew the Earl had left.

He has given his orders, she thought, *and all we have to do is to obey them to the letter!*

Because she was so tired she fell asleep.

Waiting behind the curtains which separated the main Dining-Room from the dais on which they were to perform, Ilouka could hear the voices and laughter of the guests the Earl was entertaining.

She was also vividly aware how nervous Mr. Archer was, and she thought with a smile of amusement that he might be the amateur and she the professional.

She was not worried for herself because she knew that if the Earl's guests did not appreciate her it would not matter at all to her, and only Mr. Archer would suffer.

She wanted to give a good performance for his sake, and because she had already conceived what was almost a dislike of their host, she longed to make him realise that he was not omnipotent.

At the same time, she was being needlessly critical when it would have been impossible to find fault with the way in which they had been treated so far.

Although Ilouka was aware that the rooms which they had been given were certainly not the best in the house, they were nevertheless very comfortable, and the piano had been provided especially for them.

The meal which had been served in their Sitting-Room, at the same time as the Earl and his guests dined downstairs, was excellent, and there was a bottle of wine which D'Arcy enjoyed, although Ilouka preferred lemonade.

All the time she knew that within herself there was a growing resentment at finding herself in an inferior position, which was something she had never known before in her life.

Mockingly she told herself it was a salutary experience which she would never forget.

However, there was nothing she could put her hand on positively that brought it home to her so vividly.

It was just the Earl's tone of voice when he was speaking to Mr. Archer and the way they were served the dinner, which although correct made Ilouka feel that the footmen, like the housemaids, were regarding them with curiosity rather than respect.

Then there was the house itself.

As they walked through it on their way to the Dining-Room, Ilouka had a glimpse of a huge Salon lit with crystal chandeliers and saw a unique collection of paintings and fabulous furniture.

As she peeped surreptitiously through the curtains into the Dining-Room itself, she told herself again that the Earl possessed too much.

She was looking at his possessions when she saw him.

He was sitting at the end of a long table which in the fashion set by George IV was polished and without a table-cloth, and on it were ornaments of both silver and gold which were breathtaking.

After a quick glance at them, Ilouka found herself looking at the man who sat at the far end in a high-backed armchair and knew that the Earl was actually exactly as she had expected him to be.

His friends whom he was entertaining, and there were about twenty or more, all men, were laughing uproariously and appeared to be enjoying themselves with an exuberance which she thought must have come after a good day's racing.

But she thought that the Earl in contrast looked supercilious and almost bored.

He was better-looking then she had expected, with straight classical features, hair swept back from a high forehead, and even at a distance she thought that in his evening-clothes with a high cravat round his long neck he was magnificent.

At the same time, he gave the impression of sitting aloof on a pinnacle of his own making, and with no intention of stepping down from it to mix with the common herd.

He is too proud and too puffed up with his own importance, she thought.

She pulled the curtain to, in case he should be aware that there was someone peeping at him.

The small stage or dais on which they were to perform stood between two pillars in the Dining-Room.

Ilouka thought it was probably used on other occasions by a Band or perhaps quite frequently for entertainment such as they were to give tonight.

The piano, D'Arcy Archer found with satisfaction, was an excellent one, and there were several lamps on the edge of the dais to act as footlights.

After some consideration as to what she should wear, Ilouka had chosen what she thought was one of her prettier gowns, which her mother had bought for her to wear at smart parties or a Ball.

It was not white, which would have been conventional for a débutante, but very pale green, with a full skirt which billowed out from a tiny waist and with puffed sleeves of the same material.

The décolletage displayed Ilouka's white skin, which her father had said had a magnolia-like quality about it.

The only ornamentation she wore was round her neck: a little cameo set with tiny diamonds that was hung on a ribbon of the same colour as her gown.

She had taken a great deal of trouble in arranging her hair in a much more elaborate manner than her mother felt was correct for a young girl.

Because she had long hair and the colour of it shone in the light, she arranged it in curls at the back of her head so as to make her look, in her own eyes at any rate, very theatrical.

It certainly framed her small heart-shaped face, and because despite her resolution to remain very calm she was excited, her eyes seemed enormous.

They had little glints of gold in the green of them, which made anyone who looked at her find it hard to look away.

As a concession to her theatrical appearance she had tied ribbons of the same colour round her wrists and added to each one a small white rose which actually belonged to another gown.

At the last moment she placed two of the same roses on top of her head and knew that they gave her the spring-like look of Persephone that Mr. Archer had envisaged.

When she had gone into the Sitting-Room where he was waiting for her, he stared at her for a long moment before he said:

"You look exactly as I hoped you would, and there is nothing more I can add to that."

"Thank you," Ilouka replied. "I am only afraid that I may let you down."

"I think that is impossible," he said. "We shall know by the end of the evening whether we are a success or a failure, but I am quite certain that the latter is a word which we need not include in our vocabulary."

Ilouka smiled.

"Papa always said that if you want to win the race you must believe yourself the winner."

"And that is what we must do," D'Arcy Archer said. "Now come, it is time we went downstairs, but before we do so, let me thank you once again for coming to my rescue."

As he spoke he took her hand in his and kissed it with a theatrical gesture which made Ilouka want to laugh.

Instead she accepted his tribute gracefully and they walked down the Grand Staircase side-by-side, while the footmen in the Hall watched them appreciatively.

When they were shown into the back of the Dining-Room and heard the noise made by the diners, Ilouka wondered how it would be possible for them to hold the attention of the Earl and his friends.

She thought it would be extremely humiliating to their self-esteem if they were either ignored or hissed off the stage.

Then she knew that even if they were not interested in her personally it did not matter, and only Mr. Archer would suffer.

I will do my best for his sake, she thought. *Then it is in the lap of the gods.*

She knew the dinner was coming to an end when the port had been taken round the table and decanters and others filled with brandy were set in front of the Earl.

He raised his voice and Ilouka heard him say:

"Now, Gentlemen, there will be a short entertainment to amuse you, and tonight it will be something that has not appeared here before."

"You are making me curious, Vincent," one of the Earl's guests remarked.

"Then I will reveal my surprise," the Earl said. "I am sure all of you know Madame Vestris!"

There was a murmur of assent and approval before the Earl went on:

"Madame unfortunately could not join us this evening, but we have in her place her understudy, and one who I am told is as attractive and as redoubtable as Lucy herself and—dare I say it?—somewhat younger in years!"

There was laughter at this and the Earl went on:

"Madame has captured the hearts of far more of us than I wish to disclose. Let us hope that her understudy will prove to be another Lucy as she was when she first captivated, entranced, and undoubtedly scandalised the *Beau Monde* eleven years ago."

There was more laughter and one or two men clapped their hands.

Then as if this was his signal to begin, D'Arcy Archer started to play the lilting, gay tune he had described to Ilouka.

Hidden behind the curtains, she heard the hush from the Dining-Room as the music started.

Then as Mr. Archer burst into song she realised that he had a deep baritone voice, which had however deteriorated with age, although his enunciation made it easy to hear every word he said.

She realised from the laughter that he evoked with almost every line that the song was appreciated by those listening to it.

At the same time, she found it hard to understand.

She told herself there must be a *double entendre* of some sort because a quite simple phrase had those listening laughing uproariously.

After a number or two she ceased to listen, and moving back to her peephole in the curtains she looked through it to discover the Earl's reaction.

As she had somehow expected, he was not laughing. Instead she thought there was a faintly contemptuous smile on his face, which annoyed her.

As he leant back in his chair, very much at his ease with a glass of what she thought must be brandy in his hand, she had the idea that while his friends had all eaten and drunk well, he had been abstemious.

She might have been wrong, but while their faces were flushed and in some cases riotously red, the Earl looked cool and athletic, and the jokes, if that was what they were in the song, did not make him laugh.

Perhaps he will recommend Mr. Archer even though he personally is not very impressed with him, Ilouka thought.

She had a feeling he was far from impressed and told herself that if Mr. Archer could not please the Earl she must certainly do so.

When the song came to an end, D'Arcy Archer told two or three jokes, which again Ilouka did not understand, and now she realised that at any moment it would be her turn.

She had an uncomfortable feeling that everything depended on her being a success.

The laughter died away as D'Arcy Archer said:

"And now, M'Lords and Gentlemen, I have the privilege of introducing a Lady who, when you see her, you will agree is like a nymph rising from the lake below the house, or perhaps a sprite who has crept in from the woods which surround us, or more likely, just a goddess who has stepped down from Olympus because she wishes to bemuse and bewitch the human race.

"Yes, that is right! It is a goddess I have here, and therefore, Gentlemen, let me present to you the Goddess Ilouka, here in person, for one performance and one only, before she returns to the place from whence she came."

It was all very dramatic, and it took Ilouka by surprise that he should call her by her own name.

At the same time, she was glad that she was not in fact having to impersonate somebody who was dead.

Then as D'Arcy Archer returned to the piano and played the first chords of *The Mountain Maid* she came slowly and gracefully onto the dais to stand in the centre of it.

Just for a moment she felt as if her voice had gone, then as if she was drawn to him like a magnet she looked towards the Earl.

As the words of the ballad rang out in her very musical voice, which, although she had no idea of it, had an almost hypnotic quality about it, she sang to him and him alone.

She saw that he was watching her, and while he leant back in his chair, apparently uninterested, she was almost certain that she held him with the vibrations of life flowing towards him from within herself with a magnetism which she forced him to acknowledge.

When the ballad had finished she made a little curtsey and the applause from the Earl's guests was unanimous and noisy.

The Earl did not clap, but his eyes were still on her face and Ilouka had the idea that although he would not show it, he had thought her good.

D'Arcy Archer was already playing the gypsy music they had chosen to which she would dance, and she stood very still, drawing in her breath, trying now to think not of the Earl but of the music itself so that it should inspire her.

Almost like a picture in front of her eyes she could see the Hungarian Steppes as she envisaged them, the mountains in the distance topped with snow, and a band of gypsies camped round an open fire, their piebald horses cropping the grass, the women sitting in the doorways of the painted caravans.

The men placed their violins under their chins and the dancers came running towards them to dance to the music which ran in their blood.

It was then as she saw it all happening that Ilouka became one with the dancers, and her feet began to move.

Because D'Arcy Archer was a professional he knew instinctively what she wanted. At first the music was slow and soft and spoke of the gypsy's yearning which came from his soul as he searched for love, which was part of his heart.

Sometimes he found it, but sometimes he must move on to search for it in other lands, an El Dorado which was always beyond the farthest horizon, then beyond again.

Ilouka moved and swayed and translated into rhythm the music which flowed from Mr. Archer's fingers.

There was complete and absolute silence as her whole being stirred towards the adventure of life, not only of the spirit and the soul but also of the body.

The music quickened and Ilouka's feet seemed to fly over the polished floor until to those watching her it was as if she flew in the air above it.

She moved quicker and quicker, her arms in graceful harmony with her feet, her head thrown back, her eyes brilliant with a strange ecstasy which was part of the music, part of the feelings rising within herself.

Then those who were watching began to move their feet and hands in rhythm like the slow thump of drums.

They moved quicker and quicker until finally, as if she had attained what she sought and desired, she stood for a moment absolutely still.

Her arms were flung up towards the ceiling and her head was thrown back in rapture before finally she sank down to the floor, an indescribable gesture of surrender to forces greater than herself.

At a signal from D'Arcy Archer, with the final crescendo of music, the footmen closed the curtains.

The applause in the Dining-Room was deafening and several of the guests rose to their feet, shouting: "Bravo!" while others cried: "Encore!"

D'Arcy Archer rose from the piano to take Ilouka's hand and raise her to her feet.

He realised, as only a professional could, that for a moment it was difficult for her to come back to reality from the magic world into which her dancing had taken her.

"You were magnificent!" he exclaimed.

She gave him a faint smile before the curtains were pulled open, and the pressure of his hand told her that she must curtsey as he bowed to the applause in the Dining-Room.

Then as the curtains were shut again, there was a cry of: "Join us, join us. We went to talk to you!"

The footmen in charge of the curtains hesitated a moment, but Ilouka, as if suddenly aware of the men applauding her, remembered that she was the only woman in the room and said quickly:

"No! No!"

She did not wait for Mr. Archer to accompany her, but before he would say anything, taking her hand from his she fled through the door by which they had entered the Dining-Room and ran along the corridor and up the stairs.

She could not put it into words, but she knew that what she was encountering, although she had not expected it, was another dangerous situation.

Chapter Four

Upstairs in her bedroom, Ilouka sat down on the stool in front of the dressing-table and waited for the tremulous beating of her heart to subside and her breath to come more easily from between her lips.

She felt as if she had been through a deep emotional experience and it was hard to face normality and herself again.

She knew that she had never before danced so well or put so much feeling into her movements.

She was aware that first it was because she was trying her best to help Mr. Archer since for his sake so much depended on her, but also because she had been carried away by having an audience and especially the Earl.

It had not been her main object to impress him, but because she wanted to help Mr. Archer she had somehow stepped into the part so that she became temporarily the Hungarian dancer she imagined herself to be and was no longer Ilouka Compton.

Now she had to make the transition back to what she thought of as her ordinary, prosaic self, and journey to Bedfordshire to stay with an extremely disagreeable old woman because her step-sister was jealous of her.

And yet for the moment that was the fantasy and what she had been feeling inside herself was real.

Slowly her heart-beat returned to its normal pace and she looked at herself in the mirror opposite her.

Although her eyes were still shining brilliantly, she felt that her face now looked familiar and she had in fact become Ilouka again.

Then there was a knock on the door, and thinking it was one of the housemaids she called out:

"Come in!"

To her surprise, when the door opened it was a footman who stood there.

"His Lordship's compliments, Miss, and he'd be obliged if you'd join him in the Salon."

This was something which Ilouka had somehow not expected, and her first instinct was to refuse.

After all, she had played her part, she had entertained His Lordship's guests, and she thought it was unreasonable of him to demand more.

Then as the words of refusal sprang to her lips, she thought that if she did not do what he asked, perhaps it might harm Mr. Archer.

She was quite certain in her own mind that the applause she had received from the Earl's guests would have impressed him.

If that was so, he would probably ask Mr. Archer to entertain his guests at other parties he gave and also might recommend him to his friends.

However, she remembered that the Earl had not applauded her as his friends had done, and if she refused to obey his request, he might in his authoritative way make Mr. Archer suffer for her omission.

It is the sort of thing he would do, Ilouka thought, *because he thinks everybody must obey him, and he ignores our personal thoughts and feelings because we are of no consequence.*

It made her angry to think such things, and yet they were inescapable.

If she were her own master, she thought, she would send a message to the Earl saying that she had fulfilled her part of the contract for which he had paid, was tired, and had no wish to do anything else except retire to bed.

Then she thought that if she sent such a reply it was doubtful if the footman would be brave enough to repeat it.

She felt herself smile at the thought of how angry the Earl would be simply because he was being defied by an actress of no importance whom he expected to be obsequiously grateful for his even noticing her.

Whatever my own feelings, I must help Mr. Archer, she decided.

She knew that the footman was looking at her curiously, as if he could not understand her hesitation, and after a deliberate pause she said:

"Please inform His Lordship that I will join him in a few minutes."

"Very good, Miss," the footman replied, then with a grin he added impudently: "You'd better make 'em short. His Lordship don't like waiting."

He shut the door as he spoke and did not hear Ilouka laugh.

Then because she refused to be hurried she deliberately tidied her hair and smoothed down her gown, and after quite a long look at her reflection in the mirror she walked slowly along the passage which led to the Grand Staircase.

As she went she could not help thinking how horrified her mother would be if she knew what she was doing.

It was also a pity that Muriel was not in her place to enjoy the experience of meeting a large number of gentlemen without any competition.

The thought of Muriel made her begin to hope fervently that Lord Denton, who was now staying at The Towers, would become so enamoured of her that he would propose marriage.

If they get married quickly, I can go back home to Mama, she thought, and knew that was what she wanted more than anything else.

As she reached the Hall a footman went eagerly ahead of her to open the door to the Salon.

As she reached it there was the noise of voices and loud laughter. But although it sounded very gay, Ilouka thought it was not the sort of party that would be considered correct for a débutante.

"But that is what I am not allowed to be," she excused herself.

At the same time, as the footman flung open the door she had to force herself to lift her chin and walk forward slowly and with a composure that she was not feeling.

There was quite a distinct hush as she moved down the big room beneath the lighted chandeliers, and although she felt shy and tried to focus her eyes, she could see nothing but a blur of faces.

Then, almost as if he were spot-lighted for her, she perceived the Earl and standing beside him Mr. Archer.

Then two gentlemen began to clap and others cried out: "Bravo!" as they had before, and one said in a loud voice:

"The goddess has returned from Olympus! Let us hope she does not recognise us for the swine we undoubtedly are!"

There was a roar of laughter at this, but Ilouka did not turn her head as she moved forward, fixing her eyes on Mr. Archer.

He walked to meet her, took her hand in his, and raised it to his lips.

"Thank you for coming," he said in a low voice that only she could hear.

She knew then that she had been right in thinking it was important.

Still holding her hand, he drew her towards the Earl.

"M'Lord," he said, "may I present *Mademoiselle* Ilouka!"

She dropped the Earl a graceful curtsey, and the

Earl said in the deep voice she had heard when she was trying to sleep:

"I am delighted to meet you, and of course I want to thank you for a very brilliant performance."

"You are very kind."

When she had risen from her curtsey she looked up into the Earl's eyes and found he was staring at her in a manner that somehow made her feel more shy than she was already.

She had been right in thinking that he was overwhelming and insufferably superior.

But she was determined not to give him the satisfaction of letting him think that he intimidated her.

"I have been admiring your house, My Lord," she said in the tone her mother would have used on such occasions, "and although I have often heard of your superlative horses, I did not realise you also owned such outstanding paintings."

She thought that for the moment she had surprised him, but he replied almost without a pause:

"I hope I may have the pleasure of showing them to you, *Mademoiselle,* but now my friends are anxious to meet you."

While she had been talking to the Earl, Ilouka realised that his guests had crowded round her.

Because there were so many of them and their faces were red and their eyes appraised her in a manner which she felt was impertinent, they seemed almost to be menacing her.

Without really meaning to, she took a step away from them, which took her to the Earl's side.

As if he understood, he said:

"I think, gentlemen, it would be rather embarrassing for *Mademoiselle* Ilouka to meet you all at once. It would be easier if I introduced you one by one, so that you each have a chance of conversing with her."

"I would prefer to dance with her!" one man replied, and another of the gentlemen retorted:

"That is only because you want to get your arms round her, Alec."

As this was a way Ilouka knew no gentleman would have spoken in her mother's Drawing-Room, she stiffened.

Because she suddenly had no wish to be left all alone with men who she thought had been drinking too much and were still holding glasses of wine in their hands, she said to the Earl:

"I am somewhat tired, My Lord. We have been travelling for two days, and I would prefer, if it is possible, to talk to you alone."

As she spoke she thought it might be the one opportunity she would have of putting in a good word for Mr. Archer.

"The choice of course, is yours," the Earl replied, "and what I am going to suggest is that we sit down on the sofa before I offer you a glass of champagne."

As he spoke he indicated the sofa which was at the side of the fireplace, and Ilouka immediately walked towards it to seat herself so that she faced the room.

There was a table covered with exquisite pieces of china directly behind her, so it was impossible for any of the guests to approach her unawares.

It was almost as if they had become a threatening pack of wolves, and only by avoiding direct contact with them could she feel safe.

As she was speaking to the Earl she had noticed that Mr. Archer had deliberately moved away.

He knew he was not wanted and tactfully had walked to where at the other end of the room stood a large and impressive piano.

He sat down and began to play very softly the sort of music which would make a suitable background to conversation without intruding on it.

As the Earl joined Ilouka on the sofa, she heard his guests making remarks to the effect that it was no use competing against Vincent, while another said:

"I never bet on the favourite."

They were certainly laughing and joking amongst themselves because they thought that the Earl was monopolising her.

At the same time, she had the feeling that they were too much in awe of him both as a man and as their host to protest about it.

As the Earl sat down beside her he said:

"Did you say you would like a glass of champagne, or would you prefer a liqueur?"

"I want nothing, thank you," Ilouka replied, "except to hear that you enjoyed our entertainment tonight."

"I thought that there would be no need for me to express the obvious."

"Then you were pleased?" Ilouka insisted.

"Far more pleased than I could possibly have anticipated."

She gave him a smile before she said:

"I am glad, so very glad!"

"Why?" the Earl enquired abruptly.

"Because it means a great deal to Mr. Archer," Ilouka said. "Like many people in the theatrical world, he has been going through a very difficult time, and your request for an entertainment here this evening came at just the right moment for him."

She paused, and as the Earl did not speak she bent forward to say pleadingly:

"Please ask him to come here another time, and perhaps you will tell your friends how good he is."

The Earl raised his eye-brows.

He was sitting sideways so that he faced her rather than leaning against the back of the sofa, and there was an expression on his face that she did not understand as he said:

"I thought we were talking about you."

"I am of no importance," Ilouka said quickly, "and as Mr. Archer made clear, I am here to give one performance and one only. But for him it is different . . ."

She could not say more because the Earl interrupted her to ask:

"Where in London are you performing? And why have I not seen you?"

For a second Ilouka hesitated, wondering what she should reply.

Then she said a little mockingly:

"I thought Mr. Archer made it quite clear that I was here to amuse you before I returned to the place from whence I came."

"And where is that place?"

"Where could it be but Olympus?"

She thought she was being rather clever in preventing him from being too inquisitive, but the Earl said:

"You cannot expect me to be content with such an imprecise address, but it is something we can talk about later."

"I want to help Mr. Archer."

"Why? What does he mean to you?" the Earl enquired.

"I am sorry for him."

As she spoke she thought that perhaps she had taken the wrong line.

The Earl might be the type of man who liked success and was interested in obtaining only the best.

Perhaps, she thought, in trying to help Mr. Archer she might have done him a disservice, in that the Earl, with all his money, would wish to employ only those entertainers who could command a large audience and a high fee elsewhere.

Because she felt so deeply concerned for Mr. Archer she said quickly:

"He is not begging for himself, but I am aware that because you are so important in sporting and in the Social World, you could do much to help him."

Shc thought there was a cynical twist to the Earl's lips as he said:

"Most young women in your position want me to help them."

"I am in no need of help," Ilouka said quickly.

"Are you sure of that?"

"Very, very sure."

"Are you now speaking as a goddess, or as an aspiring young dancer whom I have not yet seen on the stage at Covent Garden, which would be a far more prestigious place for you to perform than at the Royal Olympic Theatre?"

There was silence while Ilouka wondered what she could answer, and the Earl went on:

"I presume that you are intending to remain with Madame Vestris when the next Season opens. I consider you are wasted as an understudy, and I could promise to find you a part in a very much more important Theatre where I can undoubtedly arrange for you to play a lead."

"That is very kind of you," Ilouka replied, "but I was not asking you to help me, but Mr. Archer."

"Why is he so important to you? Or let me put the question I asked you just now in a different way: why are you so concerned about him?"

It flashed through Ilouka's mind that perhaps the Earl thought he was a relative of hers or that in some way she was indebted to him.

Because she had no wish to lie, and at the same time she wished to try to make the Earl understand why she wanted to help Mr. Archer, she hesitated before she said:

"I am sure you are finding this conversation very boring, My Lord. Let us talk about something more interesting."

"I want to talk about you," he replied.

"I would rather talk about horses, and Apollo in particular. How is he?"

"What do you know about my horses? This is the second time you have mentioned them."

"I know how sucessful you have been on the racecourse," Ilouka answered, "and I remember when you won the Derby with Apollo what a magnificent race it was, and how in fact he only won by a nose."

As she spoke she recalled her father describing it to her and saying it was the most exciting race he had ever watched.

"I did not even mind losing my money, which I can ill-afford," he had said to her mother, "because I wanted the best horse to win, and it was not until the very last second that we were aware which one that was."

"*I* mind you losing it, darling," her mother had replied, "because we cannot afford losses, however small."

"Do you know how much I lost in the whole day's racing?" her father had asked.

Her mother shook her head and Ilouka was aware of the look of anxiety in her beautiful eyes.

"Nothing!" her father laughed. "In fact, I won!"

He had taken a large handful of notes and coins from his pocket and put them into her mother's lap.

"My lovely doubting Thomas does not trust me!" he said. "But I return to you on this occasion the winner!"

"Oh, darling, I am glad," her mother replied.

Her father had laughed and pulled his wife into his arms, forgetting that the money was in her lap.

The coins had rolled all over the floor and Ilouka picked them up.

As she did so she thought how it made everybody happy when her father won when he gambled, but unhappy when he lost.

It was the same with people, she thought now, and while the Earl might worry about his horses, he did not understand how much the losers in life suffered.

"If you do not leave too early tomorrow morning," he was saying, "which is something I hope I can persuade you not to do, I will show you Apollo."

"He is here?"

"Yes, he is here, and actually he ran in a race today, heavily handicapped, but he won."

"Oh, I am so glad!" Ilouka exclaimed. "I would love to see him! It would be very thrilling for me."

She spoke with such excitement in her voice that the Earl looked at her curiously.

She was aware that if she could see Apollo it would make her feel close to her father, as in the days when he would describe to her in the evening the races he had watched and explain how the winner had managed to beat the rest of the field.

"Is the fact that I have a horse in which you are interested the reason why you agreed to come here?" the Earl asked. "I was certainly not expecting anybody quite so talented, or quite so beautiful."

He spoke in a dry, rather cold manner which did not make the compliment embarrassing.

Because he had asked her a direct question, Ilouka answered truthfully:

"When I agreed to come here with Mr. Archer," she said, "I was not aware that you were the owner of Apollo, because when he won the Derby your name was Hampton."

"I am very flattered that you should be interested in me," the Earl said. "At the same time, I cannot believe that you were very old at the time of that particular race, nor were you appearing in any London Theatre, or I would have seen you."

"That is true," Ilouka answered.

"How old are you?"

Iouka saw no reason to lie and replied:

"I am just eighteen."

"When did you join Madame Vestris at the Royal Olympic Theatre?"

Ilouka was thinking quickly what she should reply, when they were interrupted by one of the Earl's guests.

He was obviously older than the Earl himself. In fact, Ilouka thought, he was almost middle-aged. His face was not only red but somewhat puffy under the eyes, which gave him the debauched look that she found repugnant.

"You are being distinctly unfair, Vincent," he said as he stood beside the Earl at the sofa. "You are behaving like a dog in a manger, and if you are not careful you will have a revolution on your hands."

The Earl smiled.

"I am sorry, George," he said, "but as you will understand, I find *Mademoiselle* Ilouka absorbingly interesting, and I have no wish to surrender my position to anybody else."

"Well, I think it is too bad," his friend expostulated.

"Very well," the Earl said with a sigh. *"Mademoiselle,* may I present Lord Marlowe, a gentleman who will flatter you outrageously, so I suggest you take everything he says to you with the proverbial 'pinch of salt'!"

As he spoke the Earl rose from the sofa, and because Ilouka had no wish to talk to Lord Marlowe, who she was quite certain had drunk far too much, she also rose.

"I hope, My Lord," she said, "you will not think it rude if I retire. I am in fact feeling exhausted."

"Now that I cannot allow," Lord Marlowe said. "I want to talk to you, lovely lady, and I have a lot of things to whisper into those pretty little ears of yours which will be greatly to your advantage to hear."

As he spoke he put out his hand to touch her, but Ilouka looked at the Earl and said:

"I would like to say good-night to Mr. Archer, then go to bed."

She did not wait for his approval or for the words which Lord Marlowe was already beginning to say to her.

She moved swiftly across the room with a grace that made everybody she passed stand watching her until she reached the piano.

D'Arcy Archer looked at her from the piano-stool, then lifted his fingers from the keyboard.

"I want to go to bed," Ilouka said quickly in a low voice.

"I am sorry," he said, "but they insisted upon your coming downstairs and there was nothing I could do about it."

"I understand," she said. "Now, please, may I go?"

"It will not be easy . . ." D'Arcy Archer began, then was silent as the Earl joined them.

"I have an idea to which I hope you will agree," he said as D'Arcy Archer rose to his feet.

"What is that, My Lord?"

"It is that you stay with me tomorrow and give another performance for my dinner-party tomorrow evening."

Ilouka wished to say that was impossible, but she saw the delight in Mr. Archer's eyes as he realised what the Earl had asked.

"I have in fact," the Earl continued, "engaged another type of entertainment to amuse my guests, but I feel sure there is nothing they would enjoy more than a repetition of your performance, or a variation of what occurred this evening. I assure you I will be very generous for taking up so much of your time."

"Your proposition is something which I shall be only too delighted to accept, My Lord," D'Arcy Archer replied, "but of course, I first have to have the agreement of *Mademoiselle*."

He looked at Ilouka as he spoke, and she knew that he was pleading with her, begging her almost on his knees to agree.

"You have already told me," the Earl said to Ilouka, "that you would like to see Apollo, and I would enjoy showing you the rest of my stable. We could make the visit tomorrow morning before I leave with my friends for the races at about noon. And while I am away, the house and gardens are at your disposal, and those too I think you will find of interest."

As he spoke Ilouka was thinking that if she behaved as she ought to, she would refuse the Earl's invitation and insist on Mr. Archer taking her to where she could find a Stage-Coach to carry her to Bedfordshire.

But if she did that, she knew she would feel that she was being cruel in depriving Mr. Archer of the opportunity he craved so fervently. It would be a selfish act which would be of no real benefit to herself.

Strange and unusual though this party was, reprehensible though it might be for her to be alone with a large number of gentlemen, some of whom had undoubtedly imbibed too freely, to her mind it was certainly preferable to sitting in the ugly, stiff Drawing-Room at Stone House and being nagged by Aunt Agatha.

Both men were waiting for her decision, and she had the feeling that the Earl was very confident that he would get his own way and she would not refuse him.

Because she thought there was a smile of victory on his lips and an expression of triumph in his eyes, she longed to say "no."

But one glance at Mr. Archer decided her.

Once again there was that pleading spaniel look on his face that made her feel he was very pathetic.

"It would be a pity," she said slowly, "if after pleasing Your Lordship tonight we disappointed you tomorrow."

"I am quite certain you will not do that," the Earl replied, "and anyway, let us say it is a risk I am prepared to take."

Now he was definitely smiling, and as she thought it annoyed her she said:

"Very well, I agree to do what Your Lordship wishes, but I would still like to retire now."

"Then I will allow you to do that," the Earl answered, "but before you go will you agree to sing once again for my friends, who are feeling upset at enjoying so little of your company? I would be extremely grateful if you would oblige me."

He looked at D'Arcy Archer as he spoke, and Ilouka knew that without saying so he would be ready to pay for the extra song.

"It will not be too much for you?" D'Arcy Archer asked as he seated himself once more at the piano.

Ilouka knew he was elated at the success she had been, and most of all at the thought of staying another night and earning more money.

"No, I am all right," Ilouka replied. "What am I to sing?"

"Sing a song they know well," he suggested.

He lowered his voice and added:

"By this time, after such a good dinner, they will appreciate almost anything! So do not be nervous."

"I am not, as it happens," Ilouka answered.

As she spoke she saw Lord Marlowe staring at her and realised that while they had been talking to the Earl he had come up the room and moved until he was quite near to the piano.

The Earl turned to his friends.

"Gentlemen, I have persuaded *Mademoiselle* Ilouka to sing us a good-night song, and she has also promised to entrance us again tomorrow evening with her dancing."

There was a murmur of approval at this, and without waiting any longer D'Arcy Archer struck the first chord of the Bavarian Girls' song *Bring My Broom.*

Ilouka stood beside him at the piano, and as she did so she saw the Earl move towards the door, open it, and speak to a footman on duty outside.

She wondered if he was not interested in hearing her sing, but even before the piano introduction had finished he had shut the door again and was leaning against the wall beside it as the song started.

As it was a sprightly German tune, Ilouka realised it appealed to the audience as Mr. Archer had expected it to do.

When she finished, there was a burst of applause which started even before she curtseyed.

Then as she smiled at Mr. Archer and they moved towards the door, Lord Marlowe was at her side.

"That, *Mademoiselle,* was quite entrancing! And I want to have the opportunity of telling you so," he said in a thick voice.

He would have taken her hand, but Ilouka managed to avoid him, and before he could prevent her from doing so, she sped towards the door where the Earl was holding it open, waiting for her.

"Good-night!" she said as she reached him.

The Earl followed her out into the Hall and shut the door of the Salon behind him.

"I enjoyed your singing," he said, "but your dancing is something very different—so different that I cannot think why you have not been discovered before now."

"You are very complimentary, My Lord," Ilouka said, "but actually, although you may find this hard to believe, I have no wish to be discovered and am quite happy as I am."

"Are you telling me," he asked as they walked towards the staircase, "that you are not infatuated, entranced, and obsessed about the stage, which you have chosen as your career?"

"I think the answer is," Ilouka replied, "that I do not particularly want to do anything but be myself, and to express myself in my own way."

As she spoke she thought she had been very clever.

She had not lied, she had told the truth, and if he put a different construction on what she was saying, that was not her problem.

But she was aware as they reached the bottom of the staircase that he was looking at her penetratingly and searchingly, as if he thought she had a reason for being elusive and was determined to find out what it was.

She held out her hand and curtseyed.

"Good-night, My Lord."

He did not reply, but took her hand in his and held it for a moment while his grey eyes were still searching her face.

She looked up at him and something frivolous that she had been about to say died on her lips. Instead, she could only look at him, feeling that he had something important to say to her, but she had no idea what it was.

Then because she heard the sound of voices and laughter coming from behind them and knew the Salon door had opened again, she took her hand from the Earl's clasp and without saying any more hurried up the stairs.

She did not look back, although she knew he had not moved from where she had left him.

"I am puzzling him," she told herself. "He must not become too inquisitive, but it will do him good to know that I am different in a way he cannot explain."

She walked up the staircase, but when she would have turned left, towards the room she occupied, an elderly housemaid appeared.

"Excuse me, Miss," she said, "but I have had to move you to another room."

"Move me?" Ilouka enquired. "But . . . why?"

"His Lordship felt you were not as comfortable as you could be," the housemaid replied. "Come this way, Miss, and I'll show you where you are sleeping now."

Ilouka thought it was rather strange, for actually the room in which she had been had seemed very comfortable.

She followed the housemaid along a passage towards another part of the great house.

They walked for some way until the housemaid opened a door to a room which was very much larger, more impressive, and certainly more beautiful than the one she had occupied.

The room was exactly what she would have expected the State-Room of an early Georgian house to be.

It had a painted ceiling, panelled walls, long windows draped with fringed pelmets, and a beautiful four-poster bed, carved and gilded, with curtains of silk embroidered skilfully in a manner which Ilouka knew would send her mother into ecstasies.

She wanted to ask questions as to why her room had been changed, and as she was about to do so she saw that there were two housemaids in the room hanging up her gowns that had previously been unpacked and that her two trunks were there too.

She decided it would be wrong to ask questions in the circumstances and could only say:

"I would be grateful if you would undo my gown. I am very tired, and I am sure I shall sleep peacefully."

"I certainly hope so, Miss," the housemaid said in a voice that seemed almost an echo of Hannah's.

The thought of her old maid brought her back so vividly that Ilouka somehow thought she was there, disapproving strongly of the way she was behaving, and even more so because she had agreed to repeat the same reprehensible act tomorrow.

"Poor, dear Hannah!" Ilouka murmured beneath her breath, as the housemaid undid her gown and hung it up in the wardrobe.

Another housemaid showed her that opening out of the bedroom was a sunken bath similar to the drawings she had seen of Roman baths.

"How extraordinary to find one here in a Georgian house!" she exclaimed.

"His Lordship had it built in what was originally a Powder-Closet," the housemaid explained again, in a somewhat disapproving voice, "but most ladies prefer to bathe in their bedrooms, as is usual."

Ilouka wanted to laugh, knowing how servants always disliked anything different and out of the ordinary.

She thought that while she was staying with the Earl

she would certainly avail herself of his modern innovations, whatever they might be.

The housemaids curtseyed and went from the room, and when they had gone Ilouka went to the door to turn the key in the lock.

The last words her mother had said to her before she left for her journey to Bedfordshire had been:

"I only hope, dearest, that the Inn where you will stay the night is not too uncomfortable, and do not forget to lock the door securely. If it has a weak and ineffective lock, put a chair under the handle."

Ilouka had smiled.

"I will remember, Mama, but I think it unlikely that robbers will creep in to steal anything from me."

"It is not only robbers who might disturb you, darling," Lady Armstrong had replied. "So promise you will not forget."

"Of course I promise, Mama. Do not worry," Ilouka had said. "I will lock my door, say my prayers, and not forget to clean my teeth."

She had laughed as she spoke, and Lady Armstrong had put her arms round her to say, almost as if she spoke to herself:

"You are far too lovely, my precious one, to be travelling about the country in Stage-Coaches instead of in a private carriage with two men on the box."

"I shall be safe enough," Ilouka had replied. "I cannot believe that even the stupidest farm yokel would think I would make him a competent wife and begin to pursue me ardently with Hannah's full disapproval."

Lady Armstrong had laughed again.

"That is true enough, darling. At the same time, I am worried, so do not forget everything I have told you."

Ilouka had kissed her mother good-bye and thought as they drove away that she was being needlessly apprehensive.

It was unlikely that anything so eventful as thieves,

robbers, or highwaymen would trouble her while Hannah was there.

Instead, she had dropped dramatically into the most fantastic adventure she could possible have imagined.

"I certainly never expected to sleep in a room like this," she said to herself.

She washed in the Roman bath, which also had an elegant wash-hand-stand with hot water in a polished brass can which was covered with a quilted cosy to keep it warm.

Then she blew out the candles, except for two by her bed, and knelt down to say her prayers.

She prayed for Hannah and the poor actress who had died beside her, she thanked God for what had been a very exciting evening, and she prayed that the Earl would be kind to Mr. Archer after they had left Lavenham House.

Lastly, Ilouka prayed that she would be forgiven for the lies she had told and for doing something of which she knew her mother would not approve.

"But I am sure she would also think it wrong not to help poor Mr. Archer," she said.

As she finished her prayers she thought it would be nice if one could ever hear the answers to the questions one asked, then decided it would be very disconcerting if one did.

She took a last glance round the room and got into bed.

As she had expected, the mattress was very soft and comfortable, the pillows were filled with the finest down, and the sheets were of finer linen than she had ever slept in before.

His Lordship certainly lives in comfort, she thought.

For a moment she did not blow out the candles because the room was so beautiful and she wanted to look at it, picturing the Countesses who had slept there in the past.

She wondered if the Earl's guests had ever included

Queen Adelaide, for this room was certainly fit for a Queen.

Then unexpectedly, surprisingly, when everything was quiet, she heard a knock on the door.

It was very faint, and she thought for the moment she must be mistaken, until it came again.

As she listened she wondered if it was a housemaid who had returned because something had been forgotten.

But before she could decide whether or not to ask who was there, she heard a voice which she recognised say:

"Let me in, pretty lady. I want to speak to you."

Ilouka sat upright in bed.

It was Lord Marlowe! There was no mistaking the thick voice in which he had spoken to her before, only now it seemed even more slurred.

"Let me in!" he said. "I must talk to you! I insist!"

Quite suddenly Ilouka was frightened, more frightened than she had ever been before in her life.

She leapt out of bed to run to the door and look at the lock.

She touched it and it seemed that because it was so large it would be strong and secure.

But as the handle turned and re-turned she realised that Lord Marlowe was putting pressure on the door from outside, and she had the terrifying feeling that it would give.

She looked round frantically and saw a chair painted white and gold with a brocade seat. Dragging it to the door, she fixed the frame under the handle as her mother had told her to do.

Her heart was beating frantically in case Lord Marlowe should break in, and she was frightened to the point where she wanted to scream, but she knew it would be useless.

The room where she knew Mr. Archer was sleeping was a long way away, and she had the idea that even if she screamed no-one would be interested, except for

Lord Marlowe, who would renew his efforts to reach her.

There was an armchair on which the maid had placed her dressing-gown.

It was quite heavy, but by using all her strength Ilouka managed to push it over the carpet towards the door, but now Lord Marlowe was not whispering and his voice had grown louder as he said:

"Let me in! Let me in!"

She thought, although being so inexperienced she could not be sure, that he was too drunk to know when he was beaten and too befuddled to move away.

She gave the armchair another push, still hoping it would hold the door closed.

Then, as she wondered frantically what else she should do, the door on the other side of the fireplace, which she had not noticed before, opened and the Earl entered the room.

She turned her head and saw him there, and with a leap of her heart she knew he had come to save her.

"Please . . . please . . . help me!" she cried before he could speak. "If the lock breaks . . . Lord Marlowe will be able to . . . come in."

She was not aware of what she was saying, she was only concerned that the Earl seemed like an angel of deliverance, there when she least expected it.

Then she saw the expression of anger on his face.

"I will deal with this!" he said, and left the room by the door through which he had come.

CHAPTER FIVE

Ilouka stood clasping her hands together and listening.

She could still hear Lord Marlowe's voice and he was still pushing against the door.

Although she knew now that even if he did burst in the Earl would save her, at the same time without realising it she was holding her breath until she heard his voice.

Then it came, and although she could not hear exactly what he said, she realised from his tone that he was being sharp and commanding.

She could hear Lord Marlowe expostulating. His voice was raised so that she could have heard what he was saying, but she was no longer listening.

Instead, she was standing dazed and immobile until finally she heard Lord Marlowe, grumbling and protesting but moving away until his voice faded altogether.

Then she turned round to look towards the door by which the Earl had entered her room.

Vaguely at the back of her mind she supposed there must be a Sitting-Room attached to her bedroom as there was in the room she had first been given.

She had little time to think before the Earl came back, and she thought as he walked towards her that he seemed taller and more omnipotent than he had seemed in the Dining-Room.

She thought perhaps it was because he was wearing not his evening-clothes but a dark robe which almost reached the floor.

When he came to her side, she had intended to thank him.

Instead, perhaps because of the relief she felt that he had saved her from Lord Marlowe, or perhaps because she had not been exaggerating when she said she was very tired, she felt the room begin to swim round her.

She put out her hand to hold on to the Earl to prevent herself from falling.

"Are you all right?" he asked.

"I . . . I was so . . . frightened," Ilouka said incoherently.

"You have had a long day . . ."

He picked her up in his arms, carried her to bed, and put her down against the pillows.

As he did so, far away at the back of her mind Ilouka thought he must think her very foolish, but it did not seem to matter.

"Go to sleep," the Earl said, "and I will say what I want to say another time."

She wondered vaguely what that could be, but was really too exhausted to ask questions.

Then she knew that the Earl had moved from her bedside and was pulling the armchair back to its proper place from where she had pushed it against the door.

He also moved back the chair she had placed there first.

"Y—you . . . do not think . . . Lord Marlowe will come . . . back?" she asked.

"You may be certain he will not do that," the Earl answered.

"He is . . . horrible!" Ilouka murmured. "And he . . . has had too . . . much to . . . dri . . ."

The last words faded away into silence, and the Earl placed the chair with the brocade seat down beside the bed and stood looking at Ilouka.

Her hair was falling over the pillow and over her shoulders, and as it caught the light from the candles it seemed to glow as if with little flames.

Her eye-lashes were very dark against her cheeks and she looked very young, child-like, and vulnerable.

The Earl stood looking at her for a long time, realising from the rhythmic rise and fall of her breast that she was in a deep sleep.

Then with a faint smile he bent forward and kissed her very gently on the lips.

Ilouka made a little movement but she did not wake.

The Earl picked up one of the candles beside the bed, blew out the other, and went from the room, closing the communicating door behind him.

Ilouka came back to consciousness feeling as if she moved through layers and layers of sleep until she was aware that there was a light in the room and the maid was pulling back the curtains.

For a moment she could not remember where she was and thought she must be at home.

Then as she clutched at her dreams as if they were precious, she suddenly remembered everything that had happened the day before.

She was not at The Towers but was staying with the Earl of Lavenham and was supposed to be an understudy for Madame Vestris at the Royal Olympic Theatre in London.

It seemed even more ridiculous than any of her dreams had ever been. Then she opened her eyes wide and as she did so the maid came to the bedside to say:

"Excuse me, Miss, for disturbing you, but His Lordship'll be leaving for the races in a short while and wishes to speak to you before he goes."

Ilouka sat up in bed.

"What time is it?"

"After eleven o'clock, Miss."

"Oh no! It cannot be!" Ilouka exclaimed in dismay.

She remembered that the Earl had promised to show her Apollo and his other horses, and by oversleeping she had missed seeing them.

Then she remembered that she and Mr. Archer were to stay another night and there was therefore every chance that she could see them tomorrow.

"How could I have slept so late?" she asked aloud.

"I expects you were tired, Miss," the maid replied. "I've brought your breakfast."

As she spoke she carried a tray to the side of the bed and set it down on the table.

"Thank you," Ilouka said.

"Shall I fill the sunken bath, Miss," the maid enquired, "or would you prefer one here in your bedroom?"

Ilouka smiled.

"I am longing to use the Roman bath," she replied. "I have never been in one before."

"Very good, Miss."

She spoke in a tone which told Ilouka she thought it would be far more proper if she bathed in her bedroom.

Hannah would have felt the same, Ilouka thought, and felt a pang of grief for the old maid.

It was Hannah's death that had prevented her from sleeping the previous night, which had made her miss seeing Apollo.

Besides which, although she had not been aware of it, the singing and dancing in front of an audience of strangers had been a strain that she had never encountered before.

And heaped upon it had been her fear, which had

amounted to terror when Lord Marlowe had tried to force her bedroom door open.

Thank goodness the Earl came to save me when he did! she thought, and wondered how he knew what was happening.

She supposed that he slept nearby and must have heard Lord Marlowe pleading with her to let him in.

"How could he imagine I would do such a thing?" Ilouka asked herself indignantly.

She supposed that when men had drunk too much they had strange ideas and behaved in a way which they would not do in ordinary circumstances.

She ate her breakfast, which was delicious, and there was also a peach which she knew must have come from a hothouse.

She thought as she peeled it that it was a mistake to stay another night here, comfortable though it might be.

She had helped Mr. Archer because she had been sorry for him, but he had in fact said that she was appearing for one performance and one performance only.

Tonight she would be forced to meet Lord Marlowe again, or at least to be aware that he was watching her and trying to attract her attention as he had done last night.

"Mama would be horrified!" Ilouka told herself. "If I behaved properly, I would go away today."

Even as she thought of it she knew she could not be so cruel as to let down Mr. Archer when he was so thrilled by the Earl's appreciation of the entertainment he had provided for him.

"I shall just ignore Lord Marlowe," Ilouka told herself. "In any case, I want to see the horses, and I also find it interesting to talk to the Earl."

He might be slightly superior, but he had certainly used that quality to her advantage when he had sent Lord Marlowe away from her door.

Thinking back, she remembered how he had tidied

the room so that the housemaids would not think it strange when they called her in the morning.

She supposed that the maid had come in through the Sitting-Room as he had, as she had not awakened in time to unlock the door to the passage.

He was very kind, Ilouka thought.

She remembered that he had lifted her into bed, and for the first time she was aware that while she had been pushing the furniture in front of the door to keep out Lord Marlowe she had been wearing only a thin nightgown.

It fastened at the neck and had little frills over her wrists. At the same time, because it was of such fine lawn it must have appeared almost transparent.

She felt herself blushing to think that a strange man had seen her so immodestly garbed.

I do not suppose he noticed, Ilouka comforted herself.

It was difficult to remember what he had said or if she had thanked him before he left.

He must have blown out the candles, and vaguely, so that it was difficult to put into a coherent idea, she thought that he had said something which had made her heart leap before she had finally faded away into the deepest depths of sleep.

What can it have been? she wondered.

Then she knew it could not have been anything the Earl said but was part of her dream in which she thought that somebody had touched her lips, and she had been kissed for the first time in her life.

That would be a dream, she thought; but it was different from any dream she had dreamt before.

She finished the peach, jumped out of bed, and went into the closet where the sunken Roman bath was.

Two maids were pouring into it cans of hot water. There was another of cold water in case the bath should be too hot, then they left her to bathe herself.

It was exciting to step down the three marble steps into the bath and sit below the surface, feeling as if she had slipped back into the past and was the daughter of a Roman General or perhaps the Emperor himself.

I must tell Mama about this, she thought, and wondered if she would ever dare to do so.

She did not linger long, knowing that the Earl was waiting. Back in the bedroom, the maid helped her dress and she put on a very pretty gown of pale green muslin sprigged with tiny flowers.

The material had come from Paris and had been made for her by one of the Royal dressmakers in London, and only when she had glanced at herself in the mirror did she think that she looked far too richly gowned to be an actress who had to earn her own living.

However, it was too late to change, and she said to the maid:

"Where will I find His Lordship?"

"He is waiting for you, Miss, in the *Boudoir* next door."

Ilouka had expected him to be downstairs and was embarrassed because it somehow seemed so intimate.

The maid opened the communicating door and she went into the *Boudoir*.

It was far bigger than she had expected, and far more impressive. The walls were hung with exquisite French paintings, the furniture was French, and there was the fragrance of carnations which filled several vases.

The Earl was sitting in a comfortable chair, reading a newspaper.

He put it down and rose as Ilouka walked into the room, and as she saw his eyes glance at her gown, she thought he was aware that it was not suitable for the role in which she appeared.

"Good-morning . . . My Lord," she said hastily. "I am very . . . upset that I overslept . . . and I must . . . apologise. It is my loss, because I was so looking forward to seeing Apollo."

"I have something to tell you," the Earl said quietly, "and I am afraid it will come as rather a shock."

"A . . . shock?" Ilouka repeated in surprise.

"I suggest you sit down."

She looked at him wonderingly, trying to guess why he was speaking in such a grave tone.

At the same time, she could not help admiring the elegance with which he was dressed, and she saw that in the daylight he seemed if anything to be better-looking than he had the night before.

Because he was obviously waiting for her to sit, she did so obediently, but she raised her eyes to his apprehensively, wondering what he could be about to say.

She was suddenly afraid that by some terrible mischance he had discovered who she was.

"What I have to tell you," the Earl said very quietly, "is that when Mr. Archer was called this morning by the footman who was valeting him, it was found that he had died during the night."

For a moment it was impossible for Ilouka to take in what the Earl had said.

Then she exclaimed:

"What are you . . . saying? It . . . cannot be . . . true!"

"I am afraid it is," the Earl said. "After all, he was I think a very old man. Perhaps he suffered from heart trouble and was not aware of it, but I think it will be some consolation for you to know that he died with a smile on his lips."

"I cannot . . . believe it!" Ilouka said. "He was so happy to . . . come here, and so very . . . happy that you asked him to stay . . . another night."

The Earl sat down beside her on the sofa. Then he said in a rather different tone of voice:

"What did this man mean to you?"

"I was so sorry for him," Ilouka replied. "He told me this was his . . . last chance and unless he could . . . please you he faced . . . starvation."

"Is that the only reason you came with him?"

"He pleaded with me and begged me to save him, and I thought it would be cruel to say 'No' . . ."

"I had a feeling it must be something like that," the Earl said.

"It does not seem . . . possible that he is . . . dead."

As she spoke Ilouka was thinking that Hannah always said that things happened in threes, and on this occasion it was certainly true.

Three deaths in a row, Hannah's, Lucille Ganymede's, and now poor Mr. Archer's.

She was aware that the Earl was watching her face, and after a moment she said:

"Perhaps in a way it was the . . . best way for him to . . . die. He knew he had been a success last night, and you had asked him to give another performance, and that meant he would have enough . . . money to last him for a . . . long time."

"That is a very sensible way to look at it," the Earl said. "I want you to leave everything to me, Ilouka. I will see that he is buried in the Churchyard in the Park, and unless you particularly wish to do so, I see no point in your upsetting yourself by being present at his Funeral. But of course, you will wish to notify his relatives."

"I do not know . . . who they are."

"You mean you only know this man professionally?"

Without thinking, she told the truth.

"I met him only the day before yesterday."

As she spoke she realised she had made a mistake, because the Earl said:

"When he asked you to come here?"

There was a little pause.

"Yes . . . that was it," Ilouka agreed.

"Then I think we can leave notification of his death to the Agent who was contacted by my secretary," the Earl said. "It was he who arranged the entertainment for my party, and he will pay any money Archer has left to those depending on him."

As he finished the Earl smiled at Ilouka and added:

"That leaves you to be provided for, and I want you to have no worries on that score. I will look after you."

"Thank you," Ilouka said quickly, "but I . . ."

She had been about to say that there was no need for anybody to look after her, when the Earl rose to his feet, took her hand, and pulled her to her feet.

"Now listen, Ilouka," he said, "we have a great deal to say to each other, you and I, but now I have to leave with my friends for the races. I want you to stay here, explore the house, walk in the garden, and rest until I return."

"But . . . I think I . . . ought to . . . go away," Ilouka managed to say.

The Earl smiled again.

"Do you really think I would let you do that?" he asked. "I intend to protect you and prevent you from getting into this sort of trouble again."

Ilouka stared at him as if she could not believe what he was saying.

Then as she was trying to find words, he put his fingers under her chin and turned her face up to his.

Just for a moment he looked down into her eyes, then incredibly, so that she could hardly believe what was happening, his lips came down on hers.

Ilouka had never been kissed and she had no idea that a man's lips could make her feel as if she were his captive and it was impossible to try to escape.

For a moment she was too amazed, too astonished to even think clearly of what was happening.

When she told herself that she must struggle, she felt as if a streak of lightning swept through her body.

It was the strange ecstasy she had felt when she was dancing, which seemed to come from some music within her heart and which she felt must be in the Earl's heart too, and that they listened to it together.

It was so enthralling and so mesmeric that it

seemed to pulsate through her, and even as she felt it moving within herself and flowing out in little waves, she knew that the same feeling came from him.

They were linked together not only by their lips but by every breath they drew and the life within themselves.

It was so rapturous, so ecstatic, that when the Earl raised his head she could only stare at him, her eyes seeming to fill her small face.

Her voice had died in her throat.

"Now do you understand?" he asked in a deep voice. "We will talk about it when I return. Until then, take care of yourself."

As he finished speaking he walked away and opened the door of the Sitting-Room, then went out and shut it behind him.

For a moment it was impossible for Ilouka to move.

She could only stand where he had left her, conscious that her heart was throbbing in her breast and her whole body was pulsating in a manner she had never known before.

It was an extension of the emotions she had felt last night when she had danced to the gypsy music and known that she was searching for love.

Then because it was so overwhelming, so unlike anything she had ever dreamt of or imagined, she sat down again on the sofa and covered her eyes with her hands.

She seemed to be sitting there for a long time.

Then gradually as the throbbing of her heart returned to normal and the rapture that was in her throat and in her breasts seemed to fade into the distance, she knew that she must face facts and try to be sensible.

She tried not to think of the wonder the Earl had aroused in her, and with some critical part of her brain she forced herself to think clearly.

She knew that what the Earl was saying was something which would shock and horrify her mother and to which it was impossible for her to listen.

She could hear Mr. Archer saying to her that Lucille Ganymede had lost her "Protector" and that was one reason why she was willing to come with him to entertain the Earl of Lavenham.

Ilouka had not realised exactly what the word "Protector" meant.

Now vaguely she remembered things her father had said which she had not understood at the time but which now became more clear.

He had not known she was listening when he had said to her mother on one occasion:

"Madame Vestris has fallen on her feet. She is under the protection of one of the richest men in London."

"I thought she was married," Mrs. Compton had replied.

"They have parted company," the Colonel answered, "which from Lucy Vestris's point of view is about the best thing that could happen to her financially."

"I cannot think why the affairs of such women interest you, darling," Mrs. Compton protested, and her husband laughed.

"If you are jealous, my love, there is no reason for it. I am just telling you the gossip of the Club. Living here, we usually get the news weeks or months later than anybody else."

Ilouka knew by the note in her father's voice that he was regretting once again, as he did so often, that they were too poor to spend much time in London and were unable to afford the sports that he found so engaging.

As if her mother thought the same thing, she quickly put her arms round her husband's neck and said:

"Oh, darling, I wish I were a rich heiress."

"In which case you would doubtless have married a

Duke," the Colonel laughed, "and I would not have got a look in! I love you just as you are, and money is not really important where we are concerned."

"No, of course not," Mrs. Compton answered.

They had walked away with their arms round each other, unaware that Ilouka, sitting reading behind the curtain on the window-seat, had overheard what they said.

Not that she had been particularly interested at that time, but now she understood exactly what the Earl was offering her.

Moreover, it was not only a shock but positively frightening that his kiss had made her feel sensations she had not realised existed.

I must go away! she thought frantically. *How can I stay here and go on deceiving him? How could I ever let him know that when he kissed me it was like dancing on the top of the snow-capped mountains?*

She thought that expressed all that she had felt.

Yet it was even more than that, for the feelings he had evoked in her were not as cold as snow, but warm and glowing like the sunshine, or perhaps the flames of a gypsy fire leaping higher and higher as she danced round it.

"I must go away!"

She repeated the words as if she forced herself to listen to them.

Yet as she rose to her feet she had an irrepressible desire to stay where she was and await the Earl's return from the races so that she could talk to him, and perhaps, although it was wrong to think it, he would kiss her again and she would feel the pressure of his lips on hers.

"I must be crazy!" Ilouka said to herself. "What . . . would Mama . . . think of me?"

She walked across the room to the window and as she did so she saw that she was looking out over the front of the house towards the lake and the Park.

To the left was the centre block of the building, and

outside the front door she could see several Phaetons drawn up one behind the other, and she knew they were waiting to carry the Earl and his friends to the races.

As she watched, the gentlemen began to come out through the front door.

They stood for a moment on the steps, then the Earl was with them, his top-hat at the side of his dark head, his polished Hessian boots gleaming in contrast to the pale champagne-yellow of his tight-fitting pantaloons.

He stepped into the first Phaeton and one of his friends climbed in beside him.

A groom sprang up into the small seat behind, and when they moved off the Earl drove his horses in a way which told Ilouka that he was an expert with the reins.

The other vehicles were filled quickly with his friends, and those who had no wish to drive in a Phaeton travelled in a very comfortable and luxurious brake.

Ilouka stood at the window watching them until the last sign of the cavalcade vanished beneath the thick foliage of the oak trees, then she gave a little sigh and went to her bedroom next door.

She knew that what she had to do was difficult, not only because she had never travelled alone before, but also, although she was ashamed to admit it, because her heart urged her to stay where she was.

Two hours later Ilouka was being driven down the drive.

She had given orders to the housemaids to pack for her and for a carriage to take her to the nearest Posting-Inn with an air of authority which prevented the servants from arguing or even suggesting that she should wait until their Master returned.

She was fortunate in that the Earl's secretary, who ran the house, had also gone to the races and there was therefore no-one of any real authority left behind to tell her what she should or should not do.

Only when she was dressed for travelling and her trunks were strapped and ready to go downstairs did she say to the Housekeeper:

"I would like to see Mr. Archer before I leave."

"Is that wise, Miss? It may upset you," the Housekeeper replied.

"I would like to say a prayer beside him," Ilouka answered.

Without saying any more, the Housekeeper led her down a passage towards the room she had occupied when she first arrived.

The blinds were drawn, but there was enough light to see that Mr. Archer had been laid out with his hands crossed on his breast.

He looked, Ilouka thought as she neared the bed, almost as if he were carved in stone and lying on top of a tomb in a Church.

Now that she saw him dead, he looked younger, as if there was no more for him to worry about, and the lines on his face were less deep-cut than they had been when he was alive.

The Earl had been right when he said he had died with a smile on his face, and he did in fact look happy.

He was *happy,* Ilouka thought.

She was certain that the Earl would not only have rewarded him well but recommended him to his friends.

But she knew his recommendation would not be of very much use unless Mr. Archer could ensure that the entertainment he provided would include herself.

Because the Earl had very different ideas on that score, it might have meant that when the money was spent, once again he would fall on ill times.

She knelt down beside the bed and said a prayer for his soul and asked that he would find peace.

As she rose to her feet she found herself thinking that perhaps God knew best, and Mr. Archer through his death had been saved a lot of misery and anxiety about a future in which every day he would be growing older.

She went out of the room to find that the Housekeeper was waiting for her in the passage outside.

"The coffin'll be coming this afternoon for the poor gentleman," she said. "You'll not be staying for the Funeral, Miss?"

"I am afraid I cannot do that," Ilouka replied.

"If His Lordship wishes to get in touch with you, Miss, have you left an address?" the Housekeeper enquired.

"I think His Lordship knows all that is necessary," Ilouka replied evasively.

She thanked the Housekeeper, gave her a large tip for the housemaids who had looked after her, and thought she took it with surprise.

Then, going down the Grand Staircase, she knew she was saying good-bye to the most magnificent house she had ever seen, and also to the owner of it.

Only as she drove away did she think a little wistfully that after all she had not seen Apollo, nor had she been able to explore all the rooms in the house.

"For the rest of my life I shall just have to imagine the things I did not see," she told herself.

But she knew she would not have to imagine what it was like to be kissed, and in future would understand what the poets were trying to say in their poems and the writers in their prose.

"How could I have been kissed by a man I had only just met, and who knew nothing about me?" she asked herself.

And yet his kiss had been more ecstatic, more rapturous, than anything she had imagined or read about.

When she reached the Posting-Inn she thanked the Earl's servants for driving her there, tipped both the coachman and the footman, again to their surprise, and ordered a Post-Chaise.

She thought that although it was unlikely, perhaps the Earl might try to trace her movements, and she therefore deliberately took the Post-Chaise only as far as the nearest town on the border of Bedfordshire.

She then changed vehicles, and after the conveyance which had taken her there drove away, she travelled on towards Stonefield village, in which Mrs. Adolphus's house was situated.

She felt that in that way she had covered her tracks both cleverly and successfully.

At the same time, she thought she was being extremely conceited in thinking that the Earl would be anxious to find her once she had gone or would make any effort to trace her.

He must never know who I am, she thought.

She wished Mr. Archer had not used her own Christian name when he had introduced her after the dinner-party, because that was the only clue the Earl might have to her identity.

"As far as he is concerned I am just an unimportant actress," Ilouka said aloud as she looked out from the Post-Chaise over the flat, dull fields of Bedfordshire.

He would return to the actress from Drury Lane and the beauties who pursued him relentlessly.

It was a pain like a dagger in her heart to think such things.

Then she told herself she was being ridiculous.

"I must remember that the Earl and Lord Marlowe are prepared to kiss any pretty women they meet."

She meant nothing serious in their lives. To them one woman was very like another.

And yet to me he will always be different, Ilouka thought.

Once again she felt that strange rapture moving within her, the music flooding from her heart, and the vibrations reaching out to touch the vibrations from the Earl and make them for one rapturous moment not two people but one.

No wonder men and women seek for love all their lives, Ilouka thought.

Then she started and felt that what she had thought was revolutionary because she had admitted to herself it was love.

"Riding alone in a Post-Chaise? I have never heard of such a thing!" Mrs. Adolphus exclaimed.

Ilouka had been ushered into the stiff, ugly Drawing-Room where she was seated in the window, a piece of embroidery in her hands.

"I had no alternative, Aunt Agatha," Ilouka replied. "There was an accident with the Stage-Coach, and poor Hannah was killed when it turned over."

Mrs. Adolphus stared at her as if she could not be speaking the truth.

Then she threw up her hands in horror to say:

"You travelled alone? How could you do such a thing?"

"What else could I do?" Ilouka answered. "It was only a small village and I do not suppose anyone there had ever heard of a lady's-maid, let alone having been trained as one."

"Surely there was something you could have done if you had taken any trouble over it," Mrs. Adolphus said, always ready to find fault. "And where did you stay the night, may I ask?"

"The Vicar was kind enough to give me a bedroom in the Vicarage," Ilouka replied.

She thought that at least that would sound highly respectable.

But Mrs. Adolphus asked cryptically:

"He was a married man?"

"No, but he was well over seventy-five, and his

Housekeeper was an elderly woman and I promise you a most efficient Chaperone."

"There was nobody else with you?"

There was just a little pause before Ilouka knew that to tell the truth would be to evoke a thousand suspicions, so she answered:

"No . . . no-one else."

Mrs. Adolphus gave a sigh, not as if of relief but almost as if she was disappointed. Then she said:

"Well, you are here safely, although I must say I think your whole story is extremely bizarre, and I cannot believe there was no alternative to your travelling so far alone."

Ilouka did not answer because she felt that if she did so, the argument would go on forever.

"I would like to go up to my room now, Aunt Agatha," she said, "to wash my hands and face. The last part of the journey was very dusty."

"It is not surprising, for we are sadly in need of rain," Mrs. Adolphus replied. "Goodness knows what will happen to the crops if we do not have a shower soon."

Ilouka turned towards the door and as she reached it Mrs. Adolphus said, almost as if she hated to give her good news:

"By the way, Ilouka, you will find a letter from your mother lying in the Hall. I recognised the handwriting. I expect she is missing you."

"A letter from Mama? How wonderful!"

Ilouka did not wait to hear any more but went out into the Hall and saw, carefully placed on one side of the table where it would not be obvious when she arrived, a letter addressed in her mother's handwriting.

She picked it up and ran up the stairs where she could be alone to read it in the plain, rather austere room that she had occupied the last time she had stayed at Stone House.

She went to the window, feeling that although it

was still quite light, the gloom inside the house made it difficult to see clearly.

Then as she opened her mother's letter the very first words danced before her eyes.

She read:

I have good news for you, my darling. Lord Denton has proposed to Muriel and she has accepted him. The engagement will be in the "Gazette" tomorrow morning.

What I know will make you happy is that His Lordship's Mother is living in France for the good of her health, and Muriel is going there with his sister as a Chaperone, so that she can become acquainted with her future Mother-in-Law.

Lord Denton is insistent that they should stay with his Mother for at least a month, which means you can come home immediately, and I will present you to the King and Queen before Muriel returns.

I have discussed the matter of Muriel's presentation with Lord Denton, who is a charming young man, and he thinks that his Mother would wish to present Muriel on her marriage, so that makes everything much easier for you and me.

I am afraid your Step-Father is unlikely to send his horses so far as Stone House, even though I think in his heart he will be very glad to see you back.

Will you and Hannah therefore take the Stage-Coach as far as St. Albans, and I have persuaded your step-father to send our horses to await you there at The Peacock Inn.

You will get this letter on Wednesday and they will be waiting for you on Friday, which will give you time to make yourself pleasant to Mrs. Adolphus, as she might not like you to leave immediately you arrive.

Ilouka gave a little exclamation of delight before she read any more.

Because today was in fact Thursday, this meant she could leave first thing tomorrow morning.

"Thank goodness!" she said to herself. "I can go home and not stay here more than one night!"

It was such a lovely thought that for a moment, although the sky was overcast, the sun seemed to be shining.

While she was reading the letter her trunks had been brought upstairs and an elderly, rather disagreeable housemaid was regarding them balefully.

"You need not unpack them, Josephine," Ilouka said. "I am leaving tomorrow. My mother needs me at home."

She did not wait for the maid to answer, but throwing her bonnet down on the nearest chair she ran down the stairs to tell Aunt Agatha the news, already anticipating how annoyed she would be at having to send somebody with her as far as St. Albans.

She could not be allowed to travel there alone, after Mrs. Adolphus had made so much fuss about it already.

I am going home! Home! Ilouka thought delightedly, and her feet seemed to fly down the stairs.

Then as she walked more sedately across the Hall she found herself thinking of the Earl and wondering if by now he had returned from the races to find that she was no longer there.

What will he do? she wondered.

Without meaning to, she stood still.

She could almost feel his fingers under her chin, turning her face up to his.

She could see the smile on his lips which was different from any smile she had noticed before.

She felt again the strange sensation his lips had given her pulsating through her body, her vibrations reaching out towards him.

He was carrying her to the top of the snow-capped mountains to the music of a thousand gypsy violins.

Chapter Six

Because the sun was shining as she looked out over the London Street, Ilouka kept thinking of the glinting gold on the lake at Lavenham.

She did not see the traffic moving past, the horses drawing a smart Phaeton or a closed Brougham, but instead the swans, black and white, moving serenely over the silver water, which made her think of the music to which she had danced.

Ever since she had left the Earl's house when he was away at the races, she had found it impossible not to think of him a thousand times a day, and at night she would like awake reliving the rapture of his kiss.

At the same time, she told herself that he had forgotten her very existence and the quicker she forgot him the better.

But somehow he was always with her, in a shaft of sunlight, in a Hurdy-Gurdy playing a sentimental song in the street.

An errand-boy whistling *Bring My Broom* would bring him back to her so vividly that she felt she must cry out with the pain of it.

"How can I have been so ridiculous as to fall in love with a man who only wanted to make me his mistress and would doubtless have become bored with me very quickly?" she admonished herself.

Yet she knew there was something between her and

the Earl that was timeless and part of eternity, and however long she lived and however many men she knew, she would never be able to forget him.

Because her mother was so elated at the idea that she could take her to London for the Season and present her to King William and Queen Adelaide without Muriel, Ilouka tried for her sake to enter into the excitement of it.

However, she knew that all the time her heart was aching, and although she told herself it was absurd, the ache continued.

It is just because I had met so few men, she thought, *that the Earl seemed to me so impressive, so handsome, and so irresistible.*

She was aware now that her initial feeling of resentment against him was merely because from the very first moment she heard about him, and certainly when she saw him, he seemed different.

Lady Armstrong had been horrified at hearing of Hannah's death.

But she accepted without asking too many uncomfortable questions that after Ilouka had stayed at the Vicarage and attended Hannah's Funeral she had hired a Post-Chaise to take her to Bedfordshire.

"That was very sensible of you, dearest," she said, "although perhaps unconventional."

"There was nothing else I could do, Mama. Aunt Agatha of course was shocked, but quite frankly, I could not face a Stage-Coach again after what had . . . happened."

"Of course not," her mother agreed, "and you did the only thing possible in the circumstances. I am only thankful that you had enough money."

"Only just enough, Mama. I have come home penniless!"

"That is easily remedied," her mother answered. "Your step-father has been very generous over your Season in London and he has not only given me a large sum of money for your clothes and mine, but also promised that you shall have your Ball before Muriel returns from France."

"Oh, Mama, that is wonderful!" Ilouka replied.

She had to force the enthusiasm into her voice, for the mere idea of dancing brought back only too vividly how she had danced in the Earl's Dining-Room.

They had set off for London two days after Ilouka's return home.

The preoccupations of packing, finding a lady's-maid to replace Hannah, and opening Sir James's house in London made it easier to think of other things rather than the Earl.

But at night there were no distractions, and Ilouka would find herself recapturing the rapture and ecstasy she had felt when his kiss had lifted her up to the snowy peaks of the mountains and the world was left behind.

"I had no idea that love was like this," she told herself over and over again.

If she was a little quieter than usual and sometimes there were dark shadows under her eyes in the morning, Lady Armstrong did not appear to notice.

She was so ambitious that her daughter should be acclaimed for her beauty that she was concentrating on supplying her with gowns that would accentuate her white skin and bring out the red lights in her shining hair.

There was no doubt of Ilouka's success from the moment they attended their first dinner-party.

It was given by the Duchess of Bolton, who was an old friend of Sir James Armstrong, and when Ilouka entered the Drawing-Room, in which a large number of people were already assembled, there was a hush.

Ilouka did not realise that her appearance was so sensational, but Lady Armstrong did and she was very proud.

After that the invitations poured in and Lady Armstrong said to her husband with a smile:

"I do not think we shall have Ilouka on our hands

for very long. She has already had four proposals of marriage, and I can see the words trembling on the lips of two very eligible young Peers."

"There is no hurry for her to make up her mind," Sir James replied. "At the same time, my darling, I cannot pretend that I would not like to have you to myself."

"You are very kind," Lady Armstrong answered, "and you know I am grateful."

"What I want is that you should be happy."

Lady Armstrong lifted his hand to her cheek with a gesture that he found very touching.

"I am happy," she said, "and sometimes I can hardly believe it when after I became a widow I was so desperately miserable."

"I will never allow you to be that again," Sir James said and kissed her.

"I ought to be the happiest girl in London," Ilouka told herself.

Yet she felt guilty because she knew that despite her resolution to forget the Earl she found herself looking for him at every Ball she attended, at every dinner-party, and searching for a glimpse of his Phaeton when they drove in the Park.

"Forget him! Forget him! Forget him!" she said to herself over and over again.

But still she could feel his fingers under her chin, turning her face up to his, and feel the strength of his arms holding her close against him.

"Tomorrow we are going to the 'Drawing-Room,' " Lady Armstrong said one evening. "I hope, darling child, you will enjoy it as much as I shall. It is eleven years since I was last at Buckingham Palace."

"I expect it still looks very much the same," Ilouka replied.

"It had only just been altered by King George IV and was a sensation!" Lady Armstrong went on. "It certainly seemed to me to be very impressive, but I was very shy in those days, which is more than you have ever been, my dearest."

"I have not been shy," Ilouka replied, "because you and Papa always treated me not as a child whom you talked down to as an inferior but almost as if I were grown-up. That prevented me from being shy and also sharpened my brain."

"It seems almost too much that you should be clever as well as beautiful!" her mother said. "And any man you marry will appreciate that you are not just a pretty face with which he will quickly grow bored."

Ilouka did not reply, but she was thinking that the Earl had appreciated only her face, and they had not been acquainted long enough for him to find her intelligent.

The next evening when she was dressed in the new gown which Lady Armstrong had bought for her presentation, she had to admit that she looked sensational.

Because plain white was not really a colour that complemented the magnolia-like quality of her skin, Lady Armstrong had chosen a gown that was predominately silver.

It had silver ribbons, and the pure silk of which it was made was embroidered all over with a silver design picked out in diamanté.

It had a full skirt, a tiny waist, and was very much a young girl's gown.

At the same time, it was so imaginative that it instantly made Ilouka remember that Mr. Archer had described her in his introduction as "a nymph rising from the lake."

The silver of her gown made her think of the lake at Lavenham, and her step-father gave her as a present a small collet of diamonds to wear round her throat, which glittered with every movement she made.

"You look lovely!" he answered. "Really you need very little ornamentation."

It was a compliment which she knew was sincere, and it illustrated how lucky her mother and she were to have somebody so kind to look after them.

Mama does not love him in the same way that she loved Papa, she thought to herself, *but she does love him, although in a different way, and perhaps I could feel the same about some other man and therefore feel I could marry him.*

She knew if she was honest that what she wanted was the same love that her father and mother had had for each other and which she knew in her heart was what she felt for the Earl.

Last night when she had lain awake thinking of him, she had wondered what would have happened if, instead of running away, she had stayed on for another night at Lavenham as he had wished her to do.

When he had kissed her it had been so wonderful that she could still feel herself tremble as she thought of his lips touching hers.

It suddenly struck her that he might have to come to her bedroom for another reason other than to save her from Lord Marlowe.

It now occurred to Ilouka that she had been very stupid and obtuse.

She had taken it for granted that the Earl had come to her through the communicating door because he had heard the noise Lord Marlowe was making outside in the passage.

It was only now for the first time that she remembered that when she had turned round and begged him to save her, he had looked astonished at the furniture she was staking against the door and seemed for a moment not to realise why she was doing it.

Then he had gone away to deal with Lord Marlowe.

If he had come to her room without realising what was happening, what was the point of his visit?

Because Ilouka was so innocent and inexperienced, and because the Earl seemed so aloof and in her own words "omnipotent," it had never crossed her mind that the reason why her room had been changed and that he had come to her wearing a robe and obviously undressed was that he had intended to make love to her.

What that entailed she had no idea, but she knew it was something wrong and very improper when a man and woman were not married.

It could occur, she thought, between gentleman and actresses like Madame Vestris, but it was something that was too immodest and wicked to be suggested to a Lady.

"He believed me to be an actress, and that was why he assumed I would agree to something so outrageous," Ilouka told herself.

Suddenly she was extremely unhappy not only because she had lost the Earl but also because she realised that he did not think of her as a Lady to respect and admire, but as an actress whom he could treat insultingly in the same way as Lord Marlowe had insulted her.

It was a revelation which hurt even more than she was hurt already.

Then she knew she had no-one to blame but herself for having agreed in the first place to Mr. Archer's proposition to go with him to entertain the Earl and his friends.

Because she now recognised what she was sure was the truth of the whole situation, she could only pray even more fervently than she was doing already that her mother would never discover what had happened.

Mama would not only be horrified, Ilouka thought, *she would be deeply hurt and upset that I should behave so badly.*

"You look really beautiful, Miss!" the maid who helped her to dress exclaimed when Ilouka took a last look at herself in the mirror before she went downstairs.

"Thank you," she answered.

The three ostrich-feathers at the back of her head were very becoming.

It was at the Battle of Crecy in 1346 that the Black Prince won both his spurs and the famous ostrich-plumes which adorned his seals as Prince of Wales.

Young girls when they were presented to the Monarch had worn them ever since then.

"There won't be anyone as beautiful as you are at the Ball, Miss. I'm certain of that!" the maid went on.

Ilouka smiled her thanks, but she was thinking that there was one person who would never admire her except for her looks, but whom she wanted above all things to admire her character, her personality, and her mind.

"Forget him! Forget him! Forget him!" her feet seemed to say as she went lightly down the stairs.

As they drove to Buckingham Palace in Sir James's smart London carriage, she thought the wheels were repeating the same words.

Lady Armstrong looked lovely in a gown of pale mauve and wearing a tiara of amethysts and diamonds with a necklace of the same stones.

She carried a bouquet of mauve orchids which Sir James had given her, while for Ilouka there was a little posy of white roses that were just coming into bloom.

It made her think of the roses she had worn on top of her head and round her wrists when she had danced at Lavenham.

"You look like Persephone going down into Hades," Mr. Archer had told her.

Because of what had happened, she thought she would never be able to escape from the darkness but must remain there and never again find spring in her heart.

Then because she told herself she was being extremely ungrateful, she smiled at her step-father sitting opposite her and looking extremely smart in his uniform as Deputy Lord Lieutenant of Buckinghamshire.

"I know one thing," he said to his wife, "no man in the Palace will be able to present two such beautiful women as I am doing!"

"You cannot say that until you have had a look round," Lady Armstrong teased, "and Ilouka and I will be very apprehensive in case, dearest James, we are eclipsed by one of the beautiful women whom you knew before you married me."

"Since I married you," Sir James replied, "I have never been able to notice any other woman."

Ilouka was not listening but was thinking that the actress from Drury Lane in whom the Earl was interested must certainly be not only more beautiful than she was but much more talented.

"He will watch her performance night after night," she told herself, "and will soon forget the very amateur way in which I danced for him in his Dining-Room."

There was a little wait as they reached the courtyard of Buckingham Palace, where there were at least a dozen carriages ahead of them.

Then gradually, as the occupants were set down to enter the Palace, they drew nearer and eventually a powdered footman opened the door and Lady Armstrong stepped out.

Ilouka followed her and after they had deposited their wraps they went up a wide staircase covered in red carpet towards the Throne-Room, where the King and Queen were holding court.

It took some time to move up the stairs where the Gentlemen-at-Arms were on guard, and Ilouka thought it would be interesting to see Queen Adelaide, who had married King William in 1818 although he was very much older than she was.

People were always talking about her at her mother's parties, and while some spoke of her as "an amiable little woman," others, more critical, described her as "small, mouse-like, and excessively dull."

There were always those who were ready to gossip about the Royal Family, and Sir James said now in a low voice to his wife:

"I suppose you have heard that the odious Duchess of Kent has refused to allow Princess Victoria to attend any of the Royal Drawing-Rooms?"

"Has she really!" Lady Armstrong exclaimed. "That is too bad, when she knows that the King is so fond of his niece."

They moved on slowly until at last they reached the Throne-Room. Ilouka could now see that Queen Adelaide, seated at the far end of it and blazing with jewels, did in fact look very small and mouse-like beside her large, stout, ageing husband.

The King was almost bald, and what hair he did have was dead white, but he smiled at everybody who was presented and Ilouka was sure that the stories about his being very kind and unpretentious were true.

A friend of Sir James's came up to speak to them, and Ilouka heard him say:

"These formal affairs bore me stiff! I must admit that things were far more amusing when King George was alive."

Sir James laughed.

"You certainly have to behave yourself better these days, Arthur."

"That is true," his friend replied, "but the evenings at Court are insufferable. The King snoozes, the Queen does needlework, and we are not supposed to discuss politics."

Sir James laughed again, and Ilouka thought that the Earl certainly had more lively evenings than those her step-father's friend described.

Now she could see the presentations taking place and a Lord-in-Waiting was calling out the names:

"The Duchess of Bolton presenting Lady Mary

Fotheringay-Stuart! Lady Ashburton presenting the Honourable Jane Trant and Miss Nancy Carrington!"

The Lord-in-Waiting had a somewhat monotonous voice and Ilouka looked round at the gilt and white walls against which the sparkling tiaras of the ladies seemed to glow almost as if they held the sunlight in them.

Then it was her turn and she was in a line where every lady was being careful not to stand on the train of the one in front of her.

The Lord-in-Waiting was intoning their names almost as if they were in Church.

"The Countess Hull, presenting Lady Penelope Curtis!"

Then in exactly the same tone:

"Lady Armstrong, presenting Miss Ilouka Compton!

Her mother moved forward ahead of Ilouka to sink down in a low curtsey in front of the Queen, who inclined her head, and then Lady Armstrong moved on to curtsey to the King.

Ilouka took her place.

As she curtseyed very carefully, her back straight, holding her head high, the Queen smiled at her, and she instinctively smiled back.

Then as her mother walked away she moved on to the King.

She made an even lower curtsey than she had to the Queen, and as she rose she heard the King say in his blunt manner:

"Pretty girl! Very pretty!"

His comments were known to be often disconcerting, but because it was a compliment Ilouka could not help smiling at him, thinking that he was speaking to himself.

Then distinctly she heard a voice say:

"I agree with you, Sire."

She raised her eyes and her heart seemed to turn over in her breast.

At the same time she felt unable to move, for standing behind the King's chair, resplendent in glittering decorations, the blue ribbon of the Order of the Garter across his chest, was the Earl.

Ilouka met his eyes, until with what was an almost superhuman effort she rose from her curtsey and moved away to follow her mother.

For a moment she could not think, and was aware only that her whole body was pulsating with the fact that she had seen the Earl again and, what was more, that he must have recognised her.

She wondered frantically what he would think or what he would say now that he knew who she really was.

She was so bemused with the shock of seeing him in such circumstances that it was impossible to think, let alone speak.

Sir James had joined them and was introducing her mother to his friends. They spoke to Ilouka, and she supposed that she answered them coherently.

At the same time, she felt as if she were in another world, having stepped into a "No-Man's-Land" where it was impossible for her to feel that anything was real but the beating of her heart.

She must have talked to dozens of people in the next hour, accepted compliments and apparently answered the questions they asked her with some degree of sense.

It was only when the King, leading the Queen by the hand, had left the Throne-Room and passed through the midst of their guests to speak occasionally to someone in particular before they finally disappeared, that it was possible for anybody to leave.

"Can we go now, Mama?" Ilouka asked.

"There is no hurry, darling," Lady Armstrong replied. "I am enjoying myself, and your step-father is anxious to find a particular friend to whom he wishes to introduce me."

Ilouka could not tell her mother that she wished to leave before she was forced to encounter the Earl.

She looked apprehensively about her at the people gossipping, expecting him to approach her at any moment with an accusing look in his eyes.

Then unexpectedly when she was looking in another direction she heard his voice say:

"Good-evening, Armstrong! I did not expect to see you here!"

"Hello, Lavenham!" Sir James replied. "That is what I should say to you. I thought you would be too busy with your horses to have time for such formalities as this."

"I was pressured into doing my duty," the Earl replied.

"I do not think you have met my wife," Sir James said with a smile. "Dearest, let me present the Earl of Lavenham, who, as you are aware, has the finest stable in the country and wins all the Classic races so that none of the rest of us ever get a look-in."

Lady Armstrong held out her hand.

"I have heard of you for years, My Lord," she said, "and I am so pleased to meet you in person."

"You are very kind."

The Earl's eyes turned towards Ilouka and Sir James said:

"Now you will meet the reason for my appearance here today. My wife and I wished to present my step-daughter to their Majesties."

The Earl bowed as Ilouka curtseyed, and because she found it impossible to look at him, her eye-lashes were dark against her cheeks.

"I am delighted to make your acquaintance, Miss Compton," he said.

Ilouka was sure there was a sarcastic note in his voice, but because she thought it would seem strange if she said nothing, she forced herself to reply:

"I have . . . heard of your . . . magnificent horses . . . My Lord."

"I hope one day to show them to you," he said. "when you can spare the time to visit my stables."

Ilouka drew in her breath.

She knew he was reproaching her for having left before she could see Apollo and his other horses.

He was looking at her and she wondered if he was regarding her with contempt.

Then she was suddenly afraid, desperately afraid that he would say something which would reveal to her mother that they had met before and the whole story of her deception would have to be unfolded.

Because she was so apprehensive, it was impossible for her to judge the expression in the Earl's grey eyes.

Instead, she could only feel her vibrations pulsating towards him and was afraid that what she was feeling would be obvious not only to him but also to her mother and her step-father.

Then, coming to deliver her at the eleventh hour from a predicament which she felt totally unable to cope with, a lilting voice exclaimed:

"James! How wonderful to see you! And why have you been neglecting me for so long?"

A woman glittering with sapphires, and wearing a blue gown that echoed the blue of her eyes, moved between the Earl and Sir James and slipped her arm through his.

For a moment the newcomer isolated Ilouka and the Earl from her mother and step-father, and when he would have started to speak, Ilouka said unhappily:

"I . . . I . . . must . . . explain."

"I have to see you," the Earl said, "and as you say, you have a lot of explaining to do."

"I . . . know."

"Where can I meet you alone?"

She tried to think coherently of some place where they could talk without being overheard.

As if the Earl understood her difficulty, he said:

"I shall be riding in the Park early tomorrow morning and will be at the Achilles statue at seven o'clock."

Ilouka had only just heard the words before her mother was at her side, saying:

"I want you, dearest, to meet the French Ambassador and his wife."

"Yes, of course, Mama."

"And I must return to my duties," the Earl remarked. "Good-night, Lady Armstrong. Good-night, Miss Compton."

He bowed somewhat formally and moved away towards a group of foreign Royalty and Ambassadors who were obviously waiting to be entertained by the senior members of the Royal Household.

As Ilouka watched him go she felt as if he was walking out of her life as she had walked out of his.

Then she told herself with a sudden leap of her heart that at least she would see him tomorrow.

It would be embarrassing to have to tell him why she had pretended to be an actress, and he would doubtless be angry and reproachful. At the same time, she would see him and that was all that mattered.

She could never remember exactly what happened for the rest of the evening.

As they were driven home her mother was talking excitedly about the grandeur of the Palace, while Sir James was, Ilouka thought, a little apologetic about the effusive manner in which he had been greeted by a lady who was quite obviously an "old flame."

But their voices seemed far away and nothing she heard appeared to make sense.

Only as they reached the house did Ilouka realise that she had somehow to ride in the Park the following morning without either her mother or Sir James being aware of what she was doing.

If she said she was riding, undoubtedly Sir James would accompany her, or her mother might think it best for her to rest in the morning, as she had done since she had been in London, because there would be another Ball in the evening.

I have to see him! Ilouka thought to herself, but she could not imagine how it could be managed.

In the end, after they had had a late supper, she went up to bed, still thinking of how she could leave the house without anybody being aware of it.

It was impossible to sleep, and a dozen times during the night she rose to go to the window to look up at the star-lit sky, wondering what the Earl was thinking about her.

She was certain that he would be angry and inevitably shocked by her behaviour.

But what was really important was to make him promise not to reveal to her mother or Sir James the reprehensible way she had behaved.

It was the longest night Ilouka had ever spent.

When as she stood at the window she heard in the far distance a clock strike the hour of five, she thought a century had passed since she had seen the Earl and had known as he walked away from her that she was no longer of any importance to him.

The position he had offered her in his life was that of a woman whose only asset as far as he was concerned was that she had a pretty face.

It was an humiliation that Ilouka had somehow never expected would happen to her.

She had been brought up to believe that it was personality that counted more than looks, and while she was deeply grateful that people thought her beautiful, she knew that she had something more to offer them.

This was intrinsically *herself,* and therefore very valuable as far as she was concerned.

But as a dancer, an actress, a woman who could become a man's mistress, she was a dispensable possession who counted far less than a race-horse.

That is what he feels for me, she thought.

She felt at that moment that she was in a deep, dark hell from which she would never be able to escape.

Then as gradually the first rays of the sun appeared over the roof-tops and the sky lightened, she knew the night had passed and she would be able to see the Earl.

But she knew bitterly that while she would see him and be near him, she would have to humble herself and apologise for a deception which he would condemn utterly as an outrageous action by a woman who he now knew had been born a Lady.

She thought perhaps it would be wiser not to go to him where he would be waiting for her at the Achilles statue.

Then she knew that if she did not go, he might come to the house and tell her mother that they had met in very different circumstances.

Suddenly she decided what she would do and quickly dressed herself in her riding-habit.

Sir James's horses were stabled behind the house and could be reached from a back door which opened onto the Mews.

Because they were out every night, Lady Armstrong would not be called before nine o'clock, and because Sir James always breakfasted downstairs at eight-thirty, Ilouka knew if she left at half-past-six she would be safe from being seen.

She dressed herself with care, arranging her hair in a neat chignon beneath a riding-hat with a high crown which was encircled by a gauze veil.

Riding-habits had become very much fuller in the skirts in the last year or so. They had small waists and neat little jackets over white muslin blouses which fastened with a bow at the neck.

Her habit made Ilouka look very young, and yet beneath the severity of her hat her hair glowed like the flames from a gypsy fire.

Her eyes too seemed to fill her small face because she was apprehensive.

Having ordered a horse to be saddled, she rode out of the Mews towards the Park, accompanied by a sleepy groom who was resenting being called out on duty so early in the morning.

He rode several paces behind her, and because Ilouka knew she had to kill time before the Earl would be at the Achilles statue at seven o'clock, she went not towards Hyde Park Corner but the other way round the Park.

She crossed the Serpentine by the bridge, galloping her horse over the unfashionable grass where there was nobody to see her except a few small boys kicking a ball about.

Then she rode slowly down Rotten Row, which was also empty save for some athletic young gentlemen who preferred to ride before there was any sign of the fashionable ladies in their carriages who would require them to stop and chatter.

It was only as the statue of Achilles appeared ahead of her that Ilouka felt her heart beating convulsively.

Then she saw the Earl seated astride a huge black stallion and she had a sudden longing to turn her horse round and gallop away.

But it was too late. He had seen her, and as if he drew her like a magnet she rode slowly towards him, feeling as if she were being carried to the guillotine.

She drew in her horse and stared at him, her eyes very wide and, although she did not realise it, frightened.

The Earl swept his hat from his head.

"Good-morning, Miss Compton!"

"Good-morning . . . My . . . Lord."

There was a little tremor in her voice that she could not repress, and she thought there was a cynical twist to his lips before he said:

"Shall we ride towards the Serpentine?"

"Yes . . . that would . . . be very . . . pleasant."

She thought her voice seemed to come in a strange jerk, and yet it was impossible to control it.

They turned their horses and walked side by side, her groom keeping well behind them.

Because Ilouka felt it was impossible to speak, there was silence and the Earl seemed to have no inclination to talk.

They rode until they reached the Serpentine, which was glittering gold in the morning sun.

The Earl reined in his horse.

"I think it would be a good idea," he said, "if we left our horses with your groom and walked a little way in the trees to find a seat where we can talk."

"Yes . . . of course . . . if that is what you . . . want," Ilouka replied.

The Earl beckoned the groom forward as he dismounted and handed him the reins of his stallion, giving him an order in a voice that sounded to Ilouka a little sharp, as if he was in a bad temper.

Then he came to the side of her horse and lifted her down.

As he put his hands on her small waist and she was close to him, she felt a sensation like a streak of lightning flash through her and she knew that however angry he might be, she loved him.

If only he would kiss her once more, she thought, that would be the most wonderful thing that could happen.

Then she was free and the Earl gave the reins of her horse to the groom.

Slowly she walked ahead along a little path which led them towards a profusion of bushes underneath the birch trees.

Almost before she expected it she came upon a seat that was set back amongst some shrubs. This seemed the obvious place and she sat down.

As she did so she realised that it would be impossible for anybody to see them unless they were boating on the Serpentine.

Because she was nervous she arranged her skirts very carefully, aware for the moment that the Earl had not sat beside her but was looking down at her from his great height.

He might, she thought wryly, be on the pedestal she had imagined him to be occupying when she had seen him sitting at the end of the dining-table and knew that he would never step down from it to mix with the common herd.

Then he seated himself beside her, and turning sideways as he had done when they sat on the sofa in the *Boudoir* together at Lavenham, he put his arm along the back of the seat.

At the same time he lifted his tall-hat and set it down on the ground beside him.

Then with what she thought was a grim note in his voice he said:

"Well, Miss Ilouka Ganymede, what have you to say for yourself?"

Ilouka drew in her breath.

"I . . . I am sorry," she said. "I did not . . . mean to do anything wrong . . . but I know now that it was in fact very . . . very wrong of me to . . . come to your . . . house."

"It was not only very wrong, it was crazy!" the Earl replied. "How could you pretend to be understudying Madame Vestris, and . . ."

He stopped. Then he said:

"Never mind *what* you did. I want to know *why!*"

"If I . . . tell you the whole . . . truth," Ilouka said in a very small voice, "will you . . . promise, will you swear by . . . everything you hold sacred . . . that you will not tell Mama?"

"I suppose to tell her is what I ought to do," the Earl answered.

Ilouka gave a little cry.

"Please . . . please . . . I beg of you . . . if you tell her she will not only be angry with me . . . but very . . . very hurt that I should behave in such a reprehensible manner."

"I am not surprised," the Earl said grimly.

"I did not . . . expect to see . . . you at the Palace," Ilouka said impulsively. "I had thought . . . if I saw you elsewhere . . . I would be able to . . . ask you before you . . . met Mama not to . . . reveal to her my . . . indiscretion . . ."

"So that is what you call it," the Earl said. "I can think of a far more positive description of your behaviour."

"I know," Ilouka said unhappily, "but it just . . . happened that I became . . . involved, and I did not . . . realise what might . . . happen."

"I suppose you were unaware of the dangers you ran."

Ilouka thought of Lord Marlowe and shuddered.

"But you . . . saved me."

There was a little pause. Then the Earl remarked in a dry voice she knew so well:

"Yes, I saved you from Lord Marlowe—but not from myself!"

He watched the colour flood into her cheeks before she said in a low voice:

"I never . . . thought for a moment that . . . sort of thing would . . . h—happen. I was just trying to . . . help Mr. Archer."

"Did you not realise that when you pretended to be the understudy to Madame Vestris there would be men approaching you as Marlowe tried to do?"

"I swear to you it . . . never entered . . . my head. I had of course heard of . . . Madame Vestris . . . and I knew that . . . Mama thought her . . . improper because she wore breeches on the stage . . . but I had not thought of her in any other way until after . . ."

She stopped, as if she had no words, and the Earl finished quietly:

". . . I offered you my protection. I presume you understand what that means?"

"I do . . . now," Ilouka said in a low voice, "but only because Mr. Archer said that Miss Ganymede . . . whose place I had taken, had lost her . . . Protector, which was . . . why she wanted the money that you were . . . prepared to pay for the . . . entertainment."

"What happened to Miss Ganymede?"

Iouka drew in her breath.

"She and my lady's-maid, Hannah . . . were killed when the Stage-Coach in which we were travelling turned over."

The way she spoke was very revealing, and as she looked up at him she saw that the Earl was staring at her incredulously.

"The Stage-Coach in which you were travelling turned over?" he repeated, as if he thought he could not have heard correctly what she said.

"Yes, my step-father did not wish to send me in a carriage because it was too tiring for the horses, so H—Hannah and I were . . . going in the Stage-Coach to Bedfordshire."

"Why were you going there?"

"Because my . . . step-father's daughter . . . Muriel, hates me . . . and Lord Denton, whom she hoped would marry her . . . was coming . . ."

Ilouka suddenly threw up her hands and said:

"Oh . . . it is all so complicated . . . and such a long story . . . and if I tell you . . . you will never believe it!"

"I am trying to believe it," the Earl said, "but it is certainly somewhat involved."

"Of course it is involved," Ilouka retorted. "You do not suppose for a moment that I would have deliberately . . . impersonated an actress or come to your . . . house if I had not been put in the . . . position where it seemed . . . cruel and heartless to . . . refuse?"

She spoke passionately. Then she said in a different tone:

"Please . . . please . . . try to understand . . . and do not be angry with me."

"Why should it worry you if I am?" the Earl asked.

There was silence for a moment. Then Ilouka said:

"I am afraid of your being . . . angry with me and I am . . . afraid too that you might . . . tell Mama."

"I will not tell your mother," the Earl answered, "if you promise me that never, never again will you do anything so reprehensible. But I am still interested to know why you should be afraid of my anger."

Ilouka knew she could tell him exactly why she was afraid, and that she wanted him not to be contemptuous and ashamed of her but to admire and respect her.

Then she thought the real truth was none of these things: she wanted him to love her!

She wanted him to kiss her as he had done before, and if that was impossible, then what did it matter what he thought?

She looked away from him, her small straight nose silhoutted against the shrubs as she said:

"You have . . . obviously made up your mind . . . about me . . . and there is no . . . real point in my . . . telling you any m—more."

"That may or may not be true," the Earl said. "At the same time, I am interested in your reasons for behaving as you did."

Ilouka did not speak and he went on:

"You came to my house to give a performance which was different in every way from anything I have ever seen before, and as a result you incited one of my guests to behave in a very reprehensible manner!"

His words stung Ilouka and she said angrily:

"That is unfair! Lord Marlowe is a horrible man who had drunk . . . too much, and you cannot blame . . . me because he came knocking on my door. I never . . . dreamt that any gentleman would . . . behave in such a way."

"No gentleman would . . . towards a Lady."

"I thought of that," Ilouka said, "and as I know you do not think I am a Lady, and as you . . . despise me . . . there is no point in our going on talking. I can only say that I am . . . ashamed of myself . . . and yet I know I would have felt guilty for the rest of my life if I had . . . refused to help Mr. Archer when it was his . . . last chance."

"That is the story which I am waiting to hear," the Earl said quietly.

"W—why should you be . . . interested?" Ilouka asked.

Her voice trembled a little because she felt he was making it difficult for her, and also because it was all too impossible to explain.

Then as she spoke she turned to look at him.

Her eyes met his and her anger ebbed away.

She could only see his grey eyes and feel as if they filled the whole world.

CHAPTER SEVEN

"That is what happened," Ilouka said. "I promise you it is the truth, and there seemed to be nothing else I could do."

She had told the Earl exactly what happened from the moment her step-father had said Lord Denton was coming to stay and Muriel had insisted that she was not to be at The Towers when he was there.

She felt that the Earl looked a little sympathetic as she explained how jealous Muriel was of her.

When she went on to describe how after the Stage-Coach had turned over Hannah and Lucille Ganymede had been crushed to death, she thought his eyes hardened, and there was a tight line to his lips.

Because she was nervous she faltered and stumbled over the part where she had not only wanted to help Mr. Archer but had also felt it would be a relief not to hurry on to Bedfordshire.

She knew that in a way she was condemning herself by being so honest, but at the same time something compelled her to tell the Earl the truth, whatever he might think of her.

"It was so exciting to see your . . . wonderful house," she said, "and because it was an . . . adventure which Papa would have . . . enjoyed, I did not feel as . . . guilty as I suppose I ought to have done."

"It did not strike you that you should have a Chaperone when staying in a house where all the guests were men?" the Earl asked.

The colour came into Ilouka's face and she said a little incoherently:

"Of course I . . . knew I would have . . . needed a Chaperone if I had been staying there as . . . myself, but I did not . . . think Miss Ganymede would have . . . required one."

"And you did not wonder why there was no need for her to be chaperoned?"

"No . . . not until after Lord Marlowe . . . tried to . . . get into . . . my bedroom."

"The only excuse I can find for your behaviour is that you are very young and inexperienced," the Earl said as if he spoke to himself.

"And very . . . foolish," Ilouka added miserably.

She sighed and the Earl said:

"What do you expect me to do now?"

"All I am asking is that you . . . promise not to tell Mama . . . or my step-father."

"I will not do that," he said. "At the same time, you are aware I was not the only person present at my dinner-party."

Ilouka looked at him with wide eyes. Then she said:

"I had . . . forgotten that your . . . guests might . . . know my step-father, as you . . . do."

He did not speak and she said frantically:

"Surely they will not . . . connect me as a . . . débutante with . . . somebody who danced and sang for them once as . . . an entertainer?"

"You are not a person one forgets easily," the Earl replied, "and without flattering you, I must say that your dance was unusual. Inevitably, anybody who saw it will talk about it, especially as it took place in my house."

Almost as if he conjured up a picture, Ilouka could hear the gentlemen who had sat round the table with its gold and silver ornaments telling their friends at the Club what sort of entertainment the Earl of Lavenham had provided for them after they had been racing all day.

She clasped her fingers together and asked:

"What . . . shall I do? What . . . can I do?"

"I think for the moment," the Earl replied, "we must just hope that the gentlemen present, who were mostly older men devoted to racing, will not be present at the Balls to which you have been invited."

Ilouka gave a deep sigh.

"Why did I not . . . think of this . . . before?"

"Unfortunately, none of us can turn back the clock," the Earl said drily, "and because you cannot risk being talked about again, I think the best thing you can do at this moment is to continue your ride, then try to forget what happened before you started your Season in London."

"And will you . . . forget that you ever . . . met me before last . . . night?" she asked.

"Shall I say I will not speak of it," he answered.

"But supposing one of your friends asks you how he can meet Miss Ganymede?"

The Earl's lips twisted a little mockingly.

"I shall refer him to Madame Vestris, who will

doubtless be aware by now of what has happneed to her understudy."

Ilouka was silent before she said:

"Thank you for not being so . . . angry with me now as I . . . think you were . . . last night."

"I was astonished to see you," the Earl replied. "I never imagined I would meet at Buckingham Palace the dancer and singer I employed to amuse my guests."

"It does sound . . . strange when you put it like . . . that," Ilouka said unhappily.

"And shall I add that I was delighted that my search for you was ended."

For the moment Ilouka was still. Then she turned to look at him.

"You were . . . searching for me?" she asked incredulously.

"I was extremely perturbed as to what had happened. I could hardly believe that you would sneak away without saying good-bye and without telling me where you were going."

"How could I do . . . anything else?"

"In the circumstances, I suppose it was a sensible thing to do!" the Earl answered. "But at the time I could not imagine what reason you had for leaving in such a reprehensible manner."

She knew as he spoke that he was thinking that any woman to whom he offered his protection would be only too willing to accept it.

It flashed through her mind that it was strange that he should have wanted her when he already had the actress who played at Drury Lane to amuse him.

Then she knew it was a question she could not ask, and said:

"I suppose I was being very . . . foolish in thinking I would . . . never see you . . . again."

"It obviously did not perturb you," the Earl replied, "while I was afraid you might be in trouble of some sort."

"You . . . wanted to . . . help me?"

"I was willing to do so."

"That was kind of you, but you know now that I do not need your help."

"I am well aware that your step-father is a rich man," the Earl said drily.

As he spoke, Ilouka thought she did not need help from him, but something very different; something he must never know or realise.

She wondered what he would think if she asked him to kiss her just once more before, now that he knew who she was and was aware that she was well looked after, she no longer concerned him.

Instead she said in a very small voice:

"I suppose . . . now I shall . . . never see Apollo . . . or your other horses."

The Earl was silent and she wondered if she had been too forward in deliberately asking for an invitation.

Then he said:

"It might be possible when I return to the country, but perhaps because our previous association was rather different, I should ask your mother and step-father and of course you to dine with me one evening."

Because it was a chance of seeing him again, Ilouka felt her heart leap as she said:

"Would you do . . . that?"

"I presume you have an evening free amongst your other engagements?" the Earl remarked.

"Yes, of course."

Ilouka tried to think frantically what they were doing and said:

"Tonight we are dining at Devonshire House."

"I also have been invited," the Earl remarked, "so that will be a good opportunity for me to talk to your step-father and suggest an evening when you can be my guests."

"We shall be free the following night," Ilouka said

eagerly, "and I know there is nothing in Mama's diary for next Wednesday."

"I will remember both those dates."

He rose to his feet, saying as he did so:

"It is getting late in the morning and it would be a mistake for you to be talked about. I suggest you ride back through the Row and I will go in the opposite direction."

He spoke so formally that Ilouka felt her heart sink.

She had the frightened feeling that although he had said he would ask her to dinner, when he left her he might change his mind.

Then she remembered she would see him tonight at Devonshire House and that at least would be something to look forward to.

They walked back along the side of the Serpentine in silence.

Then when the horses were just ahead of them the Earl said:

"Enjoy yourself, Ilouka! The Social World can be very entrancing when you are young, before you become bored and disillusioned."

"Is that what you are?"

"I was talking about you," he replied, "and young ladies should not probe too deeply into things that do no concern them."

She thought he was snubbing her and she blushed before she said:

"I am sorry if that was . . . something I should not have . . . asked, but as you have already pointed out, I do not . . . behave as a . . . conventional young lady should do."

The Earl gave a short laugh.

"That is certainly true. You are very unpredictable, Ilouka, not only in what you say but in how you look and also in the way you dance."

He stood still, looking at her, before he asked:

"Who taught you how to dance like that?"

"Nobody," Ilouka answered. "It is my Hungarian

blood which when I hear gypsy music conjures up pictures which make my feet move as if they can think and feel for themselves."

"What sort of pictures?" the Earl enquired, and it sounded as if he was really interested.

"I see the Hungarian Steppes," Ilouka replied, "and the gypsies in their colourful clothing and their painted caravans. I hear the music of the violins and in the distance see the snow-capped mountains."

She wondered as she spoke a little dreamily what the Earl would say if she told him that when he kissed her it had felt as though he carried her to the top of the mountains and they danced in the snow.

"And your Hungarian blood accounts for the colour of your hair," he said quietly.

"I am like my great-grandmother."

"That explains many things that puzzled me," he said.

But before she could ask him what he meant, he walked towards the horses.

When they reached them he picked her up and lifted her onto the saddle, and as she put her foot in the stirrup the Earl arranged her skirt in an experienced manner.

He then walked to take his stallion from the groom and swing himself into the saddle.

Ilouka watched him, thinking that no man could be more handsome, or, when he was mounted, look finer or more impressive on a horse.

The Earl raised his top-hat.

"Good-day, Miss Compton," he said. "It has been very pleasant meeting you again."

Then without waiting for her reply he trotted off beside the Serpentine.

As she watched him go Ilouka thought that while he had not been as angry as she had expected, it was quite obvious that he was no longer interested in her.

Outrageously, she thought to herself that perhaps

she would have been very much happier if she had been under his "protection."

As they passed through the gold-tipped gates of Devonshire House, Ilouka was aware that her mother was not only delighted at having received the invitation from the Duchess but was also far more excited about the evening ahead of them than she was.

Because all day her thoughts had been only on the Earl, she could not help anticipating that he would pay her little attention at the dinner-party and that she would be left later to dance with the younger men.

Although there had been a number of other girls at the Balls she had attended so far, Ilouka was intelligent enough to realise that the people who enjoyed them most were the older married couples who knew one another intimately.

The ladies too were so elegant and spectacular in their tiaras and fabulous jewels that she could understand that in their simplicity and inexperience the débutantes were not particularly attractive and the gentlemen found older women much more amusing.

She could understand this even better when she talked with the débutantes themselves.

She found that despite the fact that she had always lived in the country and was extremely poor, she was not only better educated but certainly quicker-brained than they were.

She also had a variety of interests that apparently did not appeal to them.

Because her father had always talked of his successes on the Turf, Ilouka knew a great deal about horses.

She suspected that her contemporaries not only knew little about the Classic races but were frightened to ride anything that was not quiet and docile.

They also had no interest in politics, and one girl to whom she talked even confessed that she had no idea who was the Prime Minister and had never heard of the Reform Bill.

I find them extremely boring, Ilouka thought scornfully.

Then she wondered if that was what the Earl felt about her.

Apart from the fact of loving him, she knew he was an extremely intelligent man, and because she had searched the newspapers for every mention of his name she found that he frequently spoke in the House of Lords and was an authority on Foreign Affairs.

If only I could be alone with him for a little while, she thought wistfully, *I could make him realise I am not a nitwit, and there are also so many questions I would like to ask him.*

At the dinner at Devonshire House she looked down the long table at which she was at the far end and saw the Earl seated on the left of the Duchess.

He was talking to a very beautiful and heavily bejewelled lady on his other side in a way which made Ilouka suspect there was a special intimacy between them.

Perhaps that lady is one of his loves, she thought unhappily.

Because she was so curious, she asked the gentleman next to her:

"Do you know who the lady is sitting next to the Earl of Lavenham?"

He was rather a vacant-looking youth, with a receding chin, and he replied:

"That is the Marchioness of Doncaster."

"She is very beautiful."

"Lavenham obviously thinks so," her partner replied, "but then he is noted for having an eye for a horse and for every pretty woman who comes within his orbit."

He laughed rather spitefully and Ilouka felt as if there were a heavy stone in her breast which made it impossible for her to eat any more.

It was with an effort that she turned politely to the gentleman on the other side of her, who told her a rather dismal tale of how much he had lost at cards last week.

He was obviously trying to drown his sorrows by quickly emptying his glass every time it was refilled.

She tried hard to keep herself from looking at the Earl and to concentrate on her dinner-partners, but it was impossible.

When the Marchioness made him laugh it only increased the agony within her to the point where it was a physical pain.

Finally, and it seemed after a very long time, the Duchess took the ladies from the Dining-Room, leaving the gentlemen to their port.

They went upstairs to the bedrooms where Ilouka tidied her hair. As she did so, she did not see her own face in the mirror or the very attractive gown she was wearing.

Instead she saw only the seductive eyes of the Marchioness of Doncaster as she looked at the Earl and the provocative movement of her red lips as she talked to him.

"I wish I could go home!" she said, and did not realise she had spoken aloud.

"You must not say that," a girl standing next to her remarked. "Now we can really have fun. There will be dancing and the gardens are lit with fairy-lights and there are little arbours where you can sit with your partner and no-one can see you."

The girl who spoke looked coy, and Ilouka without speaking went to her mother's side.

"Are you enjoying yourself, darling?" Lady Armstrong asked. "I think the dinner was delightful and now the Duchess tells me there are a hundred or more people arriving for the dancing, and I know you will have a wonderful time."

"Yes, of course, Mama," Ilouka answered dutifully.

The music had started in the Ball-Room as they went downstairs.

It was a beautifully proportioned room filled with flowers and had several long windows opening into the garden.

Ilouka saw the fairy-lights edging the borders of the paths and the Chinese lanterns hanging from the branches of the trees.

She thought that a month ago she would have been thrilled to be in such a party.

Now, because she was certain that in a few minutes she would see the Earl dancing with the alluring Marchioness, all she wanted to do was to go away by herself and hide.

When the gentlemen finally began to leave the Dining-Room, she was asked to dance by the young man who had sat next to her at dinner.

As she could not think of a reason for refusing, she danced with him, but all the time she was watching the door for the Earl.

When he appeared he was talking to the Duke and two other men and Ilouka guessed their conversation was about horses.

That made her feel happier, and she danced more animatedly than she had done before so that her partner paid her compliments and asked her how soon he could dance with her again.

As was correct, she returned to her mother's side and as soon as she reached Lady Armstrong the Duke detached himself from the Earl and came towards her, saying:

"As a very old friend of your husband's, Lady Armstrong, I claim the privilege of dancing with you before he does!"

Lady Armstrong laughed.

"I should be very honoured, Your Grace."

"Then let us show him what we can do," the Duke said.

They moved onto the dance-floor and Ilouka looked round, then suddenly was very still.

Coming through the door with a group of other people who had obviously just arrived she saw something which she knew would be impossible to forget—the red, florid, dissipated face of Lord Marlowe.

She made an inaudible little sound, then slipped out of the room through one of the open windows into the garden.

She ran into the shadows under the trees to stand looking back at the house, hearing the music, and seeing the couples who were dancing past the window.

"What . . . shall I do? What shall . . . I do?" she asked, and knew there was only one person who could answer that question and save her.

She was almost certain that when the Duke had left the Earl to dance with her mother, the Earl had remained where he was talking and was not dancing.

I must speak to him! she thought.

Several of the guests were coming from the Ball-Room into the garden and moving amongst them was a footman carrying some satin cushions which he placed along the seats arranged under the trees not far from where Ilouka was standing.

She went up to him.

"Do you know the Earl of Lavenham by sight?" she asked.

"Yes, Miss," the footman replied. "His Lordship's some fine 'orses."

"I think you will find him just inside the door of the Ball-Room," Ilouka said. "Could you draw him aside and tell him I want to speak to him?"

The footman grinned and she knew that he was thinking that the Earl was not only notorious for his horses but also for his love-affairs.

"I'll do that, Miss."

The footman hurried away into the house, entering it by one of the open windows.

There seemed to Ilouka to be a long pause and she was afraid the man could not find the Earl, when suddenly she saw his broad shoulders silhouetted against the light and knew that he was coming to her as she had asked.

She held her breath.

As he reached the top of the steps she saw the footman beside him, indicating to him where she was hiding.

Without hurrying, and walking in a manner which made Ilouka afraid that the Earl thought it was indiscreet for her to have sent for him like this, he crossed the grass to within a few feet of where she stood beside the trunk of a tree.

"Ilouka?" he asked, as if he was not certain she was there.

She came towards him from the shadows.

"I . . . I had to ask you to . . . come here," she said. "I . . . need your help . . . and I need it . . . desperately!"

There was no need for the Earl to see the expression on her face in the light of the Chinese lanterns, for he could hear the fear in her voice.

"Let us go further away from the house," he said quite calmly, "then you can tell me what is worrying you."

They walked onto the grass, and as the Earl obviously knew the garden, he moved between the trees until they reached a high wall which formed the boundary on that side of the garden of Devonshire House.

There, set amongst the lilac and syringa bushes, was an arbour in which was placed a wooden seat made comfortable by cushions.

Here there was a little light furnished by a ship's lantern containing a candle, which gave it an intimate atmosphere, and those who occupied the arbour could not be seen from outside.

Ilouka sat down on the seat and the Earl in his characteristic manner half-turned to face her.

"What has upset you?" he asked.

"Lord . . . Marlow! He has just arrived . . . and I saw him . . . I am so . . . afraid he will . . . recognise me."

The Earl frowned and said almost as if he spoke to himself:

"I did not anticipate that Marlowe would be here at Devonshire House."

"He is!" Ilouka cried. "Please . . . you must tell me what I am to . . . do. Shall I go . . . or shall I just . . . stay here in the garden until Mama is ready to leave?"

"That would certainly invite comment," the Earl replied, "and it is doubtful if anybody would believe you were alone."

"Then . . . what can I do?" Ilouka asked, "and this . . . may not be the . . . only Ball at which I shall . . . see him."

"It is certainly unfortunate that it should happen tonight," the Earl said.

"Even if it were not tonight, it will be another night," Ilouka replied desperately.

There was a little pause before she added:

"Perhaps I had better tell Mama, but I know it will . . . upset her . . . and my step-father, who has been so very kind to me, will also be . . . horrified."

"You should have anticipated that this might happen."

"I know now that I should have done so . . . but as I explained to you this morning, I was only thinking that it would be . . . unkind to refuse to help Mr. Archer, and it never entered my head that I might meet . . . elsewhere any of the . . . gentlemen you had to . . . stay."

There was silence, then because she thought the

Earl was not going to help her Ilouka looked up at him and her eyes filled with tears as she said:

"I am ashamed . . . bitterly ashamed that I was so . . . stupid, and you despise me . . . but please tell me . . . what I can do . . . there is no-one else I can ask."

She sounded very pathetic, but she thought the Earl's expression as he looked at her was grim.

Because she was so upset, and because she thought he despised her even more than he had before, her tears overflowed and ran down her cheeks.

"You say I despise you," the Earl said at length. "If I do not do so, what would you wish me to feel about you?"

Because she was so distraught, Ilouka told the truth.

"I want you to . . . admire me and to think I am . . . intelligent and someone you . . . like."

There was a perceptible pause before the last word as she almost said "love."

Her voice was choked with tears, and as she fumbled for her handkerchief the Earl put his arms around her and pulled her against him.

"You certainly need somebody to look after you."

Ilouka hid her face against his shoulder.

"There is . . . no-one who will . . . help me . . . but you," she sobbed. "I . . . I could not . . . marry one of those stupid . . . young men."

"Why could you not marry one of them?"

Because he was holding her and she could cry against him, Ilouka found it so comforting that she could answer him quite naturally.

"I do not . . . love him . . . how could I . . . when I . . ."

She stopped, realising that because for the moment he had seemed impersonal, just someone safe and secure, she had almost betrayed herself.

"What were you going to say?" the Earl asked.

"N—nothing . . . it is not . . . important."

"I think it was," he replied, "and if you lie to me again, Ilouka, I shall be very angry."

"No . . . please . . . do not be . . . angry with me . . . I cannot . . . bear it."

She turned her face up to his as she spoke, and in the light of the lantern he could see her wet eyes, the tears on her cheeks, and the trembling of her lips.

He looked down at her for a long moment.

Then when she was still wordlessly beseeching him not to be angry, he pulled her close against him and his lips came down on hers.

It was what Ilouka had longed for, dreamt of, and prayed for ever since he had first kissed her.

Her heart leapt at the wonder of it and she felt once again her vibrations reaching out towards him and knew they joined with his.

He pulled her closer and still closer, and his kiss became more demanding, more insistent, and very much more possessive.

Then, as the ecstasy she had felt before arose within her, she heard the music that came from her heart and knew that this was love—the love that was life itself!

She thought that if she died at this moment it would not matter because she had known and touched the glory of Heaven.

The Earl kissed her until she felt that once again he had carried her to the top of the snow-capped mountains and there was nothing else in the whole Universe but love.

After what seemed a century of time he raised his head and Ilouka said incoherently:

"I . . . I love you! How can a kiss be so . . . wonderful when you . . . do not . . . love me?"

The Earl did not answer, he merely kissed her again.

Then—it seemed much later—when he looked at her Ilouka's eyes were shining like stars, her lips were red from his kisses, and there was a radiance in her face which was as if he had lit a light within her.

As she looked up at him, he could see the love in her eyes.

"I did not mean this to happen tonight," he said.

"I . . . know, but now you have . . . kissed me . . . nothing matters . . . not even . . . Lord Marlowe."

There was just a little tremor in her voice as she spoke his name.

"Unfortunately, he is still a menace," the Earl answered, "and as I have already said, somebody has to look after you, so I suppose it will have to be me!"

"That is what I . . . want you to do . . . but how?"

"As your sins have caught up with you, you must expect to be punished for them."

Ilouka drew in her breath, and because she was a little frightened by what he had said, she moved nearer to him.

"How . . . shall I be . . . punished?"

"Because Lord Marlowe, and perhaps other men from my party, will recognise you," the Earl said, "you will have to go away."

Ilouka stiffened and asked:

"But . . . how can I . . . and where can I . . . go?"

"If I am to help you, it will have to be with me."

Ilouka looked at him, not understanding what he was saying.

Then it flashed through her mind that he was making the same suggestion to her as he had at Lavenham.

The Earl read her thoughts and smiled.

"Yes, I am offering you my protection, but on a rather more permanent basis, as my—wife!"

For a moment Ilouka felt that she could not have heard him aright. Then she said, and her voice trembled:

"Are you . . . asking me to . . . marry you?"

"Can I do anything else?" the Earl enquired. "I have certainly compromised you when you slept in the room next to mine, and I carried you to bed when you were wearing nothing but a nightgown."

Ilouka gave an inarticulate little murmur, and as the colour rose in her cheeks she hid her face against the Earl's shoulder.

"I did not . . . mean that to . . . happen," she whispered.

"But I did!" the Earl replied. "I wanted you, and I meant you to be mine."

Ilouka raised her head to look at him in astonishment.

"I have just . . . realised that was . . . why you . . . changed my bedroom."

"Of course it was."

He held her closer to him.

"Oh, my darling, you behaved so abominably that I am appalled! It terrified me to think what might have happened to you."

"And yet . . . you are still ready to . . . marry me?"

"I love you!"

Ilouka gave a little gasp.

"You love . . . me . . . you really love . . . me?"

"I adore you."

"I cannot . . . believe it . . . I love you so overwhelmingly . . . but I never . . . thought you would love me."

"It will take me a long time to tell you how much."

"Tell me . . . please . . . please . . . tell me."

"I did not mean to tell you so as quickly as this, but unless you are to have a very dubious reputation, which is something I cannot tolerate in my wife, we will have to use our brains and certainly not allow Marlowe, or anybody else who was at Lavenham, to recognise you."

"How are we to . . . prevent them from . . . doing that?" Ilouka asked in a small voice.

"By going away," he answered, "and as it happens, I have a very good excuse for doing so."

Ilouka looked at him questioningly.

"Only today I was asked by the Foreign Secretary to make an unofficial but important diplomatic visit to several countries in the Mediterranean, even as far as Turkey and Egypt. I was considering whether or not I should accept. But I think I might find the journey tolerably interesting if I took my wife with me on our honeymoon."

Ilouka gave a little cry.

"Can we do that? Do you really . . . mean you will . . . take me with . . . you?"

The radiance in her face seemed to light the whole arbour, then she said in a different tone:

"Are you . . . sure you really want to . . . marry me? I could not . . . bear you to do so unless you . . . really wanted me."

The Earl gave a little laugh.

"I have never asked another woman to marry me, but I want you with me and I do not intend to lose you!"

As he spoke he pulled her roughly against him and kissed her differently from the way he had before.

Now his lips were fierce, passionate, and demanding, and Ilouka felt the fire on them and knew as she did so that a little flame flickered within herself.

It joined with the ecstasy that he always aroused in her to make it so intense that it was almost a physical pain.

"I love you . . . I have loved you . . . ever since you first . . . kissed me," she said, "but I cannot . . . believe you really . . . love me."

"I will make you believe me," the Earl answered. "But, my naughty one, we still have to get ourselves out of the very uncomfortable situation into which your disgraceful behavior has landed us."

"I am sorry . . . very sorry," Ilouka said. "Can you ever . . . forgive me?"

"I suppose I shall have to," he answered, "because if you had not come to my house it is doubtful that I should ever have met you."

He paused, then he said:

"No, I am sure that is not true. I believe it was fate that we should meet, and when I watched you dance I knew you were what I had been looking for all my life, although I had not been aware of it."

"You . . . love . . . me?" Ilouka asked.

"I felt as if you were reaching out to me from the moment you began singing," the Earl said, "and something within me, which I had never known existed before, responded."

"I *was* reaching out towards you," Ilouka said, "and when I danced, I was . . . dancing just for . . . you."

She paused before she added shyly:

"And when you . . . kissed me I felt as if you . . . carried me to the top of the snow-capped mountains and we . . . left the world . . . behind."

"That is exactly what we will do."

There was a deep note in his voice.

Ilouka thought he would kiss her again and she lifted her lips, but instead he moved his mouth along the line of her chin and then went lower to kiss the softness of her neck.

It gave her a strange feeling of excitement which was different from what she had felt before, and she thought that little flames were running through her breasts and up into her throat.

"I love . . . you," she said, but her voice was only a whisper and her breath came quickly in little gasps.

The Earl looked at her and there was a fire in his eyes.

"You are so ridiculously absurdly beautiful," he said unsteadily, "and unbelievably innocent. I have so much to teach you."

"About . . . what?"

"Love, my darling, and it will be very exciting for me."

"And . . . for . . . me!"

He held her lips captive and she felt as if she gave him not only her heart but her soul and her body.

When it was almost impossible to breathe, with what she knew was an effort he released her, but she was aware that his heart was beating as frantically as hers.

"Now listen to me, my precious," he said. "We have to be sensible. Yet all I want to do is to kiss you, and go on kissing you for the rest of the night."

"I would . . . love that."

"It is what we will do when we are married," the Earl said, "but now we have to be intelligent, and I need you to help me make a plan to ensure that Lord Marlowe will not hurt us and that your mother and step-father will not be suspicious."

Ilouka gave a sigh of happiness, put her head against his shoulder, and asked:

"What can we . . . do?"

"First of all," the Earl replied, "have you any other names besides Ilouka, which is not only unforgettable to anyone who hears it, but so unusual as to cause comment."

"I was christened 'Mary Nadine Ilouka.' "

"I like Nadine, it suits you," the Earl said, "and we must somehow convince your mother that as I prefer that name it is what you will be known as in future."

He smiled and kissed her forehead as he said:

"But to me you will always be Ilouka, which, although you did not tell me so, means 'She who gives life.' "

"H—how did you . . . discover that?"

"From a friend who speaks Hungarian," the Earl answered, "and it is what you have given me, my lovely one—a new life—a life which is different from what I have known before. But for the moment the Social World must know you as Nadine."

"Then what . . . must we do?"

"I will accept the Foreign Secretary's proposition. We will be married immediately, but in the country with nobody there except for your parents and one of my special friends who was not staying with me when I was entertaining a very beautiful, very naughtly little dancer."

"All I . . . want is to be your . . . wife."

"That is what you will be," the Earl promised, "and one thing is very certain, my alluring, adorable Ilouka, never again will you do anything so outrageous as to dance for any man except me, and never in any circumstances will you pretend to be an actress."

Ilouka looked at him to see if he was angry, but his eyes were twinkling and there was a smile on his lips.

"I love you! I love you!" she cried. "I will do exactly what you want me to do, and I promise you I will be very . . . very good for ever . . . and ever."

The Earl laughed.

"I very much doubt it," he said. "At the same time, my darling, we have a great deal to discover about ourselves, and although our hearts know already that we belong to each other, there are other things I want to learn about you."

"As I want to know everything about you," Ilouka added, "and of course to meet Apollo."

The Earl laughed again.

He held her close to him and kissed her fiercely and passionately until the arbour and the garden vanished and the music they could hear was not from the Band in the distance but from their hearts.

Then he was carrying her up into the starlit sky, above the snow-capped mountains into a Heaven where there was only the love which came from the life pulsating within them.

That was theirs for Eternity.

About the Author

DAME BARBARA CARTLAND, the world's best known and bestselling author of romantic fiction, is also an historian, playwright, lecturer, political speaker and television personality. She has now written over five hundred and sixty books and has the distinction of holding *The Guinness Book of Records* title of the world's bestselling author, having sold over six hundred and fifty million copies of her books all over the world.

Barbara Cartland was invested by Her Majesty The Queen as a Dame of the Order of the British Empire in 1991, is a Dame of Grace of St. John of Jerusalem, and was one of the first women in one thousand years ever to be admitted to the Chapter General. She is President of the Hertfordshire Branch of The Royal College of Midwives, and is President and Founder in 1964 of the National Association for Health.

Miss Cartland lives in England at Camfield Place, Hatfield, Hertfordshire.